Somewhere in her delirious happiness, he had lowered her to her bed, and his body gently covered hers. If she had been naive and innocent moments ago, her wanton abandon was now a fiery greed, ignoring those puritanical convictions that might have clung to an ordinary girl. But she was not ordinary, and she was not in the arms of an ordinary man.

His mouth claimed hers, over and over, bruisingly, caressingly, taking her breath and making it part of his own. Their magic was omnipotent, their bodies fused into a violent storm from which they could not, would not flee. Let it wash them overboard into a sea of passion. That was all that mattered now, the tender yet brutal, gentle yet commanding, primal desire that made them as one.

But was it all that mattered? Diana's senses flooded back to her. This beautiful thing she was experiencing, the heat racing through her body, the pounding of her heart against his chest . . . it was all new and frightening. She took short, deep breaths and whispered, "I am frightened. Will you hurt me?"

His fingers entwined through her hair. He was a blur above her; his finely chiseled features could gain no depth and clarity. She was aware of his strong maleness, promising pleasure her body had never experienced, except in her dreams.

"Do not be frightened, dear lassie," he whispered into her hair. "I will be gentle with you."

THE BEST IN HISTORICAL ROMANCES

TIME-KEPT PROMISES   (2422, $3.95)
by Constance O'Day Flannery

Sean O'Mara froze when he saw his wife Christina standing before him. She had vanished and the news had been written about in all of the papers—he had even been charged with her murder! But now he had living proof of his innocence, and Sean was not about to let her get away. No matter that the woman was claiming to be someone named Kristine; she still caused his blood to boil.

PASSION'S PRISONER   (2573, $3.95)
by Casey Stewart

When Cassandra Lansing put on men's clothing and entered the Rawlings saloon she didn't expect to lose anything—in fact she was sure that she would win back her prized horse Rapscallion that her grandfather lost in a card game. She almost got a smug satisfaction at the thought of fooling the gamblers into believing that she was a man. But once she caught a glimpse of the virile Josh Rawlings, Cassandra wanted to be the woman in his embrace!

ANGEL HEART   (2426, $3.95)
by Victoria Thompson

Ever since Angelica's father died, Harlan Snyder had been angling to get his hands on her ranch, the Diamond R. And now, just when she had an important government contract to fulfill, she couldn't find a single cowhand to hire—all because of Snyder's threats. It was only a matter of time before the legendary gunfighter Kid Collins turned up on her doorstep, badly wounded. Angelica assessed his firmly muscled physique and stared into his startling blue eyes. Beneath all that blood and dirt he was the handsomest man she had ever seen, and the one person who could help beat Snyder at his own game.

Available wherever paperbacks are sold, or order direct from the Publisher. Send cover price plus 50¢ per copy for mailing and handling to Zebra Books, Dept. 2957, 475 Park Avenue South, New York, N.Y. 10016. Residents of New York, New Jersey and Pennsylvania must include sales tax. DO NOT SEND CASH.

ALLEGHENY ECSTASY

CAROLINE BOURNE

ZEBRA BOOKS
KENSINGTON PUBLISHING CORP.

ZEBRA BOOKS

are published by

Kensington Publishing Corp.
475 Park Avenue South
New York, NY 10016

First printing: April, 1990

Printed in the United States of America

For Sandra, Valerie, David and Shirley

As the moonlight conjures
So shall the mist betray
The shadows of foreboding
That existed yesterday

Like a shooting star
I felt
The essence of
your being
quickly pass me by

Like love,
spurned, lost,
A gentle dove
tossed hither
by the stormy winds.
Tho I tried
I found
I could not fly

You fled
Into the moonlit mist
Upon a haunted ground;
An unearthly masquerade.
The wake
of your departure
clinging to my heart
Like indigo dye

The midnight toll
is but a lonely cry
That love and trust
cannot defy.

Chapter 1

Wills Creek in the Allegheny Mountains, December, 1786

Diana Rourke sat on the large boulder overlooking the foam-capped creek where she had spent her happiest moments. Honey Boy, a bobcat she had raised from a kitten, lay against the folds of her tattered gown, its eyes lazily closed and its chin resting upon one large paw. Neither the coolness of the winter evening nor the fact that it was the Lord's day had affected her choice of attire, as she sat barefoot upon the rock, her knees drawn up so that only her toes protruded from the tattered hem of her skirt. She had worn only a thin shawl over her thick cotton shirtwaist, yet she did not feel the cold. She bathed in the warmth of past memories so vague they were mere dreams moving through her, like the bass leaping in the wide creek.

The men of the region referred to the agile Diana as an alluring wood sprite, because she moved with the grace of a doe and could disappear among the flora and fauna as quickly as an early morning mist. Diana, though, felt there was more to her than that. Though she hesitated to admit it, she felt that she had been blessed—or cursed—with the gift of insight.

She knew that something strange and exciting was about to affect her life, though she did not know from what direction it would come. She knew only that an adventure was upon her, and she wasn't sure whether it would be for the better or the worse. While Diana had her faults, she did not consider weakness one of them. She felt she could face anything life handed her.

A flawless beauty in her own right, Diana, like the ancient goddess whose name she bore, had been blessed, also, with the charm and grace seldom seen in one so tall, so slim. Even her feet were narrow and unblemished despite their lack of shoes through the seventeen years she had lived on the creek. Her golden hair was long and disheveled as it whipped about in the wind, her ragged skirt scarcely hiding her ankles when she stood tall and straight. Her violet gaze watched the creek, her imagination forming shapes in the foam that broke upon the waves, much as it did with the clouds on a cloudy day. The forest had metamorphosed into an array of bright colors against the black timberline. Far beyond, the azure skies beckoned her attention, as a flock of geese moved silently to the south. She wished she were one of them, moving away from this place of barren solitude.

She was melancholy this evening. Perhaps it was because of Aunt Rufina's mood earlier in the day when she had fussed and found fault with Diana's chores, always performed quickly so she could spend the day roaming through the forest. She could not recall Aunt Rufina's mood being so black before her husband, Mr. Chambers, had died ten years before. Back then she had been pleasant to be with; Diana could only assume that she'd loved Mr. Chambers very much, indeed. After his death, she had become much stricter with Diana, limiting her activities and enjoyments and piling many more chores upon her.

Diana had never been allowed to visit the settlements along the creek, or to make friends with other young people, although she knew that Rufina only wanted to protect her from the cruelties of the world. Still, Rufina's overprotectiveness had been a bit of a burden, though Diana had become accustomed to the loneliness. Perchance her mood had been affected by Aunt Rufina's derogatory reference to Diana's dead mother — she had called flighty and fuddle-minded the woman Diana remembered, instead, as being slim and milk-white, with sad eyes and a mouth that had never smiled. Diana snatched greedily at her few vague memories of the woman who had given birth to her. She remembered the letters her mother had received for two years, letters that had always been tearfully tossed, unopened, into the cooking fire. Diana remembered watching with sad fascination as the paper had caught in the flames and burned until nothing remained but ashes of what might have been written there. She remembered that ritual occurring frequently until her mother had died, only two years after they had moved into Aunt Rufina's modest living quarters at the rear of the Pine Creek Trading Post she operated.

Now, at twenty years of age, Diana was worried about her future. She had seen many men come and go at her aunt's trading post — men who were grizzled and hairy and who smelled like the furs they traded for Aunt Rufina's imported Eastern goods. The Iroquois Indians who inhabited the region had proved little menace and cordially patronized her aunt's business, even as their brothers might have been off

9

scalping the trappers who provided Rufina with the furs she needed for her trade. Many times one of the Iroquois braves had come upon Diana in the forest, but even they had placed her on an invisible pedestal, daring their brothers to so much as cast a bold eye upon her.

In the past few months, there had been an emptiness inside Diana that she could not understand, and ofttimes she felt that she might explode with want of something she could not quite grasp.

In those moments when her body felt like a boiling hot cauldron, a fleeting memory caused Diana to draw in a quick, cool breath. Somewhere in the past, before her arrival in the Allegheny Mountains that had become both her prison and her refuge, she had known the clean-shaven features of a handsome man in beautifully cut clothing. But was that face just a figment formed by her desire to believe that there were, indeed, men who were not grizzled and reeking of rum and filth? The man had been her father; she knew that for a certainty. She could remember him holding her, and she could remember her own plump arms holding fast to his neck. Her last memory of him was so painful that tears filled her eyes. She remembered watching through the back window of a fast-moving carriage, hearing the haunting reverberations of his screams as he had raced across the lawn in an attempt to stop the carriage. But he had fallen, and her last recollection of him was of a sobbing heap upon a spring-green lawn, the house where she and her mother had lived with him becoming a tiny speck against the horizon of a stormy gray afternoon. She remembered a young, majestic city called Philadelphia, but she had never been allowed to visit there. Aunt Rufina refused to speak to her of the past and Diana had learned long ago not to question her about it. She had been forced, through fear of Aunt Rufina's unpredictable moods, never to ask questions of the woman who was at times as grizzled as the men she served.

How different Aunt Rufina was from her sister, Diana's mother. Aunt Rufina was big-boned and homely, her hair ragged and unkempt, its sparse remains scarcely held back by a dirty brown scarf, her lips a thin line of bitterness and frustration. Diana's mother, Rowanna, had been slim and delicate, with big violet eyes, and a full, pouting mouth. Diana especially remembered her hands, so perfect and flawless, with well-groomed fingernails that were lustrous without manmade varnishes. She remembered their gentleness. She remembered the melodious hum of her mother's voice lulling her to sleep, and the thought of her mother's goodnight kiss could still bring a smile of security to Diana's own youthful lips. But why had her mother been so sad? Why had she never smiled? Why had she taken her daughter and fled from a husband who must truly have loved her? Sometimes Diana's obsession to know ate at her like a cancer, and she would spend these long moments of solitude on the boulder by the creek, trying to remember the events that had immediately preceded the departure of the fast-moving carriage. But for some reason, that memory had managed to evade her all these years.

Suddenly, Diana lifted her forehead from her drawn-up knees. She heard the gruff cacophony of Aunt Rufina's voice, carried upon the wind so heavily that she thought it might fell the tall fir trees surrounding her. There was annoyance in the way she called her. "Diana, you ragamuffin brat! Come to me at once!" Diana shot up from her perch, startling Honey Boy, and prepared to rush back along the trail through the thick underbrush of the forest.

At her age, she did not like being referred to as a ragamuffin brat, though she knew beyond a doubt that Aunt Rufina dearly loved her and meant nothing by it. Diana had enough respect for her aunt not to have voiced her objection to the derogatory way she'd described her mother earlier. As she rushed along, knowing where each stump crossed the path and where the pine cones had fallen earlier in the day, she tried to remember the morning's activities. Had she only half-heartedly performed a chore? Had she forgotten something? She had fed the chickens and milked the cow. Had she swept out the stable where the horse and mule were housed? Yes, she was sure that she had. She had stocked the trading post shelves with the last of Aunt Rufina's jarred fruits and vegetables. She had swept the store and stocked the bin with the wood she had chopped at the woodshed. She had performed all of her daily duties. Why, then, was Aunt Rufina's voice even more gruff and commanding than usual?

So deep was she in her worried thoughts that she was unaware of the figure blocking the narrow path until she was within touching distance of a tall, dark-haired man loosely holding the reins of a white stallion which pranced majestically in place. She gave a small cry of alarm, and her eyes cut to the thickness of the evergreen forest where no escape seemed to exist. She drew her hand to her slim throat, her violet eyes wide with awe and wonderment. She began to back away from the handsome and prepossessing man—black-haired, with somber gray-black eyes, his tight-fitting buckskins dusty from travel.

12

Though she was fascinated, he was a stranger and his intentions unknown. Almost immediately she felt the rough bark of a fir at her back and stood there, her palms firmly planted at her sides.

Diana certainly was not what Cole Donovan had expected. Standish Rourke had greatly underestimated the beauty of his daughter. Because Standish had hinted that the girl's mother had been emotionally unsettled, Cole had half-expected to find that unattractive state in the very alert, wide-eyed beauty standing before him now. But the illusion he saw before him took away his breath. He had never seen hair so golden, or eyes so purple. She was tall and graceful, her flesh supple with youth. Just moments before he had seen her running gracefully along the narrow trail with a bobcat dogging her steps, so perfect in her beauty that he had convinced himself that she was, indeed, a mere illusion. Then he saw a quiver settle upon her full, sensual mouth and, gathering together his wits that had scattered to the wind upon first seeing her, he stepped forward on the trail and approached her almost menacingly.

"Will you be Diana Rourke?" he asked.

"I am, sir," she replied, her voice trembling with uncertainty. She was not familiar with his very distinct foreign accent.

"It is imperative that I speak with you," Scottish-born Cole Donovan said. "Your life is in grave danger and you must not journey to Philadelphia." He wished he could explain further, but Standish had given him a one-word explanation: Webster.

Though his words frightened her, Diana did not feel threatened by his nearness. "And why, sir, would

I be in danger?" She was surprised by the articulate voice of a man whose tall, broad-shouldered frame was clothed in new buckskins, fringed down the sleeves, and leggings in the Indian fashion. She was mesmerized by the powerful stallion digging impatiently at the ground, its large body splendid in new saddle and bridle. She had never seen a horse as white as the snow that clung to the branches of the trees in the damp shadows of the forest.

Suddenly, a man's voice bellowed on the trail, "You there! What are you doing?" In that moment, as Cole Donovan was caught off his guard, Diana scooted past him. A strong urge compelled her to turn back for one last look, but her good sense forbade it.

Undaunted by the bellowing—and glaringly threatening look—of the older man into whose arms Diana fled, Cole Donovan did not immediately mount the impatient stallion. He stood there until the two had disappeared around the bend of the trail. Standish's nephew, Webster, who had spoken often of his younger cousin, had certainly distorted his account of the elusive Diana Rourke. She was magnificent in her beauty, innocent, yet seductive, agile and graceful as she moved barefoot upon the winter-hardened ground. He felt an almost painful stirring inside as he recalled that last fleeting glimpse of her. It would burn forever in his mind. Then, gathering his thoughts, he remounted the stallion and moved swiftly along Wills Creek toward the trading post operated by her aunt. He had to warn her. He had promised Standish Rourke that he would prevent her from journeying to Philadelphia. The girl's father was an enigma. One moment he was sending his solicitor to this wild region to fetch the girl, and the next he

14

was sending Cole to tell her not to answer the summons. Perhaps when he returned to Rourke House, Standish would favor him with an explanation.

Diana had scarcely moved more than a hundred yards with her friend, whose grizzly, familiar form had been salvation for her when the stranger had blocked her path. And yet, contradiction tugged at her heart, since she also felt that Hambone had appeared at a most inopportune moment. His thick, burly arms had opened wide to receive her and, had she not forced him to accompany her on the trail, he might have raised his loaded musket at the man who had accosted her.

"That man frightened me near to death!" Diana whispered, easing her frail arms beneath the thickness of his beaver-fur coat. Hambone had been the one bright spark in her otherwise dreary existence, and the mystery surrounding him had always stirred Diana's curiosity. He was well-educated, having himself taught her to read and write fluently, yet he was content to trap in the mountains and avoid the company of other trappers. She knew that he was very old—probably fifty or so—yet he had been her best friend in all the world. He was always willing to listen, and to offer an encouraging word when she felt that her whole world was crumbling beneath her feet. He had always assured her that a better life lay just over the horizon.

"He's lucky not to be scrubbing black powder off his backside, girl," Hambone said gruffly, the deep lines in his forehead suddenly pinching into a frown. "I wanted to talk to you before you got back to the Post. Thank God I came along when I did."

Diana's mood lightened. "You are always my salvation, Hambone. That man knew who I was and warned me not to go to Philadelphia. Why on earth would he even think I was leaving the mountains, Hambone?" Even as she spoke, Diana remembered every twitch of the stranger's firm, masculine features, the tiny lines at the corners of his eyes that hinted he was at least a dozen years her senior, the ample mouth that did not smile. He had posed no threat to her, other than his presence and his ominous warning, thus Diana's mouth turned slightly upwards into a smile. "Well, that is of no matter. Did you come in search of me? What is it you must tell me?" Her lovely oval face slightly tilted to the side. Then her wide, almond-shaped violet eyes became as worried as Hambone's. Perhaps it was the somberness in his expression. "Have I done something wrong?"

"Nay, girl," Hambone replied, taking her arm with a strange gentleness. "Come, sit beside me for a minute." Diana followed his direction and sat on the fallen tree branch beside the man she adored. He saw her bare feet and clicked his tongue in chastisement. "How many times, girl, have I told you to wear shoes in this cold weather? Didn't I give you a fine pair of fur boots last time I was here?"

Diana shrugged absently. "I don't like shoes, or boots. But I wear them when it is really cold."

"Today is cold!" he argued, "You'll get your death one day!"

Quickly, Diana took his rough hands between ones almost as flawless as her mother's had been, though Diana's bore tiny calluses on her palms from hard work. "You have not come to talk to me about my lack of shoes, Hambone. Something bothers you. Please tell me what it is."

"It is, indeed, a message from Philadelphia, girl."

16

Confusion marred her features. "Then who was that man back there? He said I should not go to Philadelphia. How very odd. Has a message arrived from some member of my father's family?"

"Your father would like the pleasure of your company for a few weeks. I think you should go."

Diana remembered the premonition that had flooded her that morning on awakening. "Visit my father? He is but a vague memory to me."

"He is a kind man," Hambone replied.

"How would you know the character of my true father? Has Aunt Rufina said something to you?"

But that was preposterous! Aunt Rufina had never spoken a kind word about Diana's father, or her father's family.

Hambone shook his head. "Nay, girl. I've a confession to make. All these many years that you've lived here with Rufina, I have kept your father aware of you, sending him letters, keeping him abreast of you as you grew into womanhood. Rufina never knew, and your father forbade me to tell you. And you certainly must not tell Rufina about it."

Diana shot up from her seated position as though a bullet had struck her. She looked at Hambone, so bewildered that she could not speak. Were there, indeed, any words she could say in reply to such a confession? But from somewhere deep inside, an overwhelming strength brought her voice back to her. She looked at him, not with anger and confusion, but with curiosity and something akin to desperation.

"You know my father? How is he? Why would he want to contact me? And who was that man back there?" The questions popped into her mind so quickly she gave him no time to respond. "I cannot imagine why he would want to see me after all these

17

years. Surely, he knows that mother has been gone for quite some time. Why hasn't he ever contacted me himself? Why did mother—"

"Hush, girl!" Hambone spoke sharply, yet with underlying affection. Diana saw the pain in his eyes, and certainly heard it in his voice. He had kept this secret all these years, and it must have grieved him terribly. He must have had a good reason, and the least she could do was give him a chance to explain.

"Very well, Hambone. But you had best explain quickly, before Aunt Rufina comes after me with a strap."

"She tries it," Hambone came immediately to Diana's defense, "and she'll be the one feelin' the strap, the old wench! She's treated you badly, and it's inexcusable." Why, he would never know, but Rufina was the one woman in all the world Hambone felt he could spend the rest of his life with. Perhaps it was her independence and indomitable pride. It certainly was not a physical attraction; she was gaunt and homely and gruff like a man. And she had a vicious tongue when she took a mind to it.

Diana, of course, was ignorant of Hambone's true feelings toward her aunt. She felt an overwhelming need to defend her. "She raised me, Hambone. She has taken care of me and she has loved me, despite her arguments to the contrary. Yes, she is gruff and tries to be hardhearted, but I believe somewhere there must be an underlying softness. I'll find it one day." Even as she spoke, Diana sincerely doubted that Rufina's soft spot would ever be found, though she would never give up on the idea that she had one. But her aunt was the least of her worries right now. She wanted to hear about her father. "Please, Hambone, you intercepted me for good reason. I'll be quiet long enough to listen."

"I intercepted you before you could get to Rufina and allow her to poison you."

"Poison me?" Curiosity again brought her finely-chiseled eyebrows together. "What do you mean?"

"I know I refer to you as a child, but you are no longer a child. You are a young woman, and there's no reason for you to be tied to Rufina's apron strings. There is a man at the trading post waiting to speak to you, a gentleman from Philadelphia who claims to be a solicitor for your father's estate."

Strangely, the tone of Diana's voice did not change. "My father's estate. Does this mean he is dead?"

"No, he is quite well. He merely wishes to spend a few weeks with you and hopes to encourage you to remain at Rourke House with him."

Diana sniffed indelicately, "I'll do no such thing! I belong here in the mountains with Aunt Rufina. Who would help her with the chores?"

"You need refinement, Diana," Hambone argued. "Sure, I was able to teach you to read and write, but you need more than that. You need to learn the graces of a lady."

Diana shrugged her slim shoulders. "Who wants to be a lady?" She feigned a yawn, putting the back of her hand to her mouth as she did so. "Sounds terribly boring, being a lady."

Hambone laughed hoarsely. "You just don't want to wear shoes, lass. Now," Hambone rose and took her firmly by her right arm. "On your feet, my young friend. You'll meet with this gentleman, even if I must carry you over my shoulder. He wants to take you back to Philadelphia to visit with your father. Rufina will poison you against going. She's worked you like a galley slave, and she'll not be wanting to pay someone else to do what you've been doing all these years."

The words Hambone spoke did not fully sink in. Despite her earlier objections, Diana now had only one thing on her mind, and that was a temporary release from the confines of the mountains and her labors at the trading post. "Leave Wills Creek," she murmured. "After all these years, I have a chance." Then a thought came to her. She closed her eyes, picturing the distance between Wills Creek and her father as so short she could almost extend her hand to touch him. But in the moment that anticipation filled her, anxiety and fear were not far behind. "But I cannot understand it. Why did my father never contact me before? Why now?" She spoke the words almost harshly. "I had almost convinced myself that this was the only life I would ever know. Philadelphia seemed as remote as the moon."

"Nay, the city I told you about a long time ago," Hambone said, "truly exists. Dear girl," Hambone's arm roughly circled her shoulders. "Don't allow Rufina to frighten you. Go to Philadelphia and visit with your father. Harbor no resentment against him. Surely there is a good reason why he has not contacted you personally. It will be good for you to see where you were born, Diana. This wild country is no place for a girl as lovely as you. You will grow old and mean and bitter if you stay, just like your Aunt Rufina. Why do you think your mother left?"

"But she came back," Diana reminded him quietly.

"For good reason I'm sure, lass. Aye, for good reason. You hear what the solicitor has to say and you go to Philadelphia. You deserve better than this, certainly something better than being Rufina's slave. But when you go, I implore you to be wary of your cousin Webster. I understand from your father's letters that his brother's son is a bit of a rogue at times."

"I have a cousin?" Diana smiled up at him. "Will I have to wear shoes in Philadelphia?"

As he rose to his feet, Hambone laughed heartily. "Aye, lass, you'll have to wear shoes and fine dresses and live in a fine house. Your father is a very, very wealthy man."

"Oh, Hambone!" Diana rose to move into her friend's arms. "Why don't I feel happy about seeing my father again? You want me to go, to leave Rufina, and yet I feel emptiness at doing so. I know that my father is a kind man, and I remember that he loved me. Why am I not overwhelmed by the idea of seeing him again?"

"Because, I'd imagine, you were but three years old when your mother took you away from Philadelphia. Now!" Hambone roughly put her away from him. "Let's go see this fine gentleman that's awaiting you and get you ready for your trip! And don't you be frightened."

"I haven't decided whether I will go," she admitted. "But if I do go, I promise you I will not be frightened." Suddenly, that handsome face from back on the trail eased its way into her thoughts. "Are there other men without beards in Philadelphia?"

Hambone laughed as he turned her on the trail and coaxed her ahead. "Aye, girl. Come. We'll get into the rack of ladies' garments your Aunt Rufina has hidden away in that back room and have you fit for a king's court."

As they moved quietly up the path toward the trading post, an array of emotions flooded Diana's head. She felt pity for her mother who had died, young and troubled, without explaining why she had left her husband. She felt sympathy for her widowed Aunt Rufina who found it very difficult to speak kind words to her, though they surely rested in her heart. She felt anger toward her father for turning his back on her. Surely, if he had been keeping in contact with Hambone, then he knew that she and Rufina were barely able to scratch out a living. Why hadn't he provided for her? Or had he? Suddenly, doubt filled Diana's heart. She remembered times that Rufina made extravagant purchases for the trading post when she said there was no money. Had she been spending funds sent for Diana's comfort? But even that could not absorb Diana's thoughts. Rufina had provided for her when her own mother had died. And now she felt sadness at the thought of leaving Rufina—even for a little while.

Back at the trading post, Diana sat in the company of a short, stocky, clean-shaven gentleman who appeared to be in his forties. She was a little disappointed. She had hoped that the handsome stranger she had met back on the trail was the man who had been sent by her father's estate. Hambone sat in a chair across from them, keeping a watchful eye on the silent, scornful Rufina, making sure she did not interfere in the affairs of her niece. Diana felt a flood of insecurity fill her heart. How long would she be expected to stay in Philadelphia? She was excited at the prospect of travel yet apprehensive of it, also. She learned from the solicitor that her father's sister, Jocelyn, her husband, Philip Mayne, and their son, Webster, all lived in Rourke House. The mere mention of Webster's name sent a chill down her spine, though she knew not the source of that particular apprehension.

"My cousin, Webster. Is he a kind man?" Diana

asked, surprising Mr. Rowell with the question, but only because she had singled out Webster for her inquiry.

All of Philadelphia was aware of Webster's reputation, but Mr. Rowell could not believe that rumor had made its way into the Alleghenies and into the heart of the curious young woman sitting across from him. "Webster is a bit of a ruffian at times," Mr. Rowell replied after a moment. "Unmarried at the age of thirty-three, he possesses quite an eye for the ladies. I believe he will pose no threat to his young cousin, Miss Rourke. Your father allows no mischief among members of the family."

Despite the uncertainties that darkened her immediate future, Diana saw light at the end of a very long tunnel. Curiosity compelled her to accept Mr. Rowell's offer to accompany her to the home of her father, but Diana knew she would wish to return to Aunt Rufina before a fortnight was over. After all, Aunt Rufina, not her father, had raised her, and it was to Rufina that she owed her loyalty. Thus, she stood, approached her aunt, and gently took her protesting hands between her slim ones.

"Aunt Rufina, I promise that I will return."

"Will you, girl?" Rufina asked dryly.

Diana's gaze caught a fleeting glance of softness in Rufina's deeply lined features. "Yes, I will return. You are the only family I have ever known, and I will return. One day soon you will call for your little ragamuffin brat and I'll be here."

For the first time in her life, Rufina pulled Diana into her strong, bony arms, but only for a moment. "You take care, girl. I do—" Rufina did not have to finish the statement. Diana was well aware of the words of adoration resting, unspoken, in her aunt's heart.

The moment Cole Donovan had seen Diana
Rourke on the trail he had known that his future
would be altered. He was more than a little annoyed
that his plans to journey westward, to view the magnificence of the land that lay between New England
and the Pacific Ocean, had been delayed. He could
not turn his back on his good friend, Standish, and
leave the beautiful young Diana at the mercy of her
cousin Webster. He wished that Philip, Webster's
father, was a stronger character. Unfortunately, he
was weak and irritable, close-minded and unyielding
in his belief that Webster had at least a tad of
familial loyalty in his heart.

Seeing Mr. Rowell's horse at the trading post, a
very disappointed Cole Donovan had had no choice
but to allow Diana Rourke to accompany the man to
Philadelphia. He would have to delay his travel plans
until he had resolved the problem of the young
woman.

Even as he moved the powerful white stallion onto
the trail to begin the long ride back to Philadelphia,
passing simple log cabins and homesteads, occasionally watering his horse at a trough and accepting the
generous hospitality of the colonists who treated him,
not as a stranger, but as a friend, Diana Rourke
monopolized his thoughts. He wanted to return to
Rourke House before she arrived so he could assist
her father in looking out for her welfare. Despite her
remarkable beauty, and the spirit he had witnessed in
her as she had fled through the forest with a wild
animal at her side, Cole groaned inwardly at the
image of himself with the responsibility of a woman

under his wing.

Diana might have enjoyed the horseback ride to the coach station ten miles away had it not been for the cramped, uncomfortable lace-up shoes she'd been required to wear. She also did not like the velveteen traveling dress, its waist pinched so tightly she could hardly breathe, or the cumbersome undergarments that were, by themselves, more clothing than she normally wore on the coldest of days. Mr. Rowell was pleasant enough, though rather dull. While on the coach, Diana met a couple who provided charming company for part of the journey, though the young woman's interests were quite different from her own. Whereas Diana knew of nothing outside the forest and the mountains where she had been raised, she was cultured, refined, interested in the arts and politics. Diana hoped that by the time they arrived in Philadelphia she might be able to hide her ignorance of worldly affairs.

Chapter 2

Walnut Street City Jail, Philadelphia

The only thing Cole Donovan had in common with the other two men in his cell was that they had all been condemned to the gallows. The echo of last night's New Year's revelry still reverberated through his head, but all Cole could think about was the hangman's noose he would face in two days' time. He wouldn't mind dying so much if he was guilty of the murder of Standish Rourke, a cousin so distant he was hardly kin at all. The trial had been a travesty, false witnesses produced through fear and under duress, and the odds had been stacked against him from the very beginning. He should have been suspicious the day Webster Mayne had so generously offered him lodgings at Rourke House, when all he had wanted to do was journey into the vast unexplored American wilderness that had drawn him away from his native Scotland. But the young English-educated Scotsman had been intrigued by finding distant family in the City of Brotherly Love.

At Rourke House, Cole had found a magnificent portrait of the black sheep of the Donovan family, his own namesake who had arrived in Philadelphia in

1699 to find a prosperous settlement of over seven thousand people. From the beautiful Diana's father, Cole had learned many things about the Donovan and Rourke families, and about the settlement of Philadelphia itself. Founded in 1682 by William Penn, who had been granted the land by royal charter in payment of a debt, the settlement had become a refuge for Quakers, and for men of all religious beliefs. The word "Philadelphia", derived from two Greek words, *philos* meaning love, and *adelphos*, brother, had been a magnet to the handsome young Scotsman, who had been forced to leave his native land to avoid marrying a woman of his father's choosing. Outcast from his family and disowned by his father, the original Cole Cynric Donovan had soon found romance in the young city.

He had met and married Miss Emilia Fairmount, whose family had been one of the earliest to settle in the region. Before the first houses had been built and the city laid out in checkerboard fashion, Emilia's family, like the other early settlers, had lived in a cave, dug six feet deep and twenty feet long, beside the Delaware River.

Considering physical attributes, Cole and Emilia had been the perfectly matched couple. Tall and slim, with black hair and gray-black eyes, he was tender and loving. She was slender and graceful, with auburn hair and blushingly pretty features, a fragile woman who saw beauty not in diamonds and rubies, but in the Mammoth butterflies, the ruby-throated hummingbirds and the bumble bees that flitted among the scarlet Bee Balms, the pink and yellow horsemint and the Blue Curls that grew in profusion along the Delaware River. Now, as he sat in his tepid cell, Cole wondered just how much of Standish's

27

story about the family had been fact, and how much romantic dreams.

As the story went, when Emilia had made the announcement of the impending birth of their first child, the delighted Cole had used most of his financial resources to begin construction of a massive brick house less than a mile away from the bustling settlement of Philadelphia. Donovan had employed thirty men who worked eleven and twelve hours a day for generous wages, and the house was completed within seven months and fully furnished just days before the birth of their tiny daughter. While the house was being built, Cole had made a long journey through the woods along the Delaware River, gently extracting the bulbs of Emilia's favorite wildflowers so that, when they moved in, a large garden of wild flowers greeted her in well-manicured profusion. But the long, agonizing labor took Emilia's life less than three hours after the birth of their daughter. Cole Cynric Donovan had found it very difficult to celebrate the birth of his daughter while his beloved wife was being laid to rest in a small cemetery established on the west lawns of the house he had built for her. For weeks he had refused to gaze upon the tiny, cherubic face of his new daughter.

But in the months and the years ahead, Cole had mended his sorrows in the vibrancy and animation of his daughter, their first encounter having been forced upon him by a loyal, stubborn servant who would not allow the child to be ignored by her grieving father. Days later, he had named his daughter Emilia, after her mother. She became his life and the reason he drew breath. She was the image of her mother, and as the years went by, Cole had enjoyed the transitions as she grew from infancy into a curious toddler, then into a charming little lady who soon needed a tutor to begin her education. Cole Donovan had enjoyed taking her riding, leading her small Welsh pony on a long rope, refusing to listen to her impish entreaties that she was quite able to handle the pony herself. She had been quick-witted and lovable, dark and beautiful like her mother, and Cole's only happiness. When Emilia had turned seventeen, he had commissioned portraits of both of them, only to be riddled with guilt when he had looked upon the finished portrait of his daughter and had seen his wife's features.

At the age of nineteen, Emilia had met a man by the name of Moss Rourke. The meeting had come about quite by accident—Emilia, accompanied by her father's groom, was exiting a haberdashery where she had chosen a gift for her father's birthday, just as Moss had exited a tavern next door. He had knocked her down, scattering her purchases, then had offered his hand to help her up. That first touch had melted Moss Rourke's heart, and Emilia, too, had fallen hopelessly in love.

For weeks, because of her father's overprotectiveness, Emilia and Moss met in secrecy, enjoying moments together as they picnicked along the Delaware River or walked hand in hand on the trails surrounding the bustling settlement. It was, however, inevitable that Emilia's father would learn of her escapades from one of his many acquaintances. He forbade her to see Moss again and Emilia wept for days, refusing to see anyone or to eat the meals brought to her.

But, unlike her obedient mother, Emilia possessed a haughty, independent nature. As soon as she was able to gather her courage, she had announced that she *would* marry Moss Rourke and that her father could attend the ceremony if he so chose.

Three weeks thereafter, gently weeping beneath her bridal veil for the absence of her father on what should have been the happiest day of her life, Emilia married the man she loved. As her grieving father's health declined, his house servants became concerned. Emilia made daily trips to Donovan House, but her father refused to see her. As the story went, one evening after she had made one of her trips, Cole Donovan plunged his gold-gilted sword into a small oak sapling beside the grave of his dead wife. From that moment on, his life had consisted of brooding and drinking and cursing the darkness, until exhaustion took away conscious thought.

Thus it had come as no surprise to the servants when Emilia had to be summoned in haste from her husband's house. Her father was dying. When she had cautiously approached and sat in the chair beside her father's bed, he cursed Emilia and every child conceived of her union with Moss Rourke. With that last spoken curse, Cole Cynric Donovan's eyes had glazed in death.

After his burial, Emilia and Moss moved into Donovan House and immediately renamed it Rourke House. For eighteen years they conceived no children and Emilia, never forgetting her father's curse, was sure that it had left her barren. She had reluctantly accepted the fact that she would never give Moss children until, after nineteen years of marriage, she gave birth to a son, Standish, and two years later, a daughter, Jocelyn.

After the deaths of Emilia and Moss, the Bank of North America had petitioned for appointment as financial guardian and had appointed a custodial guardian—a longtime servant of the family—to care for the two young children. To hear Standish tell his distant cousin the tragic story of the family made Cole's blood run cold. Standish had been convinced that his mother, Emilia, had died in spirit on a lonely July night, clinging desperately to the cold, dead fingers of her father's hand, his curse reverberating through her fragile young mind.

Suddenly, a clink of metal at the narrow cell door jarred Cole's thoughts back to the present. But it was merely a guard, taking out another prisoner in need of medical attention.

Cole wished he could kick himself in the britches. If he had not been so interested in the American branch of the Donovan family, he would not be in this mess right now. His mind kept drifting to the portrait of his great-grandfather's brother, his American namesake — a portrait that could easily have been of Cole himself. Standish Rourke had told Cole that his ancestor's hair had been black and wavy like his own, though in the portrait he wore a powdered white wig. Cole's eyes were gray, as were his namesake's, and they both had firm, square jawlines and ample mouths. But that was where the similarities ended. His great-great uncle had been content to settle near Philadelphia, marry, and begin a family. Cole wanted only to be rid of this black curse of death hanging over him and flee into the American wilderness, which had been his intention in coming to America in the first place. He wanted to find that golden-haired beauty who had been foolish to flee from him on a narrow mountain trail when all he had wanted to do was warn her of the dangers of traveling to Philadelphia. She might be, even now, in the hands of her maniacal, greed-corrupted cousin, Webster Mayne.

It had come as no surprise to Cole Donovan when, upon returning to Philadelphia from his journey westward, he found Standish Rourke in fear for his life. That very night the kindly gentleman had been murdered and the poor lass, snatched from the safety of her Allegheny Mountains, would arrive in Philadelphia only to find that her father had been brutally killed.

Although he had reluctantly accepted his fate, Cole felt a deep longing for home and country. The magistrate who had sentenced him to death had not allowed him time to inform his parents in Edinburgh so that he might see them once again, nor had he been allowed to appeal the sentence. There was absolutely no hope for salvation. He had sealed his fate by coming to this treacherous country.

It was something of an amazement to Cole that his thoughts frequently roamed through his memories and settled on the happy, carefree days he had spent at Cambridge University in England. It seemed like a thousand years ago, and he scarcely felt like a man who had just celebrated his thirty-fourth birthday, a birthday spent in the squalid conditions of the Walnut Street City Jail. Perhaps thinking of those pleasant times, and the frequent journeys with his friends down to London, was an escape from his present predicament. He imagined he was again in England, watching boats move lazily along the Thames, listening to his classmates plot ways to skip classes without the burden of well-earned demerits.

Then he had made this fatal decision to emigrate to the Americas he and his classmates had only dreamed about. Immediately upon arriving in Philadelphia, he had been welcomed by the very kind Standish Rourke whom he'd met, by chance, at one of the more colorful taverns on the outskirts of town. Standish had been drawn by Cole's remarkable resemblance to his grandfather and had invited him to Rourke House, where their family ties had subsequently been revealed. Cole remembered the long talks he had enjoyed with Standish, who had spoken frequently and longingly—and yet bitterly—of the daughter he had not seen in seventeen years. Standish had spoken of the fur trapper who kept him informed of his daughter's progress, and had spoken with sullen regret of the death of his wife, Rowanna, as if it had happened yesterday rather than fifteen years before. Only once had he mentioned her departure from Philadelphia with their only child, and Cole, aware of the pain the memory caused, had never questioned him about it. He did, however, glean from the conversation that Standish Rourke did not know what had compelled Rowanna to flee with their child. He admitted only that he had always suspected his nephew, who had been sixteen at the time, of some heinous mischief that had caused it.

Cole shuddered. He could see again the glint of steel gripped firmly in the hand of Standish's murderer. He had hidden in the shadows of the corridor until the killer left, unaware that the murderous weapon plunged into the man's heart had been Cole's own letter opener. By the time Cole had rushed back to his bedchamber, hurriedly dressed and saddled a horse at the stable, Webster Mayne had sent the stableman, Tuxford, to the police. Provoked by threat and duress, the two house servants, Mrs. Sanders, and her daughter, Claudia, testified against Cole, and Webster gave testimony that he had witnessed the actual murder. The saddling of the horse and Cole's preparations to ride away from Rourke House at the hour of midnight had been taken as proof that he was fleeing the scene of the crime.

Cole had never felt so alone. The stench of the cell was unbearable, the human excrement in the chamber pots uncleaned for days, the two other prisoners making no attempt to clean themselves at the basin of tepid water. No shaving implements or other toiletries were provided to the prisoners, and Cole knew he must look a mess. He could not run his fingers through his hair without encountering tight knots, and his eyes were drawn and haggard from lack of sleep. There was absolutely nothing more frightening than the imminence of death, and he had found himself counting the hours down—forty-eight, forty-seven, forty-six . . .

He almost wished the countdown was over. Every passing hour chiseled away at the facade of strength he tried to maintain.

The heavy iron door opened. Cole's thick muscles jumped at the unexpected intrusion. One of the guards stood in the portal, his eyes sweeping over the small cell and settling on Cole. Their gazes met. With a macabre grin, the guard summoned Cole, immediately manacling his wrists at his back when he moved into the corridor.

"You've got a visitor, Donovan."

Cole was surprised. He could not imagine who would be visiting him, or for what reason. He was taken down the corridor and to the left, into a small antechamber. From there he could see a small window, and the tall, familiar form of Webster Mayne. He wanted to spring and kill, but his efforts would have been futile without the use of his hands.

Webster Mayne spun arrogantly on the heel of his patent leather shoe, crossing his arms as he did so.

"It appears to me, Cousin," he said sarcastically, "that you have a bit of a problem on your hands."

"My only problem, *Cousin!*" Cole shot back venomously, his voice, through education, more English than Scottish, "is that I am not free to throttle you!"

"Tch! Tch! What hostility. It is a wonder my poor Uncle Standish lasted as long as he did with you in the house!" He straightened his velveteen waistcoat and smoothed down the ruffles of his jabot. The large emerald ring he wore, one Cole remembered seeing on Standish Rourke's hand, glistened in the fading light of the dusk. "Here I am, out of familial love and honor, coming to you with a final reprieve. And to be so ungentlemanly about it, dear Cousin!" Cole's hostile look became one of skepticism. What reprieve could a murderer offer him, a man who had perjured himself in court and threatened two servants so they would do the same? With a lump choking in his throat, Cole could not find his voice. "Don't you know what I am willing to do for you, Master Donovan?"

As Cole watched that insipid, narrow face, he thought back to that night he had arrived back at Rourke House, reliving it again, as he had relived it over and over since his imprisonment.

Dusk had fallen. A cold rain mixed with sleet and snow fell on the city of Philadelphia. Cole had ridden long and hard from the Pine Creek area of the Alleghenies where he had confronted Diana Rourke. Wanting only to reach Rourke House before Mr. Rowell arrived with the innocent young woman, Cole had scarcely eaten a bite in three days. He was weak from hunger, and he felt that frost flowed through his

35

veins rather than blood. He had entered Rourke House, only to find a quaking shell of a man hiding behind the locked doors of his bed chamber.

"Standish? Standish, are you in there?" Cole had called, rapping firmly at the door.

"Wh-who is it?"

"It is Donovan."

Within moments, the door opened. A trembling hand moved out and firmly grasped Cole's arm to drag him into the room. "Thank God you are back. Did you reach my daughter in time?"

"I'm sorry, no. Mr. Rowell had left too far in advance. He was at the Pine Creek Trading Post when I got there."

Standish Rourke's eyes were wide with terror. "Did you see her?"

"I did. I tried to talk to her, but as I was a stranger, she was wary of me. Then a mountain man came along, someone she knew. . . ."

"Then she is coming here?"

"I would assume." Frowning severely, he asked, "Will you tell me what this is all about?"

Standish Rourke tunneled his violently trembling fingers through his thick hair. "God . . . God, my poor girl. What have I done to her?"

Cole had poured himself a brandy from Standish's private stock. But the fiery liquid in his stomach only nauseated him due to his immense hunger. "What has transpired since I left, Standish?"

"It is my sister, Jocelyn."

"What about your sister?"

"She's—" Suddenly, footsteps clicked on the stairs, were momentarily muffled on the footcloth, then began moving swiftly up the second flight of stairs. "You must leave, Cole. It is my nephew. We will talk later. Come here to my chamber when the house has settled down."

"Of course."

Standish's hand desperately grasped Cole's arm. "Swear that you will return."

Cole's gray-black eyes narrowed to study the man's face, so lined with distress that he scarcely resembled the Standish Rourke who had become his good friend. His hand fell patiently to Standish's. "There is no reason why I would not."

Standing by the door, Cole listened to Webster's approaching footsteps. They paused just outside Standish's chamber, then slowly moved on. Only then did Cole slip from the room and move toward his own.

Mrs. Sanders had heard him enter the house. He had scarcely entered his chamber before she knocked at the door. Opening it, he asked, "What is it?"

"I heard you enter, Master Donovan, and I thought you would be hungry." She carried a silver tray of covered plates.

"Thank you, Madame." When he took the tray, she turned to make her retreat. "Mrs. Sanders?" She turned back. "Mr. Rourke is upset about his sister. Do you know what is wrong?"

"No, Master Donovan. I know only that he entered her chamber yesterday morning when Claudia had neglected to lock the door behind her. Then Mr. Mayne — Webster Mayne — made him leave. They exchanged harsh words, and Mr. Rourke locked himself in his bed chamber until you returned. You are the first person he has spoken to since yesterday. Is there anything else you wish to know?"

"No, thank you, Mrs. Sanders."

"Then good night, sir."

Cole closed the door, so curious about what had upset Standish Rourke that he was scarcely able to eat the ample meal Mrs. Sanders had brought him. He was anxious to speak to Standish Rourke, and when he heard what he thought was the sound of Webster's retreating footsteps, he crept from his chamber and into the corridor. Unfortunately, Webster's footsteps were moving toward Standish Rourke's chamber, not away. By the time Cole arrived at the chamber door, Webster was leaning over his uncle's bed, his hands firmly grasping the handle of a knife. A horrified Cole Donovan moved into the shadows of a doorway across the hall and watched Webster's hasty retreat from the chamber of death.

Suddenly brought back to the present by Webster's gloating stare, Cole's fists clenched, causing a greater pain in his wrists. A tremendous desire to live brought animation back to his face and sound back to his throat. Delving into his memory, he remembered the last words Webster had spoken to him: *Don't you know what I am willing to do for you, Master Donovan?* He asked Webster, "Why don't you tell me?"

"Allow me first to relate a story to you." Webster Mayne flipped his wrist weakly, and his even weaker jawline made a feeble attempt to harden. Then, resting his velvet-clothed arm on the narrow window sill, he continued, "There is an unfortunate fellow here in the city by the name of Hogan Linford who has a fat wife and thirteen drooling brats. The poor gentleman has been told by a physician—Dr. John Redding—that the sickness of his throat is a cancer and that he has a matter of weeks—even days—to live. Such a gallant fellow! He is willing to give up

38

what little time he has left of his life in exchange for a trust fund I have offered to set up for his family until the last of his children are grown. He has offered to trade places with you on the gallows, and a guard will be handsomely paid for, shall we say, not betraying the exchange?"

"Even if I agreed to such an inhumane act, why would you wish that I live?"

Webster Mayne dramatically cleared his throat, then rubbed his balding pate. "It seems that I have a little problem. My uncle chose a most inopportune time to send for the daughter he had not seen in seventeen years. As you might know, dear Standish willed half his estate to this wood brat, with very annoying stipulations."

"And half to your mother! Wasn't that enough for you?"

"It was not. I cannot take the chance—" Webster paused. Whatever he had been about to say remained unspoken. Continuing, he said, "My father and I need desperately to inherit all of my uncle's estate. That is where you come in."

"And what can I do, you bastard?"

Webster remained undaunted. "I need your assistance in dealing with my young cousin."

Animation sprang to Cole's features. "Is the woman in Philadelphia?"

"Not yet. But she will come to see her father." Webster's wry grin creased his right jaw. "She will come despite your journey to try to stop her." Cole's dark eyebrow shot up. "Yes, I know all about it. I overheard you and Standish talking in his study, and I know he sent you to persuade his daughter not to come . . . after he had sent Mr. Rowell to fetch her to him."

"Why don't you tell me why he changed his mind? And why he was so frightened when I returned to Rourke House?"

"I'm afraid my uncle and I exchanged rather harsh words. A threat or two might have been dropped."

Cole's tall, slim figure slightly wavered. He braced himself against the doorjamb, outside of which the guard stood—the one, he assumed, who was in on the conspiracy. In the short span of time that followed—as he tried not to think of the tragic young woman within Webster's maniacal clutches—Cole had to make a choice between saving his own life or saving the life of a man dying of an unfortunate disease, a man who had only a few days—at best, weeks—to spend with a family he must love very much. Cole wanted to live more than anything, but he could not agree to anything as heinous as having another man executed in his place. Therefore, he replied, "There is no need to tell me your plan. I will not agree to exchange my life for another."

With an irate "harumph!" Mayne clicked his finger, catching the guard's attention. "Bring the man in here."

Almost immediately, a thin, dark-haired man was ushered into the chamber. His skin was jaundiced, and his eyes were almost blood-red. He could not stand without the guard's support and it was only too obvious he was, indeed, dying. In a scarcely audible whisper, Hogan Linford asked, "Is this the man?"

Webster replied, "It is, but he will not agree."

Strength without a visible source surged through the dying man's veins. He staggered the few short feet toward Cole and held firmly to the lapels of his ragged muslin shirt. "You cannot do this, sir. You are a strong, young man, with many years ahead of you. You cannot wish to die. I have so little time left and you must—" desperation rose in his voice, "you must think of my family. Without me to make a living for them, they will surely perish. Mr. Mayne has so generously agreed to provide for them. Please, you must agree!" The desperation in his voice drained him of his strength. He half fell to his knees and Cole, chained like a dangerous animal, was powerless to offer him assistance.

"I'm sorry for your misfortune," Cole replied in a strangled whisper. Tears moistening his eyes, he hoarsely ordered the guard, "Please, take him to a place he can rest. I cannot bear his suffering." When the muffled sobs of the man faded into silence, Cole turned his tearfully enraged eyes toward Webster Mayne. "I hate you for this! Tell me your plan! But before I agree to this exchange, I wish you to summon a trustee of my own choosing, and I will first see that you hand over the funds for that man's family! And you make it worthwhile! Every last farthing of your personal resources!" Cole's jawline firmly clenched. "God have mercy on your black soul! Because one day I will see you dead!"

Webster returned to Rourke House within the hour, well pleased with the scheme he had devised. He set Tuxford to work in the basement, work that Webster's father was not to know about. Then he moved up the stairs to the east wing of the house and soon unlocked both the doors to his mother's bed-chamber.

Moving about the large, dusty chamber, Webster sighed deeply. He liked coming here. His mother was the one person in all the world who loved him, and he loved her in return. She was unusually quiet this morning. Soon, he took a chair beside her bed and touched his hand to hers.

"How are we today, Mother? I do hope your brother didn't upset you the other day. But you needn't worry. He will tell no one about you." Silence. Webster leaned back in the chair, a bit weary. "You see, Mother, I had to kill him. He was going to change his will, cut you out of it completely and leave everything to that little wood brat who will be arriving at the house any day now. I am going to have to deal with her, too. Your blasted brother has tied up what you should have gotten when your blasted mother died. You do not get your inheritance until she gets hers. And hers will be tied up for a year. Standish was worried that his daughter suffered the same mental illness as his late wife—I am afraid that misunderstanding was my fault completely, tch, tch, tch—and therefore, the girl must be proven to be sane before she can inherit. If she is declared insane, then you will get everything . . . everything, mother. You must not worry. Your Webster will take care of it for you."

Chapter 3

It had come as a great shock when Mr. Rowell and Diana Rourke arrived at the large brick house after a week-long journey only to learn that Standish Rourke had been brutally murdered in his sleep by the amiable young Scotsman he had befriended. Diana had felt a very disturbing moment of calm, despite the loss of the father she had never known, but as fleeting memories of early childhood came back to her, she became saddened at the news of his death. She had not even had the opportunity to attend his funeral.

She found her Uncle Philip to be a kindly gentleman in his late fifties, though he struck her as a trifle weak of character. He suffered from a nervous disorder that affected his hands and made them tremble almost violently. She felt sympathy for him when he tried to take her hand in comfort and his own hands shook too uncontrollably for it. He eventually settled for a brief, firm pat, then ordered his elderly servant, Mrs. Sanders, to direct her to the private suite that had been reserved for her. She was quite intrigued by a life-size portrait nestled among a wall of mirrors. The strong, masculine face, surrounded by an immaculate white wig seemed strangely familiar to her. A small brass name plate identified him as Cole Cynric Donovan. She would have to ask someone his relation to her, since she knew so little of her father's family. Unbeknownst to her, the mysterious stranger she had mét on the trail just the week before, lurked in the shadows of the massive house.

The following morning she met an almost befuddling array of characters. Her cousin, Webster made goose bumps suddenly pop up on her cool skin. Balding at the age of thirty-three, he wore the remains of his light brown hair in a queue. She remembered Hambone's warning to be cautious of him, and wondered what her old friend knew that she did not. The elderly housekeeper, the widowed Mrs. Sanders, was standoffish and visibly irritated by having to serve an additional house guest, yet there was a fleeting moment in which Diana was sure she wanted to be friendly. Mrs. Sanders's son Tuxford, ever-present with a Brown Bess musket, was a man whose very size was intimidating. Her daughter, Claudia, was a nine-year-old trapped in the body of a nineteen-year-old woman. She smiled and laughed inappropriately, then immediately launched into a silly game of hide and seek with Diana, who was not sure she would adjust to her new surroundings — and to wearing shoes — for even a fortnight.

But her first few days were not so terribly unpleasant, though she did miss the gruff, homely ways of her Aunt Rufina. She also missed dear Hambone and her bobcat, Honey Boy. The experience of new surroundings excited her but she did not feel the security she'd felt in the mountains.

The day after her arrival at Rourke House, she

had asked Philip, in the presence of Mrs. Sanders, about her Aunt Jocelyn, but he had replied simply, "Jocelyn is a very frail woman and can see no one. You need not concern yourself with her."

"But," Diana argued, though without malice, "wouldn't she enjoy the company of her only niece?"

"She has Claudia." Philip had not meant to be cruel. But the remark still stung. "A stranger in the house would be upsetting to her."

"But I am her niece. I could not possibly upset her. Will she come down to dinner?"

Mrs. Sanders had lived in the house many years. She knew Philip did not like discussing his wife's condition. She saw him squirm in his chair beneath Diana's innocent interrogation. "She won't," Mrs. Sanders replied in her usual crisp manner.

"Surely she comes downstairs sometimes."

"Never . . . hasn't left those rooms in fourteen years."

"Fourteen years! But that cannot be!"

"It is, miss." Philip rose from his chair and swiftly left the room. He did not mind Mrs. Sanders and Claudia discussing his wife, but he would not remain to listen to it. He knew that Mrs. Sanders would not be discreet, but it did not matter.

Diana watched Philip leave the room. "Did I say something to upset him?"

"It is painful for him to discuss his wife."

"I am sorry. I didn't know. Now — about my aunt, why has she isolated herself? Is something wrong with her?"

"Only in the mind. She'll allow no one in the chamber but her husband, her son, and Claudia."

"I find that very odd, Mrs. Sanders."

45

"It isn't my place to question the things that go on in this house."

Diana was confused and a little frightened by the prospect of a woman who had not left her private suite in so many years. But for the time being it would be best not to press her uncle about visiting Jocelyn Mayne. Uncle Philip would allow it when the time was right.

Here, in this big house set apart from the city of Philadelphia, its several acres surrounded by thick hedges and well-manicured rows of timber, she felt almost more isolated than she had in the mountains. Now that the dreadful news had fully sunk in, she found it abominable that her father had been murdered in his sleep by a man he had befriended. The murderer was even now awaiting execution in the Walnut Street City Jail! Diana shuddered to think about it. For days, all she'd been hearing from everyone who came to the house was a countdown to the gallows.

The day had been foggy, warm for the season, with no wind. Diana had walked the immaculate grounds, amazed at the massiveness of the house, built of red, slave-made bricks. It had cast a dark, brooding outline against the midnight sky on the night she had first arrived, and she still could not imagine that she had once lived here, that she might once have played in the nooks and crannies that were now dark, foreboding, and unfamiliar. For some reason, she felt a cold tremor settle in her throat when she stood at the edge of a creek that ran through the property, a spring-fed creek so clear she could count the pebbles lying on its bottom.

Her very first day in her new temporary life had

brought many readjustments. Mr. Rowell had informed her that in less than a year's time she and her Aunt Jocelyn would inherit in equal portions this large house, the whole of its lands, and a large fortune being held in trust in the Bank of North America, the country's oldest bank and one of only three in the nation.

"Why a year?" Diana asked. "Is that a standard waiting time?" She cared not about owning the house. She had only one thought in mind: financially assisting her Aunt Rufina and making life a little easier for her. Perhaps if she did not have to work so hard she would not be bitter and unfriendly. At least, it was something to think about. Without her, Diana would have had no family.

Mr. Rowell frowned severely. "Miss Rourke, I do not wish to be cruel, but since you have asked . . . your father's will was written just a few weeks after your mother took you away from Rourke House. He was very confused by the abandonment and did not know why you had been taken away from him. He convinced himself your mother suffered a mental illness that compelled her to flee back into the mountains where your father had first met her, and he feared that you, as your mother's daughter, might suffer from this same malady. You must prove yourself worthy of inheriting your father's estate during this year following his death—"

"I can return to the mountains then?"

"If you wish."

"I am not imprisoned here for the purpose of proving my mental stability?"

"Indeed not! Though it would be more proof to the courts of your strength of character if you remained

47

in your father's home and proved your abilities to handle your own financial affairs."

Diana drew her slender hand to her chest. "Is that all?"

"No . . . your Aunt Jocelyn's inheritance is directly tied to yours. She does not inherit until you do. If you are declared an unstable woman, then she inherits your half. If she should die, you inherit her portion. But only if you are declared competent. If neither of you inherit, then the municipality of Philadelphia becomes sole legatee."

"Oh, dear. I believe I've been insulted by my own father. Tell me, Mr. Rowell, how my father could question my mental state, when the only other legatee has locked herself in her private suite for fourteen years?"

Again, Rowell frowned. "That, Miss Rourke, is a question that I cannot answer."

"I see."

After Mr. Rowell's departure, Diana felt terribly uncomfortable in her father's house. She walked for a long, long time on the grounds, then with the approach of evening twilight and cooler weather, she forced herself back to the dreary, dark-paneled interior of Rourke House. She had found the parlor her favorite place to be. There, above the massive hand-carved fireplace, hung a portrait of her mother, Rowanna, when she might have been about Diana's age. A life-size portrait of her father handsomely astride a fine white stallion almost filled another wall. His eyes were kind and smiling in their lustrous liveliness. They brought back vague memories of those days so long ago when he had held her and whispered endearments to her. Why, when was she able to remember those tender moments and the tragic day of their parting, could she not remember the reason her mother had fled from so loving a man?

She joined Webster for dinner that evening, but he'd had a bit too much brandy to be good company. "Webster, where is my father buried?"

"In our private cemetery," he replied in a tone much too sharp to suit the conversation.

"Is that far?"

"Across the bridge and at the bottom of the hill near the hedgerow."

"I shall go there tomorrow in reverence to my father."

"I wouldn't, Diana. The ground is extremely muddy this time of year. Why not wait until your father's tombstone has been properly erected."

"And when will that be?"

"After the new year. It has been specially ordered from Virginia."

"Webster?"

Annoyed by her chatty mood, Webster replied, "What is it?"

"Are we going to celebrate Christmas?"

"We never celebrate Christmas. Your father ceased the tradition seventeen years ago."

Diana shrank. "Since my mother and I left this house?"

"Yes."

"Very well. It would not be appropriate to celebrate now that he is gone."

"You are being sensible, Cousin."

Within the next few minutes, Diana retired to her sleeping chamber on the upper floor. It was something of a mystery why she had been housed in the massive bedchamber which, with its oversize furnishings, was very masculine. An antique portrait of a Scottish ancestor, Cole Cynric Donovan, monopolized the wall among the row of ceiling high mirrors. She could lie on the great bed and see many reflections of the portrait in the mirrors, as though they surrounded her. From the first moment she had seen the portrait, she had been intrigued by it. The face in the portrait seemed somehow familiar, though she could not imagine why. The gray eyes of the man the portrait were staring almost blankly and his arms were crossed; his attire reflected the European fashions of the early eighteenth century. He was clean-shaven, with tiny lines at the corners of his eyes probably caused by the weathering of time rather than the artist's brush. His brocade waistcoat was meticulously detailed, as though its buttons could be unfastened by nimble, living fingers. He had a crooked little smile, as though mischief had passed fleetingly through his mind at the precise moment of the artist's rendition of his features. Diana felt a familial attraction to the image of her relative who had been dead for almost seventy years.

With a small sigh, Diana closed her violet eyes, his features firmly ensconced in her memory. Then she sat up, so quickly she felt dizzy, to lock her gaze to those exquisite eyes in the portrait. Of course! Free of the white wig, wearing buckskins rather than the ancient garment of the early 18th century, he could very well be the man who had blocked her path on the Allegheny trail. What a strange, yet warming coincidence. Cloaking her eyes with the darkness, allowing dreams to fill her, she quickly felt sleep overtaking her. She did not hear the sounds that suddenly broke the silence, or feel the soft whisper of the gauze draperies above her bed slightly touch her cheek as the third of the five mirrored panels opened on recently oiled hinges. Then Cole Donovan, staring down at her for just a moment with a strange sadness in his eyes, disappeared into the darkness behind the panel.

The following morning, Diana rose early, drawn from her bed by another unseasonably mild day. She went through her armoire, examining the dresses that had been made especially for her in the days before her arrival at Rourke House. She was amazed that they had been sized so perfectly when her father did not know her, or her size. Having lived in the Alleghenies most of her life, owning just one ragged skirt and blouse at a time, she felt overwhelmed by the wealth of so many fine dresses. Still, she eyed the shoes with consternation. They hurt terribly, and Mrs. Sanders's assurance that they would soon conform to the shape of her feet was very little consolation. They were ugly, thick-soled, encumbering things, and she decided to go barefoot in the house, her feet unnoticed because of the voluminous skirts Mrs. Sanders suggested — indeed, ordered — that she wear.

That day, Uncle Philip and Webster brought Dr. John Redding home to have dinner with them and meet Diana. She enjoyed Dr. Redding's company. He promised that with the consent of her uncle she could accompany him and his wife on a proposed visit to New York City.

"But I cannot," she said quietly, cutting a quick glance toward her uncle. "I want only to return to my home in the mountains."

51

John Redding arched a graying eyebrow. "Do you, indeed?"

Philip Mayne immediately cut in, "But, my dear, you cannot leave Philadelphia until after your father's will has been probated. That will take a year."

"Only because my father thought I might be insane," she pouted. "Mr. Rowell said I could return if I wished, that there was no stipulation in the will preventing it." Even as she spoke, she remembered Aunt Rufina and her promise to return within a fortnight. "I certainly cannot stay a year."

Dr. Redding took her hands and gave them a gentle squeeze. "Have you met your Aunt Jocelyn?" John Redding had been made very curious by Mrs. Sanders' frequent remarks that the lovely Jocelyn had isolated herself to her suite.

"We do not speak of Jocelyn!" Philip intervened rather rudely.

"No, we don't," Webster added. "The subject of my mother is not open to discussion."

"I see." As John Redding looked into the lovely, bewildered eyes of Standish Rourke's daughter, he wondered why she was not allowed to visit her Aunt Jocelyn. Though he did not understand the reason, he would honor the request of the Mayne men not to bring up the subject of Jocelyn. His personal opinion was that the visits would be good therapy for the very disturbed lady, though he had not told Philip so. To relieve the tension that had suddenly arisen, John got back to the subject of New York. "Perhaps, if you stay for a while, you might change your mind about visiting New York . . . if you have not been snatched from society by a handsome young bachelor."

Diana blushed prettily. "I doubt, sir, that such a

man would look at a wood sprite such as me."

John Redding laughed. "Young lady, I believe that they would!"

When the men began discussing politics, and where to purchase the best snuffs and teas, Diana politely excused herself.

She was just moving up the stairs toward her chamber when the spry, petite Claudia jumped from the shadows of a corner in the bend of the stairs.

Diana drew back with a small cry of alarm, her hand instinctively clutching at her throat. "You bad girl! You scared me to death!"

Claudia's animated features suddenly drained. A pout turned down the corners of her mouth. "Sorry, miss. Just want to be your friend."

Diana was suddenly very ashamed. In all the years of living in the mountains among bushy men and Indians, she had ached for friends her own age. But the only friends she'd had were old Hambone—whose real name she had never known and had never really thought to ask—and the trappers and Indians who patronized her Aunt Rufina's trading post. "Please, forgive me. It's just that you startled me and I reacted without thinking. You will forgive me, won't you?"

"Sure, miss." Straight brown hair whipped across her shoulders as she looked to be sure they were alone. "Going to the hanging tomorrow, miss?"

"Hanging? What—" Then it occurred to her—the man who had killed her father. "No, of course I won't go. What a dreadful thing to ask me!"

"Why, miss? Everyone from hereabouts will be there. Even Master Philip has given mum and me permission to go. They'll bring him out of the jail all

53

hooded, with his hands tied at his back—"

"Hush!" Diana spoke harshly, closing her eyes tightly against the ugly picture forming in her mind. She rushed toward her bedchamber and slammed the door, leaving a very confused serving girl standing on the platform of the stairs.

Philip and Webster were engaged at the liquor cabinet far past midnight. Webster, as usual, was arrogant, his father tolerant, and certainly neither was good company for the other. Whenever they were together, tension was very thick about them.

"I am going to take care of the will," Webster told his father, swirling brandy in his goblet, its amber liquid catching the glow of the fire.

"You'll not cause any harm to that lovely young woman," Philip ordered, his voice suddenly gaining more force. "I'll not have her hurt. From what I have heard, she wants only to return to the home of her mother's sister."

Webster had not told his father that he'd traded a dying man for the life of Cole Donovan. Webster had made sure Cole was well aware that he could still go to the gallows if the deed he had proposed to him was not accomplished in the appointed time. "Has Mother found out yet about her brother's death?"

"Don't be preposterous!"

Webster enjoyed baiting his father. "You'd better hope, father, that no one finds out before the year is out."

"If you keep a level head, and keep out of the liquor, perhaps no one will find out."

"And suppose they do, Father? Standish found

54

out—"

"Of course he found out! He overheard us discussing her! Why do you think he sent Donovan to warn Diana not to come? Why do you think he was so determined to get into Jocelyn's chamber?"

"He had no right to impose himself on Mother."

"He had every right. What we have done all these year is—" Philip shuddered violently. "My God, Webster. Any reasonable man would have reacted the same."

"Then you see why—?" Webster immediately bit off his words—his near confession. His father was pouring another brandy. He appeared not to have caught Webster's truncated statement.

"Suppose Claudia one day opens her eyes," Philip continued glumly, turning back.

"Claudia?" A dark eyebrow rose. "Claudia doesn't have the sense to close her eyes in sleep, let alone open them. Just remember, Father, if we don't inherit, we don't pay our debts. And if we don't pay our debts, some of our unscrupulous creditors will not hesitate to slit our throats!"

Philip Mayne shuddered. "Thank you, Webster. I could not have made it through the day without that little reminder." Slamming his fist into the palm of his left hand, he continued, "I cannot believe Cole killed my brother-in-law. He and Standish had become very good friends."

"But all the evidence pointed to him. If not he, then who?" Philip gave his son a long scrutinizing look, flustering Webster. "You do not think that I killed him, do you? Dear God, do not take out your irritability on me!"

Philip wished he was strong enough to answer

from his heart. He'd suspected his son all along, but had quietly denied it since the murder. He evaded Webster's inquiry. "With my brother-in-law dead and his daughter in the house, things are going to change. The house will be half hers, and as soon as the will is probated, she will have a voice in what becomes of it. I do not want Diana annoyed to the point where she will request we move from the house."

"She cannot do that. Because of Mother—"

"Shut up about her!" Immediately, Philip's voice softened. "I believe we can live in harmony here, and perhaps she will keep the house in the family in reverence to her father."

"And I repeat again . . . what if someone finds out about Mother, as Standish did?"

Drawing his violently trembling fingers to his eyes, Philip replied, "We will not think about that now. We must concentrate on Mr. Donovan. I must presume he killed my brother-in-law. Perhaps things will settle themselves after his execution."

That is what you think! Webster thought, replying instead in his curt, calloused manner, "Our poor distant cousin, Cole, who cannot decide whether he is Scottish or British. What a shame to die so young!" Webster, a bit of a boaster, found it very difficult not to gloat of the switch that had been made at the Walnut Street City Jail. But he had to be discreet; Cole's services to the Rourke household were too valuable. Because of his uncanny resemblance to the original Cole Cynric Donovan, whose portrait hung upstairs, he was the only one who could accomplish the deed that had to be done, driving the tall, slim beauty who would be one of

Standish Rourke's legatees into an asylum. Webster thought it a bit of bad luck that his uncle's will had not stipulated that "if she die within the year, etc., etc. and etc." Killing her would have been so much easier than having to go to the trouble of proving her mentally incompetent. Nevertheless, whatever the late Standish Rourke's intentions had been, Webster silently thanked him for the loophole he had provided. Threading his greed through the narrow eye of that loophole was another matter.

Webster frowned, thinking how the Scotsman had, for the time being, bested him when, at the hour of ten o'clock yesterday morning, a canvas bag containing every last farthing of Webster's personal wealth had been passed to a bank trustee for the benefit of a fat woman and her thirteen drooling brats. *But he will uphold his end of the bargain. I guarantee that!* Webster thought, a wry grin twisting his face as he left the parlor.

Diana changed from her burgundy velvet dress into a light-weight cotton sleeping gown with long, lace-fringed sleeves. She unpinned her golden hair, allowing it to cascade over her shoulders and back. Upon her arrival she'd found a lovely silver filigree brush and comb set. Now she sat before the boudoir mirror—the one feminine item of furniture in the chamber—and brushed her hair with a vengeance. She remembered her years in the mountains, caring not whether her long tresses were disheveled, caring not whether it took three days to untangle the knots braided there by the whipping wind. But Mrs. Sanders had suggested that she had to assume the

57

position of a lady of wealth, and such ladies did not allow themselves to be untidy and unkempt. Diana had even been required to take a bath last night and this morning in a tub filled to capacity with lathers and perfumed oils. What had happened to her former life, when she had simply abandoned her ragged garments on a rock and swam beneath her favorite Allegheny waterfall?

Tonight she was unusually sleepy. Perhaps she did not want to think of the dawn, when the young man who had killed her father was to be hanged. Even this mile's distance from the town of Philadelphia she had been able to hear the gathering of carriages and wagons throughout the night, the faraway, haunting echo of voices; even children were being brought to view the gruesome spectacle. Diana was sickened by it. The event was treated like a picnic, the three condemned men the main course for the bloodthirsty colonists who were gathering. What had happened to humanity?

She knew she must have slept very heavily, for when she was suddenly awakened by a sound so close it seemed to be in her room, she sat up sluggishly, rubbing her eyes as she did so. The room was almost foggy, like the night outside the window. Moonlight shone through the chamber and caught the features of the portrait of Cole Cynric Donovan, reflecting it hauntingly among the long panels of mirrors. She rubbed her eyes sleepily. Then, as though something had suddenly popped into her mind, she became aware that there was a difference in the portrait. She tried to focus in the semi-darkness, drawing the heavy covers over her drawn-up knees. Then she saw it. The arms were crossed differently. The smirk at the corner of his full, masculine mouth was not there. Rather, he frowned. She froze with fear. One of the hands moved and she saw the brocade waistcoat tighten across his chest. Animation suddenly sprang to the portrait; it was three dimensional — and the long-dead ancestor was slowly and surely moving toward the foot of her bed.

With a scream of fear gathering in her throat, Diana scooted from her bed, traversed the room, and pulled the door wide open. She stood there, quaking so violently that she could scarcely keep her knees from buckling. The cry continued to freeze in her throat. Then, drawing her hands to her ears, she found the strength to let out a loud, piercing scream, which immediately alerted the household.

She was hysterical by the time Philip Mayne reached her. Soon, supported between Philip and Webster, she was led to a sitting room just down the corridor. His niece sobbing uncontrollably, Philip called for Mrs. Sanders, who had donned her dressing gown the moment she'd heard Diana's fearful cry.

Mrs. Sanders showed her first moment of kindness as she rocked Diana gently against her plump shoulder and soothed her with comforting words. "Calm down, girl, and tell us what has frightened you so."

Philip stood sternly just a few feet away. Webster had thrown himself lazily on a settee across the room and his right leg hung over the arm. He sighed wearily.

"He—he came to my room!" Diana stammered, her sobs becoming choking lumps in her throat.

"Who, girl? Who came to your room?"

"Him! The man in the portrait. He moved. I saw him."

"My God!" Webster feigned annoyance. "You are referring to a man who has been dead for sixty-eight years. Your own great-grandfather, Diana!" He flipped his wrist, turning his head just in time to catch his father's disapproving look.

Suspicion immediately pinched Philip's brows. "Mrs. Sanders, take my niece back to her bed. I'm sure she has just suffered a nightmare."

Diana flicked away her tears. "Yes, that's all it was." She did not want to upset her afflicted uncle her first week in the house. "Thank you for understanding."

Then Diana saw the way Webster was looking at her—with hatred. He seemed oddly pleased at her frightened state. Since the nightmare was the first she'd had in many, many years, she'd had a right to react as she had. But as she met Webster's gloating look, she vowed that she would not be weak. She pulled away from Mrs. Sanders, rose unsteadily to her feet, and moved toward the sitting room door.

"Perhaps I did have a bad dream," she said quietly. "I apologize for disrupting the household. It will not happen again."

"Go with her, Mrs. Sanders," Philip ordered, his voice soft with kindness.

"No!" Diana turned and gave him a strong, unwavering look. "I said I am fine. I do not need a nursemaid in my chamber."

"Very well." As she walked away, her head held proud and erect, Webster Mayne smiled sardonically. "I believe it's going to work," he murmured.

As soon as Philip retreated down the corridor,

Mrs. Sanders started to step past Webster. But he brutally took her arm, causing her to wince from the pain. "I'll have your soul if you breathe so much as a word to the girl of what's going on. You and your simple-minded girl will have your throats slit if my father and I do not inherit my uncle's property."

"I thought it was your mother who would inherit."

Webster smiled wickedly. "Her inheritance is our inheritance."

Mrs. Sanders recalled the evening before, when she'd seen Cole Donovan slipping into the cellar from the darkness of the winter-barren shrubbery. Since he was supposed to be hanging the morning after, she had, without thinking, gone immediately to Webster with the news. He'd had no choice but to bring Mrs. Sanders in on the conspiracy, and she had no choice but to go along with it. After all, as Webster had callously reminded her, she had no other home but the one she had made for herself and her children at Rourke House. She would go along with him, or he would make all their lives a living hell.

When he released his brutal grip, Mrs. Sanders, tears filling her eyes, returned to the bedchamber which she'd been reassigned, beside the one in which Diana Rourke slept.

Chapter 4

As a brave, hooded young man named Hogan Linford was being hanged along with two other men, an early morning drizzle fell on Philadelphia. The bodies that went limp beneath the gallows brought loud cheers and boisterous laughter from the large crowd of men, women and children who had gathered to witness the gruesome sight. Many had moved as close as the guards would allow them, because the fog was thick and the condemned men mere black outlines upon the gallow traps. As was the custom, the bodies were displayed in their simple pine coffins for several hours before being buried. Only one remained hooded; a guard telling the crowd that it had been "his last wish" — an explanation that brought a round of protests from the viewers.

Diana tried not to think about the hanging. Actually, she was enjoying her first trip to a major city. Like other cities, Philadelphia was a mixture of land uses, with stables, breweries, blacksmith shops, soap boilers and tanyards intermixed with taverns, offices, shops, and opulent residences. Unlike other cities that had been hastily thrown up without sensible thought, Philadelphia had been carefully planned, and its streets followed a regular grid pattern. A center of foreign trade, it was a fine place to shop for china, silks, stays, and wine, for wimble bits and pickled mangoes, for weathervanes, stoves, and venetian blinds. It was also a center of medicine, the arts, science, and literature. But Webster was intent on spoiling Diana's journey to the city. When Uncle Philip left early on business, Webster insisted that they pay a visit to Dr. Redding, in the hopes of planting the seed of Diana's mental instability. Greed for his dead uncle's wealth compelled Webster to drag his protesting cousin into John's small, neatly furnished offices.

"I told him that I was all right," Diana whispered quietly, glad to be alone behind the curtain with the kindly doctor. "I had a frightful dream, but Webster insists that I confessed to seeing ghosts. My goodness! I admit that the handsome fellow in the portrait—regardless of whether he's my great-grandfather," she continued in an attempt at humor, "would certainly stir the romantic wiles of a healthy young woman, but I assure you, Dr. Redding, that I *do not* see ghosts."

The short, stocky physician patted her hand in a paternal gesture. He was a little surprised that Webster Mayne would react so dramatically to something as trivial as a nightmare. After all, the young woman had recently been taken from an environment she had known for seventeen years. She was a stranger in Philadelphia and at Rourke House, the place where her father had been murdered. It was only natural that her state of mind might be a trifle ruffled. She would, after all, need adequate time to adjust to a new way of life, and he fully intended to explain that to Webster Mayne. Looking at the lovely face of the young woman, he sensed the panic she must feel. Holding her hands just moments before, he had felt tiny callouses on the palms of her otherwise flawless hands. She had been a hard worker in her other life. She must be overwhelmed by the suddenness of so much wealth—the Rourke wealth—when she had probably lived in abject poverty. John Redding's heart went out to the young lady who had been dragged from one insecure world into another. And he was suddenly very angry with Webster Mayne for even suggesting that she was mentally unsound. Perhaps Webster had other motives. He would certainly have to look into it. Momentarily, John Redding approached a glass-fronted medicine cabinet and took a brown medicine jar from it. "This is laudanum," he explained. "Take only half a teaspoon at night if you cannot sleep. And," he smiled warmly, "if you happen to see any more ghosts, just close your eyes and tell yourself that it is just a dream. Can you do that for me?"

Diana nodded her assent. "Yes, I believe I can. I'll just close my eyes." Dramatically, smiling, she firmly shut her eyes and whispered, "You are not there—you are only a figment of my imagination."

John Redding rose from his chair, then took her hand to help her up. "Perfect! And should you need female company outside that dreary old house, you let me know. I shall fetch you into town to spend the day with my wife, Rosa."

"Thank you." Diana was not sure why she felt so comfortable with the middle-aged physician. "If my persistent ghost argues with me, I shall demand that he kiss me. After all, one cannot feel the kiss of an apparition, isn't that so?"

"It is, indeed!" John Redding favored her with a comforting smile, charmed by her affable character, then turned her toward the outer office. Just before he parted the curtain for her, he whispered, "Do not tell your cousin about the laudanum. Use it only when you feel it is necessary."

"Very well. Now we shall see what my cousin thinks about my visit with you today."

Webster certainly was not receptive to John Redding's explanation about the change of environment and exchanged insecurities. "Her mental state is in question here, John," he retorted persistently. "I insist that she be more thoroughly examined!" He knew that was not necessary. But it was vital that the seed of doubt be planted early.

"And what shall I do?" John shot back with equal annoyance, "Hack open her head and see what goes on in her brain?" He smiled apologetically at Diana Rourke. "She is fine. Take her back home and give her time to adjust to life at Rourke House. And for mercy's sake, take that damned portrait out of her sleeping chamber, or else make other arrangements for her. Surely, there are other rooms in the house more suitable to her needs."

"Perhaps I should do that." Webster had no intention of following either suggestion, but he could not allow John Redding to see that he was desperate to have the girl declared insane. Webster and his father had many creditors, many of unscrupulous reputation. They would have no way to repay them without the wealth tied up in his dead uncle's estate. And he was not willing to wait the rest of the year, the time Mr. Rowell had told them to expect the final probate. If Diana was declared insane, then his mother's inheritance would also be freed for distribution. They needed the money now.

John Redding escorted the two to the door of his office. "It is the middle of the week, Webster — not much going on. Take your cousin on a tour of the city. Show her the shops. Introduce her to some of the ladies about town. She needs to make new friends. Don't confine her to that stuffy old house day in and day out.

Take her to meet Mr. John Fitch and Noah Webster. It might be her only opportunity to meet men of importance." Webster Mayne frowned. "That is, important men in addition to yourself," John amended hastily. "Noah might acquaint her with the art of lexicography. She'd enjoy that."

"Whatever it is," Diana quietly responded, "I am sure I will enjoy learning about it. Are you agreeable, Cousin? Might we see a bit of the city before returning home?"

Reluctantly, Webster agreed. "But we cannot tarry long. I have business about town and you really must tend to your correspondence. You said you would write to your Aunt Rufina today."

"There is always tomorrow," she replied, smiling in anticipation of the tour. "My letter can go out in Friday's mail." As they began their descent of the stairs onto Market Street, Diana turned and smiled at John Redding. "Thank you for your kindness. Won't you come to visit us again very soon?"

"Of course, I will."

"Come to dinner tomorrow?"

John cut a look at the tall, frowning Webster Mayne. Webster slighted nodded his assent. "Very well. I'll see you then."

Cole Donovan could not complain about the basement suite to which he had been condemned, except that it had only one painfully small window that allowed light. The brick walls had been freshly painted in a soft cream color, the doorways refurbished with decorative facings, and a deep green carpet installed throughout the large three-room suite. It had been furnished with a comfortable bed and an armoire large enough to hold the several historical garments that had been sewn for him in secret—fashions that might have been worn by his ancestral namesake eighty years before. The suite was accessible only through a door behind a shelf that at present housed bottles of aging wine, a door that one unfamiliar with the basement would never find. That one door gave him access to the three stories of the house through the narrow passageways built between the walls. He could enter any room at will . . . except one. The passageway entrance of the suite where Jocelyn Mayne lived had been bricked up years before.

He sat in a comfortable chair beside a shelf well-stocked with books and other reading material—Webster Mayne did not want him to become bored in his "prison." He could not stop thinking about that lovely oval face he had first seen on a narrow wood trail in the Allegheny Mountains. Seeing her again last night had merely added fuel to the fire consuming his heart. He had witnessed her in sleeping innocence, her mouth petulant and full, her eyelids violet and almost translucent in the light of the moon, her tresses spun by the moonlight into strands of gold that blinded him with their beauty. He remembered a small, slim hand lying gently beside her cheek, the single satin bedsheet outlining a tall, graceful, feminine form such as he had never before seen. He had felt his heart race with unexpected pleasure, and regret. He did not like what Webster Mayne had ordered him to do in exchange for his own life. And in these past few hours he had made an important decision. He would flee Rourke House and Philadelphia to begin his journey into the American interior. And he would take Diana Rourke with him, even if he had to kidnap her.

Certainly, Diana Rourke was not as Webster had described, and he had only half listened to Standish—a parent always saw beauty in the homeliest of children.

67

Cole had expected a whimpering, hump-shouldered woman with a mentality two shades above a moron. But even in her sleeping loveliness, Cole had sensed keen intelligence. He could imagine her quick wit.

Cole could hardly bear to meet his reflection in the mirror above the washstand as he rose to wipe the perspiration from his brow. Why, he wondered, had he been born with the same face as his ancestor? Even though Cole had caught the eye of many women who had been only too willing to point out his remarkable physical traits, Cole, himself, tended to disdain them. For all he cared, his dark, wavy hair could be thin and mouse-brown, his strong jawline weak, his broad-shouldered, virile body thin and malnourished. At the moment, he wished he were dead. But if he truly wished that, he'd have gone to the gallows as planned, and damn the unfortunate rogue who had wanted to provide for his large family after his death.

He couldn't help but remember the shock he had seen in the eyes of the beautiful Diana Rourke when she had suddenly awakened from her sleep. How he must have startled her! He had entered through the secret mirror and had stood precisely where Webster had told him to stand, before the portrait of the original Cole Donovan, where the moonlight would catch his features. She had scarcely touched the floor to race hysterically from her bedchamber. Cole had then disappeared behind the mirror and before to the hidden suite in the cellar.

He turned from the washstand just as the secret door opened and a very irritated Webster Mayne entered, removing one of his riding gloves. Cole felt his hands clench in rage as his eyes met the man's sarcastic gaze.

"Well, our dear Dr. Redding feels that my young cousin is merely having trouble adjusting to her new surroundings."

With sudden ferocity, Cole pulled the brocade waist-coat down his arms and threw it to the back of the chair. "So! You are already attempting to plant the seeds of suspicion against that poor girl. God, man, have you no conscience?"

"Not where my uncle's estate, or your life, is concerned. Don't forget, Cousin," he continued with abating sarcasm. "I can snap my fingers and you'll find yourself back in that fetid hole on Walnut Street, charged with not one, but two murders. Hogan Linford."

"I had nothing to do with that!" Cole raised his hand to his forehead to brush back an unruly lock of hair. "Could Walnut Street be any more confining than this prison?"

Webster arched an eyebrow. "You don't like your new quarters, Cousin? I had them specially renovated and furnished for your comfort and convenience. It is ungracious of you to complain." He turned and poured himself a brandy from the bottle on a small mahogany table. "I see you have not partaken of the liqueurs I brought for you. Would you care for one?"

"No!"

"Mind if I do?"

"Would it matter if I did?"

Webster chuckled with undaunted calm. "Not in the least, Cousin. I came here, not to exchange insults and barbs with you, but to go over our little plan. The household has been apprised of your presence. Poor Mrs. Sanders, who fears for her life and that of her stupid daughter—"

"You treat her like a slave," Cole shot back. "She has nowhere else to go."

"She is a capable woman."

"That may very well be. But who is going to take into domestic service a girl who sees ghosts . . . a girl who

69

hasn't the sense to come in out of the rain! And your blasted man, Tuxford! He's lucky someone hasn't cut his damned throat!" Some had suspected Tuxford of being a traitor during the revolution. There were some who believed him to be the ten-year-old boy who had carried messages back and forth between General Thomas Gage and his top officers on the front.

"Mrs. Sanders," Webster mused with imperturbable calm. "It is a good thing some women will do anything to protect their children, isn't it? But enough of Mrs. Sanders. Getting back to my young cousin, until my further orders you are not to make an appearance except in her chamber, or out on the grounds at night when no one is about, with the exception of Claudia. And, God help you if my weak-minded father finds out about this! You must convince my young cousin that you are the apparition of our long-dead ancestor. No one else in the house will ever admit to your presence, and if that simple-minded Claudia says she sees you, I can easily refute her statements. She has collected half a dozen ghosts by now. Another will not matter one way or another. If seeing ghosts does not break my cousin's resistance, you are in a lot of trouble, Cousin."

Cole fell lazily to the chair where he had thrown his waistcoat. He had no intentions of following Webster's orders.

Webster gulped his brandy. "I have business I must attend to in New Jersey. While I am gone, I expect you to make covert appearances every night. And," he waved a bony finger, "I am serious, Cousin. My father is not to find out about this. What he does not know will not hurt him." Webster cleared his throat with a little too much melodrama. "When you enter my cousin's suite, always make sure you awaken her."

Cole pressed his thumb and forefinger to his closed eyes. "Of course! Sleeping beauties can see no apparitions, can they?"

"Don't be flippant!" Webster approached the door and searched for the tiny latch that would swing it open on well-oiled hinges. "Once she is declared insane and institutionalized, you will be free to return to Scotland, or England, or wherever the hell you wish to call home."

"In the meantime, you get away with murder?"

Webster's mouth twisted into a wry grin. "I am a bit impatient, I'll admit. But it's my damned cousin's fault. Once my uncle reunited with her, he'd have written my mother out of his will and left everything to her. At least this way we still have mother's inheritance. And, if you play your cards straight, we'll have my cousin's, also."

"I don't like having been condemned for murdering a man who was my good friend when it was you who did the foul deed."

"You will get over it, Cousin. Besides, you are not a Mayne, a most respected name throughout Pennsylvania. You are dispensable. The Maynes are not."

That was a point Cole would certainly find time to refute at a later date.

Cole Donovan took advantage of Webster Mayne's journey to New Jersey to confine himself to his basement suite. He did not make nightly visits to Diana's bedchamber on either Wednesday or Thursday night, though he wanted to — not to frighten her, but simply to look at her, even to hold her and feel the warmth of her mouth against his own. He had imagined such a kiss a thousand times since the night he had appeared at her bedchamber and sent her fleeing hysterically into the corridor.

Webster's absence would have provided the perfect cover to flee from Rourke House with Diana, except for one thing. At Webster's orders, all the horses, save one aging, winded mare, had been taken to stables ten miles to the north of Rourke House. They were, in effect, prisoners at the bleak house Cole wished to God he'd never seen.

He slept restlessly that Thursday night but awoke to a day turning fair and windy. Mrs. Sanders brought his breakfast around seven o'clock. Cole always said "Good morning," but she never responded. Guilt pinched her mouth into a thin line and she always left as silently as she had come.

Shortly after the hour of eight he heard feminine laughter in the winter-barren garden outside the one window of his basement suite. It was not the familiar, high-pitched laughter of Claudia, but a laugh that was almost like a whisper on the wind. He wanted so much to see Diana, to watch her fresh, early morning loveliness flitting across the grounds, and with that thought in mind he dressed in the attire matching that worn by his ancestor in the portrait, leaving the wig on its wooden stand. He left his suite, his breakfast untouched.

He exited through the cellar door and instantly saw her sitting on a stone bench, playing with Mrs. Sanders's big yellow cat. He leaned against a pole and watched from the shadows of the cellar door. She was lovely, lithe, dressed in a pale blue skirt and white long-sleeved shirtwaist. Her foot kicked out from beneath the hem of her skirt, betraying that she wore no shoes. He smiled. He wanted to make his presence known to her, but knew he could not. She was only to see him in the evenings, surrounded by darkness. Thus, regretfully, he turned back to his suite and disinterestedly picked at the ample breakfast Mrs. Sanders had brought to him.

Webster returned to Rourke House shortly before the evening meal. "Well, how have you been, Diana?" he asked, taking her arm as they moved toward the dining room.

"I've enjoyed the mild weather," she said. "It's so lovely. I wish I could recall more of my childhood here. Perhaps one day some little thing will bring back a pleasant memory. Where is Uncle Philip, by the way?"

Webster frowned as he absently replied, "Here and about, I would assume. Now, about your nights? Any more of those ghastly nightmares?"

"Heavens no!" she laughed quietly, choosing not to tell him of the laudanum she took at Dr. Redding's direction. "And no more ghosts!"

Color rose in Webster Mayne's face. He was angry at the possibility that Cole had disobeyed him. He escorted Diana to her chair to the right of him and said, "Excuse me for just a moment. I'll see if father is going to join us for dinner."

For some strange, unexplainable reason, Diana was not overly fond of Webster. Except for overreacting to her nightmare, he had been a perfect gentleman, quite cordial and polite. Yet she did not trust him. Perhaps it was his narrow, naked scrutiny of her at times when he didn't think she was watching. Webster had just exited through the foyer when her uncle entered from the kitchen, nibbling at a small piece of roast they would have for dinner. "I thought I heard Webster."

"You did," Diana replied. "He went in search of you. I'm sure that when he doesn't find you, he'll return."

Actually, Webster was gone for almost twenty minutes. He then assumed his place at the table across from Diana, spread his napkin and clapped his hands as a cue for Mrs. Sanders and Claudia to serve dinner.

Webster was quite red-faced, his eyes narrow and

angry. Diana was concerned. "Are you all right, Webster? You were gone a very long time."

Webster smiled wryly, thinking quickly. "When I didn't find father, Diana, I chose to freshen up a bit before dinner."

Ever since writing her letter to Aunt Rufina yesterday, something had been on Diana's mind. "Uncle Philip, I know this may not be an appropriate time to bring this up, but do I—is there—" She stammered nervously. "Are there any monetary provisions for me while I am waiting out probate of the will?"

Philip quietly placed his fork beside his plate. "Of course, Diana. A bill of exchange shall be deposited in a special account for you at the bank once a month."

"For how much?"

"Fifty pounds sterling."

"Is that a lot?" she asked.

"It is a considerable amount for a young woman to spend in a month's time."

"Is it mine to do with as I please?"

Greedly little wench! Webster thought.

"It is," Philip replied, again taking up his fork.

"Good! Then I wish that all but five pounds of it be sent to my Aunt Rufina on the very day the money is deposited to my account each month. Will you arrange it with my banker?"

Philip was pleasantly surprised at the generosity of his niece, even as Webster frowned in dismay. He wanted nothing more than for his cousin to be a greedy little snip. "If it is what you wish," her uncle consented.

"It is."

The remainder of the meal was spent in near silence. Though he had returned home in a good mood, Webster had now grown dark and somber. He was short and at times rude in his replies to both Diana's and his father's inquiries about conditions in New Jersey, and did not even answer when his father began telling him of the bill of exchange Robert Morris had been required to pay Mr. William Bell that day. Nothing interested Webster and he seemed anxious to retire to his private quarters.

Diana also retired early. She took up an old diary she had earlier found in the downstairs library. No name had been inscribed in the front cover, but after several pages of reading she realized that the diary had belonged to Cole Cynric Donovan, the man whose portrait graced the chamber where she slept. She read with fascination the account of his days, until the final entry, written just a few days after his death. She knew that only because another hand had written on that final page, "Sir Cole Cynric Donovan died two days past. He has been buried on the grounds of Donovan House beside his dear wife . . ." The house had once been called Donovan House. Only through marriage had the house been assumed by the Rourkes. Her gaze returned to the same spot where she had been reading just moments before: ". . . beneath the oak where he buried his sword a few weeks ago. How long will it be visible, the gold gilt that his loving hands once caressed? My dear father once said that he would rather bury his sword in a young tree than bury it in the heart of a man, and it pains me so to think that at the time my own heart was the young sapling in my father's eyes. Even so, he should have died more nobly than to have wasted away in bed . . ." Emilia Rourke's signature was the last entry in the diary that had been her father's.

Diana did not realize tears had moistened her eyes until her cheeks suddenly felt damp. Feeling a trifle foolish, she flicked the tears away, tucked the diary into a small drawer beneath the table, and rose to ready herself for bed. But she was much too excited to even think about sleeping. She made no attempt to gather her sleeping garments from her dresser drawers. She paced the room, thinking of the diary, thinking of the tree, on these very grounds, where a gilded saber had been thrust by the hands of Cole Donovan. She thought about his grave beneath that very same tree. She had walked the grounds several times since her arrival at Rourke House, but she could not remember having seen the cemetery Webster had told her about. Had it fallen to neglect, buried among overgrown hedgerows? And now, with darkness veiling the night skies, she felt an overwhelming desire to rush out into the haunting fingers of the darkness and find his grave. But was she that brave? Her shoulders slumped. No, she didn't think so.

She resigned herself to the bed, the covers of which had been turned back. She dressed slowly, absently, removing each item of clothing as though it were the last thing she wanted to do, until she stood naked before one of the ceiling-high mirrors. She imagined that even these few days had taken the healthy color from her skin. She was accustomed to long days out of doors and even the winter sun had bronzed her skin. Perhaps she only felt pale because she felt so confined. She was not barred by puritanical convictions from studying her nakedness, relieved that the delicious meals Mrs. Sanders prepared had not begun to pad her slender frame with even a pound of additional weight. Her small, firm breasts were not the least fuller, her waist still tiny and lean, and her hips and thighs smooth and unflawed. Hers was a body that had never been seen by man, at least, not until that moment.

Cole Donovan's body felt like a boiling cauldron. Through the tiny crack in the mirror he saw her standing there, her nakedness glowing in the moonlight flooding the large chamber. He had never seen such feminine beauty, her breasts pink and upturned, her waist so small that he was sure he could span it with his hands, her hips and buttocks curving into long, lithe legs and slender feet. After that first blind, virginal look, he felt air gulp into his lungs, and his gaze instantly settled on her eyes that seemed to turn straight to his direction.

It might have been only a mouse moving in the wall, but the alarmed Diana moved quickly toward the nightclothes she had laid out on her bed. She dressed as though she were suddenly in a room full of people, staring at her nakedness. A hot flush rose in her cheeks and she almost breathed a sigh of relief as the hem of her gown touched the floor. Quickly, moving between the sheets of her bed, she drew the covers up to her neck. After a few minutes she snuffed the candle at her side and was content to lie in the semi-darkness of the January night.

Then Diana remembered her laudanum and removed it and the spoon, wrapped in a linen napkin, from beneath her pillow. She took half a teaspoonful as Dr. Redding had directed, then returned the items to their hiding place. "There," she said quietly, dropping her tousled head to the pillow, "a good night's sleep should be more rewarding than looking for your—" she spoke directly to the picture, "—grave on such a dark night." As she closed her eyes, she heard a rumbling at the stables and assumed that Tuxford was bringing back the horses. She still thought it rather odd that they had been removed two days before. But it was too trivial a matter to worry about.

Cole's silver-gray gaze watched her oval features in the moonlight. Soon, very soon, when the laudanum had taken effect, he would commence his masquerade. He would obey Webster's orders only until the proper time came to flee into the American interior, taking the lovely young victim of Webster's scheme with him. He had initially thought she would be a burden to him, but now he could think of nothing more pleasant than having such an alluring siren at his side.

Chapter 5

The tiny bit of laudanum Diana had taken flowed smoothly through her veins. She felt her body become heavy, then feather-light, just moments after she had taken it. She felt her eyes gently close. A cool breeze from the slightly opened window whispered across her exposed hands and her cheeks. In the twilight of her sleep she was again a wood sprite half running, half floating through the forest along Wills Creek in her beloved Allegheny Mountains, her long hair caught momentarily on a thin, bare twig, her slim feet moving gracefully over the large, smooth rocks at the edge of the creek. She heard the sounds of the forest, the hoot owl, the geese flying overhead. Everything beautiful floated through her mind—the whistling wind that drowned out the gruffness of Aunt Rufina's call, the pine trees that swayed to touch the horizon. Tonight the laudanum had a hypnotic effect on her. It did not only make her sleepy; it made her happy and contented, too. She felt that she could face anything tonight.

A large canopy of gauze suspended from the ceiling above her bed suddenly floated over the coverlets. She felt the whisper softness of it against her hands. She heard the distant sounds of the city—the clatter of carriages dimming with distance, the calls of rowdy, larcenous urchins seeking niches in alleyways in which to sleep for the night, the brawling of men at the taverns as they gathered enough courage to return home to scornful wives.

Then she heard something not so distant, something that seemed to be in the room with her. Strangely, she felt no fear or alarm. It was as though her thoughts had taken her away to a place of safety, to another world where there was no harm or insecurity. Her thick, blond eyelashes flickered and her blurred vision slowly, oh, so slowly, focused on the firm, masculine features of a dark-haired man. Half-closing her eyes, she smiled, remembering the first time she had seen him on the trail running parallel to Wills Creek. But he had been different then. His coal-black hair had not been covered by the antique powdered wig he now wore.

"Dr. Redding said there are no ghosts," she whispered. "He says I am to tell you that you do not exist."

Diana Rourke's voice was like music to Cole's ears. He knelt beside the bed and, without touching her, whispered in reply, "And you are right, Diana. I am as alive as you are." He tore off the wig to expose his coal-black hair. "I am the man you met on the trail in your beloved mountains." His life was still in danger from Webster, who expected him to continue the charade until she rambled like a madwoman. He was not sure from whence the courage came to tell this lovely, half-sleeping beauty the truth.

Diana was only half lucid, her euphoric state clinging to her like the gentle embrace of loving arms. She turned her head and stared at the features of a man who seemed so real that she was sure she could reach out her hand and touch him. She smiled, and its inappropriateness hinted that the laudanum had, indeed, taken her to a far, distant world. "But you cannot be alive when I said you do not exist," she replied softly. "Certainly, you are an apparition, and I must deny you. Dr. Redding told me so. Don't you see your portrait? You, sir, are dead, and have been for almost seventy years." Cole wanted to touch her but Webster had made it clear that he was not to have physical contact with her. He was never to allow her to touch him either, to feel that he was, indeed, flesh and blood. But Cole stopped to think about it. If no one would believe she had seen a ghost, they would certainly not believe she had touched one. It was not as if he would leave visible marks on her body. She was an innocent; she did not deserve what her cousin was doing to her. And Cole himself was an unwilling pawn, though he expected to end that as soon as he could flee from Rourke House with Diana and be sure they would not be caught. The wondrous sight of the Allegheny Mountains had tugged at his adventurous heart. That was what he wanted — to flee with her, into her own world, and fate be willing, to share it with her. For the time being, though, he had no choice but to do as Webster had ordered. Webster's ploy of removing the horses while he was away from the house had made it impossible for Cole to put his plan into action. When he left, it would have to be beneath the treacherous eye of Webster Mayne. When he did not reply, Diana continued, "You have not answered me, sir. Didn't you hear me? I said you have been dead for almost seventy years."

"I heard you," Cole replied, rising to his feet,

81

straightening the replica of the antique waistcoat as he put his hand out to her. He had seen her read the diary that he himself had read many, many times. He had been close enough to see the page she was reading, and had watched her eyes light in anticipation of seeing his namesake's grave. "Come with me, Diana. I shall show you the grave of Cole Cynric Donovan. And then I shall take you far, far away, to your beloved mountains where you will be safe."

An invisible force brought Diana to a sitting position, then placed her hand in Cole Donovan's. Despite his assurance that he was flesh and blood, she had expected his hand to be cold, like a crypt. Rather, it was warm and dry. She rose hypnotically, allowed him to hold her dressing robe for her and again took his hand so that he could lead her toward the corridor. "No! No!" Life suddenly sprang to her voice, though she remained shielded by her dream world. "Someone might see us."

"No one will see us, Diana," Cole replied, wanting only to be alone with her outdoors, where they could not be overheard. He wanted to tell her of the vicious plot against her, and to assure her that he would help her. But at the moment, she seemed to be existing in a dream world that was strangely confusing to him.

Mrs. Sanders had heard the muffled voices through the wall. She knew Cole Donovan was playing the vicious masquerade ordered by Webster Mayne. She knew he would continue to do so to save his neck from the gallows. She did not fault Cole because she knew he was innocent. She remembered the panic in his voice when he had found Standish Rourke dead. She remembered the desperation with which he had held her arms as he had told her he would ride for a constable. Yes, she knew he was an innocent victim and had been set up to take the blame for the crimes of Webster Mayne. As she moved into the corridor, she prayed that Webster would draw his last breath that night. She wished she had the courage to tell Master Philip her suspicions that Webster had killed Standish, but that courage was denied her.

Cole and Diana met Mrs. Sanders in the corridor. She deliberately did not meet Cole's gray-black gaze. "Miss Diana, where are you going this time of night?"

"Master Donovan is taking me out to the grounds to see his grave," she replied, her voice low and almost inaudible. She then took Cole Donovan's hand and walked with him down the stairs and out into the cool, dark evening, ignoring the harsh entreaties of Mrs. Sanders, who hesitated for a moment, then moved slowly toward Webster's chamber. She, too, was expected to play her part in this masquerade, for her safety and that of her children. At that thought, her mouth pinched in frustration. Her son, Tuxford, had fallen too easily into the role of watchdog for Webster Mayne. She feared the loyalty of her son to his own family was lost.

Diana's feet felt like lead, yet they floated. Her mind whirled with thoughts, yet her head felt empty. She knew only that a tall, slim man held her hand, leading her farther into the darkness toward a small bridge that crossed a narrow stream. Suddenly she hesitated, her body beginning to quiver with a fear that surfaced from deep inside. She could see the moonlight reflecting off the gently flowing waters of the creek, and something wild and frightening caused

83

her heart to beat with frantic rhythm. But in the same moment, Cole coaxed her on ahead, to the right, toward a hedgerow and a massive oak, barren of its leaves, the ground so thickly blanketed that at first she did not see the small, simple stone half buried in the roots of the tree.

"There it is," Cole whispered hoarsely. "That is where the original Cole Donovan lies, between his wife and his daughter. That is the man I have been ordered to portray in order to—" He halted in mid-sentence, releasing her hand, and moved to the side of the tree, where he stroked the very tip of the sword that had been run through the sapling seventy years before. "This is all that remains of a once proud sword. It lies forever in this great oak, and will soon be forever hidden from the eyes of mortal man—and woman. Touch it now, while it still exists."

Hypnotically, Diana stroked the smooth metal surface. "I feel it." She turned and her pert face lifted to the apparition before her. Without warning, she whispered, "Kiss me, Master Donovan."

It might have been a request a ghost could turn down, but it was not a request to be denied by mortal man. Cole's hands lifted to her satin-clothed shoulders and held them firmly. Her eyes closed, her mouth lifted to him. Slowly, savoring the delicious aroma of her hair and her perfume and the sweetness of her mouth, he kissed her tenderly.

Diana was suddenly overwhelmed by the musky, masculine scent of a man who was alive and animate. This was not a ghost. He was as mortal as she. He had been about to confess a conspiracy, yet she could not find the strength to question him about it. She wanted only to be with him and to feel his arms around her. That someone was playing a vicious trick on her didn't seem very important at the moment.

What she did not know was that Webster Mayne had found the bottle of laudanum she'd hidden beneath her pillow and had added a small portion of a rare hallucinatory drug imported from the Caribbean islands. The drug was lethal if used in large doses, but Webster had known precisely how much to add to the bottle. It might not have mattered if Cole Donovan were not there, in flesh and blood. Her hallucinatory state could have produced the illusion of him regardless.

"Come away with me, Diana. Come now, while there is a chance."

"Yes, take me with you —"

Even as she consented, approaching footsteps and mumbled voices broke the silence of the late evening. Diana was unaware that the alarmed Cole had disappeared into the darkness of night. She was suddenly surrounded by an array of people: Philip Mayne and his son, Mrs. Sanders, Claudia, Tuxford, and Dr. John Redding. Had so much time passed that Tuxford had been able to ride into Philadelphia for the doctor? She panicked as arms reached out to confine her, and tried to struggle free. "Stop it! Leave me be! Cole! Cole, why don't you stop them?"

Then, in a brief moment of lucidity, she heard Webster Mayne say harshly, "Don't you see, John? My young cousin is mad! She believes she is here in the darkness with a damned ghost!"

Before John Redding could reply, Philip interjected, "I believe you're overreacting, Webster. I'll take care of my niece! You leave her alone!" Although his words were harsh, sympathy eased across the darkness toward Diana.

Still, she flung her arms, her hair moving in a slow, golden cloud about her head and covering her half-conscious features. Then she slumped in her uncle's arms. She remembered only the gleam of eyes that might have been Cole Donovan's in the darkness. She reached out to him, but he was instantly lost in the mist that rose from the ground around her. She remembered nothing more of the night.

John Redding sat at Diana's bedside throughout the night. He was confused by her condition. Even twice as much laudanum as he had prescribed would not have induced the hallucinations that plagued her and the intermittent moments of deathly silence in which he was hardly able to feel her pulse. In one moment her skin was hot and flushed and in the next, cool and damp. Webster Mayne had stood behind him, repeating in magpie fashion, "She's insane! My poor cousin is insane," until John was sure he himself would go mad. Finally, he'd requested that Webster Mayne leave the room, which Webster had not taken kindly to. Sullenly, he had retired to the study to read his latest copy of *Die Philadelpsiesche Zeitung,* a weekly German-language newspaper begun in 1732 by Benjamin Franklin. Webster and his father were two of the few non-Germans living in and around Philadelphia who could read and speak German fluently, and Webster's expletives were often in that language.

The following morning a courier arrived at Rourke House to summon John to Jacob Hiltzheimer's house. John would not leave the unconscious young woman and sent the courier to Dr. Kuhn, whom he knew would order Jacob bled despite John's adversity to the practice. All the while John stayed at Diana's bedside, Cole Donovan stood behind the mirror, his eyes tear-moistened, his mouth moving with unspoken curses directed toward Webster Mayne. He prayed that Diana would be all right. He knew that Webster had not poisoned her—she was of no use to him dead. But he wondered what he had done to her that had gone awry.

Cole decided at that moment that he would no longer participate in this vicious masquerade. But he would not die either. At mid-morning, when he saw that Diana Rourke was beginning to come around, he returned to his suite, changed into his buckskin attire, and moved toward the hidden door. He was going to take the still sleeping Diana Rourke to a place of safety.

Unbeknownst to him, however, Webster had crept up on him in the passageway behind the wall of mirrors. He had seen pain in the way Cole had slumped against the wall, heard his muttered oaths. As Cole had turned back to his cellar suite, Webster had been one step ahead of him. When Cole stepped from his rooms, he came face to face with Webster Mayne and the burly stableman, Tuxford, who held a loaded musket.

"Going somewhere, Cousin?"

"Away from here," he snapped. "I will not go through with this!"

"Oh, but you will." Webster crossed his arms in a threatening gesture, his hands clenched around his elbows. "Tuxford, what are your orders?" Webster asked over his shoulder.

Mrs. Sanders's muscular son replied, "To shoot Master Donovan if he steps so much as a foot off this property."

"Then do it now," Cole said between tightly gritted teeth. "Because I am leaving! And I am taking your cousin with me!"

Webster snapped his fingers. "Tuxford!" The man stepped forward. "Do as my cousin has ordered."

Tuxford stood forward, pulled back the cock of the British Brown Bess Webster had taken off a dead soldier during the Revolution, and aimed it squarely between Cole's eyes. "Now, Master Mayne?"

"What are your sentiments, Cousin?" Webster restrained a chuckle. "It is entirely up to you whether you die now or go free after my dear little cousin has been locked away in an asylum."

The determination that had surged through Cole just moments ago suddenly waned. "You can't kill me. It would be murder."

Webster Mayne laughed maniacally. "Ah, but you are already dead! Hanged on the gallows just days ago. I can bury you on the grounds and no one will be the wiser."

Webster was right, of course. And Cole was certainly not ready to die. If he had been, he'd have gone willingly to the gallows. He wanted to live, and he would do it at almost any cost. As he allowed his gaze to move from the musket to Webster Mayne's viciously narrowed eyes, he knew that, somehow, he would extract himself from this mess, and see to it that the lovely Diana Rourke got what she deserved—her share in the house and the land and the wealth that had been her father's. He would continue the masquerade only until the right moment came for escape. He needed a cohort, someone he could trust. In his mind, he knew who that person should be — Philip Mayne — but the man was spineless and would be of no help at all.

"No, I do not wish to die," he said with emotion. "I'll do as you have ordered me."

Webster put his hand on the musket and lowered it. "You may leave now, Tuxford. Master Donovan and I have reached an agreement." Tuxford turned away but halted when Webster again spoke. "But my order stands, Tuxford. If my cousin leaves the grounds of Rourke house, you are to shoot him on sight."

"Aye, Master Mayne."

As soon as Tuxford was out of sight, Cole drew back his hand and hit Webster across his right cheek. Undaunted, Webster merely rubbed his stinging flesh. It was, after all, a small price to pay for getting his way. "I suppose I deserved that," he smarted. "Don't tell me you have developed a soft spot for the wood sprite?"

"She is a lovely, intelligent young woman. And she does not deserve what you are doing to her."

"That is your opinion," Webster snipped, turning back as he continued to rub his aching cheek. "But you had better convince John Redding that the girl is insane. Perhaps I am being a bit impatient. Give it a few weeks but no longer. I need the funds that are tied up in probate. By the way," Webster half turned back. "Despite your extremely bad humor this day, why don't you join us for supper this evening?"

"What do you mean?"

"Just what I said, and wear the costume, not those blasted buckskins. I would like to see how my young cousin reacts."

"And Philip?"

"He will be dining in the city this evening."

Mrs. Sanders kept Diana in her bed long after John Redding had departed. She brought her a lunch tray and sat with her while she picked at the food. Diana lost her appetite the moment Mrs. Sanders remarked that her activities of the previous evening had been bizarre. Diana had no recollections of the night, except that she had fallen asleep very soon after slipping between the sheets. Thus, she was a little surprised when Mrs. Sanders began telling her what had happened.

"That cannot be!" Diana argued, her gaze lowering. "I slept soundly the entire evening."

"Nay, Miss Diana. You went out on the grounds with the ghost of him there," she said, pointing to the portrait of Cole Donovan, "and we found you at his grave."

Diana dug deeply into her mind but could not remember having left her bedchamber. She remembered only awakening at mid-morning with a terrible headache. Mrs. Sanders had told her that Dr. Redding had been summoned, but she could not remember seeing him.

"I don't know what is going on here," Diana said, stabbing at a bit of tripe on her plate, "but I believe someone is playing an awful trick on me."

" 'Tis none of the household," Mrs. Sanders replied guiltily. "You might ask Dr. Redding. He was here, miss, and you were out of your head the whole night."

"I will ask him. I promise you that I will question him about it. I don't believe I was out on the grounds last evening looking for a grave."

Nevertheless, when Diana dressed at mid-afternoon and ventured out of the house, she moved on a deliberate course across the lawn and the small bridge over the frightening creek, to the big oak that did, indeed, seem vaguely familiar to her. And there it was. The roots of the oak half obliterated the small headstone upon which were legible only the letters "N-O-V-A-N" and beneath that, "1720". She absently rubbed the engraved lettering. Then, looking at the unkempt graves of the two women lying to either side of Cole Donovan, she rose and found the oval of brass still visible in the oak tree. She had a feeling that she had been here last evening, though she had no recollection of it. Diana did not find the condition of the ground half as bad as Webster had told her. She spent a few silent moments beside the freshest grave—that of her father. In departing, she whispered, "I wish I could have known you."

She whiled away most of the day, roaming the grounds. When, later, she received a brief visit from Dr. Redding, Diana bombarded him with questions which he quickly and discreetly answered—though not to her satisfaction. She sat with him in an arbor badly in need of paint, then bade him farewell and moved toward the house just as the sky was beginning to darken. Mrs. Sanders had just rung the dinner bell. Diana startled her in the hallway, where she was moving toward the stairs with a large tray. "Claudia? Claudia, come here girl," Mrs. Sanders called up the stairs.

Instantly, Claudia appeared. "Yes, mum?"

"Here is the mistress's dinner."

"Yes, mum." Claudia took the tray and started up the stairs.

When Mrs. Sanders turned, Diana asked, "Do you ever take the tray to my aunt?"

"Never do," she replied shortly.

"Why?"

"Master Philip will allow only Claudia in there. Says the mistress feels more comfortable with her."

"Claudia could only have been about five years old when my aunt confined herself to her suite."

"And she's been taking the tray to her since then. Now," annoyance had sifted into Mrs. Sanders voice, "are you going to dine with your cousin this evening?"

"Yes, I am."

Diana was surprised to find that three additional places had been set at the table. She had just settled into her regular chair when her cousin entered. Claudia returned momentarily, and she and her mother brought out silver bowls of steaming meat and side dishes. A shadowy movement caught Diana's eye and she watched Cole Donovan, resplendent in antique garb and periwig, enter the foyer, then approach the dining room and sit at the table opposite Webster, who had assumed his father's place at the head of the table. Wide-eyed, Diana watched Cole, even as Webster continued as though he had not entered. She remembered nothing of Cole Donovan's confession last evening that a conspiracy was being woven against her, and had almost convinced herself that the man now sitting quietly at the end of the table had, indeed, been an apparition. Claudia entered from the kitchen and began serving their individual plates, serving portions of food at the empty places and at Cole Donovan's place. Diana dared say nothing. She turned her eyes swiftly and watched as Claudia placed small portions of food on her plate. Then Claudia took up the wine bottle and began pouring the cool, amber liquid into their goblets. When she poured at the empty places, Diana's curiosity could no longer be controlled.

Diana found that she could not simply sit there and say nothing. It was not her nature. "Claudia, who are you serving at the end of the table?"

Claudia gave her a quizzical look. "Why, Master Rourke," she said, referring to Diana's dead father.

"No." Annoyance laced Diana's voice. "At the other end of the table."

"Master Donovan," Claudia replied.

Immediately, Diana came to her feet, allowing her fork to clatter to her plate and then to the floor. "You see! I'm not mad! You're trying to make me believe I see ghosts, and there is no ghost there. That man is as alive as we are!" Diana gave Cole a smug, almost nasty look, then rested her hands arrogantly on her hips.

Webster drew back and brought his fingers to his clean shaven chin. "Claudia, whom else are you serving at the other end of the table?"

Claudia smiled broadly. "Why, it's the Mistress Donovan and their daughter, Emelia."

"Don't be ridiculous!" Diana snapped. "There is no one else there! Only Master Donovan! And he is certainly not dead!"

Webster rose, traversed the short space separating him from his cousin, and put his hand on her shoulder. "Come, dear, perhaps you should retire to your chamber. You had a terrible episode last evening."

With fury darkening her violet eyes, Diana slapped his hand away. "Don't patronize me!" Silence. "Why, Webster?" She turned pleading, tear-moistened eyes to her cousin. "Why are you trying to trick me?" Her gaze turned to Cole. "Say something, won't you? Don't let me stand here feeling every bit the fool!"

But Cole said nothing, though his eyes glazed with pain. Webster then shrugged absently. "I'm sorry you're not well, Diana—"

Every human emotion flew through Diana's slender frame: anger, rebelliousness, pain, humiliation. Melodramatically throwing down her napkin, she approached Cole Donovan. When he came to his feet she drew back her hand and hit him very hard. She knew she had not flayed insanely at air. The palm of her hand stung from the blow. Then, sobs wracking her body, she turned and fled toward her bedchamber, refusing to listen to the falsely sympathetic entreaties of Webster Mayne.

Only when she was out of sight did Cole Donovan mumble threateningly, "One day I am going to see you dead!"

To which Webster countered, "I am damned sick and tired of hearing that!"

"Don't get too sick and tired of it! You'll hear it often." Cole wanted to add, "until I take the girl out of your clutches," but maintained his composure and did not confess his true intentions. He did not want Tuxford watching him more closely than he already was.

Cole fled through the kitchen but was stopped by Mrs. Sanders. "Please, young master, forgive me for what is happening."

Cole's voice softened. "I know it is not your fault. You have your daughter and son and yourself to think about."

Diana threw herself across her bed and sobbed uncontrollably. Her chest began to ache from the intensity of her sobs and she wrapped her arms around her middle. "Oh, why? Why is this happening to me?"

After the sobs died down to scarcely audible whispers, Diana's hand went beneath the pillow for the bottle of laudanum. She sat forward and held it between her fingers for a moment, feeling the coolness of the dark brown bottle, watching the fluid sway with the movement of her hand. It would make her sleepy. She wouldn't have to think about anything or anyone—not her cousin Webster or Cole Donovan. But she knew that she could not allow herself to become addicted to the bitter elixir. Thus, she rose, crossed to the bureau, and buried it beneath her underclothing.

Diana had been strong and independent living on Wills Creek, and now, as she slid the bottle beneath her garments, she made a vow that she would not be dependent on anything at Rourke House—not laudanum to help her sleep, not the other members of the household for company. Not anything! And, by heavens, she would not be intimidated by an apparition or conspirator or whatever he was. She remembered seeing a case containing dueling pistols in her uncle's study downstairs. She waited until the house quieted down, until she heard Webster ride away from the house—it was Saturday night, after all, and a favorite night for the taverns in town. She waited until the servants had retired to their own quarters. Then she moved stealthily down the corridor and stairs, making sure that no one was about. She eased into her uncle's study and closed the door. A lamp had been left lit. She opened the dueling case that had collected dust of several weeks' neglect, took one of the fancy pistols and loaded it with powder from the pouch and a large caliber ball, then used the brass tool enclosed in the case to firmly lock the flint in place. Her ghostly visitor would surely make his nightly appearance again! She couldn't frighten him to death if he were already dead, but if he was alive—and she had little doubt that he was—that would be a different story.

Diana crept back to her bedchamber and placed the pistol beneath a scarf on the table beside her bed. She dared Cole Donovan to make his appearance. She dared him to try to make her appear mentally unsound when all she wanted to do was accept the legacy her father had left her and do with it as she pleased. She would give it away before Webster got his greedy hands on the money.

Yet, in the same moment that she swore she hated them all, especially Cole Donovan, she knew she was drawn to the tall, slim, black-haired man whose handsome face had been ever so close to her own last night . . .

She gasped, feeling her knees suddenly become weak and flaccid. She remembered! Dear God, she remembered last night so vividly now. He had, indeed, come to her bedchamber. Her hand had been enfolded within his warm, alive, strong one and he had escorted her out into the darkness! He had asked her to go away with him. But his plea so contradicted the masquerade and the conspiracy he was engaged in. Her mind revolved at an incredible speed as she tried to put the pieces together.

Then another memory flooded her mind: full, masculine lips claiming her own in a tender yet passionate kiss, hands that firmly held her shoulders, then became a gentle embrace.

Oh, why wasn't Hambone here? He would know what to do and how to advise her. He would offer a comforting shoulder, something she certainly hadn't gotten in this dreary old house. Perhaps if she sent a message to him, he might come to visit her, even stay for a while and investigate the strange things that had been happening to her these past few days. Hambone was sensible and a bit of an investigator. He enjoyed a good challenge.

Diana felt terribly tired but she had firmly decided not to sleep. Last night had drained her, and eating very little during the day had taken its toll on what remained of her strength. She drew a deep, steady breath and began unfastening the stays of her cream-colored gown with its thick rows of tatted lace. Only when she had slipped her favorite bed gown over her head — a ragged thing she had brought with her from the cabin on Wills Creek — did she feel her nerves begin to settle.

She slipped into her bed and took the pistol from beneath the table scarf. Falling to the mound of pillows against the headboard, placing one pillow upon her lap as a prop for the pistol, she made herself comfortable and waited.

She would find out once and for all just who her nightly visitor was.

It he wanted to masquerade in the moonlight and frighten her to death, then he would pay the price for it.

Despite her exhaustion, Diana was wide awake. Nothing in the world could have forced her to sleep that night.

Chapter 6

Cole's gray-black gaze pierced the veil of darkness surrounding Diana Rourke until he was able to see her, sitting so stiffly against her pillows that he wondered what she was up to. Her beauty was almost luminous in the dark as a glitter of gold threading through the lace of her pillows momentarily caught the moonlight cast into the room in a thin triangle.

Tonight Cole stood behind the mirror, not to play the damnable role meant to drive Diana insane, but simply to look at her through the crack between the mirror and the wall. Soon he would be able to approach her and draw her into his embrace. He knew that she awaited him—and there was rebellion in the stillness of her features—yet there was no way she could uncover his deception. There were, after all, only two in the household who were not part of the plot against her: one a spineless man and the other a confined woman.

Her loveliness drew him from the deep darkness of the corner. He moved slowly, until he stood directly before the life-size portrait of his ancestor. All the while his gaze held Diana's, and he was fascinated by the lack of animation in her face. It was indeed as though she had expected him and remained deliber-

99

ately unmoved by his appearance.

Cole stood with his feet slightly apart, then crossed his arms in the direction opposite those of the man in the portrait. Cole was, after all, left-handed while his namesake had been right-handed.

Ever so slightly, a smile touched Diana's mouth. She watched him, the firm set of his jaw refusing to flex, his breathing very gentle against the brocade waistcoat, the dying embers of the hearth giving the right side of his face an eerie glow. Then, without any warning, the pistol came up from the coverlet of the bed and she propped it on her drawn-up knees.

While Cole did not move, his eyebrows arched in surprise. He had suspected she was up to something, but he certainly had not expected a weapon. It was a betrayal of sorts. She was sure he was not a ghost — his cheek still stung from the proof of that — and she knew the gun would prove a threat to him. He tried not to show his fear, but that was like asking the sun not to shine.

Attempting to still the violent pounding of his heart, he asked her, "Why do you raise a weapon against me, Diana? Have I done you any harm?"

"You have done me no physical harm," she replied quietly. "But you conspire with my cousin to try to drive me mad. It seems so unnecessary, since I would really prefer not to be here."

Yes, he knew that she had come to Rourke House out of curiosity, and that she would much rather be roaming the familiar mountains of her home. He knew that she remained at Rourke House so that she could financially assist her Aunt Rufina, and he respected and admired her for her generosity and unselfishness. In a way, their lives paralleled; he

100

would rather not be here either.

He wondered if the gun was loaded. He wondered how proficient she would be with it if it were. She had been raised in the woods. She'd had to learn to fend for herself at a very early age. Yes, he was fairly certain she could put a hole in the middle of his forehead if she chose to do so.

But on the other hand, he wondered if she wanted to.

Almost as if she had heard his thoughts, she said very quietly, "Well, Master Donovan, let us see if ghosts bleed. Shall I aim for the left shoulder, the right, or would you prefer to be crippled for the rest of your life?" As she spoke, she moved the weapon so that the muzzle pointed to the different areas of his body she mentioned. "Or shall it be . . . ," the weapon rose from his knee and pointed directly at his groin, "a part of your anatomy much more vital to a mortal man."

Try as he might, Cole could not remain unscathed by her threats. Slowly, his arms unfolded. He hoped that she would at least allow him a moment to ponder her question and make the choice. He could not simply stand there, looking like a simple-minded dolt, but he could not allow her to make the decision for him either. And he certainly was not in a mood to be shot by so beautiful a woman as Diana Rourke, a woman who had stirred his desires when he thought he had risen above such foolishness.

He chose another mode of reasoning. "If you fire the gun, Diana, you will certainly miss me. The household will come running, and how will you explain having discharging a weapon in your bedchamber?"

"I am willing to take that chance," she shot back with sudden vehemence. "They already think I am a bit touched. If I am not and you *are* a mortal man, then you will not have to worry about what the household thinks, will you? You'll be just as dead as the man in the portrait behind you. Of course, if you wish to tell me what is going on here and why you are doing this . . ."

She had him backed against a wall, literally. Cole recrossed his arms and reassessed the situation. He had told her only half-truths in the past, and he suspected that she knew much more than she let on. He could tell her what was happening, admit who he was and what had brought him into this heinous conspiracy, and then perhaps he could help her to beat the odds and win the battle with her devious cousin. Or he could continue the masquerade, which would certainly result in him being shot. "Very well, if you will lower your weapon, I will tell you the whole truth."

Diana was too smart to fall for that one. If she lowered her weapon he would dive back into the darkness and be gone before she could react. "No, you approach and sit at the end of my bed. I will listen to your story. Then, if I find it reasonable— and believable—I might decide not to shoot you."

She certainly drove a hard bargain. Cole did not take his eyes from the muzzle of the gun as he approached. He sat on the bed so lightly that she did not even feel the pressure of his movement on the mattress. She continued to aim the gun, watching him as he drew his leg up and bent it, so that only one foot touched the thick rug. "Where do you wish that I begin?" he asked, shrugging his shoulders.

102

"Start with your name," she replied, arching a pale eyebrow.

Blasted! he thought. This was a hell of a way to start a truthful conversation. His name would be the first thing she would not believe. "If I tell you the truth — no matter how preposterous it may seem — will you promise not to shoot me?"

"If it is the truth, I guarantee it," she replied in the same even tone.

Without hesitation he responded, "My name is Cole Donovan." To hear the familiar name took her quite off her guard. For the first time, her body trembled, and this gave Cole just enough time to lunge forward and snap the gun from between her fingers. She gave a small cry of alarm as his sudden move made him fall to his knees with the weapon. But just as quickly, he lunged for her again, clamping his strong hand over her mouth just as she was about to cry out with more intensity. "Hush! Hush, you little fool! I fully intend to explain, but not with a weapon pointed at my head!"

Since coming to Rourke House, Diana had enjoyed very few happy moments, and oddly, the time she had spent in Cole's arms had been one of them. She remembered that night, though it was still a bit foggy to her. She knew this man had entered into a conspiracy with her unscrupulous cousin, but somehow she trusted him. Thus, coaxing his hand away from her mouth, she whispered hoarsely, "Just tell me that you are not as devious as my cousin! That is what I want to know right now. And," she quickly added, "assure me that you are no ghost."

"The answer is 'no,' Diana, to both questions. If you had fired the weapon, you would have killed me."

Diana threw herself forward and into his arms. "Then hold me. I don't care what your name is, be it George or William or Cole. Just hold me. Hold me as if I am dear to you. Oh, but I have been so lonely!" She did not know why she trusted him so deeply, but she did. She saw something in him that did not fit with the puzzle of conspiracy being worked against her.

Her pleading entreaties won that small part of his heart he had been trying to keep from her. Slowly, Cole drew her into his arms and held her trembling body against his own. He entwined his fingers through the thick masses of her hair, feeling its richness. How sweet, like lilacs, she smelled. How soft her body was against his. It gave him a thrilling sense of pleasure to feel her trembling slowly subside and her slim arms move to encircle his neck. He felt the gentleness of her ample mouth brush his cheek.

Again he could see her sprinting through the woods, knowing every bramble, every rock, every leaf that had fallen from the trees. He imagined her splashing happily in an isolated stream, away from the eyes of men. He could imagine her sitting on a boulder, her arms encircling her drawn-up knees, dreaming her dreams and wishing her wishes. He had seen enough of her these past few days to know that he wanted to be part of her life. She was like no woman he had ever met. He smiled to himself as he remembered her stinging slap at the dinner table, but wept inside as he remembered the tears that had shined in her lovely violet eyes.

He was not quite sure how the tender, noncommittal embrace became a hotbed of passion, but suddenly their mouths flamed against each other's. His mind and body seemed to separate as his hands slid beneath the thin fabric of the gown at her shoulders to feel the suppleness of her flesh. She was round and smooth, her skin youthful and vibrant. Her hands slipped beneath his thick waistcoat and settled on the silken fabric of his shirt. Passion caused the buttons of the tight-fitting waistcoat to snap free one at a time as their bodies molded one to the other, their almost violent movements sending the coverlet into a heap at the foot of the bed.

Diana was lost in a fantasy, one of those rare, tender moments when she imagined a man such as this one who claimed to be Cole Donovan, holding her, loving her, erasing all her inhibitions, caressing her with strong yet gentle hands. Suddenly, she despised the fabric that separated their bodies. She wanted to feel the warmth of him against her, above her, claiming her, throwing her inhibitions to the wind as if they were so much rubbish. And she might readily have done so if the man who held her had not cast her off as easily as he might have a clinging leech.

"No, Diana!" Cole shook his head with frustration and despair. Quickly, he refastened the buttons of his waistcoat. "It is true that I am a mortal man. I cannot be so near a woman like you." He turned swiftly to her and his silvery eyes were suddenly as dark as the corner from which he had emerged. "No, Diana, not a woman *like* you. It is you I want. It is you I crave. And you deserve so much better. You do not deserve what Webster Mayne is doing. I ask you again! Come away with me—to your mountains, if you wish!"

At that moment, a rap sounded at the door. It was

Mrs. Sanders. "Miss Rourke, are you all right?" Immediately behind her Webster Mayne was muttering curses and Cole, taking Diana briefly and firmly by the shoulders for only an instant, rushed back into the dark corner untouched by the moonlight.

Before he disappeared from her sight, he whispered harshly, "Tomorrow, I shall come to you and we will talk about leaving this place together. For now, I beg you to say nothing."

Diana heard a soft, haunting creak and he was gone. Only then did she arise, slip into her robe, and approach the door. "What is it, Mrs. Sanders?" She looked across the housekeeper's shoulder. "Cousin Webster? What brings you out at the midnight hour?"

Webster Mayne viciously elbowed the housekeeper aside and Diana could not help but notice her venomous look as he did so. "Mrs. Sanders said she heard voices. She was concerned for you. Have you been having more hallucinations?"

Diana laughed lightly. "Goodness, no. I must have been talking in my sleep. At home I was notorious for it, and more than once I got a good nudge with the end of Aunt Rufina's broom to halt my nocturnal chatterings."

Webster's look was skeptical and disbelieving. He did, however, notice how flushed and pretty his cousin appeared, with her disheveled masses of golden hair and a high crimson in her cheeks. Her mouth appeared dew-kissed, and he wondered if perhaps his reluctant conspirator was disobeying his orders and drawing the lonely young woman into a web of seduction. Although Webster loathed his distant cousin, he was very envious of his God-given graces and the natural attraction women felt for him. He did not want Cole Donovan enjoying Diana's attention.

"Are you sure it was nothing else?" Webster replied after a moment.

"I am very sure," Diana laughed, closing her delicate fingers over his clothed arm. Immediately revulsed, she withdrew her hand. "You really mustn't worry about me. I am adjusting to life here. I have even managed to forgive you for, shall I say, trying to pin a label of insanity on me? I do wonder if you have my best interests at heart."

Webster frowned severely. "Indeed," he replied shortly. He turned toward Mrs. Sanders, who held a lantern. "I will leave you to your rest then." he continued gruffly. "Mrs. Sanders will be nearby should you need her."

I am sure that she will! Diana thought. "Thank you, cousin, for being so thoughtful." She was not sure if she had successfully disguised her sarcasm.

Diana closed the massive door and stood with her ear against it until she heard retreating footsteps. She wished they hadn't appeared at such an inopportune time, and vowed that in the future she would keep her voice low enough that Mrs. Sanders could not hear.

Disrobing, she climbed back in bed and stared into the dying embers of the fireplace. Sparks flickered into the hearth and disappeared into nothingness. She wanted her visitor to return, although he had lied to her again by telling her that his name was Cole Donovan. She knew now that a conspiracy was being carried out and that he was part of it. But he seemed kind and sensitive. He had held her so gently, enveloping her with his warmth and understanding. He had said he wanted to return to the mountains, taking her with him. She had felt a certain kinship to him, and a sexual attraction such as she had never before felt. Her body still surged with the fire of his nearness.

Diana forced herself to remain awake for another hour, hoping that he would return. Then, dismayed and disappointed, she eased down among the pillows, immediately feeling the cold hardness of the pistol against her thigh. She removed it and slid it beneath her bed.

She vowed that tomorrow she would find the place where her visitor was entering her bedchamber. It would give her something to do for the day.

On Tuesday, the weather was a mixture of snow and rain brought in by a northeast wind. Uncle Philip and Webster attended the wedding of Elliston Perot and Sarah Sansom, which Mrs. Sanders said would be a typical Quaker ceremony. Diana was a little hurt that she was not asked to attend as a member of the family. It would have given her a chance to wear the new lavender dress, cape, and bonnet that had been made for her. She was tired of being pent up in the house and would probably have enthusiastically attended even a funeral that day.

Her close scrutiny of the bedchamber had not yielded the secret of the hidden door. She tried each of the mirrored panels but they were securely locked in place. She imagined that there must be a catch somewhere that when flipped would swing the mirror open. But she had not been able to find it and so had moved on to other ventures.

In the kitchen, Mrs. Sanders attempted to question her about the night before but Diana remained noncommittal. "I do apologize, Mrs. Sanders. Perhaps I ate too much supper. That always causes restlessness at night. I'll try not to disturb you in the future."

"No more ghosts, eh, Miss?"

Diana shrugged lightly, spreading jam on a biscuit as though she were stroking smooth satin. "No more ghosts, Mrs. Sanders. I think I'm adjusting well to this musky old prison." Immediately, she wished she hadn't made a derogatory remark about the house. Mrs. Sanders would surely pass the trivial statement on to her master. "Forgive me, Mrs. Sanders," Diana continued, attempting to excuse her tactlessness. "It's just that I would love to have gotten out of the house today."

Mrs. Sanders was busy kneading the dough for the evening meal. "It's a sluggish day, Miss, certainly not a day for a young lady who—" she looked down at Diana's bare feet, which were immediately drawn back beneath the hem of the skirt, "who doesn't take to wearing shoes," she ended quietly. In an attempt to change the subject, Diana asked, "What are those stuffed birds in Uncle Philip's study?"

"They were your father's," Mrs. Sanders replied. "They are gold and silver Chinese pheasants, sent to your father by Lafayette, who also sent some to our Mr. Washington."

"The same Lafayette who fought so nobly in our revolution?" Diana asked.

"The same," Mrs. Sanders replied. "I'm afraid the poor things could not adjust to the weather and died

109

within a week. Your father could not bear to dispose of the lovely creatures, so he packed them in wool and sent them to a Mr. Peale for preservation."

"They are very lovely," Diana replied, propping her pert chin in the palms of her hands. "But I would imagine they were much lovelier alive."

"Indeed, they were," Mrs. Sanders agreed.

"Mrs. Sanders?"

"Aye, girl?"

"If I were to try to leave Rourke House and return to my Aunt Rufina, would you stop me?"

"Nay, Miss, but I'm afraid Tuxford would. He has orders from the master."

"Mrs. Sanders?"

"What is it now?"

"Do you think my Aunt Jocelyn is really up there in those rooms?"

Mrs. Sanders sucked in a ragged breath. "Why ever would you think otherwise, miss?"

"Just a hunch," she replied, shrugging. "I cannot imagine anyone voluntarily confining herself for fourteen years. It is not natural."

Mrs. Sanders bit her tongue to refrain from replying. She had her own opinions about matters of the house, but had learned long ago that she was expected to keep them to herself. She began pounding the biscuit dough with a vengeance. It hurt her deeply that the gentle-hearted Jocelyn Mayne might, indeed, be up there, denying herself the company of the pleasant—if somewhat frisky—young woman sitting across from her. Philip had explained that he did not want his wife to know of her brother's death. Diana continued to watch the housekeeper, expecting some sort of response, until finally Mrs. Sanders said, "I don't question, miss, and I would suggest that you don't either."

"I do wish I knew why she won't come out," Diana replied. "I would so love to meet her."

"I wish you could, too. Perhaps one day. Now, go about yourself, miss. Find something to do. And I wouldn't give another thought to running off if I were you. After probate of your father's will, I'm sure you will be free to go about your own enjoyments if that's what you want to do."

"If I survive my cousin's antics, the house will be half mine and he will be very furious."

How did she know about Webster? "I expect he would."

"And if I am declared mad within the year, the house will belong entirely to Aunt Jocelyn, and hence, to Webster and my uncle."

"I expect so," Mrs. Sanders again replied.

Diana got to her feet, then smoothed down the ruffles of her burgundy-colored gown. "Do you know what I'm going to do, Mrs. Sanders? I am going to see the probate through to its conclusion. Then I am going to donate my share of my father's property to the city as my father truly wished, and venture back to the Alleghenies."

"And what about Master Philip and poor Mistress Jocelyn who lives in this house? If you demand a sale, Mistress Jocelyn will also be required to sell her part."

Diana hadn't thought about that. "Then she had better come out of there and let us all know she—" Diana had been about to say something the house-keeper would certainly have related to Webster. She caught herself in time and smiled mischievously. "Well, I just think she needs to give up this ridiculous isolation. You know, of course, that regardless of what happens, I plan to return to the mountains."

"Not afraid of being scalped by the Iroquois, Miss?" Mrs. Sanders inquired matter-of-factly, her flour-coated hands suddenly ceasing their brisk caress of the biscuit dough.

Diana shrugged. "Pooh! I have many friends in the Iroquois nation. Now," she rose, smoothing down the gathers of her gown, and moved slowly toward the kitchen exit. "I shall return to my chamber, put on those god-awful shoes, and venture out on the grounds for a while."

Webster was in the cellar suite having a talk with his reluctant co-conspirator. He swirled brandy in a crystal goblet, the amber liquid creating an almost hypnotic effect on the narrow-eyed Cole Donovan.

"I heard you last night in her chamber," Webster said evenly. "I heard you say that you would tell her everything. Need I tell you what will happen if you do?" Silently, Cole dragged his index finger across his neck. "Precisely, though your death would be a little less messy," Webster promised. "I intend to have this property, and I will see my cousin locked away in an asylum." The glaring Webster couldn't help but notice the look of anguish that fleeted across his handsome cousin's face. "Don't tell me you're falling for the foolish thing? I don't believe it!"

Cole did not want Webster to suspect that he planned to take Diana back to the mountains. He attempted to disguise his true feelings. "Of course not! I simply do not believe she deserves what you are trying to do. She is what you said, I imagine.

112

I've seen little spirit in the girl!" As he spoke he remembered the honey sweetness of her kiss, the gentle fragrance of her skin, the smoothness of her voice even as she had threatened to shoot him. No, he was not falling for her. He had already fallen.

"What I *will* do!" Webster amended. "With your help. Now, assure me that you were not serious when you said you would tell her the truth."

"Of course I was not serious. It is part of the plan. All I want is to get this deed done and for you to keep your promise to allow me to return to Scotland."

Webster quickly drank down the brandy and set the goblet on the small butler's table. "You shall have your freedom, cousin, when the deed is accomplished. Now, I would prefer that you not visit the chamber of my cousin this evening. I will be away until the morrow." Webster pushed open the door, then turned back with a half-cocked grin on his thin face. "Tuxford will keep an eye on you tonight. You are to remain in your chamber. Read a good book or otherwise entertain yourself."

Cole arched a dark eyebrow. "Do you not trust me, Webster?"

"No further than I could spit, Cousin, if I were a spitting man."

In the days he had spent in the cellar suite, Cole had found another exit to the outside behind an unused armoire. The window, just large enough to accommodate his body, was a discovery he was sure neither Webster nor Tuxford knew about. Therefore, though Tuxford was posted outside the door with his Brown Bess propped against his chair, Cole felt confident as he quietly pulled out the armoire and crawled through the window hidden from outside view by an elaborate iron railing. During the spring and summer seasons, he had seen the ground inside the railing profuse with wild flowers, but now the dirt was cold and sterile, the window partially covered by withered brown vines. He moved stealthily through the darkness and was just about to enter the house when he saw Diana Rourke, her long, filmy gown floating hauntingly in the January wind as she moved toward the cluster of graves far across the lawn. Picking himself up and brushing off the dirt that had gathered on his clothing, he ran across the lawn until he stood in her path and caused her to halt suddenly.

The moonlight reflected in her purple eyes as they shared a long, searching look. Then very quietly, she said, "I was lonely when you did not come tonight. I could not be cooped up in my chamber."

Cole removed his jacket and drew it over her slim, shivering shoulders. "You shouldn't be out on this brisk night so scantily attired," he said. "Come," he swept her into his powerful arms. "I will return you to your bedchamber."

It was far past midnight; no one moved about the house. Cole enjoyed the gentle pressure of her arms around his neck, the feel of her head resting against his shoulder as he nudged open the door of her chamber with his foot. He took her not to her bed, but to the small sitting room separated from the sleeping chamber by French doors, their tiny glass panes recently cleaned and clear like the crystals that sparkled from the chandelier where the candles remained lit. He gently put her on the wide, spacious divan and adjusted a mass of pillows beneath her head. Kneeling beside her, he again met her silent gaze.

"Why do you look at me like that?" he questioned quietly.

"Like what?" she asked.

"I don't know." He felt that he belonged with her, despite the mixture of emotions in her lovely oval features. "You should hate me, but I do not see hate. You look at me as though," he fought for the proper words, "as though I am no threat to you."

"You aren't," she replied. "While I do not understand your association with my cousin, I believe that you mean me no harm. I believe I am being tricked. And I believe you are, too." He started to speak, but instantly her fingers lightly touched his mouth. "Say nothing, Cole. I want no explanations, and certainly no lies. Just stay with me for a while. Will you do that?"

Cole rose from his knee and sat on the sofa beside her. Tenderly, he took her slim hand between his strong ones. "If you wish it. We must speak softly so that Mrs. Sanders will not hear us together."

Diana propped herself up and cocked her head slightly to the side. "We need not speak at all, Cole. Please, will you just hold me? Hold me tightly?"

His jacket had slipped from her shoulders. When he reached for her to hold her gently in his arms he felt warm, feminine flesh, supple and smooth, felt the whisper softness of her breathing against his cheek. Her thick golden tresses covered his hands and he could not help but entwine his fingers through the rich masses. "Diana," he whispered against her hair. "We must leave Rourke House until the completion of probate. I swore the first moment I saw you on

115

your mountain trail that I would protect you from all harm. But I cannot successfully do so here. Come away with me. We will return to your mountains, and I will take care of you."

"No, I cannot. I must stay here to accept my inheritance so that I can help my aunt."

"Your Uncle Philip is a good man. He will see that your wishes are carried out and that your aunt receives compensation each month. You must come away with me for both our sakes. God! I have never met a woman so lovely, so fragile yet strong, as fragrant as lilacs in spring. Do you not know what you do to me? You make me forget what I was brought here to do. You might very well destroy me, but I want these tender moments, feeling your arms about me, holding you and knowing that I can be of some comfort to you in your loneliness."

"You are not an apparition, are you?" she teased.

"You know I am not," he replied firmly, "I am a man, and you are a woman."

"Cole, I want you to care for me, perhaps even love me one day. That is what I want." She laughed lightly. "And certainly I would not wish to have romantic notions for my own great-grandfather."

Even her attempt at humor did not erase his moment of melancholy. "Then I am as you wish it," Cole replied, a lump of rage and regret choking in his throat. "I am here only for you, Diana. I care for you and, God knows, a man would have to be insane not to fall in love with you." Without warning, Diana drew back and began unfastening the buttons of his brocade waistcoat. Surprised, Cole took her hands and halted their movements. "What are you doing, Diana?"

116

Her eyes bright and animated, she smiled so lovely a smile that it melted his heart. "I want only to feel your heartbeat, Cole."

His fingers wrapped around her hands became a gentle caress. His other hand rose, so that he could unfasten another button of his waistcoat. Then with that done, he slipped her left hand beneath the silky fabric. "There, do you feel it?"

Beneath her, his heart thumped gently. Closing her eyes for the briefest of moments, she enjoyed the elation rising within her. "Yes," she said, her violet eyes opening to hold his steady gaze in the semidarkness of the sitting room. "You are warm and alive, just as I suspected." Withdrawing her hand, she again encircled his neck with her arms and drew close to him in an almost desperate plea for his company. "Don't leave me, Cole. Stay with me."

Putting a mere breath of space between them, Cole gently captured her mouth in a warm, sincere kiss. How sweet were her lips, how soft and warm her cheeks. Although the temperature outdoors had dropped to below freezing and only a glowing ember remained of the evening's fire, he felt a hot flush fill his body. He could not prevent his hands from roaming down her arms, finding her tiny waist and briefly encircling it, moving over the gentle curves of her hips and thighs. Then he drew back and uttered, "Not here, Diana. We must leave in all haste. We must leave tonight while it is overcast."

Diana was all aflutter. "Not tonight. I have decided to remain at Rourke House until the will has been probated." She had never felt such a sensual pleasure; indeed, she had never even imagined it. Her fingers clutched his clothed shoulders and, unconsciously,

117

she arched her shoulders so that her breasts brushed his ample mouth. "Cole," she whispered, "what is this wonderful thing I feel for you?"

Even as she spoke, his hands suddenly ceased their intimate explorations. With a protesting groan, he pushed himself away from her and began pacing back and forth across the small sitting alcove, his hands clutching at his dark, wavy hair. After a moment, his gaze returned to her imploring one, twinkling with a sheen of tears that magnified the violet of her eyes.

"I cannot do this," he murmured, refusing her arms that slowly eased out, inviting him back into her embrace. "I can kidnap you, by damn, but I cannot take advantage of your vulnerability."

"I am not vulnerable," she whispered, drawing up her knee, caring not that her smooth, satin thighs were suddenly revealed. "Is it wrong for me to want to be with you?"

Cole stood for a moment more, fighting a losing battle. The victor sat enticingly on a wide, spacious divan a mere few feet from him. Slowly, hypnotically, he followed the siren call of her mellow enticements.

He was a man, and by his own assessment a healthy one. She offered him a treasure he could not walk away from.

Chapter 7

The tingle of excitement began in Diana's neck and shoulders and moved in a slow, fluid river through her passion-sensitive body. Despite the coolness of the evening she felt overwhelmingly hot. As Cole moved back into her arms, she held him tightly, caressing his muscular back through the tight fabric of his waistcoat. "Remove this," she requested quietly. "It must be terribly uncomfortable." Cole put just enough distance between them to unbutton the waistcoat and pull it down his arms. His silk full-sleeved shirt was open to mid-chest, exposing sinewy muscles that rippled beneath her trembling touch. "It troubles me that you are so mysterious with me, Cole, or whoever you are—"

"My name really is Cole Donovan," he assured her. "That is the truth."

"And you are kin to," she pointed toward the portrait, "my great grandfather over there?"

"He was my great-grandfather's brother. Yes, I suppose we are kin of sorts. But we are very distant kin. If we want to be together, we have a right to be."

Diana continued to caress his muscular chest beneath the thin fabric, moving her arms slowly to his back, drawing him close to her. "Then we shall be," she replied with provocative innocence. "Will you hold me, Cole? And when I am precious to you, will you tell me the terrible thing that has forced you into conspiracy with my cousin?"

Cole felt his body tense, his jawline becoming so taut that pain shot through his neck and shoulders. How innocent was his little wood sprite and how cautiously curious she was. Although she had been—was being—victimized, she was willing to allow him time to divulge his role in the conspiracy against her. Guilt and self-revulsion suddenly shuddered through his body and Diana, believing him to be cold, moved more intimately into his embrace. As she held him tightly, Cole whispered against her golden hair, "You are already precious to me, Diana—so precious that it fills me with reproof to simply hold you in my arms. I am not worthy of your trust. You should cast me off like the vile rubbish that I am."

His musky, manly scent filled her senses, sending her thoughts into reeling fantasies. She heard not his words but the pleasant, flowing smoothness of his voice. She felt not the stiffness of his body but the sensual softness of his touch and the ever so gentle beat of his heart against her breasts. She was so sure she was right about him being as much a victim as she that she felt safe and warm and comfortable in his arms. He made no greedy, unprovoked moves against her but held her as though she were, indeed, more precious to him than gold. It pleased her greatly that perhaps she was.

But a thousand questions filled her mind, questions that were not answered by the security of his embrace. She moved her cheek against his shoulder, her hands higher on his hard, sinewy back, and tried to chase her queries away. For the first time in weeks, she felt safe, and that was all she wanted right now.

But was it indeed? If his arms were all she needed why did an ominous darkness, like thunderclouds, suddenly fill her heart? Why did she fight a tremendous desire to pry herself loose from his embrace and flee where he could never again find her? The mirrors through the French doors reflected hauntingly back at her. She wanted to leap into a fantasy world where there were lush green forests and babbling creeks, where nothing mattered but that life surrounded her. She wanted to lose herself in the flora and fauna of a safe and distant netherworld where no harm could ever come to her. She closed her eyes tightly, fighting the sudden revulsion that caused her to shudder.

Cole could well imagine what she was thinking, though he could not guess the magnitude of her imagination. He knew only that she might be having second thoughts about placing so much trust in him. It pained him deeply that secrets existed between them. He wanted more than anything to tell her what her cousin was doing to her, but did he dare tell her until they were well away from Rourke House?

"Diana?" Even as he spoke her name he fought to answer his unspoken question.

"Yes," she replied in a quiet, trembling voice.

Silence. Cole held her as though she were as delicate as gossamer, all the while fighting the demons inside himself. "Diana, what do you want of me?"

Diana quietly pondered the question for a moment. "What do I want of you, Cole? I want the truth. I want honesty, even if it brings me pain. I want—" She stumbled over the words, remembering how she had been sheltered from well-groomed, educated men, remembering the reeking stench of gin and filth that had surrounded the only men she had been accustomed to. Cole was the man of her dreams. He was the one she'd spent so many hours on Wills Creek

121

thinking about, wondering if he truly existed. He was the one who made her remember the fragrance of spring blossoms and the pungent, pleasant aroma of the mighty firs of her beloved mountains. Forgetting her daydream for a moment she continued quietly, "I want you to care for me, Cole."

"I do care for you, Diana. How can I convince you of that?"

"By telling me the truth." Slowly, she put a hair's distance between them, and her piqued winter-pale features tilted slightly to the side. "Why you have been engaged in trickery with my cousin?" What was wrong with her! Her thoughts were topsy-turvy. One moment she wanted to know all the details, and the next moment she didn't want to know anything. He would begin to believe she was something of a simpleton. Still, she would not drop her eyes from his thoughtful gaze lest he see that her thoughts were, indeed, in disarray.

Cole thought her anything but a simpleton. She was a warm, sensual, innocent woman and he wanted nothing more than to hold her in his arms. In order to tell her his reasons for entering into the conspiracy, he would have first to confess that he was the man believed to have murdered her father. If not for that he would tell her everything unhesitatingly, but he was much too intrigued by her beauty, her charm and intelligence, to cause a rift between them. She would be horrified to know that he was the man who was to have been hanged, less than a fortnight ago, for her father's murder. She would be horrified to know that an innocent, terminally ill man had willingly died in his stead. As he stared into her violet eyes, breathing deeply of the feather-soft scent of her perfumed hair, the warm whisper of her breath upon his cheek, he knew he could not bear to see her lovely, oval features

122

contort into a grimace of horror and hatred.

In the same moment that he would have pulled away from her and risen to his feet another thought came to him. He could admit that he had been accused of murder—a murder that Webster was blackmailing him with—and not admit that the victim had been her father. If he could get around the very delicate questions her quick mind might compose, then perhaps he could turn the conspiracy on Webster while maintaining the trust that should exist between them. But to bring about that ironic twist of fate they needed a third conspirator of their own, someone they could trust implicitly, who would lift the black veil of deception Webster Mayne would smother his niece with. They needed John Redding, and of all the men in Philadelphia that Cole had met he trusted John most of all. Thus he began the narration he had been composing in his mind for several days now, hoping his own quick thinking would avert any questions as to the identity of the man Cole was accused of killing.

"Very well, Diana," Cole said, only then turning his eyes to take in the softness of her golden hair illuminated against the flickering candles of the chandelier. "I will begin my horrid tale in the hope that you will find it in your heart to forgive me for what I have done." Slowly Diana sank back against the pillows of the divan, drew her satin robe across her breasts and, keeping his hand gently enfolded within her slim fingers, waited for him to confess his black deed. No matter the circumstances, she had already made up her mind to forgive him. "Last month I was accused of a crime I did not commit—"

"What crime was that?"

Cole's gaze did not waver from hers. "The crime of murder, Diana. It matters only that I did not commit the crime. The details are unimportant." Silence. Cole breathed a sigh of relief as she seemed to accept this statement. "Webster knows I am guiltless but vowed that, if I refused to enter into his cruel conspiracy, he would turn me over to the authorities and see me hanged. He has already borne false witness against me and will not hesitate to do so again. He plans to drive you mad before you can inherit your father's property. Apparently Webster has many debts, and he needs your father's resources to pay them."

Diana nodded as though she had suspected all along that such might be the case. "I see, Cole. Please," she prompted him, "go on."

"Since I, much to my misfortune, bear a remarkable resemblance to your great-grandfather, Webster ordered me to play the role of ghost in an effort to drive you mad—"

A thought came to Diana. She sat forward and met Cole's gray-black, guilt-sheened gaze. "But at the dinner table! Mrs. Sanders, Claudia . . ."

"They are both servants whose livelihood depends on this house. Webster could make life miserable for them if they did not go along with the plan. Mrs. Sanders likes you very much. She is deeply pained by what Webster is doing. As for Claudia—she is a bit scatter-brained and wouldn't know a true apparition from a courier delivering a missive. Her testimony could easily be refuted. She sees ghosts in every corner of Rourke House."

A fleeting smile touched Diana's mouth. But this was a very serious situation. To smile was innappropriate and she was quick to suppress it. "So in exchange for your own life you were to sacrifice my sanity?"

Cole quickly pulled away from her and rose to his feet. He smoothed down his silk shirt and tucked it into his breeches. His back to her, his trembling hand rose to sweep back an unruly lock of black hair.

Diana watched him in silence. She noticed only then how thickly muscled his calves were beneath the tight white stockings, how immaculately clean his patent shoes with their large silver buckles. Her cousin had gone to considerable lengths to duplicate her ancestor's costume. Cole Donovan did indeed appear to be the man in the portrait she could see through the French doors. Right now, he was very tense, the muscles of his broad-back almost riveted against the thin fabric of his blouse. She wondered what he was thinking, and how he would answer her question.

Cole turned back with a world of pain in his eyes. "Diana, that was what I was going to do. But you didn't give me a chance to warn you on the trail. Your father had sent me with a warning for you not to journey to Rourke House. It might have been Webster, not your father, who had summoned you. When I saw you, you were so alluring, so innocent, I wanted only to protect you."

Gracefully, Diana came to her feet and approached Cole. Guilt almost compelled him to turn away from her but she gently put her hand on his bent arm. "Suppose I had been an ugly hag—"

"I do not see women as hags!" he shot back with sudden ferocity. "I care not what a woman looks like. I care what is inside her." Without warning, Cole swung toward her and firmly gripped her upper arms. "I see the warmth and gentleness in a woman's heart, Diana," he continued, his voice mellow and soft. "It is the beauty there that creates beauty on the outside. You are the most beautiful woman I have ever met, but if you had been homely my guilt would have been no less than it is now."

With a tiny smile, Diana rose to her tiptoes and touched her mouth to his. The unexpected gesture

125

took him quite by surprise and he did not physically respond, except to look at her as if she had suddenly lost all reasoning. "And what was that for?"

"For being honest with me, Cole Donovan. Your words are those of a man with no equal. In my loneliness in the mountains I had never imagined a man such as you. Truly, sir, I wonder still if you are réal or an apparition."

Diana's softly spoken words reached deeply into Cole's heart. He felt it flutter with want of her, felt the coolness of the small sitting room suddenly surge with heat emitting from his own body to encompass her, to claim her, to possess her and hold her in his arms so closely that their bodies would fuse as one. That was how badly he wanted this lovely wood sprite who had encountered so little compassion or companionship in her life.

But could that be true any longer, now that Cole knew how he felt about her? Webster Mayne could snatch his life out from under him, but was his life more important than the sensual woman he held in his arms, whose mouth he wanted to claim, whose sweet breasts he longed to caress softly, without the barrier of silken material?

How vulnerable was the innocence in her eyes, how soft her lips, just inches from his own. Had he not closed that small space between them to gently capture her mouth in the gentlest of kisses, she might have made the bold move herself.

Diana was immediately, wondrously assailed by the masculine smell of him, commingled with the sweet taste of brandy lingering on his mouth. "Diana," he whispered huskily. "I want you so. I've been waiting long for a lass such as you to come my way."

Ah, but she was innocent and naive, he knew that. He wanted her, but he could not bear to spoil the dreams, the wants and expectations lingering behind her exquisite violet eyes. He could not deprive himself of this golden-haired treasure, but he would have to move slowly with her. He would rather die than spoil the pleasures she expected to exist between man and woman.

A fear that was not really a fear rose within her and she peeled herself from his embrace. Rushing across the bed chamber, she threw open the window and let the rain that had begun to fall beat lightly against her silk-clothed body. When she turned again, a brilliant purple hue lit her eyes and her full golden tresses lay limp upon her shoulders, aglitter with the drops of rain that had fallen there. Cole quickly traversed the floor and pulled her away from the window, relocking it immediately.

"I will not having you catching your death, you little fool," he muttered beneath his breath.

"Ah, but you are a right winnin' lad," she chuckled, employing a feigned Scottish accent created, especially, for this wonderful moment in her life. "A fool, you might say, Cole Donovan, but I am the fool you want."

There was no denying that, Cole thought, drawing her lithe body against his hard chest. He wished he had a bit of heather ale in his gut; perhaps then he would feel more confidence in making this prize his own, in seeking the pleasures she seemed so willing to relinquish to him.

He should withdraw from her, leaving this innocent and naive treasure untouched. But he was not that strong, and his lust-filled eyes lowered to her silken bed gown, its simple tie undone. The material clung to a youthful, yet womanly figure whose hard-peaked breasts pressed against the damp fabric and made his groin ache with want of her. He wanted to overpower her, to feel the delicious, inviting curves of her against his body and take her, here and now, without prelude.

Yes, yes, she wanted this! Her body shivered with heated anticipation. A wild, intense desire grew within her, begging for his nearness, his amorous attentions, the gentleness of his hands exploring her body through the offending silk garment she wore. She wanted to be free of it, but she did not want to appear wanton. She wanted to feel his sweet breath against her cheek, her eyelids, her temple, to feel his strong, slim fingers tunneling through the golden mass of her hair. Her senses reeled and suddenly, her passion-heated body no longer felt the coolness of the January night. A gentle pulse began in her heart and raced through her, and all the things she had wanted from Cole, her mesmerized body was now feeling.

Somewhere in her delirious happiness, he had lowered her to her bed and his body had gently covered hers. Her desire drew her closer, and closer still, until his hands were no longer gentle, but wondrously seeking and satisfying.

If she had been naive and innocent moments ago, her wanton abandon was now a fiery greed, ignoring those puritanical convictions that might have clung to an ordinary girl. But she was not ordinary, and she was not with an ordinary man. His possessive mouth claimed hers, over and over, bruisingly, caressingly . . . taking her breath and making it part of his own. Their magic was omnipotent, their bodies fused into a violent storm from which they could not . . . would not flee. Let it wash them overboard into a sea of passion. That was all that mattered now, the tender yet brutal, gentle yet commanding, primal desire that made them as one.

But was it all that mattered? Suddenly, Diana's senses flooded back to her. This beautiful thing she was experiencing, the heat racing through her body, the pounding of her heart against his chest . . . it was all new and frightening. She took a short, deep breath and whispered, "I am scared. Will you hurt me?"

Her tenderly spoken words were like cold water thrown in his face. Cole's movements ceased, and his fingers entwined loosely through her hair. "I'll be wantin' you so, lass, but I will not hurt you. Not now." Gritting his teeth, he started to move from her, but her arms darted to his back.

"You will not leave me, Cole? You will not leave me . . . like this? Wanting you, too?" Tears touched her cheeks at the very thought that he would even consider forsaking her. Tenderly, Cole's fingers moved to brush away the tears clinging to her cheeks, then he replaced those very tears with a gentle kiss.

"What do you want? Do you want me with you, or do you wish that I leave?"

"I want you with me, Cole, but . . ." Gently, she shrugged beneath him. "I am frightened."

Again, his fingers entwined through her hair. He was a blur above her; his finely chiseled features could gain no depth and clarity. She was aware of his maleness against her tender thigh, promising pleasures her body had never experienced, except in her dreams.

"Do not be frightened, dear lassie. I will be gentle with you."

His words were soothing, yet enflaming, the lustrousness of his eyes promising and enrapturing as his ample mouth tenderly brushed her own, his hands now massaging her shoulders beneath the straps of her gown. She felt it slipping down the length of her body, and as she arched her back against the wondrous pain bursting through her abdomen, Cole's tongue drew a circle around the rosebud of one of her breasts, then the other, enflaming her so that there was no turning back. Passion coursed a path through her body and she knew she wanted to be his prize . . . to lie in his arms, to love and to be loved by him. He was the one preordained to quell the painful thirst within her. As his hands commanded the attentions of her body, she realized that she lay fully naked beneath him.

Her fingers frantically worked the buttons of his waistcoat, then pulled it back over his strong arms. "I want you . . . I do want you," she whispered her assurance, sweetly, against his cheek, arching her back almost violently in order to imprison her passion-sensitive breast against his masterful, seeking mouth.

Cole wanted to free himself of his clothing and bury himself within the sweet, moist depth of her before his skin burned from his body; that was how badly he wanted her. With a groan of annoyance, he pushed himself up just enough to shed his breeches and boots as if they were one garment, then allowed her fingers to ease the satin material of his shirt down his arms.

Now, he was free to seduce her, to win her confidence, to make her want him so badly that her fears would vanish with the night. Instinctively, her thighs eased apart to make room for his narrow hips, and the explorations of his hands lightly brushing her silky inner thighs.

She gasped as his hand touched her . . . there . . . where she had never been touched before. She closed her eyes tightly, the breath leaving her lungs so quickly she was sure she would faint. But she willed herself into readiness, because she did not want to miss a single deliciously erotic stroke of his hands. Her lungs heaved; she arched her hips against him, against his hand that instantly rose, to circle her wrist and caressingly bring it close to her disheveled tresses of golden hair.

"You are ready for me, Diana?"

"Diana's senses soared with the clouds. "Yes . . . yes . . ." Her hips arched violently against him, begging for him, wanting him so desperately that she no longer felt rational.

Before she quite knew what was happening, she felt his partial penetration into her. There was no pain. A smile of relief came to her lips . . . but just at that moment, he drove himself with such force into her that her abdomen was seized by a violent, painful tremor. Instantly, his mouth covered hers, and tears trickled down her temples to be lost in her hair.

Cole had felt her body convulse, then stiffen beneath him. Hurting her brought tears to his own eyes and he whispered hoarsely, "Dear lass, that will never happen again."

But the pain had been of such a short duration that she now felt only desire, and her hips slowly matched his cadence, so eager was she for the fulfillment of their union. His masterful hands seared her flesh and she bathed in the pleasant waves of the flaming river consuming her, body and soul.

Now that her fright had ended, she felt free to explore his own body . . . his tight muscles, his taut, sinewy back, his narrow hips moving gently against her own. The maleness of him stroked her, his movements growing harder and harder still, tantalizingly invading her body with the writing thrills that enslaved her to him.

Cole had never taken so lovely a prize . . . a golden-haired goddess with passion darkened eyes. He could scarcely control his own body as he ground harder and harder still, until their legs and hips jerked with explosive release and he took a final plunge, hot flames exploding between her thighs and

131

raging upwards as he buried himself deep within her. His ecstasy made it almost impossible for him to breathe as he lay gently upon her, savoring the sweet receptacle of her body and her own ragged breaths upon his cheek.

Their bodies lay entwined in the aftermath of passion. Diana could not remember ever being happier. Cole was hesitant to withdraw from her, even though his body had been sated, and it gladdened her that he enjoyed being with her, like this. Perhaps he even had some feelings for her.

"I do believe I could love you, bonny lass," he whispered after a moment.

"Or perhaps lust for me," she whispered.

Repositioning himself at her side, Cole pulled her into his arms. "That too. If you still wish to shoot me, now would be the best time. I am too weak to defend myself."

Diana drew her palm up to her temple and looked down on him. His eyes were closed. Gently she traced her finger down the straight bridge of his nose. "I believe I'll wait until I am angry with you again."

His gray-black eyes opened to meet her exquisite violet gaze. A grin crossed his handsome features. "I'll remember that, Diana, when again I see anger darken your eyes. I think I would prefer that you not be angry."

Diana suddenly drew the sheet over her nakedness. Her head dropped to the pillow beside him. Pleasurable thoughts should have filled her head in the aftermath of so wonderful an evening; instead, her thoughts suddenly focused on the victim of the murder Cole has been accused of. Her father had been murdered in December, as had the victim of the crime that Webster held over Cole's head. Could it possibly be? Diana shook her head. The man who had murdered her father had already been hanged. Still, she felt a sudden desire to flee, although Cole was all the security she had ever felt in Rourke House and they had, after all, just made sweet, exquisite love. She would never believe that the kind, gentle man holding her so endearingly close could be a murderer. She forced the thought away, scattering it into a million tiny fragments that she hoped would never come together again.

With that problem resolved, she allowed him to hold her, to caress her passion-sated flesh through the thin fabric of the sheet. She eased to her side, then dropped her head of golden hair to his firm chest, feeling the gentle pulse of his heart suddenly increase in intensity. Yet even as she wrapped herself in the security of his embrace, the offending unanswered question kept popping uninvited into her thoughts. She tried closing her eyes tightly as the scattered remnants of the puzzle came back together again. But the question in her heart did not make its way to her mouth, for suddenly it was captured, in a warm, passionate, sensual kiss, by the man who held her oh, so closely and robbed her of every sensible thought. Her body was suddenly a hot, passionate receptacle wanting only to be satisfied again.

Brought to a heated frenzy by the fusion of their mouths as they sought, once again, to sate their desire, neither heard the light knock at the bedchamber door, until a thin triangle of light from the corridor reflected off the French doors. Simultaneously Cole and Diana moved quickly from the divan, pulled on their clothing, and crept into the shadows of the small room. Forcing her breathing to a respectable rhythm, Diana pulled free of Cole's arms and moved toward the French doors.

"Oh, my," she said, yawning with feigned boredom

133

when she met Mrs. Sanders's gaze. "I was just reading the most tiresome report in the *Herald.*"

Mrs. Sanders, holding tightly to the handle of a lamp, looked at her with skepticism. She looked terribly disheveled for someone who had merely been reading. "Indeed, miss? And what report was that?"

A rather sickly grin made a fleeting path across Diana's oval face. She again yawned, then stretched her shoulders as though they were wracked with tension. "It was boring, too," she laughed weakly. "I cannot even remember what I read." When Mrs. Sanders approached, Diana quickly slammed the French doors. "I left it a ghastly mess, Mrs. Sanders," Diana continued with haste. "You go on back to bed and I promise I'll tidy it in the morning."

"And you, miss? You're retiring, also?"

Diana made a rather dramatic gesture, flinging her hand across her chest. "By George, so I am! I really shouldn't keep these god-awful hours, should I?"

Diana approached and gently coaxed Mrs. Sanders toward the door. "Now don't you worry about me. I'll climb into bed this very minute and go fast to sleep."

"Shall I bring you warm milk?" Mrs. Sanders offered, surprised at being impatiently ushered from the young woman's chamber.

"No, I am fine. I am very tired and will go straight to bed."

Again, Mrs. Sanders turned and her dark, graying eyebrow arched with mild skepticism. "Very well, miss."

Only when Diana had slumped heavily against the closed door, breathing a sigh of relief, did Cole emerge from the shadows of the sitting room. Although he had heard their conversation, Diana felt compelled to reassure him, "She suspects nothing. She believes I am alone."

"We hope so. But, of course, he couldn't possibly know that," Cole reassured himself. "If Tuxford knew I had crept out—"

A thought came to Diana. She stood erect and slowly moved toward Cole. "That reminds me of something I have been wanting to know. Where are you lodged in the big gloomy house?"

"In the cellar."

Diana shuddered. "Sounds dank and uncomfortable. How do you manage to stay so immaculate in your dress?"

With a gentle laugh, Cole took her arm and coaxed her back to the sitting room, closing the door with his foot. "Because your dear cousin has provided me with all the luxuries, including a bath. It's really quite comfortable down there."

"But a prison," she said, "not a home."

Cole shrugged his wide shoulders. "A prison, yes, but not forever. I will find a way out of this predicament." He planned to take her to the mountains. But he could not do so without someone in Philadelphia to help them while they were in hiding. "We need someone willing to help us, Diana. Someone we both trust."

Diana had been standing with her back slightly toward him, feeling his hand gently caress her right arm. Suddenly she spun toward him, her eyes lit up as brightly as the candlelight of the large crystal chandelier. "I trust John Redding. He will help us."

Cole smiled a knowing smile. "We must leave a letter for him telling him what Webster is doing to you. I don't know if I can tell him that I—" He'd been about to say, "the man who was supposed to have been hanged for the murder of your father," but quickly recomposed his sentence, "That I have been framed for a murder."

Diana moved quickly toward the writing table in the corner. "That is something John definitely needs to know. I want him to help you, too." She sat, drawing to her the ink bottle and the quill which rested in a brass holder. She then took a sheet of the linen writing paper which bore the watermark of the Rourke family. Scarcely past the salutation, she looked up rather quizzically and asked Cole Donovan, "Why would I write John a letter? Why not simply tell him on the morrow?"

Cole Donovan's gray gaze suddenly darkened. He could not tell her what he planned to do as soon as the letter had been written. He could not tell her that already, with Tuxford drugged on laudanum at the stable, he had crept to the livery in Philadelphia and purchased two good riding mares, a pack horse and ample supplies for a very, very long trip. He could not tell Diana that they stood saddled and ready to go, in the fenced area beside the stable, or that he would take her with him even if she had to be bound and gagged. He imagined it would take that, though he could not picture doing that to a woman he had just made sweet, wicked, wonderful love with.

Diana couldn't help but notice Cole's frozen expression. She became suspicious and gently laid the pen across the paper. "Why have you not answered me, Cole Donovan?"

Animation sprang to his face. "I was thinking that perhaps you're right. But," he thought quickly, "go ahead and write the letter so we will know precisely what it is we must tell John on the morrow."

He must have sounded terribly sincere because, unhesitatingly, she picked up the pen. "Yes, that is a good idea. I'll write the letter right away, while everything is fresh in my mind." She looked up at him with smiling violet eyes. "You really must be going, don't you think?"

"Yes." He managed a small, guilty smile. Blast! If only she didn't trust him so implicitly! "If I stay who can say what might happen?" It was a rather feeble attempt to mask his true intentions.

The crimson rising in her cheeks, Diana's eyes dropped shyly. "Do go on with you, Cole Donovan, while I compose our thoughts for John Redding."

Cole forced himself to leave but looked at her, writing busily, as he slipped into the mirrored panel and disappeared down the narrow steps toward the cellar. Upon reaching his suite, he quickly changed into his buckskins, packed a few personal belongings in a canvas bag, then crept out to the stable. There he found Tuxford soundly sleeping and the horses nibbling lazily at the sweet feed he had left in the grain bin to keep them quiet.

It was now time to put his plan into action. He estimated that about twenty minutes had passed since he'd left Diana at the writing desk. Knowing her sentiments about leaving Rourke House, he had brought with him a strip of hemp around which he'd wound a long length of velvet ribbon. If she gave him an argument, he would not hesitate to use the hemp to bind her hands, or to quiet her with the gag he tucked into the pocket of his buckskin trousers. Quietly he turned back to Rourke House and the unsuspecting Diana Rourke.

Chapter 8

So that her thoughts would not scatter to the wind, Diana quickly composed the letter as she might to someone she did not plan to see the following day. When she got to the part about Cole Donovan and the misfortune that had befallen him, she wrote sympathetically, hoping she would be able to memorize her words, the better to successfully relay the outrage of her cousin's actions to the kindly Dr. Redding. But as she thought of Cole Donovan, she thought of the long, loving moments they had spent together, and the awakening of a passion that had lain dormant within her. It had taken a man like Cole Donovan to bring her fully into womanhood. She glowed from the beautiful moments when they had lain together upon the divan.

Sighing deeply, she brought her thoughts back to the composition beneath her hand. Having written her thoughts in the form of a letter, it came naturally to end it with her signature and two long lines beneath, in her usual flamboyant, yet feminine style. As her eyes scanned the two-page letter, her pen stood ready to make necessary changes. She was quite pleased upon reaching her signature to find that she had not even forgotten to dot an *i* or cross a *t*.

Startled by a shadow crossing the light beside her, she turned, alarmed. Immediately, her gaze lifted to the cool, gray-black eyes of Cole Donovan. "You did give me a start," she said quietly. "I did not hear you enter. Here—the letter is finished. Do you wish to read it?" Cole took the letter she offered him and his gaze moved rapidly across the two pages. When he looked up, she asked, "Is it satisfactory?"

"It is quite satisfactory," he replied, folding the letter in thirds and tucking it into the pocket of his jacket. Putting his hand out, he waited for her slim one to ease into it. "I want only to share that inviting bed with you, Diana Rourke. But we have much more pressing problems." As she smiled shyly for him, lowering her eyes, Cole eased closer to her.

In the move, the length of velvet-covered hemp he had hidden at his back was revealed. "What is that for?" Diana asked.

Before her eyes could again lift to his, Cole Donovan's right hand reached out and pulled her from the chair. His other hand covered her mouth. While she had been frozen in bewilderment just moments before, her fear now became a violent tremble against his body. "You are coming with me, Diana. You are—we are both—in danger here. If you will not come with me willingly, then I am prepared to use force." A mere breath of space separated their eyes, Diana's sparkling with rage, Cole's dark and foreboding as he awaited her reply. "Will you come with me?"

Despite the mad thumping of her heart, Diana tried to put her thoughts together. If she nodded her assent, it would give her the opportunity to scream, which would surely bring someone to her rescue. If she fought him, he could easily subdue her efforts. She had no doubt he would be able to take her from the house, using his secret routes, without awakening the family. But was he such a fool that he would fall for her ploy, were she to timidly consent to being kidnapped?

Diana had only a second to choose between the two measures. Inborn stubbornness would not allow her to give in willingly, subdued by his superior physical strength. Thus, she resorted to her wiles, weakly nodding her assent, and as his hand slowly began to slip from her mouth, she let forth a piercing scream.

But its duration hardly counted as a scream, for Cole's hand firmly, roughly covered her mouth, smothering her effort. His dark eyebrows met in an angry frown as he deftly used the velvet-covered hemp to bind her hands, then removed the gag from his pocket. Before so much as a minute had passed, she was bound and gagged.

Diana was too startled by his brutality to offer resistance at first. Only when he began tugging her across the room did her senses return fully to her. He had bound her hands and forced the clean bit of rag between her teeth, but her feet were free. As he reached the door, she kicked out, catching him full upon his knee.

"You little vixen!" he hissed. "I should beat you for that!" He pulled her intimidatingly close, his glaring eyes mere inches from her own. "But I won't." Although he knew beyond a certainty that he never would, he added, his voice low and threatening, "Not yet."

Diana mumbled rebelliously against the gag, managing only to move the offensive bit of cloth further between her teeth. When he suddenly picked her up and threw her across his shoulder, she beat against his back with her bound wrists.

So! This was the way it was going to be!

Diana's fury had somehow subsided into numb indifference. The outrageous Scotsman had taken her as his prisoner and they were moving on a northwest course toward God-only-knew where. After three days he had decided that they had traveled enough distance from Philadelphia for him to safely untie her hands, but he had humiliated her by putting ridiculous little bells on her feet so that he could tell if she removed them from the stirrups. She had not spoken a word to him in these three days of traveling at a leisurely pace, though he had repeatedly tried to draw her into conversation. To watch Cole Donovan, one might have thought he was on a pleasure outing. Who would suspect that a kidnapping was taking place and that the lady being kidnapped was planning escape—and revenge!

Except for taking her against her will, Cole had seen to her every comfort. He had bundled her in a thick rabbit cape that covered her from her head to her slim ankles, had made sure she was never hungry, and had been cordial and polite to her. What he had not tendered was an apology, and that was something of an affront to her. Certainly, he owed her one.

Evening was approaching. A deep, dark haze scattered across the far horizon, sprinkled lightly by the last golden rays of a winter sun that had not been especially kind to them in their travels. The wind was mercilessly cold, and the snow blanketing the forest blindingly bright. Diana had a bit of a headache and she had every intention of complaining of it, when and if she ever decided to speak to Cole again. She hoped her silence was painful to him.

Actually, Cole Donovan was more amused than anything. Whenever their eyes met, hers became narrow and challenging, her mouth pinched and tight as she tried to relay her disapproval. He talked to her in a light, indifferent tone, his intention not to draw her into conversation—though he knew eventually she would become bored with her silence—but simply to provoke her temper. He knew how difficult it must be for her not to lash out at him with vicious words and insults, and a few unladylike threats to boot.

Previously, they had made camp about this same time of the evening. Diana was weary from the long day in the saddle, and annoyed by the silly little bells on her shoes that insisted on tinkling despite her efforts to keep her feet still. Every time he heard one of the musical little warnings, Cole looked around and tugged at the line imprisoning her horse to his own, his expression successfully relaying that retribution would be the end result of an escape attempt.

If only she could get her hands on the musket in the casing of his saddle, she would shoot him! If she could reach out and take the long knife from its sheathing at his waist, she would stab him repeatedly. If only—oh, how perplexing! He was bigger, stronger, and, in some ways, more cunning than she was. She had no choice but to do his bidding. She wanted to see him dead. No! Worse, tortured, the skin sliced from his bones in tiny shreds while he screamed in agony.

Yet, despite the humiliation he had put her through these past three days, he had otherwise been kind to her. Although he had met only cool silence, he had explained that he simply wanted to protect her from her evil cousin. Diana had to admit that Webster was a bit of a scalawag, but was he really as dangerous as Cole would have her believe? And she had not even had an opportunity to accomplish the impossible . . . meeting her Aunt Jocelyn! Cole Donovan had taken that chance from her for the time being.

If he thought she would not get even, he was sadly mistaken.

Half an hour later, they pulled into a cool, snow-covered clearing beside a pond. Though it was frozen over, Diana knew Cole would, as he had last evening, break a hole and snag a healthy trout for their supper. Cole dismounted, tied off both his horses, then turned, disengaged the little bells, and assisted Diana down from her own weary beast. Reluctantly, she moved into Cole's arms, snapping her head away as their faces drew close. But even as she tried to put distance between them, she felt his masculine breath against her hairline. This should have made her angry, but instead only intensified her traitorous attraction to him. The musky aroma of him flooded her senses, and she berated herself for her lack of self-control.

As he went about the nightly routine of preparing for supper and making them both comfortable for the evening, Diana found a large niche in a tree that seemed to have been struck by lightning. Snuggling into the hole, she crossed her arms beneath her cape, drew up her feet, and propped her chin on her drawn-up knees. Her eyes followed Cole's every movement. Once, he glanced her way, but much too briefly to have seen her eyes narrow with loathing. It outraged her that he accepted her attitude matter-of-factly and could not be brought to the brink of ire. He was calm and indifferent; she was the only one with fury darkening her eyes.

Diana climbed to her feet, scarcely able to prevent the shiver of cold that ran down her spine when the night wind once again stung her cheeks. Her move toward the woodline immediately drew Cole's attention.

"Where are you going, lass?" he asked, his cold, methodical tone causing her mouth to press into a thin line.

"To tend to business that does not require an audience," she replied, with as much sarcasm as she could muster.

The evening twilight did not hide the fact that he shrank with embarrassment. "Then go about it!" he snapped, immediately continuing his search for firewood. "And don't wander far off. I'll be listening for you."

"I'm sure that you will!" Diana moved toward the timberline, then eased her way down the snow-covered ground into a long, winding gulley. She kicked up snow as she moved, much as she had done as a small girl, bored with life and wishing for excitement. Slowly, the sounds of the clearing and the dull thumping of the branches Cole stacked on his arm faded away. Diana's mood perked up. The dark silence was a welcome relief, and at the sight of the purple sky across the forest of firs memories suddenly sprang back to her. The familiarity of where she stood evoked a wild pounding in her heart. Her violet eyes, absently scanning the ground just moments ago, now searched desperately among the firs. Then she saw it, a lightning-rent cedar a mere hundred yards to her left. Trancelike, she moved across the snow, her grace and beauty luminous in the last dying embers of twilight. When her hand touched the fir, her fingers immediately traced the indentation of her initials — *DR* — carved into the cedar by Hambone many, many years ago when he had taken her on one of her rare trips away from the creek where she had been raised. She knew then that she was less than seven miles from Aunt Rufina's trading post. Hope! Salvation! Escape from the clutches of the madman who had made her his prisoner! With scarcely a thought of the scavenging wolves and other predators of the night, Diana began to run northward through the woods, unaware of the thin, winter-barren twigs grabbing at her tender flesh.

After five minutes, Cole became suspicious of Diana's absence. Even before she had found the familiar tree, he had begun his search in the direction where he had seen her disappear. "Damn stupid lass!" he mumbled angrily, making sure his musket was properly loaded as he moved through the ever-darkening forest. Her footsteps were easy to track. For one raised in the woods, she was not using her good sense. She should have known that she could not get away, and that it would only make things worse for her in the future. He would have to guard her at every moment — even her private ones — and if he had to tie a lead to her, like his pack horse, then

145

he would do just that! "Damn stupid lass!" he mumbled again, holding the musket so firmly that his knuckles were white with pain. "I should have made her wear the bells!" He had never imagined that she would try to escape on foot in such foul weather.

Cole could not imagine what had caused her to run, since she had made no effort to last evening or the evening before. Her attitude of acceptance must have been a ploy; she had been waiting for an opportunity such as this to make her escape from him. They had been traveling for three days. It occurred to Cole that this was the time it had taken to travel by horseback from Philadelphia to Rufina's trading post. So! That was it! She had gotten a whiff of home. Almost mechanically, Cole turned northward, hoping to cut off her escape. She would not be safe at the trading post; Webster would find her there, to be sure.

Diana soon reached a spot in the forest where men from the creek came to cut firewood in the autumn months. She had lived in the woods long enough to know that footprints in the snow could easily be tracked. Thus, after sitting there for a moment, she strapped a few twigs to the bottom of her boots with two lengths of material from her petticoat, then stepped up to the first of many large, fallen trees. Dropping twigs behind her as she went, she was able to move precariously over the wide trunks for a good half mile before having to touch ground again. She was sure she could throw Cole Donovan off-track that way. He was, after all, a Scotsman, uneducated in the ways of the American woods. Then, exhausted by her perilous journey over the fallen trees, she found a niche among stacked timber and curled in for the night. The only drawback to her escape was that she was almost too hungry to sleep. In the silent, snow-laden forest, her growling stomach might easily give away her position. Still, she was pleased with herself for outwitting Cole Donovan. Tomorrow she would be back on the creek with her Aunt Rufina.

For the time being, though, she was so cold that even her ankle-length fur cape afforded her little protection from the bitter wind. She tried to move deeper into the cavern of stacked timber, but twigs dug into her back.

Diana did not realize she'd fallen asleep until she was awakened by a low growl just a few feet from her drawn-up legs. She tried to focus in the darkness, but all she could make out was a large dark patch against the snow that had drifted into the niche.

As the clouds momentarily parted, allowing the winter moon to catch the glimmer of ice clinging to the mouth of the timbers, a pair of amber eyes turned to her. Gasping, eased tightly into the wedge of rock, she could not possibly retreat further. She was not sure what predator she faced, but it was dark with a spotted belly. She wondered if it had been drawn by the smell of her rabbit cape, and what its intentions were. Then it moved toward her and as she looked on in horror and fear, two large paws landed on her shoulders.

"Honey boy! Oh, Honey Boy," she whispered, relief sweeping away fear as she hugged the playful bobcat she had raised from a kitten. "What are you doing this far south?" The large cat fell onto its back amongst the folds of her rabbit cape and lifted its paws to her. He growled affectionately, sinking his teeth into the soft fur. "You thought I was something to eat, didn't you?" Diana laughed, rubbing his spotted belly and pulling his short, stubby tail. Then the cat sat on its haunches and waited for another hug, for which it did not have long to wait. "Now that you're here, Honey Boy, you can be my protector. There's a terrible man who has taken me against my will." She spoke as if the cat could understand her. "But you'll keep him from taking me again, won't you?"

"Will he?"

With a cry of alarm, Diana looked up to see the dark outline of Cole Donovan at the entrance to the cavern of timbers. "Get him, Honey Boy! Get him!" But the big cat merely ambled over, sniffed at Cole's soaking wet buckskin boots, and waited for his head to be rubbed. "Oh, you are a traitor!" Diana said sharply, stunned by the cat's affection for a stranger.

Cole softly petted the bobcat's head. He remembered seeing the beast moving through the bushes on the cold, December morning when he'd first met Diana Rourke. "Even he knows what's good for you," Cole said, his anger lost in his relief at finding Diana safe. "Now! Come along, before some real danger finds you hiding in here."

"I won't go!" Diana pouted, crossing her arms determinedly.

"Get her, Honey Boy!" Cole said to the cat, pointing toward Diana with an unshaking finger. Immediately the cat ambled toward her, sunk his teeth into the cape and began tugging at her. As Diana cried out with strangled indignation, Cole Donovan threw his head back and laughed. "Some friend you have there, Diana. A real Benedict Arnold! That's a good

148

boy, bring her to me."

The moment the cat had disengaged her from the tight niche in the rock, he pounced upon her and began scooting his affectionate head among the folds of her cape once again. "Don't you ever speak to me again, Honey Boy!" But even as she spoke, her fingers moved to stroke his soft chin. "What a traitor you are!" Then she said to Cole Donovan, "So, you have me back in your clutches once again. But I did give you a run, did I not?"

"That you did, lass," he mumbled, unrolling a blanket to pull around her. "Now, let us return before our horses become food for predators such as this overgrown mouser." He began a retreat but immediately turned back. "Is it possible you have officially broken your vows of silence?"

"I hate you," Diana said quietly, moving unsteadily to her feet.

"I don't think so." Cole grinned mischievously. " 'Tis my feeling, lass, that you'll be loving me one day, to be sure."

"When hell is as cold as this cavern!" she shot back with vehemence, refusing the comfort of his arms as she moved past him into the glimmering night. How could she have been so foolish as to make love to him that night in the haunting darkness of her chamber at Rourke House? "When my family comes to fetch me, you'll have the hide whipped off you for compromising my honor!"

"Your honor, lass?" Cole repeated with feigned surprise. "That is as shallow as your hatred, to be sure." Diana turned, fury blackening her violet eyes, and without warning, her hand swung out toward his face, half hidden in the shadows of the night. But he caught her wrist in mid-air and held it

149

firmly. "You don't want to do that, lass."

"You're probably right," she answered with unexpected calm, wringing her wrist free of his grip. "I'll save my energy for the knife I will one day twist into your back."

Webster was furious. For the past three days he had irritated the devil out of the Philadelphia Constable's Office. He had also hired German mercenaries to go in search of his missing cousin. Without her, he could not continue with his plan. Without his plan's enactment, half of the Rourke fortune would sit comfortably in probate for a year before passing, unmolested, into the hands of that blasted girl! Webster shuddered at the thought. While her inheritance was tied up, so was his mother's. Damn! What madness had possessed Standish Rourke to tie the two legacies together with an invisible string? If Webster did not pay his gambling debts soon, his creditors would begin letting blood, in large quantities. He had to get his hands on that money! It was all that kept his head on his shoulders. Mindless in his fury, it was not the best of times for him engage in conversation with his father.

"I don't give a damn what it looks like!" he said, referring to the German mercenaries his father had frowned upon. "I—we—must get my cousin back where she belongs!" Webster was furious with Cole Donovan. There was no doubt he was behind Diana's disappearance; he had not been seen since that night either. There was only so much Webster could say in the presence of his father, who believed that Cole had been hanged for killing his brother-in-law. He would have to keep his foolish little secrets. He didn't want his father to get suspicious of his motives.

Philip, however, could not have been more suspicious than he was at that moment. He watched the fury darken his son's gaunt face, saw his body shudder, his hands clench and unclench at his sides. He had never seen Webster like this. He wanted to question him about the disappearance of Diana, but Philip was afraid of his own son. Webster would have him believe that Diana was a simpleminded child who had turned her back on her father's estate to return to the poverty of the mountains. But how did she leave? There were no horses or carriages missing from the Rourke stables. No, Diana Rourke was not simpleminded, and she had *not* gotten a sudden whim to walk away from Rourke House in the middle of a cold January night. Someone had taken her away against her will . . . someone with motive.

"What are you thinking, Father?"

Startled, Philip Mayne turned back to his son. "Thinking?" Webster glared at him. "Nothing. While I was deep in thought, I cannot remember what I was thinking of."

"It is hardly an appropriate time for daydreaming, Father. Your only niece, Diana, is missing, and yet you do nothing but stare into nothingness?"

Philip rubbed his eyes with his thumb and forefinger. "I am tired, Webster. We are all tired. Goading me into an argument is not going to bring Diana back to this house. We must think this out reasonably. She must have had a reason to leave."

"I told you! She has returned to that frazzled witch in the mountains!"

"She has done no such thing!" Philip shot back,

151

surprised at his own vehemence. He tried to remain calm in Webster's presence, though it was ofttimes a futile effort. "Yes, she is gone, Webster. But she did not leave by herself. She was not happy here, I'll admit, but she would not have recklessly endangered her life. Someone aided her, though for what reason I do not know."

"Did you talk with John Redding again like you said you would?"

"I have talked with John several times," Philip replied, exasperation lacing his voice. "How many times must I tell you? He knows nothing."

That was not quite true. John had just tended to the last of his patients for the evening and had returned to his living quarters above his office. He again took up the sheets of paper that had been slipped beneath his door three nights before. He felt guilty for keeping it from his good friend, Philip, but he had felt it vital to do so. Diana was in trouble and so, it seemed, was another person. But how had Diana met this stranger who had been falsely accused of murder? Since Diana had been protected from people of questionable character, John was very much troubled by that aspect of Diana's letter, which had been written hurriedly, more as a collection of circumstances not to be forgotten than as a letter. What had motivated her to write the letter to him, a man she had known only a little while? That, too, troubled John. And this man she had written about? Who was he, and where could Diana possibly have met him? He could not forget that she had been virtually isolated from most outsiders. John had visited the house the morning after receiving the letter and Philip had not indicated anything amiss in the household. He had not even realized Diana was missing until John requested that a servant be sent to her bedchamber to rouse her so that he might see to her health. John had no doubts that Philip was innocent of all wrongdoing in Diana's disappearance. That left Webster, and of his culpability, unfortunately, there was no room for doubt. Webster had walked into the parlor that morning, his face a mask of guilt. He had spoken defensively even before John had opened his mouth.

Now John sat in his favorite wing chair and re-read Diana's hastily written narrative. "An innocent man was accused of a murder he did not commit . . ." John's brows pinched into a frown. *A man!* What man? Someone from Diana's past? But would such a person have had access to Diana at Rourke House? John thought not.

Then a thought came to him as quickly as a lit candle illuminates a dark room. But the idea brought an inner revulsion which caused his body to shudder involuntarily. Could it possibly be? He would have to wait until the morning to test his theory.

John slept fitfully that night, keeping his wife awake far past midnight. Finally, in desperation, she questioned her husband about "another woman," at which John laughed heartily. "Darling wife," he had mumbled, kissing her cheek and patting her tightly clenched hand, "there cannot be 'another woman' when I have the best of all." Then, returning to his prone position and pulling his wife down beside him, he had pretended to sleep.

The following morning he rose earlier than usual, dressed, and hurried toward the town magistrate's house a few blocks away. He roused the elderly gentleman from his sleep with a rather preposterous request. But because John Redding was one of the most respected men in all of Philadelphia, and because, from him, such a request would not have been made without just cause, an order was granted for the exhumation of the remains of Cole Donovan, the man executed for the murder of Standish Rourke.

At mid-morning, John hired two laborers to dig up the simple, pine coffin such as all executed men were buried in. Since it had been cold the three weeks since the execution, the ground was hard, and the task took until mid-afternoon. John Redding remained on the scene. When shovels hit the hardness of pine, he moved closer to the rectangular hole.

"Take it to the top, eh, guv'ner?" the elder of the two men queried.

"No." John threw down an iron bar. "Just pry off the lid and remove the hood from the corpse."

"Aye, guv'ner." The brawny man used the palm of his right hand to hammer the bar between the loosely driven nails holding down the lid. They popped up one at a time.

There was no odor emitting from the coffin; the coldness had delayed decomposition. When the lid had been removed, the two men in the hole remained unaffected, but John Redding gasped in surprise. The body in the coffin was that of a sick, ailing man, not a well-muscled, healthy man like Cole Donovan. Even before the older of the gravediggers removed the hood, John knew he would not see the features of Standish Rourke's houseguest. He recognized that body; he had treated the terminally ill man for several months before his disappearance.

John had tried to learn his whereabouts, but when told that the man's family had moved to Virginia, he had assumed that Hogan Linford had moved south with his family despite his illness.

John took a long, deep breath, staring narrow-eyed into the dead features of Hogan Linford. He was in a quandary. Should he report his discovery to the proper authorities? Or should he keep the secret? At least now he knew who Diana's "mystery man" was. Cole Donovan! Was he an innocent man, or just crafty enough to have pulled the wool over Diana's eyes?

They were all questions that would need answers. With a sharply spoken "Cover him back up," John threw a few coins to the men in payment of their labors. He turned from the grisly scene and moved slowly from the cemetery, his hand trembling violently as it fought to retain custody of the cane he used for walking.

Chapter 9

Diana fully intended to make up for the past three days now that her vow of silence was broken. She did not stop complaining for the half-hour it took them to return to the clearing where Cole had left the horses.

"Will you hush, lass?" Cole said finally, with a mixture of indifference and exasperation. "I have closed my ears to your incessant rambling."

Reaching the clearing just a few steps ahead of him, Diana turned and settled her slim fingers on her hips, slinging back her cape as she did so. "Have you, indeed, Mr. Donovan? Tell me, have you heard a thing I've said?"

Cole moved past her, preparing to remove the gear from the pack horse. "I've heard everything, lass. But I didn't pay attention. Fuss and complain, if you like, but my ears are closed. Be civil," he turned, winking at her, "and you'll have my undivided attention."

Diana balled her hands until they became tight, painful fists. "You're a swine!" she hissed, pivoting smartly on her heel so that she would not have to face him. "A swine, do you hear? I should like to see you in the middle of a table of laughing men, an apple stuffed in your mouth so that you'll suffo-cate!"

As she crossed her arms and tapped her toe in outraged indignation, Cole threw his head back and laughed heartily. "Were I a pig in the middle of a table, lass, I doubt seriously I would be in a posi-tion to suffocate. Now—" He approached from be-hind and his hands gently fell to her shoulders, caressing a path down her arms. "Go get those bells from your stirrups."

Diana turned sharply, slapping away his hands in the move. "Whatever for?"

"You ran away, lass. From now on, you wear the bells all the time, morning and night, sleeping or awake."

"I will not!"

Cole's eyes narrowed, though they scarcely hid the humor twinkling in them. 'Aye, you will." Cole moved back to the gear to separate the tent from the items they would not need.

Of course, Diana could not refute the fact that Cole was stronger than she was. He could easily force her to wear the bells. "You may make me wear them," she said with pinched defiance, "but I will not retrieve them for you."

Cole threw down his gear and moved steadily toward her, his muscular arms hanging loosely at his sides. He passed close enough to brush the fur of the rabbit cape. Within moments, the annoying tinkle of the bells echoed in the cold night. Diana kept her arms crossed, her eyes ahead, and did not fight him as he kneeled before her to secure the bells to the laces of her shoes. But as soon as he stood and moved away from her, she bent, ripped them from her laces, and, with a mighty heave, threw them into the timberline.

"There go your damn bells," she said, tight-lipped. "If you want them back on my shoes, you may spend the night searching for them.

Cole remained undaunted. He approached, firmly grasped her arms, and pulled her against his heaving chest. "You, lass, could not have played into my hands more easily. Now, you will sleep beside me tonight, with my arms holding you tight."

Diana gasped. "I will not!"

"Oh, but you will," he said between gritted teeth. "Since I cannot trust you — and you have lost the bells — you will sleep so close to me that you'll think we are one body . . . like that night in your bed-chamber."

Diana knew he meant it; she could see the determination in his narrowed eyes. "I'll find the bells," she offered, hesitating only for a moment. "If I find them, may I sleep away from you?"

Only now did Cole release his grip. "Aye, lass," he assented, doubting seriously that she had the slightest chance of finding them. That she might have to sleep beside him evoked a very warm feeling in him, and he silently prayed that her efforts would prove futile. "Go, find the bells," he challenged, flicking his wrist with feigned annoyance. "If you do not find them, then bring your blankets into the tent. I'll be awaiting you there. And," his words became low and threatening, "don't even think about running. I will be watching you, lass." A low growl emitted from the timberline. Honey Boy had found a warm spot against some fallen timber and was lazily washing his paws. "Watch her, Honey

Boy," Cole ordered, his voice cracking with suppressed laughter. "If she makes a dash for it, pin her down."

Ignoring both Cole and the cat, Diana moved toward the place where she thought the bells might have landed. She searched, moving twigs, brushing away snow, ignoring Cole as he pitched tent across the clearing and kept an eye on her. She searched until the tips of her fingers were so numb from the cold that she thought they'd crack and fall off her hands. She did not find the bells, but she did find a rock. Slyly, she dropped it into the interior pocket of her cape. It might come in handy before the night was out. Then, bringing her fingers to her mouth to blow warm air upon them, she turned back to the fire now blazing before the tent with quite a look of contentment upon her face.

"Did you find them?" Cole asked.

"If I had, you wouldn't have had to ask me. I'd have thrown them in your face!" Her gaze turned to the fire. "Why aren't you fixing our supper?"

"No time to fish, or to hunt. I had to track down a fleeing lass. You'll have to go hungry tonight."

So! He was going to make her pay for running away. Although her stomach was in tight knots, she was much too stubborn to let him know. "Very well. I'm not hungry anyway. You've kidnapped me. You may as well starve me, too."

"But you just said you weren't hungry anyway."

He was badgering her, and she refused to fall victim to it. She knelt before the fire, warming her hands, and declined to meet his challenging gaze.

If she had, she'd have seen love in his eyes. Cole had never seen anyone as beautiful as Diana

159

Rourke, her hair like spun gold, a rosy warmth upon her cheeks, her long, thick lashes shielding her exquisite violet eyes. He felt like a bastard for what he was doing to her, but she'd given him no alternative. Her naivete and innocence would not allow her to see the evil in her cousin Webster. But Cole had seen what Webster was capable of. He could not let Diana fall victim to the same fate that had claimed her father. Cole frowned. Diana could think what she liked of him, but he would die before he allowed Webster to get his hands on her.

Cole watched as she tucked her fingers beneath the warm cape she wore and drew her feet up to hide them beneath the hem of her skirt. He imagined that she was aware of his scrutiny, yet it did not cause her features to tighten in anger. Rather, they were soft, supple, innocent, the golden flames dancing upon them. Seeing her like this, Cole could almost imagine that they were the only two people in the world, isolated from all harm and danger, again lost in each other's embrace. Ah, what a glorious memory! Cole half reclined, resting his tousled head on his palm, and watched the fire continue its hypnotizing waltz upon Diana's ivory features.

Then a spashing sound caught his attentions and he shot up, his head turning in the direction of the pond. "Ah, lass, I believe a trout has taken the bait I offered it."

"But you said—"

Cole moved easily to his feet, then drew his shoulders back to relieve the stiffness that clung there. "I did have time to break the hole and leave a line," he said dryly. "Now, dear lass, if you can wait half an hour, I'll fill your growling stomach with fish."

"That was Honey Boy, not me, doing the growling," she argued without spirit.

"As you please," Cole murmured, moving toward the pond.

As he stood tenuously upon the ice, drawing in his line, Diana felt a sudden compulsion to rise, creep up behind him, and push him into the icy water. But she would likely lose their supper, the flopping, protesting fish, for the effort. That alone enticed her to remain seated and to simply watch him, his broad back straining against the fabric of his buckskin shirt as he fought the creature at the other end of his line.

Cole had snagged a good-sized catfish rather than a trout. Within moments he had skinned it, rolled it in a little flour from the sack tied to his pack horse, and was frying it in pig fat over the fire.

They ate in silence. The half he gave her was more than she could eat, and Diana soon withdrew to the interior of the tent that had been warmed by the fire. On previous nights she had slept in the tent, while Cole slept outside. Despite the loss of the bells, Diana felt that he would honor his gentleman's agreement to allow her a peaceful sleep. She paid little heed to his threat earlier in the evening and did not hesitate to tie the canvas down. But as soon as she got comfortable upon the mat, the ties were loosened and Cole scooted into the tent beside her.

"Ready, lass, to curl up in my arms?"

"I most certainly am not!" she protested, drawing a blanket up to her shoulders. "You should sleep outdoors like you have before!"

"So that you can slip beneath the canvas and be gone in the blink of an eye? I think not! Besides, lass, haven't we shared a bed of passion? Shall we repeat the experience?"

"Get out!" Diana was properly furious.

Cole again rested his head on his drawn-up palm. "And what will you do if I stay?"

"I'll—well, I . . . ," Diana stammered foolishly. What would she do, indeed? He would prevent her from slapping him as he bloody well deserved, and he certainly was not going to leave. "I will sleep outside!" she announced flatly.

She started to crawl out but he caught her by her ankle and yanked her back. "I am not a fool. You'll stay here with me, Diana."

Cole flipped Diana over so that she landed on her buttocks. "You're a swine!"

"Aye, so I've heard," he laughed, drawing her protesting body to him. "Now, hush, and go to sleep."

Diana lay very still. She would not give him the pleasure of seeing her fight. She did not even break her arm from his grip, which had relaxed into a gentle embrace. Flat on her back, she listened to Cole's rhythmic breathing and saw, from the corner of her eye, the rapid flutter of his eyelashes. Oh, he is enjoying this! she thought, crossing her arms across her supple breasts and closing her eyes so that she did not have to see his arrogant, smirking mouth and fluttering eyes. Then, smiling to herself, she felt the weight of the rock she had secreted into her interior pocket.

Within a matter of minutes, Diana could tell by Cole's steady breathing that he was almost asleep. She tried to move out of his arms but they tightened, proving that his instincts to keep her his prisoner were intact. Her smallest move would provoke his arms to become prison bars. There was no way to escape him. She closed her eyes and tried to drown out the sound of his breathing and the musky, manly aroma of him that filled her senses. Perhaps if he shifted positions in the night she would be able to make good use of the rock.

She had not realized how exhausted she was. The far-off sounds of the night became nonexistent, Cole's steady breathing drifted away, and she found herself relaxing in a contented half-sleep. How peaceful she felt, her breathing joining Cole's in the whisper of the winter wind. She wanted to remain alert, but truly she felt warm and happy in her twilight moment. Unconsciously, she turned into Cole's arms, then nestled her head against his strong, buckskin-clad shoulder. Purring contentedly against him, nothing mattered to her but that she was safe and secure in his arms.

Cole watched her thick eyelashes flutter against her winter-cooled cheeks. How lovely was this wood sprite, her oval face relaxed and pleasant, her mouth puckered in her sleep, her hand easing across his waist and finding a warm niche in the rough material of his shirt. Tenderly, he pulled the rabbit cape across her body, then drew her close to him. He tried to sleep, but he was too aware of her sensuality and the painful pounding of his aroused body. His blood flowed so quickly through his veins he thought they'd explode.

He had tasted the sweet nectar of this treasure only once, but he had dreamed about it a thousand times since.

163

Suddenly, the flashes of remembrance brought Diana to full alertness. Although she did not move, her mind revolved around only one thing: escaping and returning to Aunt Rufina's trading post. Thus, gathering her thoughts around her like a thick, protective blanket, she sighed dreamily, "Make love to me, Cole."

Stunned, Cole spent a few moments gathering his own thoughts. He wanted to believe she was aware of the request she had made, but in view of her hostility the past few days, he could not. "You're asleep, lass," he said."

"Is that so?"

She sounded lucid, but still Cole remained skeptical that Diana Rourke would make such a request of a man she claimed to loathe. "Do you not remember, lass? I am a swine."

"I like swine," she teased, smiling even as her eyes remained closed. "They treat us simple human beings as equals."

"Indeed, lass," Cole chuckled. He touched his full, masculine lips to her cool hairline and felt her move to meet his tender touch. Still sure she was mumbling in her sleep, Cole was surprised when her eyes opened oh, so slowly. A smile touched her mouth.

"I thought you were asleep."

"I am, Cole. I am dreaming of lying in the arms of a man who is gentle and kind and who wants to protect me from all evil. Does this wonderful dream lie, Cole? Are you not the man who cares enough to have taken me away from danger?"

Cole's mouth pressed into a thin line, and the muscles of his sinewy chest tightened. "You are ridiculing me, Diana. You are trying to provoke me into anger or . . ." His dark eyes met her violet eyes. "Are you seducing me with ulterior motives?"

Rather than reply, Diana's hand slipped to his neck and coaxed his face to her own. "You have won a prize, Cole, for guessing the right answer. I am indeed seducing you. But with no motive except the pleasure of commingled flesh, man's and woman's."

Cole remained suspicious about what she was up to. He made a quick assessment of the vicinity of the tent. Lying about were no rocks with which she could bash him in the head when he least expected it. His musket and knife were behind him and out of her reach. Yet he could not believe that her provocative words were anything other than sweet, inviting poison.

Diana knew she had him convinced. He had that hungry, lusty look in his eyes. She gingerly felt for the jagged bit of rock that was large enough to shear off his scalp if she so chose. He had only to take the bait of her proffered flesh, lose his senses to his primal lusts, and he would be missing a few follicles of hair.

Watching his eyes dart between the swelling mounds of her breasts and her own narrow, teasing eyes, Diana's mouth parted. Wetting her lips with her tongue, she eased her hands around his neck and pulled him close. The sweetest of kisses did not have to be pried from him; he gave it willingly, his mouth claiming hers gently, then with the demanding firmness she had felt before. Throwing off her cape, her fingers moved to the rawhide ties of his buckskin shirt and, with them undone, she then

165

focused her attentions on getting the tight-fitting garment off. But Cole hardly resisted. Taking the tails of the shirt, he quickly shed himself of it, throwing it into a bundle against the far side of the tent.

His thickly muscled chest invited the roving of her fingers. Responding to her traitorous instincts, Diana touched him, tracing a path with her right forefinger. She had to be convincing, so that she would catch him at his most vulnerable. His lust would put him off-guard long enough, so that she could immobilize him and make her escape. Even as her fingers moved gently over his chest, her mind whirled with the details of her escape. She would not bother to cover her tracks; it would only waste valuable time.

Suddenly aware that Cole's eyes had narrowed as he watched her features, Diana absently brushed away the perspiration caused by the heat of the fire which burned just outside the tent. It was intolerably warm, and she imagined that his passion for her added to the heat of the fire. She smiled a crooked smile, wondering why her own cold seduction did not counteract the warmth. Perplexed by her body's betrayal, she moved her fingers through the thick hair at the nape of Cole's neck.

"Do you not want me, Cole Donovan? Have you forgotten so easily that," she half-growled the words, "our bodies were made to be together?"

That Diana's cheeks did not suffuse with color made Cole question her sincerity. Nevertheless, his body responded physically to the nearness of her, to the provocative invitation of her words and the arching of her body intimately against his own. One of her ivory shoulders had been bared by her move, and, putting his suspicions aside for the moment, his mouth traced a path across her smooth flesh toward the column of her neck, then across the soft curve of her chin, her moist, parted mouth his ultimate goal. She responded warmly, her fingers moving to his taut back to draw him closer. That she was willing and wonderful made their being together natural and instinctive. Cole's doubts flew off with the winter wind that whipped against their passion-warmed canvas tent.

As Cole's hands became more intimate, Diana closed her eyes, her thoughts of escape slowly and traitorously replaced by her need and want of him. As his fingers slipped beneath the fabric covering her other shoulder, she moved to her side so that his mouth could trail the kisses there that the other had enjoyed. Her heart pounded so quickly that she was sure he could hear it, feel it against his hand that moved to circle her right breast, gently kneeding it, touching the taut pink nipple that was soon covered by his mouth. Her breathing increased in intensity, her back arching so painfully that she thought she would break in two. Oh, why, why did her body have to be her greatest enemy?

But Diana stopped to think about it. Those crucial moments after a man had sated his lust were his most vulnerable. He would be weak and defenseless in her arms, even as he congratulated himself upon his renewed conquest. Unable to say truthfully that she had despised their first union, Diana felt that nothing would be lost in giving him one last remembrance of her, one last union of their bodies. Then, only then, would he feel the weight of the rock against his arrogant head.

Thus, she threw herself into her role, sighing at the appropriate moments — she refused to admit even to herself that her kittenish moans came naturally — and gasping when his mouth or his gentle hands found a vulnerable spot upon her body. She lifted her buttocks so that he could remove the heavy skirts she wore, used the toe of one boot to unfasten the other's laces so that she could kick it off, then used her exposed toe to rid herself of the other boot. All the while, Cole Donovan masterfully caressed her body to near explosion and Diana, foolishly, continued to believe she was merely playing a deadly game.

Her mind refused to accept that her body was in a wild frenzy of passion beneath his touches, that her skin burned with a yearning for him. She gasped for air, hoping sensible thought would return to her, but even her quickly drawn breaths did not cool the fire deep within. Involuntarily, her thighs parted to accommodate his body. She had not even realized that he had shed his buckskin breeches and boots and was now fully naked beside her, preparing to shift to the heated bed of passion she had prepared for him.

"Let us be rid of these," Cole growled, pulling her pantaloons down the length of her legs. "No barriers . . . only you, Diana, and me, together . . . here, as it should be."

"Yes," she murmured, lifting her knees to press them against his narrow hips. "Yes, Cole." Her desire flaming painfully through her body, Diana's chest heaved against his powerful one, fusing her breasts against his sinewy muscles.

His body aching as painfully, Cole recaptured one of the pink rosebuds of her breasts with his mouth, his fingers entwined so tightly through her hair that she groaned. Immediately he released his grip to lightly stroke her crimson cheeks.

"Forgive me, Diana. I did not mean to hurt you." Rather than reply, Diana pressed her body more firmly to his, then cupped his strong jawline between her hands and coaxed his mouth to her own. His breath was sweet, like wine, his kiss powerful, possessing, his tongue darting teasingly between her teeth, then withdrawing, so that he could kiss each violet eyelid in turn. His body ached for her, but he knew she enjoyed these teasing moments of foreplay.

But Diana was hardly willing to wait until he had fulfilled what he thought she wanted. Her hands traveled down the sides of him, first feeling his narrow waist and hips, then moving between them to touch a part of him that made him growl in a mixture of surprise and frustration. "Damn, woman, what do you do to me?"

Diana laughed in return. "Seeing that you are ready for me, Cole. Now! Not in a few minutes, not in an hour."

Cole enveloped her soft ivory features between his palms. "You little vixen. Shall I show you what a man can do for a woman?"

"I already know," she cooed, placing her hands over his own, then gently kissing each of his palms. "But if you can show me something I do not know, I am willing."

Cole laughed wickedly. "I could show you this!" he said, nipping playfully at her earlobe. "Or this," he continued, trailing kisses down the column of her neck, between her taut breasts, down her torso, then lowering over the flat plane of her stomach.

Only now did Diana gasp in protest. "Cole, what are you—"

"Hush," he murmured, lowering, lowering still, until both were lost in a frenzy of passion. Diana had never experienced anything as wonderful as this, and her body shuddered with joy and satisfaction. Only when his mouth had fused to her own again, was she able to capture her breath. In that moment, his body joined to hers and they began to rock together on the sea of ecstasy where time was suspended and a solid earth did not exist. The vortex enrapturing their joined bodies was large enough only for the two of them.

Suddenly, snapping her back to the present, Cole held her close him and rolled to his back so that she was atop him, covering his body. She felt a sense of challenge, of control, as her hips moved gently upon him, driving his full length deep within her. He growled, lifting his manhood to her, offering himself to her to do with as she pleased. But she wanted only to maintain their union, regardless of who commanded the superior position, and when she felt the frenzy of his hips moving toward fulfillment—hers as well as his—he wrapped her to him, rolled with her, and drove himself with full force deep within her. Immediately filled with the sweet nectar of him, she shuddered with wonder, amazed that a man could satisfy a woman so fully and completely.

Cole rested his sweating brow against her hairline and breathed rapidly, his shaking hands moving up to rest on her bare shoulders. "God, what a woman you are!" he said thickly.

Instinctively, Diana's hands circled his waist and held him gently. Her right hand moved over his buttocks and slid down against his hip. When her hand felt the jagged rock she remembered what she had vowed to do. She rested her hand upon it for what seemed like hours. Then, shutting her eyes tightly, she eased the rock from the pocket where it nestled and scooted it across the ground and beneath the canvas tent.

"What was that?" Cole asked, alert.

Diana's fingers traced a path down his jawline. "It was nothing, Cole. Probably Honey Boy moving off toward the woods to hunt."

Cole's gaze held her own, then his nose touched hers, eliciting a laugh. "Your nose is cold!" she protested. "But," he had remained joined to her, "it is the only part of you touching me that is cold."

Cole smiled mischievously as he grazed her cheek with his fingers. "My pretty lass, it is you who has enflamed my body. You . . ." He attempted to withdraw from her, but his body would not allow it, the commanding length of him growing hard again even as he spoke. "You who would . . ." He moved inside her, feeling her knees draw up to press against his hips. His hand moved outward, causing him to stretch, but he immediately returned and held the rock before her widened eyes. "You who would," he repeated, "have bashed me in the head when I, having pleasured myself, lay weak in your arms. I knew all along what you were planning, lass, but I have kept an eye on you."

"Ohhhhh!" Diana cried hoarsely. "You—you black devil!" She attempted to move from beneath him,

171

but his hands held her hips against him. He cared not that she began to beat upon his shoulders. With a low growl, he captured her protesting mouth, tossed the rock aside, and calmed her, seducing her with his body's gentleness.

Diana hated herself, hated her traitorous desire for the Scotsman who had taken her prisoner.

Yet her hips pounded against him, her mouth parted, begging to taste the sweet, warm, wonderful kisses that would rob her of all sensible thought.

She was Cole's prisoner, and willingly so.

Chapter 10

Diana slept well that night, perhaps because she had decided she would not use subtle means, but would resort to drastic measures to escape Cole Donovan in the future. She would be rid of him at her first opportunity, and she did not care what weapon she used. She hated him. Hated him!

Diana touched a bit of her favorite perfume to her wrists—a last link with the civilized world she had dropped the day of her kidnapping—then crept from the canvas tent. She was angry with herself because she knew she was fooling no one, not even herself. She loved Cole Donovan as much as she hated him. Drawing herself to her feet, she pulled her cape about her to ward off the brisk morning wind, then looked about for Honey Boy. Almost as if they were kindred spirits, he appeared from the timberline and ambled over for a familiar hug. He was well rewarded. Having got his fill of Diana's embraces, he then turned and sped back into the darkness, unaware that Diana watched as he disappeared over a hill. At the trading post, the big cat had often brought freshly killed game to drop proudly at her feet, providing their meat for dinner.

Now that he knew where Diana was, perhaps he would not be far behind. Diana felt comfort in that, despite the fact that the cat had betrayed her last night. Then again, he might get a longing for the warmth of his favorite corner in Rufina's trading post.

Cole propped himself on his elbow and watched Diana move about the clearing, gathering firewood. The gentleman in him urged him to rise and do the chore himself, but he wanted to see what means she would use to start a fire. Their only bit of brimstone was in one of his packs. Patiently Diana placed the wood, along with some dry straw, on the burned-out remnants of last evening's fire, then rubbed a smooth stick briskly between her fingers, and soon had a fire burning. She glanced smugly toward her captor as she warmed her hands.

"It took you twice as long with your brimstone," she said smartly. "If you want to learn the ways of the woods, you should ask me."

Cole lazily looped the rawhide ties through the holes of his buckskin shirt then slipped on his leggings and boots. "I am always willing to learn," he replied, easing from the tent to sit across the fire from her. "And I am willing to have you as my tutor."

"I'd as soon tutor a venomous snake."

Cole laughed. "What will you do, lass, when you deplete the less popular species of the animal kingdom in your derogatory remarks of me? Last night I was a swine. This morning a snake. What will I be next, eh?"

Diana pressed her mouth into a thin line as she

174

mumbled, "Dead, if I should be so fortunate."

Again, Cole laughed, simultaneously kicking his foot out to kill the fire with a well-placed load of snow. "We'll be needing no campfire this morning, lass. It is time to move on."

"Arrogant . . ." She had been about to call him an ass but that, clearly, would have been an insult to that unfortunate beast of burden. Instead, she finished waspishly, "Scotlander! You could not stand that a woman was able to build a better fire than you."

Cole climbed to his feet, then arched his back and stretched lazily. "I am sure, lass, that there are many things you can do better. And I am quite willing to admit it. Now," he grinned, refusing to allow her black mood to nettle him. "Gather yourself together and let's get on our way."

"Why rush? We've been moving at a fairly slow pace since leaving Philadelphia."

"Indeed, I am in no great hurry, lass. I believe we are well out of reach of anyone who might take a mind to coming after us."

"And suppose Honey Boy should return to the trading post and bring back the men?"

Cole chuckled, "Did you teach the old boy to talk while I was asleep?"

"Don't be ridiculous, Cole Donovan! It doesn't become you."

They had scarcely moved an hour's distance along the snow-laden trail before mumbled voices—the language unknown to Cole—sifted toward them through the trees. Putting his finger to his lips to ensure Diana's silence, Cole dismounted his horse, crept up a low hill toward the voices, and looked down upon a band of about twenty Indians camped in a deep gulley. He motioned to Diana, who quickly alit from her horse and moved toward him.

"What tribe are they?" Cole asked, his hand on her shoulder to keep her low.

"Renegades," she said dryly. "Mostly Delaware, and a few Shawnee. See the rum barrels?" Cole nodded. "Those renegades will be passed out for hours—with the exception of those two over there—and it's lucky for you they will."

Cole looked across the gulley toward two Delawares engaged in conversation. "Not friendly then, hmm?" he questioned.

"I know them," she replied. "They frequent Aunt Rufina's trading post and would not harm me. But you—who knows?"

"You're saying then that they are dangerous?"

"Thirty-five years ago, their fathers were probably part of the band that scalped all the white children in a schoolhouse near here. You decide whether they are dangerous." With that, Diana turned away from him and moved toward her horse.

Later, having traveled several hours since the near confrontation with hostile Indians, Cole and Diana relaxed in a long-abandoned cabin nestled in the Allegheny hills. Having brought the remainder of last evening's fish, Cole offered the larger portion of it to Diana. But she merely broke off a small piece and handed the rest back to him.

"Not hungry?" he questioned.

"You wouldn't care if I were," she sniffed.

Without warning, Cole crossed the room and pulled her into a firm embrace. When she refused to meet his gaze, his fingers went under her chin to coax her face up. "I care very much, Diana. You are everything I've ever wanted in a woman. I could make you my life, my reason to breathe. If only you weren't so damnably stubborn!" Despite the harshly spoken words, his sincerity had shone like a beacon.

"Then why do you take me against my will?"

"To protect you, Diana." His grip relaxed. "You innocently went to Philadelphia to visit your father. You found him to be dead, and you are so loyal to your family that you cannot fathom the notion that Webster was responsible for the terrible deed. Aye, lass, I do indeed take you against your will. But had you listened to reason, it would not have been necessary."

She wanted to believe him, to trust him. But foremost in her mind was the trickery he had used against her that night he had taken her from Rourke House. And the trickery on so many nights before! How could he expect her to trust him when he had engaged in a vicious masquerade, supposedly on the orders of her own cousin?

Cole had noticed a change in her since last evening. She had planned to bash his head in with a rock. After they had made love and lain together in its aftermath, he had seen her ease that same rock beneath the canvas tent. His little prisoner was beginning to relax, to accept, to want him as much as he wanted her. He had to believe it. She could

177

easily have put him in danger when they'd come upon the Indians. And that, too, provoked curiosity in him.

"May I ask you something, Diana?"

Diana did not attempt to draw away. "You may."

"The Indians this morning—why didn't you make our presence known? They would probably have helped you return to your aunt."

"They would have, indeed," she replied.

"Then why?"

Diana's composure flew to the wind. She could not admit that she was fearful for his life without admitting how much she cared for him. What could she say that he would not take as a confession? But as soon as she had asked herself the question, she spoke with carefully chosen words she hoped would be taken seriously. "Blood! Blood, Cole, I cannot stand the sight of it! You're a rogue and a brute, but even you do not deserve to be split open like a hog, your hair skinned off your skull, leaving a ghastly, disgusting mess for the wolves to fight over. No! Call it compassion, though you don't deserve it. Call it selfishness for sparing myself of such a gruesome sight—"

"Or call it love," he interrupted. "Why do you not admit it, lass? You love me, and you know it."

Only now did Diana find the strength to free herself of his grip. "Love! How vain you are!" She turned her back to him and arrogantly crossed her arms. "I hate you! How many times must I tell you so?"

Cole approached. His arms easing around her, he gently touched his mouth to her windblown hair.

"So many times, Diana, that I have no doubts you love me. Your denials only reaffirm what I already know. What *you* already know. Your lovely lips hiss that you hate me, but your heart bleeds with love for me. As mine does for you."

"Oh, you awful, arrogant fool!" she gulped, spinning toward him. "Look into my eyes! What do you see?"

He met her dark purple gaze, saw the tremble at the corner of her mouth, the pinching of her brows. "As I suspected," he whispered. "I see love. *L-O-V-E.*" He spelled the word slowly, emphasizing each with a gentle touch of different features of her face—her eyelids, her nose, her mouth. "Now, my little wood sprite, why don't you make this humble cabin comfortable and begin a fire in that ancient hearth? The wood looks dry enough."

"We are resting at midday?" she asked incredulously.

"I believe you have earned it, Diana. We have traveled for four long days and nights. We will enjoy the rest of the afternoon and evening here. I'll stir up a hare or some pheasants. And," he smiled warmly, drawing his fingers soothingly over her cool cheek, "I'll even skin or pluck the blasted things. You will not try anything, will you?"

"Running away, you mean?"

"Aye, lass."

Diana shrugged carelessly. "I'm rather exhausted. No, I won't run away . . . not this time, at least. But my promise is not binding beyond the day."

"And the night?"

Again, she shrugged. "Yes, and the night."

"Then I will trust your word, Diana."

"But I will never trust you," she assured him. "You're a hideous, horrible man." The softly spoken words did not elicit the proper response. He merely smiled as he took up his long rifle. Moments later she heard their three horses being led into a lean-to against the cabin and the retreat of his footsteps in the snow.

He had left their mounts. She could easily give him a few minutes, then make off with all the horses. But she had given her word that she would not flee. Could he expect her to honor such a promise? Perhaps not, but she expected it of herself. She would not flee, nor would she leave him without a horse. He was a tenderfoot. Diana Rourke could not leave any one defenseless, not even a black-hearted rogue such as he.

She busied herself about the cabin, flicking dust off rickety furniture, dragging the mattress off a hand-hewn bed frame to be aired outdoors. Within half an hour, a roaring fire in the hearth had warmed the cabin and she was able to shed the rabbit-fur cape, which she draped over a ladder-back chair for the time being. The cabin was really quite comfortable, and a quick assessment of the roof assured her that it was sound enough to keep out foul weather. Then she grew tired and decided to lie down for a moment and rest.

But was she really tired? After a few minutes, tension prickling her shoulders, she arose, and began salvaging a few tin pots and pewter and clay bowls from a disheveled corner. Suddenly the door opened and snow-blinding light flooded the chamber. She turned, drawing in a long, stunned breath. Standing in silhouette in the doorway was Cole Donovan, wearing the masquerade of her long-dead relative.

"Trust him, Diana," he said in a haunting whisper. Diana, too surprised to utter a sound, watched the shadow slowly exit the cabin and close the door.

Instantly regaining her composure, her cheeks suffused with crimson rage as she flew across the cabin and flung open the door. Her chest heaving, she stumbled across the clearing, hardly aware of the bitter cold that penetrated the fabric of her blouse.

"Cole! Cole Donovan! Come out and show your face!"

Immediately, Cole emerged from the timberline, two large pheasants tied together by a length of twine slung across his shoulder. "I'm here, lass," he said, approaching her. "I've some fine birds to fill our stomachs."

Diana's fist flew out and caught him full upon his unguarded chin. The fierceness of the blow sent him staggering to the ground. "How dare you! How dare you pull that vicious trickery. Even here! Even now!"

Cole sat on his rump and rubbed the aching bruise. "What the bloody hell are you talking about, lass?"

"You know what! Don't you pull that innocent act on me! I'm too wise for it!"

Slowly, Cole climbed to his feet, retrieved the pheasants and moved toward her. "Humor me, Diana. Explain to me what brought about this vicious,

181

unprovoked attack."

"Humor you, indeed!" His gaze unwavering, she could see that he seriously awaited an answer. Very well, she would humor him if that was what he wanted. But he would pay for it later. "That ridiculous costume! Why did you don that—that get-up? Why would you want to frighten me?"

"And when did I do this?"

"Scarcely a minute ago!" she shot back. "I fled immediately after you!"

"I see," Cole replied with more patience than he felt. "You fled immediately after me, and I presume you say I was wearing the costume of your great-grandfather. You meet me emerging from the woods, wearing my buckskins and carrying two damn pheasants over my shoulder. Not only am I a swine and a snake, but I can change my clothing faster than I can relieve you of your own."

His insult failing to register, Diana's eyes widened. Dear God, she hadn't considered that. He could not possibly have . . . "I—I don't know what to say, Cole."

"Say 'I'm sorry, Cole,' plant a kiss here," he pointed to the tender spot on his chin, "and I'll let it pass this time."

"Well I *am* sorry," she sniffed. "But I don't believe you deserve a kiss."

Instantly Cole pulled her into his arms and captured her mouth in a bruisingly firm kiss. "Ah, but I do, lass," he said, upon releasing her. "And I've collected the debt. Now, if you've finished seeing ghosts, I'll prepare these pheasants for roasting."

His kiss still flaming upon her mouth, Diana

182

turned and entered the cabin behind him. Her vivid dream had unnerved her; she was still trembling.

At midday, her hunger satisfied, Diana lay upon her rabbit cape on the bed, absently watching Cole clean his rifle. A thousand thoughts scattered through her mind. She felt dazed and disoriented, unaware of the passage of time. Even so, she felt safe and secure with Cole. He would protect her against all harm, of that she was sure. And he cared for her. That he had not been affronted by her rash attack against him was a safe reassurance of that.

"He said that I should trust you."

"Ummm?" Cole did not look up from the long rifle.

"My great-grandfather. He said that I should trust you."

Cole's expression did not change. "You drifted off to sleep, Diana, and you had a dream. It was nothing more than that. In your dream, your great-grandfather said that you should trust me. I will not argue with that."

It seemed plausible enough. For the sake of her sanity, Diana would have to accept his explanation. But though she had been tired, she couldn't remember falling asleep. A small voice inside her kept insisting that she'd had a very strange visit that day.

A dozen or more miles to the north, Rufina was exhausted. She'd taken advantage of the absence of traders that day to dust and rearrange shelves and check supplies in the cellar and stock rooms. She missed Diana, her little ragamuffin brat, and regretted that she'd shown so little affection for her over the years. She suspected that Diana knew how much she was loved and that her spoken affection had not been necessary. Oh, how would she survive the days and the evenings without the sweet girl for company?

Thinking of Diana made Rufina remember Rowanna, Diana's mother. She and her younger sister had never gotten along very well, and Rufina had been hesitant to accept Rowanna and her child when she'd left her husband in Philadelphia. It seemed so long ago that at times Rufina did not want to remember exactly what had caused her sister to flee.

But at those times she would look into Diana's sweet features and imagine the terror Rowanna had felt when she'd found her that night, lying limp and lifeless at the edge of a black creek that ran through Rourke property. How the child must have fought as her cousin Webster, older by thirteen years, held her head beneath the water in an attempt to drown her. Battered and bruised, her memory of the horror lost from her young mind, Diana had been taken away from Rourke House. Rowanna, deeply loving her husband, had never found the courage to tell him that his own sister's son had tried to murder their young daughter.

Startled by the bell clanging as the door was opened, Rufina Chambers clambered to her feet. There, looking the proper gentleman, was Mr. Rowell, the man who had taken Diana to Philadelphia with him in December. Rufina was visibly startled to see him, and a bit shaken by speculation as to the reason for his visit.

"What brings you here, Mr. Rowell?" Rufina looked past the balding gentleman. "Bringing back my Diana?"

Rowell shook his head, then removed his long cape to shake the snow that clung to its shoulders. He had made the full trip by horseback, rather than by his preferred mode of transportation — public coach. His rump and inner thighs were sore and raw. The reason for his visit only made matters worse.

"I'm afraid not, Mrs. Chambers."

"Then what is it?" she asked with unintended abruptness, turning toward the stove where a pot of water boiled. "Hot tea, Mr. Rowell, or cocoa? I have both."

"Cocoa, indeed?" Rowell remarked. "It is very difficult to get these days. How do you manage it, Mrs. Chambers?"

"Whatever you might want, Mr. Rowell, I can usually manage to get. I assume you prefer the cocoa?"

"Yes, please." Rowell settled into a rocker beside the stove, which emitted warmth his freezing body very much required at the moment. Almost before he could settle, he was accepting the steaming cup from the middle-aged woman. "Thank you."

Rufina fixed a cup for herself, then sat across from Mr. Rowell. "Have you business in these parts, sir?"

Rowell sighed a deep, weary sigh. "Only with

185

you, madam. Only with you."

"You have brought word of my niece?"

Rowell slowly shook his head. "I bring you dismal news. Your niece has disappeared from Rourke House and no one knows of her whereabouts."

Rufina felt a sick, sinking feeling in her chest. "Has anyone checked the creek that runs through the property?"

Confusion marred Rowell's ruddy features. "Why would you ask such a thing, Mrs. Chambers?"

She had spoken impulsively, almost unaware of the words that spilled from her lips. Yet, if there was any chance that harm had come to her niece — harm engineered by Diana's cousin, Webster Mayne — then someone had to know it. Mr. Rowell was, at present, the only person who would be even remotely interested. Rufina took a long, deep breath and told Standish Rourke's solicitor the ghastly story from a day long past, precisely as her sister, Rowanna, had told it to her.

"Well, I must certainly agree that Webster is capable of murder. He may have tried to kill your niece as a child, but I assure you the death of your niece at this time would not be profitable to Webster Mayne. If something were to happen to Diana, the only one to profit would be the municipality of Philadelphia."

"Indeed? A strange stipulation. Doesn't Diana have a living aunt, her father's sister?"

"She does. But Jocelyn and Diana must inherit simultaneously, and that will take a year. I assure you, Mrs. Chambers, that Webster is, as we say, up in arms about her disappearance, and the Rourke

186

property has been extensively covered in the search for Diana."

"Then there is hope," Rufina said with gruff quietness, "that Diana is still alive."

"Not just hope. In all probability she is alive."

"Then where is she?"

"It is our hope—"

"Whose hope?" Rufina interrupted.

"It is the hope of myself and her Uncle Philip that Diana may be returning here."

"How long ago did she—" Rufina bit her bottom lip to keep from trembling.

"She was last seen preparing for bed five nights ago. A housekeeper saw her and has assured the authorities that nothing seemed amiss. Your niece was cheerful when last seen."

"If Diana was coming here, sir, she would already have arrived. No, some mischief has befallen my niece."

Only now did Rowell sip the cocoa. "Very good." He met the hard gaze of Diana Rourke's strangely gaunt aunt, hardly able to see a familial resemblance to the portrait in Rourke House of the exquisitely beautiful Rowanna Rourke. "I did not come here to worry you, madame—"

"But you have done just that."

"Then I am sorry. If Diana should arrive here, it is imperative that word be sent to Philadelphia. Bulletins are being posted throughout the colonies. We shall get to the bottom of this very unfortunate situation." Finishing off the cooling cocoa, Rowell stood. "I must be departing."

"It is getting late, sir. I have a spare room at the

back if you wish lodgings for the night."

Rowell considered the offer in a moment of thoughtful silence. His rump was terribly sore. "Yes, that would do nicely. I'll pick up a few toiletries from your stock of goods. Thank you, madam."

A few minutes later, Rufina showed the solicitor to a small, comfortable bedchamber. Then she went to her own chamber and roused the man sleeping there. "Hambone, up, you ruffian!" Even Diana did not know about their intimate involvement that was well into its tenth year.

"Go away, woman," he mumbled, pulling the pillow across his tousled head. "I'm not in a mood!"

"Not that!" Rufina argued, taking the pillow to hit him across his backside. "Diana's in trouble." Though tall and big-boned, the forty-two year-old woman possessed the agility of a much younger woman.

The words she had spoken brought Hambone to full alertness. He turned over and rubbed his bloodshot eyes. That he smelled like old, musky wood was an assault to Rufina's fine senses. "What's that you say, woman?"

"You heard me. Diana's in trouble."

It went without saying that Hambone was fond of Diana; she was like a daughter to him. "Is she not in Philadelphia?"

"No one knows. You might get more information from Mr. Rowell. He will be spending the night in the spare chamber and taking supper here. But," again, Rufina slung out at him with the pillow, though not for the purpose of physical assault, "were I you, I'd take a bath before meeting the fine city gentleman."

"You are not me," Hambone retorted, slinging his bare feet to the thick bear rug. "And the fine city gentleman will take me as I am. I've no time to be a blasted dandy."

Hambone quickly pulled on his foul-smelling clothing and move toward the trading area, where hot coffee boiled on the stove. A cup had just been poured when a low, slinking shadow moved through the partially open front door and into a dark, favorite corner. Hambone could not greet the bobcat Diana had raised with his usual playfulness.

"Back again, eh, old boy? No game for dinner?" Hambone bent and tousled the coarse fur of Honey Boy's head. But something caught his attention; nothing visual, nothing that could be seen. Slowly, he sank to his knees, again stroked the cat and brought his hand to his face. His nostrils flared. "Rufina! Rufina, come immediately!"

Momentarily, Rufina exited the back living quarters. "What are you hollering about, old man?"

"Come here. Quickly. Come here!"

Rufina approached, saw the bobcat and asked, hardly genuinely concerned, "Something wrong with him?"

Hambone took her right wrist and roughly pulled her to her knees. "Touch him. Touch the cat!" Both perplexed and confused, Rufina rubbed her hand over him. "Smell your hand."

As ridiculous as it sounded, Rufina brought her hand to her nose. "My God . . . Diana. He smells of Diana. It is the perfume you brought her from the city last summer."

189

Honey Boy, unaware that he had answered a very big question for the two concerned people, merely rolled to his back and enjoyed the attention he was getting.

Hambone knew that Diana was somewhere within a perimeter of ten miles or so. The cat, as far as he knew, had never wandered further.

Chapter 11

At the trading post, Hambone was getting some men together and gearing up for an intensive search. Ten miles away, Cole and Diana basked in the mellow warmth of the small cabin, enjoying a hot supper of roasted pheasant. Diana had found that being a prisoner had certain rewards. She could, after all, be in worse hands than those of Cole Donovan. If not for the circumstances, she could almost enjoy his company. He was a likeable sort in a curious sort of a way, though his idiosyncracies literally drove her mad. He had about him a gentleness and a quality that Diana found appealing. He was never condescending, or patronizing, and always spoke to her as if he were sure she possessed some degree of intelligence and reasoning. Diana liked that.

A light snow had begun to fall outdoors. That she would not attempt an escape that night was a fair certainty. As the remainder of the day's light faded into darkness, Cole prepared a blanket on the floor and made a pillow out of one corner of it.

"You are not going to sleep in the bed?" Diana questioned. "I aired out the musky old mattress."

"After today?" he grumbled.

191

"What do you mean?" Diana was genuinely puzzled, having forgotten about her earlier assault on him.

"You see ghosts and lambast me on the chin! I think I'll be safer down here." Just at that moment, the rumble of a wagon sounded outside the cabin, bringing Cole to his feet. Taking up his long rifle, he quickly sat beside Diana and clamped his hand over her mouth. "Blasted, lass! Did you use that cat to get word to anyone?" Actually, the thought had never crossed Diana's mind, and that it hadn't was something of a disappointment to her. She managed to shake her head, but Cole did not release his palm from across her mouth. She was as shaken as he by the sudden intrusion from the darkness. It could very well be hostile Indians, and she was in just as much danger as he, even more so. "Don't let out a sound," Cole ordered gruffly. "I'll see who is out there."

Cole released her, positioned the loaded long rifle, and was just approaching the door when it flew open, permitting a blast of cold air to flood the room. Suddenly, two men stood opposite each other, rifles aimed steadily. A tall, burly, bearded man stood his ground just inside the cabin door. Cole felt an old familiar twitch at the corner of his eye.

Frightened into silence, Diana wondered just how long the two men would stare each other down until explanations were demanded. Then, without any warning, a small, pitched voice echoed from the clearing surrounding the clearing, "Papa, will they let us in?"

The twitch eased in Cole's left eye and his musket

lowered. "You have family out in that weather?"

"My woman," the man said, lowering his musket, also. "And my little girl. Thought we could warm ourselves at your fire."

"Blast!" Cole could not keep the agitation out of his voice. "Didn't you have sense enough to knock at an occupied dwelling? I could very well have left your wife a widow, and your wee lass fatherless!"

"But you didn't, did you, matey?" The big man moved forward and extended his hand. "Ward's the name, Zebedee Ward. We been movin' due east from Kaintok."

Cole took the proffered hand. "Cole Donovan." Looking to Diana, he said, "And my wife, Diana." The narrowing of his eyes dared her to argue. Besides, Diana did not know how to do so without looking foolish, and—she shuddered—the man's eyes raked her greedily, boldly. Cole had glanced away and had not noticed, not that he would care anyway. "Bring your family in, Zebedee Ward," he said. "This cabin belongs as much to you as to us. We happened upon it, same as you."

Zebedee Ward grinned lecherously, causing the silent Diana's skin to crawl. "But you came upon it first. Callie!" A woman's quiet voice answered. Suppressed agony laced the few words she spoke. "They're friendly. Come in to the warmth." Zebedee Ward then turned to Cole and announced, "Wife's in labor. Hope it ain't inconvenient for you and your missus there for her to birth in here."

Diana suddenly found her voice. "Men, ohhh! You would allow your wife to alight from a wagon unassisted, and in labor?"

193

Cole frowned, taking Diana's arm as she started past him. "You are right, *little wife*. Some men are insensitive clods. I will assist the woman inside, if you don't mind . . . *sir*."

Cole handed his long rifle to Diana. Moving past the unyielding man, he soon returned with a very pregnant woman in tow and a whimpering, shivering three-year-old dragging at her heavy skirts. The distress written in the woman's haggard features indicated that she was in the final hour—perhaps even minutes—of her labor.

Diana went immediately to her, supporting her body against her own. "Cole, if you will be so kind as to bundle the child in my fur cape there in the corner—behind that tattered curtain where she can rest—and assist Mr. Ward with his team, I shall take care of this lady."

Callie Ward's face contracted with agony, yet she made no sound. Diana supposed that she did not want to alarm the little girl, who held fast to her skirts as Cole tried to take her in his arms.

"Come, come, little lady." Cole's mellow voice had a soothing effect on the carrot-topped child.

"My mum . . . I want to be with my mum," she said quietly, even as her arms circled Cole's neck.

"But your mum is going to give you a very special gift soon. A new sister or brother. Would you like that?" She nodded against Cole's shoulder. "What is your name, pretty lass?"

"Hester."

"Come, Hester," Cole comforted, patting her back as he turned. He took Diana's cape from the chair and, placing it in the corner behind the curtain,

194

gently laid the child there, bundling her in the warmth of the fur. Her little fingers stroked the softness, eliciting the tiniest of smiles. "Do you think you can go to sleep now?"

Hester nodded. "And when I awaken, mum will have my little brother or sister?"

"Aye, lass." Cole touched the tight red ringlets held back by a bit of pale blue ribbon. She was a lovely child, reminding Cole of the tow-headed, cherub-cheeked children of his native Scotland.

When Cole withdrew, Zebedee Ward said, "Not very manly mooning over females that way."

"Actually, quite manly," Cole argued impassively, never taking his eyes from Diana. "Will you be all right?"

She had assisted Callie Ward to the bed. "We women will bring forth a babe if you and that poor, pitiful excuse for a man will go about other business."

Undaunted, Zebedee Ward said, "Don't be that way, little lady."

Before she could retort—and it would probably have been vicious—Cole interjected, "But you have never birthed a babe before."

Diana looked up. "How do you know?"

"I assumed."

"Well," Diana's lips pressed into a thin line, "you assumed correctly. But I believe we'll manage just fine. Is the child settled?" Cole could see the tiny, cherubic face between the tatters of the curtain. Seeing the child already asleep, he nodded. "If you'll bring in some clean, untouched snow, from near the timberline, and put it in that black pot—"

she pointed toward the hearth, "so that it can be boiled, I will greatly appreciate it."

"Then you will be all right?" Worry pressed upon Cole's voice.

"We will manage just fine."

Cole had never been so proud of Diana. Her voice trembled with fear and dreaded anticipation, yet she had not hesitated to assist in something so wonderful, and unpredictable, as childbirth. Cole had not realized her true strength.

Outdoors, Cole assisted Zebedee Ward in unharnessing his team—four powerful, large, bay mares with hooves the size of dinner plates. Cole did not favor one of them stepping on the soft buckskin of his boot.

No sound emitted from the cabin. Half an hour passed, and Cole had scarcely responded to Zebedee Ward's multitude of questions, often giving only half answers, or ones intended to be curt enough to dissuade any further conversation with the man. But Zebedee Ward did not cease his rambling, and Cole assumed he had mush in place of a brain. He did not like the man, nor his view of women. This was not a man he would miss when soon they parted company. Only the needs of Zebedee Ward's wife and little lass would buy this loathsome husband and father extra time at the cabin.

The half hour stretched into a full hour, then two, then three. Cole was sure the night wind had frozen him to the marrow of his bones. Just when he was sure that ice was slowly shrinking his brain, the wail of new life emitted from the cabin.

"The damn woman better not have burdened me

with another worthless female," Zebedee Ward mumbled.

"Be thankful for a healthy bairn," Cole shot back, "be it lass or lad."

"I'll be thankful for a male child," Zebedee Ward countered in return. "A woman who cannot birth a male is not worth her weight in salt."

Cole gritted his teeth to keep from replying. Within a few minutes the cabin door opened and Diana, carrying a blanket rolled into a ball, moved to the corner of the porch where the men stood. "Your wife is fine, Mr. Ward."

"And the young'un?"

"You have a strapping son. I am sure he will now justify your wife's existence." She had, evidently, heard Zebedee's harsh declarations through the walls of the cabin. "Perhaps she might even now have earned a little tenderness from her husband." Her sarcasm was undeniable, eliciting a half-cocked smile from Cole. The man deserved to be brought down a peg or two.

Zebedee Cole walked heavily across the porch and entered the cabin. When the door closed, Cole said, "One day you and I will have a healthy bairn, lass." The grin clung to his face.

"When the sun turns black," she said flatly, handing the blanket to him. "Will you dispose of this properly? Mrs. Ward gave birth upon it."

"I will, lass," he said. When Diana turned to re-enter the cabin, Cole softly spoke her name, "Diana?" She halted without turning back. "One day you will forgive me for everything I've put you through."

"I doubt it," she whispered, exhaustion marking her words.

"You will, lass. I promise it."

In the same hour that Diana was bringing Zebedee and Callie Ward's son into the world, John Redding was delivering a daughter in Philadelphia. He had just taken the news of a healthy child to the nervously pacing father—a long-time friend—and had picked up his medical bag, when a young lad pounded at the door. The downstairs maid answered the late-hour knock and John, descending the stairs, heard his name spoken.

"What is it, lad?" he asked. Immediately a message was pushed into his hand and the boy disappeared into the darkness. John unfolded the single sheet of paper and read, "John, come to Rourke House posthaste. Must discuss Diana's disappearance." It was signed simply, "Philip."

Despite his exhaustion, John could not ignore the summons of his good friend, although he could justify complaining about its untimeliness. Perhaps there had been a new development. Perhaps Philip suspected that John knew more than he was letting on and wanted to question him. After the grisly discovery in what was supposed to have been Cole Donovan's grave, John had been conducting his own investigation. He had reached what he felt was a positive conclusion . . . Cole Donovan had not murdered Standish Rourke. A switch in the town jail could only have been made by one person. Webster Mayne was probably the one who should have been in the grave to begin with. But John could not voice his speculations; Philip was much too good a friend for that. He needed proof, and hoped that some careless mistake on Webster's part would provide the necessary proof to take the case again before the courts. The murderer of the gentle Standish Rourke deserved the maximum punishment for his heinous crime.

John bade farewell and again voiced his congratulations. Wearily he drew himself into the saddle of his equally weary horse. Both deserved a good night's sleep—John for the hours he had spent at Meta Nelson's birthing bed, and the horse for the long, patient hours he had stood in the drizzling rain dreaming, possibly, of the grain and hay-filled bin that awaited him back at his stable.

The inclement weather dragged the ten-minute trip into one of half an hour. John dismounted his horse and Tuxford appeared from the stables. "Give him some hay and sweet feed, will you, Tuxford? He's been a good boy today."

"Aye, Master Redding," Tuxford replied in his usual gruff voice.

Within moments John stood in the well-lighted foyer and was being escorted into the parlor. "Care for some tea, Mister John?" Mrs. Sanders asked.

"I think not," John replied, "but I will help myself to a bit of Philip's favorite bordeaux."

"Very well. I'll announce you to Master Philip."

John had just settled into a comfortable corner of the massive divan when Philip entered the parlor, his brows pinched and lines of worry marking his wide forehead. John stood and clasped the older man's hand. "Philip, what has transpired? News of Diana?"

"No, nothing . . ." Philip withdrew his trembling hand. "It is Jocelyn—"

"Jocelyn? Is she ill? Should I see her?"

"No, nothing like that." He did not notice the fleeting moment of disappointment, of curiosity, mark John's face. "It is merely that she knows much more than I thought. She was aware of Diana being in the house but said nothing to me."

"Did someone tell her?"

"I don't believe so. She said she was sitting at her window one night about two weeks ago and saw a woman—she described Diana—moving toward the family cemetery. Jocelyn said the moon was high and that a man met her there," Philip trembled. "Jocelyn said she met a man—someone she had never before seen. She said he took her by force."

"I should summon the authorities to question Jocelyn in more detail."

"I cannot cause her that anguish," Philip argued. "It is simply information that I thought you might well use in locating my dear niece. John, what do you make of all this?"

Again, silence. John stood with his back to the taller man, swirling the cool crimson liquid in the goblet. Was this the time to tell Philip of the grisly discovery, and of the pieces of the puzzle he felt, thus far, fit together? Was the man Jocelyn claimed to have seen in fact the Scotsman, Cole Donovan? Without turning, John asked, "Where is Webster this evening?"

"At one of the gaming tables set up in some god-awful slum in Germantown," Philip remarked. "He'll get himself killed one day."

"Indeed." A frown marked John's wide forehead. "About Jocelyn, I will honor your request that the authorities not be summoned yet. Please, if she remembers anything else, let me know right away."

"Of course, John."

Bowing slightly, John took his leave, and soon was moving toward his horse and long-overdue sleep.

He had scarcely moved to the chilly outdoors before Webster emerged from the back of the house. "That was damned foolhardy, father. Suppose he *had* insisted that the authorities speak to mother."

"But he will not. He is an honorable man. I simply had to throw suspicion off my wife and your mother."

"You must be careful. We cannot allow anyone to find out about mother until the will is probated."

"I am trying to see to that end, Webster. Can't you see that?"

Diana was exhausted. Callie Ward and her new son slept in the small bed, little Hester was wrapped in Diana's cape in the corner, Zebedee Ward lay against the far wall, and Diana was curled in Cole's arms on the dusty rug before the hearth. He held her tightly, but had made no advances toward her, not even in the privacy of the heavy blanket they shared. He had whispered an endearment to her and now slept peacefully.

As he slept, she could not help but study his

features: the straight, perfect nose, the firm, square jawline and ample mouth, the faint lines at the corners of his eyes. She had not realized how thick and black his lashes were, lying like soot upon his flame-warmed cheeks. With a man like Zebedee Ward in the room, Diana was more than happy to enjoy the safety and comfort of Cole's arms. She found that sleep came easily upon her and scarcely stirred when, at two in the morning, the newly born infant awoke to be nursed at his mother's breast.

The following morning, the two men went hunting and brought back a wild turkey Zebedee had killed, and a sack of beans and four eggs Cole had purchased from a friendly Cherokee Indian. Callie offered flour from their wagon and Diana baked a skillet of biscuits over the hearth.

Hester had not left her mother's side since "discovering" her new baby brother. She now chatted, promising the new babe all sorts of wonderful things when he "stopped all that squawling." When Hester said, in childlike innocence, "Papa's kind of mean sometimes, but you'll like mum," Zebedee Ward drew his hand back to strike the child. Cole caught his hand in midair.

"You should think about treating your wife and children like human beings. I don't take to men beating children, or their wives."

"Wasn't goin' to hit the child hard," Zebedee said, shrugging his shoulders. "She just needs to learn some respect for her pa and ma."

"He doesn't mean it," Callie said in defense of her husband, her thin face haggard from exhaustion.

"He doesn't hit her hard, Mister. He acts meaner than he really is. It is simply the way of the Kaintoks."

"Nevertheless, Mrs. Ward, I do not wish to see brutality. You remember that, Zebedee Ward."

"You know, Cole Donovan," Ward said jauntily, "if I were to stick with you a while, you might just make a real nice fellow out of me. Which direction will you be travelin'?"

"South, I suppose."

Taking the biscuits from the fire, Diana interjected, "That sounds like a challenge, Mr. Ward."

Zebedee Ward grinned. "Just might be, little lady," returning his look to Cole. "South you say?"

While Diana gave Cole a glaring look, he shrugged his shoulders and replied, "Or possibly into the interior. We have no set destination." In the event that Zebedee Ward should happen to meet up with anyone searching for them, Cole did not want the man armed with precise information.

"Travelin' mighty light. Got only one pack animal and your two riding horses."

Cole tore off a bit of the cooked bird for sampling. "While my little lady is giving me healthy bairns, I thought I'd use my hands to build whatever we need. The land will yield everything."

"How far do you plan to travel?"

"As far as God, Fate, and the Indians will allow."

"Adventurous man, eh?"

Diana glumly announced, "Everything is ready." When Zebedee Ward moved toward the food she had set out on a small table, Diana put her hand firmly on his arm. "I do not know the custom

203

where you are from, Mr. Ward, but where I am from, gentlemen allow ladies and children to be served first."

"Where I'm from the little ladies and young'uns get whatever is left over."

With cocky persistence, he resumed his journey toward the table. "Your custom is not acceptable here, Mr. Ward. You will wait until I have prepared plates for your wife, your child, and myself. Then you may heap your plate and fill your belly."

What could be seen of the man's face through his thick, dark beard suffused with color. "What do you say about this, Donovan? Can't you control your quick-tongued woman and put her in her place?"

"Sorry. Where I am from ladies and children are, indeed, served first. I wouldn't argue with my wife. She carries a long knife strapped to her thigh."

Though neither Diana nor Cole were aware of it, Zebedee Ward backed down for the first time in his life. Growing from a bully of a boy to a bully of a man on a wild Kaintok mountain where women were treated worse than the hogs, he had always gotten his own way. But now, the vicious look of a slender young woman had literally backed him into a corner. Diana felt triumphant; if only she could have that same searing effect on Cole Donovan. He had stood up for her, however, and that certainly merited her appreciation.

After they had eaten the hearty breakfast, Diana walked outdoors. Within moments, Cole joined her. "What do you say we teach the pompous court jester some gentlemanly manners and travel along with them for a bit?"

"You are serious?"

"Aye, lass. Might be a good experience."

"I might tell them you kidnapped me. Even a ruffian such as that would frown upon such an unscrupulous act."

Cole laughed lightly. "I doubt it. Besides, when I present our marriage certificate—"

"What?" Diana was visibly surprised.

"Didn't I tell you, lass? I had a marriage certificate drawn up. It looks mighty impressive, and authentic." His lie did not reflect in his eye.

"And what other mischief do you have up your sleeve?" She was seething inside, scarcely able to feel the coldness of the morning.

"I happened to mention to Zebedee Ward last night while the bairn was coming into the world that you were a runaway wife, and that you had a habit of telling terrible tales of being kidnapped. He believes you are a spoiled city girl who does not believe in the age-old custom of following the husband."

"Did you indeed?"

Of course, he hadn't. But he wasn't about to admit it to the feisty Diana Rourke. "Aye, that I did, lass. And old Zebedee offered to keep an eye on you for me."

"I imagine that he did. The crude, ogle-eyed bastard."

"Diana!" Cole could not believe the expletives she had so softly spoken. "Such language from a lady."

"Lady!" she stormed with heated inflection, flaying her hands within inches of his face. "How can I be a lady with you!" She turned her back on him, preparing to march off into the timberline where she might be alone. Tired of her walking away from their every argument, Cole took her shoulder to halt her retreat, but with much more force than he had intended. Her feet slipped out from under her on the icy ground and she fell flat. His laugh reverberated through the clearing. "Hush! Hush, Cole Donovan! Suppose I had hurt myself." Moving to the front of her, Cole offered his hand to help her up. Crossing her arms, she refused his assistance, refusing, with equal intensity, to meet his amused gaze. "Oh, I do dislike you so!"

When she continued to refuse his hand, Cole dropped to his knees to envelop her shoulders between his palms. "You are the dearest lass I have ever chanced upon. My life would be empty without you."

Only now did she permit herself the tiniest of smiles. "My derriere is getting damp," she said, finally offering her hand. When her feet were again under her, rather than in front of her, she looked up, surprising him with the warmth and acumen he had hoped for. "I'll make you a deal, Cole Donovan."

"And what is that, Miss Diana Rourke?"

"I will stay with you as long as you deem it necessary. But you must allow me to send word to my Aunt Rufina so that she will not worry about me."

"Nay, lass. I cannot allow it. If Webster found out—"

A realization came to Diana. "It is not me you are worried about, Cole Donovan. It is yourself."

She didn't really believe that. She knew only that she could not bear the thought of Aunt Rufina worrying for her. Studying his undaunted expression, she could see that her words had had no effect on him. He knew she was simply upset and did not mean what she had said. "Please, my aunt has been too good to me to be put through this."

"I cannot allow it," he reiterated his decision. "I'll compromise with you. When opportunity arises, I'll attempt to learn from John Redding if he has been able to help us."

Diana gently turned away from him. "Then will you tell me one thing, Cole Donovan?"

"If I can, lass."

"Who is it you are supposed to have murdered in Philadelphia?"

Cole felt sick. He had expected her to ask almost anything of him, but not this. Now he had either to answer her question or, by not doing so, breed conviction in her of his tacit guilt. Twice, they had been together intimately, and that, he felt, had been their mutual confession of love for each other. Would a truthful answer to her question destroy the trust and the love that might be growing in her heart for him? Inside the cabin, the little girl was laughing, and the beautiful sound reached Cole's ears, momentarily breaking his train of thought. Was there a way to evade her query?

"Listen to the child, Diana. She sounds so happy."

"You did not answer me, Cole." Diana's mind had swum with horrible suspicions for days. Cole claimed to have been awaiting execution when reprieved by Webster Mayne to be used as a pawn against her. Cole was familiar with Rourke House, a familiarity that could not have come about in a few short weeks. He had claimed that his great-great-uncle was Diana's great-grandfather. And now, Cole's features were ashen white, themselves supplying the answer she so deeply dreaded. Still, she had to hear it. "Answer me, Cole! Who? Who are you supposed to have killed?"

Holding her gaze, transfixed, Cole drew himself up erect and very calmly answered, "Your father."

Chapter 12

Diana felt her veins drain of blood, her body of life. She had to believe she was still asleep, seeing not only ghosts, but dreaming horrible dreams, hearing horrible confessions that could not possibly be true. A nightmare! It had to be! Even now, inside the cabin, her body was probably asleep; only her dream spirit stood in the cold, haunting, winter clearing, hearing Cole Donovan's hesitantly delivered confession. But no! Dear God, no, she was not asleep. Her unspoken suspicions had been confirmed. He — Cole Donovan — the man she had given her body to, and whose she had taken in return — had just whispered "your father" in response to her question.

Trembling so violently she could hardly maintain her footing, Diana clenched her hands, gritted her teeth, closed her eyes so that she would not have to see the vile vision of Cole Donovan standing there.

"My father—" she gulped. "You murdered my father?"

Cole's hands came up to grip Diana's shoulders but she flung them away, shivering as if repulsed by the very touch of him. "No, Diana, I did not kill your father. I was accused. I was convicted. I was condemned to die. But I did not kill your father. I saw the man who killed him. I was in the house that night. Dear God, if you can believe such a foul deed of me, then it is better that I give you over into the hands of someone you will truly feel safe with."

For the hundredth time since first meeting this dark, mysterious man, Diana silently admitted to herself that she was falling helplessly in love with him. She could not imagine a day without him, even though, by his own confession, he had been convicted of killing her father. She hated herself, wanted to berate herself for her traitorous love for him, and yet a tiny voice inside her kept alive the idea that perhaps he was telling her the truth. She wanted oh, so much to believe in him. She wanted to love him and be loved by him. But to want to be with a man who had killed her father was more than she could bear. Yet could she so easily accept his confession of innocence? Would she be a fool to do so?

So many things flooded her mind, threatening her equilibrium. She wanted to return to the cabin, but there were too many people there. She needed to be alone . . . alone somewhere where she could think, could cry if that was what it took to relieve her grief. Glorious, blessed solitude! Surely somewhere just beyond the timberline there was a niche where she could hide, bury her face in her hands, and release all the emotions that his words had created.

Just as she was about to follow her heart, to flee into the timberline and find that place of solitude, something else he had said flooded her mind. *I saw the man who killed him.*

He must have seen the puzzlement in her face and guessed its source, for suddenly Cole, his body rigid, half screamed, "It was Webster. Your Cousin Webster, Diana. He is the man who killed your father. I saw him do it!"

So, it was back to Webster, the old standby nemesis. What would Cole do without him? "I want to be alone for a while," Diana whispered dryly, putting one foot forward to move past him.

"Diana, please . . ."

Diana's hands went up trembling, which forced her to immediately draw them back into the warmth of her cape. "Give me some time, Cole. I cannot bear to be with you, not right now."

"I am guiltless, Diana. Do you think I could care so much if I had killed your father?" Pain marred his dark features; moisture sheened his exquisite, shaded eyes.

Her lips parted as though she were preparing to answer him, but then pressed together. Lowering her eyes, she moved past him, knowing that he would honor her request for solitude. Soon she had disappeared into the shadows of the timberline.

Cole tucked his fingers into the leather belt at his waist and watched her walk away. He wanted to go after her, but she had expressed her need for solitude. Perhaps if she sat down somewhere alone and thought out the whole situation, she would realize that he could not possibly have committed such a foul crime. Cole prayed that she was a good judge of character. He prayed that she loved him enough

211

to give him even a shadow of a doubt.

He remained outside for an hour, or possibly two—he really wasn't counting. Checking on the horses, making sure they had plenty of feed, accounting for his gear and double-checking the sturdiness of the saddle girths and accoutrements, he wiled away the time since Diana had moved into the timberline. He was sure he had seen her shoulders droop in defeat, sure he had heard a sob collect in her throat. It had taken all his willpower not to go after her, and he was sure she was well aware of that.

Cole had to make decisions of his own. Diana believed him to be a murderer. She felt no trust in him, no security, nothing but hostility toward him for taking her from her family. He knew what he had to do. Slowly, softly patting the neck of one of his saddle horses, he moved toward the cabin, knocked, then entered.

Zebedee Ward was polishing off the last of the breakfast. Callie nursed her new son at her breast and the little girl, Hester, played with a few bits of wood she'd found in a corner. Cole pulled up a chair beside Zebedee Ward and straddled it. He didn't like the man, or the idea of Diana being in his company, but with a wife and two children around, he felt reasonably sure Diana would be safe with the family.

"Can I talk to you about my, umm, wife, Ward?"

"Sure," he said, throwing a bone into the hearth.

"She doesn't want to remain with me. I assume since you've left Kaintok you're moving to the north. Can my wife travel with your family until

212

she reaches her aunt at the trading post about ten miles from here?"

"A woman belongs with her man," Zebedee Ward replied, giving Cole a narrow, disbelieving look. "If she ain't willin' to follow her man, beat her. She'll see some reason."

"I don't beat my women," Cole replied evenly, then reiterated his request. "Can she travel with your family?"

"Sure, if that's what you want."

"It is. I'll leave one of the saddle mares for her. I'll take the other, as well as the pack horse. She won't be any trouble." Cole stood. "I'll be gone by the time she gets back from her walk. You tell her you'll see her to the safety of the trading post. And," Cole hesitated, "tell her I'm sorry things couldn't work out for us."

"She'll be safe with us," Callie Ward interjected, aware of Cole's immense dislike for her husband. "You mustn't worry about her." Nestling her son onto the pillow beside her and covering herself with the blanket, Callie motioned for Cole to come to her. He sat on the bed beside her. How plain she was, her hair straight and thin, her cheeks hollow and gaunt. But her eyes were gentle and kind. "Is there, Mr. Donovan, any sentiment that I can give to your wife for you?"

Cole smiled, then tenderly touched the babe's smooth cheek. "Tell her — tell her I love her. Tell her not to return to Philadelphia."

Callie, relieved that her husband's back was to her, touched Cole's hand in a gesture of comfort. "As you wish, sir. And please, do be assured your

213

Diana will be safe with us until she reaches her aunt."

"I am," he replied, rising, arching his back to relieve the tension. "Now, I must ready my horse. She will not wish to see me again."

As he moved toward the door, Zebedee Ward remarked, "Not much of a man if you can't tame one wild little filly."

Without responding, Cole exited the cabin, quickly readied his horse, took his long rifle from the porch and rode off to the south without looking back.

For the past two hours, a whirlwind of thoughts had made Diana almost dizzy. She'd found a covered feed trough a few hundred yards into the forest and had curled up against the rough, weathered wood. It did not matter that it was cold, nor did it matter that a light, steady rain had begun to fall, turning to ice as soon as it touched her exposed hands and face.

Diana was in a quandary. She had grown to care deeply for Cole Donovan, despite his ofttimes irrational behavior. She had enjoyed the comfort, gentleness, and caring of the tall, muscular Scotsman, and now he had confessed that he should have died on the gallows for the murder of her father. What was she to think? What was she to believe? That he was innocent, victimized just as he claimed she was being victimized by Webster?

But then, all the pieces began fitting together. It would be too much of a coincidence if it had been another man's murder for which Cole had been blamed; too much of a coincidence that he had *happened* to end up at Rourke House. He bore a remarkable resemblance to her great-grandfather, the only reason he had so successfully been able to pull off his masquerade. But he hadn't instigated that cruel joke by himself. He must have been hired — coerced — by another person. Her Uncle Philip was a kind man, though weak of character, and that left only Webster. He was devious. Hadn't he tried to make her look insane in front of her uncle, Dr. John Redding, and the domestic staff at the house?

Something clicked in Diana's mind. Cole was telling her the truth. He had not killed her father. Webster had.

As a great flood of relief spread over her, Diana rose quickly to her feet and rushed back through the underbrush, caring not that twigs and twines stung her arms as her cape whipped back with the wind. She cared not that the wet ground had dampened her feet. She cared only that she had to see Cole, to tell him that she believed in him, wanted him . . . loved him. She whispered the words over and over, "I love you, Cole. I love you."

The cabin greeted her like an inviting haven when she exited the woods and saw its warm glow behind the canvas covering the north window. Her heart quickened; she felt a rush, a prickly feeling across her shoulders. "Cole, Cole," she half yelled, rushing into the cabin. But she saw only the Ward family. "Where is Mr. Donovan?"

"Gone, little lady," Zebedee Ward growled. "Gave

you your freedom, he did."

"What do you mean?"

Callie Ward smiled, extending her hand to Diana. "Come, sit on the bed."

Diana wanted only to find Cole, to be in his arms. Hesitantly, she approached Callie and found a bare spot on the corner of the mattress. "What is it, Callie?"

Callie fondly took her hand. "Your husband said you are to travel with us to your aunt's trading post to the north. He also said that you are not to return to Philadelphia, but to surround yourself with friends. And," Callie whispered these last words, "he said to tell you that he loves you."

Diana felt tears moisten her eyes. These were words she wanted to hear Cole say himself, not receive through a new friend. "Where is he? I must talk to him."

"He is gone," Zebedee Ward interrupted. "Travelin' to the south. He left you the best horse."

Diana felt frantic. That she would never see him again was something she could not face. That he was gone forever was far worse than anything she had ever imagined. She could scarcely believe that a month ago she had been a carefree, daydreaming, half-woman sitting on the bank of Wills Creek. Now her life was topsy-turvy, she was in love . . . and she was alone.

"No!" Diana rose so quickly she almost lost her balance. "No, it cannot be this way. I will not let him leave me!"

Callie smiled shyly. "Your horse is out there. Go after him if you truly want him."

216

Diana hastily gathered her few things together. Panic seized her and she was unsure how she managed not to forget anything. She felt like a mechanical thing guided by a pendulum, going through the motions because there were no alternatives.

Within moments she had bade quick farewells, wishing everyone good luck in their journeys, and had mounted the horse Cole had left for her. His tracks were easy to follow in the soft snow.

He could not have gotten more than an hour's distance away.

Less than a week ago Cole had taken a treasure from Philadelphia. Now, alone he rode along a frozen Allegheny trail, dragging a protesting pack horse behind him. He could not get Diana out of his thoughts. Things could not possibly be worse. He was in a new land, a criminal, and she—the woman he loved—was in danger. The chance that she could be protected from the irascible and murderous Webster seemed remote. Cole felt that he had abandoned her.

Should he halt, go back for her, profess his love and adoration and swear never to leave her again? Was that what she wanted? What conclusions had she reached in her solitude? Had he been too hasty to believe she would condemn him, believe that he was nothing more than a murderer and cutthroat?

It didn't matter. Cole was past the point of turning back. He had made a decision—a decision he was sure was the one she would have wanted, and he had to go on without her. She was better off without him. Her people would protect her. Perhaps she would have sense enough to see that there had been some truth in what he'd said. Perhaps she would be able to see that Webster spelled danger for her. But could she, indeed, see evil in any person, this innocent young wood sprite who had stolen his heart? He wasn't sure.

Distracted by the direction his thoughts had taken, Cole did not see the branch until it had hit him full in the chest, unseating him from his horse and gouging his side through his buckskin shirt. When he hit the ground, both animals panicked but did not move more than a few feet away. He sat for a moment, feeling his ribs, mentally withdrawing from the pain he felt. Damn! His fingers came up with blood upon them. How could he have been so absent-minded! Cole mentally berated himself.

Very soon, the sun would dip low in the west. Finding himself out of sorts at the moment, he decided not to travel any more that day. Leaving Diana Rourke was the most difficult thing he had ever had to do, and he felt that he should do it slowly, so that the pain would not be as great. He found his footing, collected his horses, and moved off the trail into a narrow gulley through which ran a clear stream. He estimated that he'd been riding for about two hours. It was scarcely past noon and normally he would have had another five or six hours of traveling. But he felt very low, despondent and alone. Diana Rourke was in his blood. The absence of her was a mortal blow. He had once prided himself on his ability to stand alone, but now it was a great hindrance to him.

As he found the small jar of salve he carried, and a length of gauze to dress his wound, he wondered where Diana was right now. Had she left the cabin with the Wards? Was she even now reaching her Aunt Rufina's trading post? Was she glad to be rid of him? He imagined that she was, and he couldn't blame her. His need to protect her had backfired. His unrequited love would always bring melancholy. The excitement he had once felt in exploring the interior of this vast land was no longer with him. He was merely fleeing from death, blending into the American wilderness in hopes that he would never be discovered. He could never again return to Philadelphia, nor to his beloved Scotland. This land that he had hoped would be his new home was now his prison. Webster Mayne had made sure of that.

Snatching up as much wood as he could carry, Cole began building a fire. He was cold, but not hungry enough to worry about catching a fish. Perhaps later, when night had fallen, he would tend to the needs of his body. Right now, he was concerned with the need of his heart. And that need was Diana Rourke.

Diana was frantic. She had been dogging the trail of Cole's horses for two hours and her own mount, which she'd ridden hard, could hardly move another step along the trail. That she was in a quandary was an understatement. She had been sure she'd catch up to Cole by this time, and yet there was no sign of him except imprints in the snow along the trail ahead.

She was a woman alone in the Alleghenies, without a weapon, but she was too concerned about Cole Donovan to worry about meeting up with hostile Indians. The possibility had not yet crossed her mind, though it would eventually. Being a sensible girl, she would realize that dangers existed in every niche and crevice of the mountains. At the moment she cared more about Cole than she did about personal danger.

Weary from travel, Diana continued to follow the trail of the two horses. But the trail ended suddenly and Diana, confused, dismounted. Then something alien caught her eye and she bent, touching her fingers to a patch of discolored snow. Blood! Alarm coursed through Diana . . . apprehension . . . fear. She drew herself erect and looked around. Cole! Cole, where are you? she asked herself, puzzled by the abrupt end to the trail, fearful that the blood meant —

No, no! she heard the words scream through her mind. Don't assume, Diana. Things are not as they seem. Again, she searched the trail, seeing the scurry of hoofprints that marked the snow as though the horses had been frightened, and the dreadful patch of blood. Perhaps Cole had been hurt. Diana brought her hands to her throbbing temples and locked her fingers through her long, loose hair. I must be rational, she thought. Cole is nearby and he needs me. Think, Diana! Think! Then she saw hoofprints disappearing into the forest to the right. Taking the reins of her horse, she began walking slowly through the dense forest of firs. Bare brambles caught at her skirts, ripping, snaring, slowing her journey. Just when she was sure she had gotten herself and her mare trapped in the underbrush, she saw the gentle swirl of smoke in the trees just a hundred feet away. It gave her new hope, new incentive, and she ignored the clawing brambles to move toward that inviting fire . . . toward, she prayed, a fire that her beloved Cole had built.

Though he'd seen nothing, Cole had heard the approach of a horse and someone afoot. Thinking it to be an Indian, he had shimmied up a tree with his long rifle. He sat wedged between the trunk and a twisted branch as the sound moved closer. Cocking the weapon, he suppressed an expletive. He'd lost the flint. Looking below, he saw it half buried in the snow. Without the flint, the quarter-pound ball in his rifle was as useless as paper. He had no time to retrieve the flint and lock it down; whoever was approaching had made an appearance in the shadows of the woods.

Cole crouched lower on the branch. If it was a hostile Indian, he was dead. There was not a damn thing he could do about it now. He just prayed.

When he recognized Diana, he was torn between hiding from her and releasing a yelp of excitement that she had returned to him. But what had transpired since her journey into silent thought? Had she decided he was guilty and, thus, deserved to die? Had Zebedee Ward provided her a weapon to accomplish the task? Did she hate him and wish only to be sure that he was aware of it before returning to her home?

221

Or was she there, scarcely a hundred yards away from him, searching frantically for him and wanting only to be with him? Did she believe him innocent? Had she risked her life to be with him because, she, God forbid, loved him? There was only one way to find out. When she entered the clearing and made a wide, sweeping gaze of his campsite, Cole, with masculine grace, jumped down from the tree branch.

Diana released a startled cry before she spun around and saw him. She saw the spot of blood on his shirt, his eyes narrowed thoughtfully as he watched her. She saw that the flint was missing from his long rifle. Relief swept over her and, rather than rush into his arms, she shrugged her shoulders absently and said, "Can't fight off enemies—or women—without a locked-down flint."

"Is there a difference between the two, lass?"

Again, Diana shrugged, kicking up a bit of snow with the tip of her boot. "It all depends."

"On what?"

"Who the woman is."

"Suppose it is you, lass?"

"Then there is definitely a distinction." Only now did Diana allow herself to smile, but again seeing the blood of his wound, her brows met in a frown. "How did you injure yourself?"

How he managed to appear so relaxed, Cole would never know. He set down his rifle and sauntered slowly toward her. "I was thinking of a pretty lass left behind and I allowed a damned branch to unseat me from my horse. What do you think of that?"

Linking her fingers at her back, Diana moved toward him, meeting him halfway across the clearing. Maintaining her composure when all she wanted was to be in his arms, was almost painful to her. When she was within touching distance of him, her fingers eased toward his wound. "Is it bad?"

"Just a scratch," he remarked. "I am not dying, lass."

Without warning, Diana threw herself into his arms. Startled at first, his arms slowly went around to hold her close. "Cole, I thought about everything you said," she whispered. "I know you could not have killed my father. I do believe it was Webster and that he put you up to ghastly mischief by threatening your life. You took me away from Rourke House, but you took me away because you care about me. When you left me before I could tell you what I had decided, I felt empty inside. Hollow, like an old, dead tree."

"What are you trying to say, lass?"

"I believe you know." She drew slightly back and met his narrow gaze. "I want to be with you, Cole. I want to love you and be loved by you. Is that so wrong?"

Cole murmured in reply, "And here I thought you were coming after me to . . ." He made a melodramatic move with an invisible knife at his throat.

Diana laughed. "No, my beloved, I will not kill you. Come." She took his hand and seductively coaxed him toward the tent he had erected. " 'Tis an inviting place over there, warmed by the fire, where a lady and her man may snuggle in privacy."

Cole returned her gentle laugher. "Aye, lass, I

believe there is, indeed. I don't think I can pass on such a sweet proposition."

Aware of the emotion possessing her, Diana took his hand and led him into the warm tent. She wanted only to be with him, to thank the little voice inside her for helping her make the right decision. She could never fall so deeply in love with a murderer. Cole was a victim, same as she, and one day in the not-too-distant future, Webster would get what he deserved.

But for now, she was with the man she adored, loving him, caressing away any doubts that might have clung mercilessly to him. She was in her beloved mountains and, God willing, she would woo his adventurous heart into staying here.

Diana lay upon the blanket, her fingers deftly unfastening the rawhide ties of his shirt. She enjoyed his teasing kisses, the gentle caresses of his hands, the firmness of his body against her. She enjoyed the tenderness with which he shed her of her clothing as she willingly assisted.

Cole's blazing eyes lingered over her suffused features, capturing a gentle smile. His mouth kissed her violet eyelids in turn, then possessed her mouth in the most sensuous of kisses. Her body burned for him, a wondrously painful tingle beginning at her shoulders, then exploding in gentle rapture within her breasts, her stomach, the now naked limbs which so perfectly accommodated his masterful body.

"Don't ever leave me, Diana," he murmured, again caressing her mouth until she felt their bodies mold together, floating upwards as if a southern wind had suddenly chased the February coldness far, far away.

In his arms, she mastered the art of loving; in her heart she formed a splendid future for them, together in the mountains for all their days.

Their splendid male and female forms were notes in harmony, his maleness flowing to her gentle, feminine beauty.

Always, there would be their love.

That alone would conquer and beat down all challenges.

As their bodies floated upward, upward still, and they were lost in passion's world, Webster Mayne and his vicious threats might well have been a million miles away.

"I love you, Diana," Cole whispered, his voice husky with passion. "I have loved you since the morning on the trail."

Diana chuckled, fusing her body more closely to his own. "And I was afraid of you, Cole Donovan. Love was the farthest thing from my mind."

Capturing her mouth in the sweetest of caresses, Cole hoped to make all her fears nonexistent, now and forever.

With his hands now lovingly imprisoning her hips, Cole thrust deeper and deeper still, until Diana moaned with wondrous ecstasy.

When, at last, they lay huddled together in the aftermath of love, legs intertwined, Diana smoothed back his dark hair, then traced her finger along his strong, unshaven jawline. "Cole?"

"Ummm?" he responded sleepily.

"Did you think I would ride after you?"

"No," he murmured truthfully. "I thought I had lost you forever."

"Would you rather have traveled on alone?"

"No, lass. I've never wanted to be parted from you."

"Cole?"

"Hush!" Cole chuckled, touching his lips to her smooth temple. "Sleep against me for awhile. Then I will run us down some supper."

Diana sighed dreamily, "You are my supper, Cole. Just to lie beside you is enough."

"And what about me?" Cole asked thickly. "Am I not worthy of supper?"

Diana's fingers circled his sinewy neck, drawing his body against her own. "Am I not enough for you?"

"Almost. But my belly still desires nourishment."

Closing her eyes, the gentlest of smiles warming her face, Diana soon fell asleep beside him.

Nothing could penetrate their wonderful world. She thought.

Chapter 13

May, 1787

Cole relaxed against a stately oak, stabbing at the ground with a twig he'd picked up moments earlier. Deep in thought, he was scarcely aware of a flock of doves landing several feet away. Feeding on the ground corn Diana had thrown out that morning, the fat, gray birds had not detected Cole's silent presence, either. The day was warm, the azure sky blending into a pale red upon the far horizon.

These last four months had been bliss for him. He and Diana had moved South because the weather had grown warmer with each day; or had the weather grown warmer because they moved south? It did not matter. They had unhurriedly traveled the routes of the Alleghenies and now were considering settling in the lovely spot some miles south of old Fort William in Virginia. He had always meant to begin a western trek, but despite this had never been able to track a course away from Diana's beloved mountains.

On the other hand, there was unfinished business in Pennsylvania. They had covered enough distance to be safe, but he wanted to stay close enough to someday resolve the unfortunate business hanging over his head. Diana was in line for a sizeable inheritance; Cole did not feel right depriving her of it, despite her protests that wealth meant nothing to her.

Cole felt secure in their love. She had become his woman and one day very soon, if she were willing, he would take her as his wife.

The approach of Zebedee Ward startled the doves, which took to flight. Despite the man's crude barbarity, Cole had grown to like Ward. He smiled when the burly man bent to the ground beside Cole. "We been in this particular spot more'n a week, Donovan. You growin' fond of this earth?"

" 'Tis paradise," Cole replied quietly. "Nothing north of Virginia can compare to it. Have you ever regretted turning south instead of north?"

"Too damn cold up there, Donovan. Every man makes at least one mistake in his life. Mine was thinking the fruits would be sweeter the more norther I traveled."

Cole chuckled. "Wasn't the way of it, eh, Ward?"

"What do you say, Donovan, about settlin' this valley? What with you and your missus," Cole had never confessed that he and Diana were unmarried, "me and my brood, the Satchetts and Duncans, the Waverly clan, an' the others, we got the makings of a real nice settlement here."

"If the Indians be willin'."

"The Indians be damned."

"They were here first," Cole argued, deliberately suppressing his vehemence. He did not like what the white man was doing to the native Americans.

"Tell you what, Ward. I'll speak to my lass, and I'll pow-wow with the locals. If we don't offend anyone, I do not have an objection to settling here. If it can be worked out amicably, I will file homestead claims in Roanoke."

"Don't think you should talk to the Indians, an' a man should make decisions without his she-male. But you do as you please, Donovan. I'll saddle up a couple of horses and we can scout the area."

As Ward turned to leave, Diana approached, her springtime freshness drifting with the breeze to fill Cole's senses with a familiar longing. Nodding politely to Zebedee Ward, Diana quietly dropped to her knees beside Cole. Raising her fingers to smooth back an unruly lock of hair from his forehead, she asked him, "What are you thinking, Cole?"

Taking the slim hand at his forehead, he brought it to his mouth to bestow the gentlest of kisses upon it. "A bonny lass I dream about, with hair like flowing gold and eyes like amethyst."

Teasingly, Diana replied, "And should I be envious of this lass?"

"I don't think so. Tell me, did you finish the washing that had you fussing this morning?"

"I did. See my fingers," she laughed, turning her hands over, "they are all wrinkled from the water. I will look like that all over one day, when I am old and gray."

Cole shared in her laughter. "And this gray-haired old man will love you just as much. Aye, just as much, if not more."

Diana eased into the comfort of his arm, pleased

by the sincerity of his words. "Have you decided yet?"

"Ummm?"

"If we will settle here for the time being."

Cole drew in a breath of clean spring air. "Aye, it's a good place, ready to be settled. I must talk first to the chief in the village."

"May I accompany you?"

Cole cut her a sideways glance. "Why?"

"I've seen how the Delawares and Shawnees live in Pennsylvania. I wish to see how the tribes of the Cherokee nation live."

"Always the adventuress, eh, little woman?"

"Your little woman," she smiled. "There is no force on the face of this earth that could separate us."

"I wouldn't say that," Cole mused. "Webster probably has men dogging our tracks even to this day. And," Cole hugged her to him, "I would imagine that John Redding has put two and two together. Now, about your inquiry. I would prefer that you not accompany us on this trip. Perhaps when we have determined whether these Cherokees are friendly, then you can visit their village."

"But—" Cole did not give Diana the chance to lodge her protest. His narrowing eyes reiterated his decision. But she loved him too much to hold this small disappointment against him. There were, after all, more important things on her mind right now. Her eyebrows meeting in a worried frown, Diana nestled against him, wanting and needing his protection. "Cole?" she met his lazy look, then took the piece of straw he had been absently nibbling on.

"Cole, there is something I have been wanting to tell you for days now."

"What is it, Diana? Are you homesick?"

"No, I'm a big girl now. I'm not homesick."

"Regretting that you stayed with me?"

"Never." Timidly, she traced a path with her fingers along his unshaven jawline. "Cole, perhaps you'd better—" She'd been about to say "sit down," but, with a smile that did not quite touch her mouth, she realized they were both already sitting. She was not sure how he would take her news, or how she should best present it. Should she ease up to it gradually with small talk, or should she simply blurt it out and take her chances? Oh, but she was a coward! She could not take the chance of alienating him, of being a burden to him, when they had so much else on their minds. She continued quietly, "If we settle here, Jim Duncan plans to ride north to his father's family, then return in several months. I am wondering if you would object to him taking word to Dr. Redding. Hopefully he could learn whether John has been able to help us with our dilemma."

Cole chuckled. "For a moment there, Diana, I thought you were going to tell me you were with child."

"Pooh!" Diana shot up so quickly one might have thought she'd been struck. "With child, indeed!" Had he seen her face suddenly suffuse with color? Had he recognized the radiance of an expectant mother? Diana turned slightly away from him, linking her fingers before her so that he would not see them tremble. She was not sure why she hesitated

231

to tell him. Perhaps it was the shadow which hung over their lives. Perhaps they could work out their priorities before encountering a new one, regardless of how untimely it had come. She had, at best, two months before the telltale signs of motherhood would give away her secret for all to see. Therefore, that much time remained for her to break the news to him.

Deep in thought, she had not realized that Cole had climbed to his feet until his hands gently encircled her arms. "My beloved, I was merely teasing you. Do not be flustered. Certainly, I would be pleased, but we have plenty of time to think about such things. For now, 'tis you and me and Philadelphia to worry about. After that, you may have a dozen babies and I will love them each and every one. Now." Turning her to him, he tried not to show his disappointment. He could think of nothing in his life more fulfilling than to know that Diana carried the seed of their child within her. Favoring her with a warm smile, he continued, "You've got a good idea about Jim Duncan. But I scarcely trust the man. He's too foolhardy."

Diana's heart had sunk. His words, though innocently recited, had fully tendered his desire that she not be with child. She was thankful that she had not worried him with this, and instantly replied to his observation. "Jim's a bit wild, but reliable enough. And he's the only one of us planning to travel north anytime soon. We haven't much choice but to trust him." Breaking contact with Cole, Diana continued, "I'll think about what I should write to John before talking to Jim. It'll be a few days before he departs."

Diana trembled. Thinking that the early morning coolness was the reason, Cole gently grasped her shoulders and said, "You should get the shawl Mrs. Ward made for you. I can't have my lass getting ill when we have so many plans to make."

Diana shrugged absently. "It isn't the chill."

"It isn't?" Confusion marked Cole's handsome features. "Then why would you tremble so?" His hands gently caressed her arms, feeling the goose bumps that formed upon her skin. "What is troubling you, Diana?"

She pulled away, trying to smile so that she would not have to answer him. But her mouth remained pinched, and her eyes would not meet his own. "Perhaps it is the chill. Sometimes I am a bit addle-brained. Mrs. Ward is preparing breakfast. I'll call you when it is ready."

When she turned, she almost ran head-on into Zebedee Ward. She said "Excuse me," and scooted past him, relieved that Cole did not call her back. Clinging to her cheeks were tears which she flicked away before reaching the campfire where Callie Ward was preparing breakfast. Her four-month-old son snuggled among blankets in a wooden bin at her side. Hester frolicked at the edge of the clearing, gathering newly bloomed wild flowers.

"Did you tell him?" Callie asked.

Diana sat on an empty keg beside Callie's son. She touched her fingers to his plump, pink cheek. "No, I didn't know how to tell him. He has so much on his mind right now."

"Are you afraid of him?"

233

"No—no, of course not!" Diana had not meant to stammer. Her words, however, appeared those of a frightened woman. "He is a gentle, kind man," she continued quietly. "He treats me as an equal, not as one subservient. He asks my opinion on important matters, and he respects it. When he touches me I feel like a princess. When he is sad, I am sad, and when he is happy, I am happy. I adore him, Callie."

A fleeting moment of envy touched Callie's soft brown eyes. She wished her husband were as kind as the man whose heart belonged to the woman across from her. "Then why did you not tell him?"

"As I said, he has more important things on his mind. There is plenty of time."

Relief swept over Diana when Mrs. Satchett and her daughter approached the camp fire. Each held a jug of milk freshly drawn from the Satchett's cow. Moments later the men were called to breakfast. Diana sat beside Cole, quietly listening to the chatter and laughter of the children, picking at her breakfast and wishing she were alone somewhere. She felt a little ill and the aroma of the bacon did not help matters much. Soon, she excused herself, explaining that she would return in a little while.

"Are you well, lass?"

Diana turned at the sound of Cole's concerned voice. "I am fine. I would like to see to my horse. She had a split hoof, and Mr. Ward was kind enough to trim it."

"The horse is fine," Zebedee Ward said.

Diana shrugged. "I would like to see for myself."

When she turned to move toward the roped-off area where the horses were tethered, Cole did not go after her. She'd been acting a little moody lately, and she seemed to require more time alone. But that was the way of a woman; a man never knew from one day to the next what kind of mood she would be in.

When she was out of earshot, Zebedee Ward said, "Woman's actin' kind of spooky, Donovan."

"Misses her family," Cole explained, knowing full well that the astute Zebedee Ward would not accept his explanation for an instant. Zebedee's reply confirmed that.

"A woman's place is with her man. Family has nothing to do with it."

The usually quiet Callie Ward interrupted. "It is the private business of Mr. Donovan and his wife, Zebedee. Leave them be." Traveling with the Donovans had made Callie Ward much more willing to confront her husband. She knew Cole would not allow another man to be brutal to a woman. She enjoyed the comfort of his gentle ways and, for that reason, could not understand Diana's hesitation to tell him about their expected child.

Momentarily, Zebedee put down his plate. "You ready to ride, Donovan?"

Cole, too, relinquished his plate to Callie for washing. He and Ward mounted their saddled horses and rode to the west. He was worried about Diana. Something was on her mind, and if she would not tell him, perhaps he should talk to Callie Ward.

They had entered a wide gulley so deep in the forest that the sun could not reach them. The ground could not be seen through the damp mulch of the autumn leaves that had fallen some months earlier.

"That woman of yours is actin' a little strange, Donovan," Zebedee Ward again observed. "Sure she ain't knocked up."

Cole deplored the crude expression. "She's not with child," he replied, gritting his teeth to keep from embellishing the terse words.

"How d'you know?"

"She told me."

"Women ain't always truthful, Donovan."

"My woman is," Cole argued with feeling. "But I do not wish to discuss my wife. I thought we were going to locate the Indian village?"

Ward laughed, "Hell, man, you lettin' that she-male make mush out of you. Come on—let's put some distance between you an' your troubles. She'll be safe until we return."

Cole's heels gently hit his horse's flanks, coaxing her into a slow gallop. He gritted his teeth to keep from replying. Zebedee Ward infuriated him at times. But he was right in one thing. Diana was safe with the others back at their camp. He would not have to worry about her.

That was a point the others at camp might have argued. Diana had seen to her horse, pleased with the work Zebedee Ward had done on the hoof, and had returned to the campfire to assist Callie with the breakfast cleanup. She was a little disheartened by the words she and Cole had exchanged earlier in the morning, and the secret she had kept was eating her alive. She felt that it was worry, more so than the morning sickness Callie had told her to expect, that made her stomach churn. She should have blurted out her news, expecting the worst but hoping for the best. As it was, Cole had ridden out with Zebedee Ward for another day of explorations in the region they wished to settle, and she was stuck at camp with the women and day guards.

She was busy scraping leftover food onto the ground for Jim Duncan's dog when the rumble of several horses approached from the forest. She turned, dropping the pot and spoon in a noisy clatter when three mounted Indians, each leading two freshly groomed horses, cautiously approached their camp. One moved forward, his glistening black hair held back by a band made of beaver fur and feathers. Since they'd begun their travels, they had met only friendly Indians, and Diana hoped these would be no different. Usually, they wanted a meal, or to trade a horse for white man's goods. Evidently, these Indians had brought their best horses, and Diana was quite curious as to what they could possibly own that would be worthy of such a trade. She wished that Cole and Zebedee Ward were here. Jim Duncan was too young and hot-headed and Ethan Satchett was too old and forgetful to deal with the haughty trio who now sat astride their horses before them.

Diana did not give Jim Duncan a chance to speak. "What do you want?" she asked, drawing her hands to her slim hips. None of the three answered her. "Do you speak English?" Still, no answer. So! They thought it beneath their dignity to answer a

237

woman.

Jim Duncan said, "We want no trouble here. If you speak English, tell me what you men want. No English, just grunt and point."

"Grunt and point is for hungry bear," a young brave said scornfully, moving in front of his Cherokee brothers.

Even as he spoke, Diana admired the exquisite horses prancing in place. One especially caught her eye—a silver and white spotted stallion with a brown eye and a white one. It danced on its slender legs, occasionally twisting in place as if to free itself of its captor.

"I asked you what you wanted," Jim repeated.

"Six fine horses," the Indian spokesman pointed out. "We trade—six fine horses for . . ." His dark brown hand moved fluidly, then began a descent toward Diana. She looked around, seeing nothing but the pots and pans she and Callie were about to take down to the stream and wash. "We trade for the golden-haired squaw. Six horses—one squaw— fair trade."

"You cannot barter for me!" The slim, white hands of the quick-tempered Diana immediately flailed the air. "I am a person, not chattel." Her fury could scarcely be contained. "Besides, I'm worth more than six ponies!"

A frown marred the smooth, bronze face of the Indian. "Silence your squaw, white man!" His hand shot up in a threatening gesture, though his only weapon—an antiquated musket—was strapped to his back. "You," he motioned to Jim Duncan, "trade squaw for six fine horses?"

Jim Duncan looked down to see that the flint was securely locked in his own musket, though he wasn't sure he would have the guts to use it. For the moment, words were his best bet. "Sorry. The golden-haired woman has a man. You savvy? Any bargaining will have to be done with him."

"Where the white man who own this squaw?"

With an outraged "harumph!" Diana turned on her heel and walked away. Her angry gaze briefly met Callie's pleading eyes before she moved toward the timberline and their own horses. As she stood there among the horses, stroking the soft muzzle of her mare, she heard the muttering of Jim Duncan and the Indian who would so callously try to bargain for her with horses. Where was Cole when she needed him? Had the Indians seen the two men ride out? It occurred to her that they might have been hiding in the woods, waiting for just such an opportunity. Surely, they had not just happened upon them? She shuddered to think that she had been *staked* out, like untamed territory waiting to be claimed and settled. She was furious.

A few minutes later, Jim Duncan approached her. "Sorry to disturb you, miss. But they won't leave. They say they'll wait and talk to Cole."

Again, Diana shuddered. "Why on earth are they doing this? Civilized people don't do this."

"Not so, miss," Jim Duncan argued. "I've been to too many slave auctions, and I've seen men, women, and children in chains. I've seen 'em branded and crippled and beaten. I've seen 'em killed by hot-tempered men."

Diana had heard of the atrocities toward the Afri-

239

cans stolen from their native shores by slave traders. "As I said, Jim, civilized people don't do this." Managing a small smile, she asked, "Who is entertaining our guests?"

"Callie has given them coffee. They seem to like it. Perhaps they'll take coffee instead of you, miss?"

Only now could Diana manage the smallest of laughs. "Indeed, perhaps they will."

Two hours after leaving their encampment, Cole and Zebedee Ward lazily sat atop their horses on a ridge overlooking a neatly grouped Indian village. Cole expected to hear children laughing, to see men engaging in games of skill and bravery, but the village was strangely quiet. Off to the right, a large corral held fifty or more fine horses.

"Village don't look hostile, eh, Donovan?" Zebedee asked.

"Doesn't to me," Cole replied.

"Think we ought to ride down there and make friends?"

"I wouldn't just yet. There is something strange going on down there." Cole's gray-black gaze swept over the peaceful village nestled in a deep, wide gulley between two high mountains. "I do not think we'd have found the village if we hadn't seen the three men riding from this direction."

"They had some fine lookin' horses with 'em. Heard Indians like to trade horses for white man's goods. Reckon they're on their way to our encampment?"

Cole chuckled lightly, his arms crossed upon the

240

MORE PASSION AND ADVENTURE AWAIT... YOUR TRIP TO A BIG ADVENTUROUS WORLD BEGINS WHEN YOU ACCEPT YOUR FIRST 4 NOVELS ABSOLUTELY *FREE* (AN $18.00 VALUE)

Accept your Free gift and start to experience more of the passion and adventure you like in a historical romance novel. Each Zebra novel is filled with proud men, spirited women and tempestuous love that you'll remember long after you turn the last page.

Zebra Historical Romances are the finest novels of their kind. They are written by authors who really know how to weave tales of romance and adventure in the historical settings you love. You'll feel like you've actually gone back in time with the thrilling stories that each Zebra novel offers.

GET YOUR FREE GIFT WITH THE START OF YOUR HOME SUBSCRIPTION

Our readers tell us that these books sell out very fast in book stores and often they miss the newest titles. So Zebra has made arrangements for you to receive the four newest novels published each month.

You'll be guaranteed that you'll never miss a title, and home delivery is so convenient. And to show you just how easy it is to get Zebra Historical Romances, we'll send you your first 4 books absolutely FREE! Our gift to you just for trying our home subscription service.

BIG SAVINGS AND FREE HOME DELIVERY

Each month, you'll receive the four newest titles as soon as they are published. You'll probably receive them even before the bookstores do. What's more, you may preview these exciting novels free for 10 days. If you like them as much as we think you will, just pay the low preferred subscriber's price of just $3.75 each. *You'll save $3.00 each month off the publisher's price.* AND, your savings are even greater because there are never any shipping, handling or other hidden charges—FREE Home Delivery. Of course you can return any shipment within 10 days for full credit, no questions asked. There is no minimum number of books you must buy.

responded, taking the cup of coffee Callie offered him. Diana approached, then eased beneath the protective wing of his arm. "What do your people call you?"

"I am called Tahchee." Meeting Diana's defiant gaze for just a moment, Tahchee asked "This squaw belongs to you?"

"We belong to each other . . . aye," Cole replied, gently squeezing Diana's slim shoulders.

"I bring six fine ponies. You give me white squaw, I give you ponies."

Cole's dark features drained of color. "You want my sq—woman?"

"Woman have fire of spirit gods in hands. I have sick son. I chief's son. He my son. I trade six fine ponies for woman with power to heal."

"But Diana does not—"

Instinctively, Diana's fingers had touched Cole's mouth, withdrawing when they had accomplished their task of silencing his words. "Cole, could I speak to you a moment? In private?"

Nodding his head to the Indians, Cole turned, moved to the other side of the Wards' wagon with Diana, and waited for her to speak. "I am quite proficient with mountain medicine," she said. "Perhaps if there is something I can do for the grandson of a chief, the chief will in turn allow us to settle this land."

"It is out of the question. If the lad dies, we might all die." A thought came to Cole. "Don't tell me, lass, that you wish to be traded to the Indian village for six ponies?"

Diana's hand came up to lightly strike his chest.

242

mane of his horse. "I doubt seriously we have anything that would be worth those fine horses they were leading."

"Maybe they'll take Callie's pianoforte."

"Callie plays? This is the first I've heard of it."

"Don't say anything, Donovan, if you know what's good for you."

Small talk eased the tension. "The entertainment would be nice."

Zebedee laughed gruffly. "When she plays, she sings, and when she sings, any God-fearin' human within hearin' distance might think a caterwauling she-cat's in heat somewhere."

"Don't you ever have anything good to say about the lass?"

"Sure . . . she's real lively under the blankets."

Cole stifled a groan of disgust and turned his horse on the trail. "Let's return to camp and inform the others that we know where the village is located."

An hour later, they emerged from the forest and into the clearing where the others awaited them.

Diana's heart began to race as Cole and Zebedee Ward approached, dismounting just a few feet away from where the Indians were drinking coffee. Silently, Cole approached, raising his hand in a friendly gesture—a gesture that was returned by the youngest of the three men.

"Do you speak our language?" Cole asked.

"I speak English, white man. What do you speak?" The astute Cherokee had detected Cole's Scottish accent.

Cole grinned. "It is some degree of English,"

241

"Of course not! We have no need of their horses."
Cole stroked his unshaven chin. "Actually, I do like the silver and white stallion—"

Diana struck him, though merely as a gentle chastisement. "Do, hush, Cole, and be serious! We want the land. If I can help the chief's son then we have a better chance of settling here."

"It's too great a gamble. The lad could be seriously ill, perhaps even dying. I cannot allow you to place your life in danger, nor the lives of the people in our party. I cannot allow it."

Diana's mouth pinched into a tight knot. Her hands rose to her hip and she tapped her toe in quite an outraged fashion. "I do not believe the decision is yours, Cole Donovan. You have always treated me as an equal, allowing me to make my own decisions without, I might add, a typical man's ridicule. I am discussing this matter with you because I respect and love you, but when it gets right down to it, I will make the final decision. I certainly will not allow myself to be traded for ponies, but I will look at the boy. We cannot know if he can be helped until we have looked at him. It could be something simple."

"Or it could be something deadly, scarlet fever, smallpox—"

"Ouf!" Diana turned away, crossing her arms as she did so. "Those men look perfectly healthy. I would not risk the lives of our traveling party by bringing illness upon them. Give me more credit than that."

Cole approached and gently folded her within the warmth of his strong hands. He touched his mouth to her hairline. "I will not argue with you, Diana. I will tell you only that you *will not* go with them, and my word is final!"

"But Cole—"

"Hush! You are accustomed to having your way, but this time I will have mine. We shall write it down somewhere so we can remember the one time I stood up to you like a man!"

He was uncompromising and sarcastic. His harsh words successfully conveyed the extent of his anger, and she could not argue further with him. Cole released her almost roughly, stepped around her, and moved into the midst of the waiting Indians. "My woman does not possess a gift of healing. To allow you to think so would go against my conscience. I am sorry, she cannot accompany you to your village."

Deep lines etched into Tahchee's forehead. He frowned ruthlessly. "Have many men . . . could take woman from you."

"And I will fight to keep her, even if I must fight alone."

"You won't have to do that," Zebedee said, holding his musket at the ready.

Tahchee turned. Muttering to his men in their native Indian tongue, he broke the silence of the morning. Diana quietly moved beneath Cole's arm as the men pow-wowed. Then Tahchee turned and approached Cole Donovan. "Let woman come to village and see son and Tahchee will promise the safety of your people."

"No! My woman stays here. And we will fight for our safety if we are forced to. Though I do not believe you are a violent people."

Again, Tahchee frowned. The white man was brave; there was no denying that. His unwavering look commanded respect. "You come now, with your woman."

Damn, the man was persistent. "No, it is out of the question." The Indians mounted and soon disappeared into the forest. Cole sensed that they'd given up much too easily. "Zebedee, let's make sure all our weapons are at the ready. I have a feeling they'll be back."

Tahchee and his men did not move farther than the shadows of the timberline. He was determined to have the white woman who was his son's only chance for recovery. The white man had been unreasonable. Tahchee would rather have purchased the woman with their six finest horses, but since that was impossible, he would now have to resort to theft. He only hoped that by taking her against her will he would not dilute her powers to heal his critically ill son.

He did not have long to wait. The women of the camp moved about, preparing the midday meal for their men. Tahchee never took his eyes from Diana. The men had put out extra guards, and when she took up a bucket and began moving toward the creek just down the hill, one of the men accompanied her. Tahchee could hear her fussing at her young guard; she had more spirit than he'd ever seen in a woman.

"Jim Duncan, will you let me be?" she protested.

"I am in no danger."

"Mr. Donovan said I should keep an eye on you."

"And where is he?"

"Tending to the horses. You're not still mad at him, ma'am?"

Diana managed a small smile. "No, he was right, of course. I wanted only to make friends with the Indians so they would allow us to settle here in peace. Perhaps I wasn't thinking prudently. Now — will you please stop walking so close to me, for goodness sakes? I am in no danger."

"Sorry, ma'am." Diana had filled the bucket in the creek and now struggled to lift it. "Here, let me carry that for you."

"Thank you, Jim," she replied, wiping her brow in the midday heat. "Let me carry your gun."

Watching the exchange, hidden from the camp by the thick underbrush of the timberline, Tahchee immediately dispersed his men, one to the right and one to the left.

Diana and Jim heard the thundering of horse's hooves at the same time, but by the time they had spun, Diana had been whisked onto the back of an Indian pony. The musket she had been carrying clattered noisily over the smooth white rocks at the banks of the creek. By the time Jim yelled for help and retrieved his musket to run after them, the pony had disappeared into the forest. There seemed to be movement all around, fading in the same direction.

Cole came running. "Where is Diana?"

"They took her," Jim puffed, only to be immediately jerked toward Cole by the lapels of his shirt.

"I was carryin' the water for her. Damn, Mr. Donovan, I didn't think—"

"You are right," Cole growled, his eyes narrowed to mere slits. "You didn't think!"

The men gathered with their horses. Zebedee brought his and Cole's. "Let's go after her, Donovan."

Cole took the reins of his horse. "I will go after her alone. I'll have better luck than if we charge into their village like a riled army."

Quickly, Cole mounted his horse and moved to the side of Zebedee Ward. "If I do not return with Diana within two days, move on."

"What do you mean?"

"I mean, Ward, that if we are not back by then it is a bad sign. Protect these people and get out of this territory."

"And what about you and your woman?"

"If we do not return within two mornings, no power on earth will be able to help us."

Cole turned the mare and coaxed her ahead. Within moments he had disappeared into the forest toward the village of Tahchee.

Chapter 14

Hambone swung his legs to the floor, pulled on his leggings and boots, then moved toward the kitchen in search of coffee. His grizzled features had worn a worried frown perpetually for the past four months. There were too many questions for which there were too few answers. Since he and the local men had lost the trail in their search for Diana, Hambone felt that he'd failed her. He had always been nearby when she needed a friend, and now she was out in the wilderness with a madman, alone and frightened, wondering if each day would be her last. It was little wonder Hambone had taken to mountain brew much more frequently these days.

He suffered an abominable headache. Rufina had a cup of coffee awaiting him when he emerged through the curtain. Taking the cup, he moved to a favorite chair near the front entrance, absently solacing his wicked mood with the thick, hot brew.

"You'll have to quit that pinin'," Rufina ordered hoarsely. "Not doin' Diana any good. Not doin' yourself any good."

His grizzled eyebrows met in an even more severe frown. Honey Boy ambled through the open doorway and fell against Hambone's legs. "Scoundrel. You were last to see our dear girl." Even the harshness of his words could not disguise the underlying affection he felt for the big cat he had brought home to Diana one stormy evening three years ago.

Rufina continued as if the bobcat had not interrupted her. "Dr. Redding will be coming along pretty soon. His letter said in a couple of months, and it's nearly that now. Remember, old man, he assured us Diana was in good hands."

"Aye, the hands of a murderer!" For the first time in weeks, a little spunk reflected in Hambone's voice. "The kindly doctor will tell us the man is innocent, but what proof does he have? This Scottisher should have been hanged for the murder of Diana's father, yet an innocent man went to the scaffold for him. What manner of beast would allow such a trade?"

Rufina poured a cup of coffee and took a chair beside Hambone. Her hair was ragged and unkempt, untidy locks escaping the cotton scarf holding it back. She smoothed down equally ragged black skirts, nearly upsetting her coffee in the move. "John Redding has vowed to get to the bottom of the mystery. In the meantime, old man, worrying will accomplish naught. I feel in my heart that Diana is safe. Were she in Philadelphia with Webster Mayne, then I would worry about her."

Hambone had heard her voice scores of negative remarks about Webster. He had never thought to question it before. But now, thinking only of his dear girl, his shaggy eyebrows arched over pale gray eyes. "The man is her cousin. What harm could he

249

do her?"

Rufina had spoken very little of her sister, Diana's mother, in the many years Hambone had known her. He never really knew why. He imagined that Rufina had always been a little envious of Rowanna's loveliness when she herself was big-boned and homely. Hambone vaguely remembered Rowanna Rourke. Her skin had been smooth and milk-white, and she'd had thick, lush hair and big violet eyes, like Diana's. But he was sure love had always accompanied Rufina's envy of her younger sister, and while she had often made derogatory remarks to Diana about her mother, she had never truly meant them. Ofttimes she had blamed Diana's shortcomings on that long dead sister, but perhaps that was her way of justifying her own existence. Being the lone survivor of the two was the only victory Rufina had ever enjoyed over her more delicate sister.

In the few seconds since Hambone had spoken, Rufina had made a very important decision. Her sister had once sworn her to secrecy about a very delicate matter, but the time had come to stop protecting the sinister Webster Mayne. Perhaps if the family had known long ago what kind of beast he was, Rowanna could have remained with her loving husband and together they could have raised Diana.

Recalling the last thing Hambone had said, Rufina calmly repeated his question, "What harm could he do her?" She sipped her coffee, then met Hambone's silent gaze. "When Diana was a tiny thing, scarcely three years old, she was taken from the nursery of Rourke House by her cousin Webster. While the sleepy child nestled trustingly in his arms, he took her to a black creek running through the grounds of their family home, dropped to his knees, and pushed her head beneath the water. As she fought for her young life, Webster laughed maniacally, rousing Rowanna and Philip from their beds. Rowanna reached him first and saved her daughter. Philip thought that Webster had saved a sleepwalking child from death, and was never told otherwise."

Hambone shuddered. "And where was Standish?"

"Away in Virginia. He arrived home that next morning to find Rowanna packing to leave Rourke House. His entreaties that she stay, or at least explain, were ignored. Rowanna loved her husband too much to tell him that his own kin, his only nephew, had tried to murder their little daughter."

"Thank God dear Diana remembered no part of this hideous chapter from her past. And Diana's father never knew. Perhaps it would have been easier on him if he had."

"That was Rowanna's decision. I believe coming back here and pinin' for her husband is what eventually killed her. In the space of one week, I buried Diana's mother, and my own husband."

"Standish loved that child dearly," Hambone argued.

"I'm not denying that he loved her."

"Perhaps he should have known what Webster had done."

Rufina shrugged. "I always thought he should have, so he would have understood. But Rowanna did not want him to know the treachery of his own sister's child." Silence. Rufina took a moment to

251

gather her thoughts before continuing, "I believe, old man, that it was Webster Mayne who killed Standish. I don't believe the Scottisher, Mr. Donovan, had anything to do with it."

"But he was the one who tried to run. He was the one condemned."

"I have a theory on that."

"And what is that?"

"I believe the young man, Mr. Donovan, witnessed Webster Mayne murdering his uncle. If he could attempt to murder a three-year-old child, he could kill a grown man."

"That may very well be, but you have no proof."

"I don't need proof. I feel it in my heart. And I feel in my heart that Diana is safe."

"You believe she's with the Scottisher then?"

"John Redding believes she is with him. He is a learned man. If he can form such a conclusion, then I can go along with it. John believes she is with the Scottisher, and I believe she's safe. I believe the man fled, not only to save his own life, but to save Diana's life. I never liked the idea of her returning to Philadelphia. That's why I was against it from the beginning."

"You should have told me all this before, Rufina. I wouldn't have encouraged her to go." Moisture sheened his eyes, but he quickly dropped them so that Rufina would not notice. He was a mountain man; tears were for dandies.

Rufina had not realized until that very moment how much Hambone loved their Diana. She set her cup on a small table, took his from him, then sat and held his hand for a long, long time. No words were spoken, and Rufina did not leave her chair until the first customers arrived for the morning.

A little while later she watched Hambone gather his musket and accoutrements from the corner and leave the trading post. The bobcat tagged his heels as he disappeared into the morning shadows of the forest.

Moving along a narrow trail toward the village of Tahchee, Diana was surprised that European culture had influenced everything from their living quarters to their costume and physical characteristics. She saw lovely dark-skinned maidens and handsome young braves with pale eyes. Many of the women wore long shirts in the manner of flowing tunics, and turbans. Their gowns, she was to learn later, were self-manufactured from cotton they raised on their own plantations.

Taken down from the horse at a large straw-covered lodge in the center of the village, Diana was met by a woman of aristocratic Scotch, French, and Cherokee descent named Sehoy. She was colorfully attired, and her soft, black, waist-length hair was braided with golden ropes. She spoke a strange mixture of French and English, but quickly dropped the French when Diana said, "I speak only English. I don't know who you are, but I was taken by force from my people."

Ignoring her declaration, Sehoy touched Diana's golden hair as if awed by it. "You are the one who will save my son. My great-grandmother, Sage Squaw, powerful medicine woman, say you come.

253

She die many years ago and we wait for you."

Diana felt a sinking feeling in the pit of her stomach that had nothing to do with her delicate condition. She had been childishly impetuous and impulsive in trying to persuade Cole to allow her to come here. Though she'd been terribly angry with him, she realized now he had done the right thing. Suppose the Indian child was too gravely ill for her to help? How could she explain to this gentle, trusting woman that she was a mortal woman, same as the people of her village?

But why should she worry? She had been dragged up onto the back of the Indian pony and forced to come to the village. They could not blame her if the child died.

She was worried, however. An ill child lay just beyond that lodge door, and that was much more important than the indignation she felt. Thus, she favored the worried Indian mother with a comforting smile.

She had just reached the door to the lodge when Cole came charging through the center of the village, jumping off his horse before it came to a full halt. Immediately he was subdued by two burly Indian braves and brought to his knees before Tahchee. Another of Tahchee's braves kept Diana from advancing toward him.

"She is my woman!" he yelled hoarsely.

Tahchee approached. He did not take his eyes from Cole's glaring visage as another of his braves took the horse and moved from the lodge of their chief's son. Sehoy's pleading, sympathetic eyes met Cole's gray-black ones. "You are husband of Healing Woman?"

So, the villagers had already given Diana a new name, to match the powers they were convinced she possessed. Who was he to argue with them? "She belongs with me. And I want her back."

Tahchee raised his hand, ordering his braves to release Cole. But they stood nearby in the event his bravado flared again. "White man will get squaw back . . . but she will first heal my son." Diana's heart thumped madly. She wanted to rush to Cole, but the brave blocked her path. Momentarily, Sehoy approached, coaxing her toward the lodge. Diana's gaze locked with Cole's for a moment, then broke away as Sehoy's hand fell gently toward her own. Hesitantly, she moved to enter the darkened lodge, looking again to Cole. He started to accompany her, but Tahchee put a restraining hand upon his shoulder. "Presence of man weaken power of Healing Woman. Remain here with Tahchee until laughter of son fills the air."

Frowning, Cole crossed his arms, his feet apart in a careless stance. He did not notice the presence of the villagers surrounding him. He was too worried about his and Diana's immediate future.

The interior of the lodge was dark. Sewn deer hides covered the windows of the octagonal building of mud and straw. In the center of the freshly swept, packed dirt floor was a bundle of blankets among which lay a thin human form. The trepidation Diana had felt disappeared as she dropped to her knees before a dark-skinned boy of about nine

255

years, his forehead dotted with perspiration. She touched him; his flesh was cool.

"He has no fever," she remarked.

"It will return," Sehoy answered. "He will burn like a fire, then the spots of water will come for a little while. Then he will burn like fire again."

Diana removed the blanket from his torso and pressed on his slightly distended abdomen. "When did the illness begin?"

"Five moons ago. He was well when he went into the forest with the boys of the village. When the sun went below the trees, Tah-he-no say he not hungry and that stomach hurt."

Just at that moment, Diana's hand moving fluidly over his chest and abdomen met the first of several hard, reddish-purple wounds. "What are these?"

"Boys stir hornet nest. All bitten. Not reason for son's sickness. Other boys are well."

"My Lord." Diana continued to touch the child's cool, damp body. In all she found seven such stings, four on his chest and abdomen, two on his neck and one on his right leg. She had once seen a man die within two days of a single bee sting, and she knew that some people were created with no tolerance for the venom of even the tiniest insects. The child was critically ill. That he was still alive after four days was the only encouragement for recovery. The poison had worked through his body. Diana felt that, even now, the child might possibly be recovering his illness. She could pretend to possess the powers of a sage woman while his body healed itself, or she could be truthful. Truth would not secure for them the land they needed to begin the settlement. But she also could not deceive these people who had put their full faith and trust in her simply because she had golden hair. "I believe your son is recovering," she said quietly.

Sehoy immediately responded, "Son is dying. Healing Woman only one to keep spirits from taking away. Sehoy get anything Healing Woman need to heal son. Tell what you need."

Diana's trembling fingers came up to sweep back her long, loose hair. The young mother would not accept her assurance; to argue would prove futile. She had never before seen such a strange mixture of hope, determination, and stubbornness as there shone in the lovely blue-eyed features of the Indian woman. "Very well," Diana surrendered. "Bring me the following items: a poultice of wet tobacco leaves, hot sage tea with a mixture of burdock, and clean cotton towels. I will also need calamus root and vinegar. Is everything readily available?"

Sehoy smiled sadly. "I will get for you." Exiting the lodge, she gingerly approached her husband and Cole. She did not meet Tahchee's eyes as she spoke, but bowed subserviently. "Healing Woman will cure son. Sehoy must collect herbs for purification ceremony."

Cole fought the urge to rush into the lodge, knowing that Tahchee would halt his flight. If only he could talk to her. If only he could be assured that she was not sitting beside a dying child, trying to figure out a way to explain to the parents that nothing could be done. Cole was in a quandary. Diana needed him and he was helpless to go to her. He turned in frustration, approached his horse and began rubbing his hand briskly down the muscular neck. Catching his bottom lip between his teeth, he almost drew blood.

Inside the lodge, Diana used a small towel to wipe the perspiration from the boy's body. He was small and thin for a boy of nine, his hair soft like his mother's, but cropped off just above the shoulders. She imagined his eyes being the same blue color, but the sudden rapid fluttering of his eyelids revealed a rich chocolate brown. When he shivered, Diana drew the blanket over him and felt his forehead. The fever had not returned. His unconscious state was troubling. With the fever broken, he should regain consciousness. Perhaps it was as Sehoy had said—perhaps the break in his fever was a temporary thing.

Sehoy returned with the items she had asked for. Diana carefully applied the poultice of wet tobacco leaves over the seven stings. She bathed his body in the cool vinegar, avoiding the areas of the poultice, and forced the child to swallow some of the warm sage tea. It was then a matter of waiting.

Sehoy dropped to her knees and chanted. Diana sat very still, holding the child's hand, feeling his weakened pulse slowly begin to show more life. The fever did not return. As the minutes became an hour, and the hour two, Diana's back began to ache and her legs from the knees down grew numb. Her head sank wearily and all the while Sehoy continued her haunting chant. Then, at mid-afternoon, Tah-he-no's eyes opened and Diana suddenly felt their penetrating, black gaze. A thin, tiny hand rose to touch the disheveled tresses of her golden hair.

For the first time in four days the child spoke, but in his father's native language. While Sehoy linked her fingers and drew them to her tear-moistened eyes, Diana coaxed the child to take a small piece of calamus root between his teeth and chew. But he soon spit it out and spoke again to his mother.

Unfamiliar with the language of the Cherokees, Diana asked the smiling Sehoy, "What did he say?"

"He ask for the meat and potatoes steaming over the fire, because his belly is rumbling."

Tears came to Diana's eyes. Her delight erased her body's exhaustion and she calmly rose to her feet. "Feed your son," she said softly. "I will inform your husband that he has recovered."

Sehoy thought she was being helpful when she said, "You are woman. You must look down when you speak to chief's son."

Diana turned and lifted her haughty chin. "I believe I have every right to look him square in the eye." She did not feel this way because she had "healed" his son, but because she was no less a human being than Tahchee. If anyone had to drop his eyes, let it be him. Within moments, she exited the lodge, shielding her eyes against the bright afternoon sun.

Tahchee stood where she had left him, his arms crossed. She approached, met his startling black gaze, and said, "You do not have to speak to me . . . since I am a mere woman and below your station." She did not try to hide her sarcasm. "Your son has recovered."

Seeing Cole exit a lodge with several pieces of

skewered venison, she started past Tahchee. "Healing Woman." She halted, surprised that he had spoken directly to her. "Tahchee will reward for saving son's life. Fine ponies. Anything you want."

Diana turned, exasperated. She did not like the deception. "I was not responsible for your son's recovery. His own little body was healing by itself. I was stolen from my people when the healing process was almost completed."

But Tahchee had taken the same stand as his wife. He replied, "Son was dying. Healing Woman talk to spirits and spirits favor Healing Woman. That is why son lives."

Though she knew the Indian braves would frown upon such an open display of affection, Diana threw herself into the approaching Cole's arms. "I was so scared when I went in there," she whispered so that only he could hear.

Cole had seen peace on Tahchee's face. "The child?" he questioned.

"The child was recovering even when they brought me here. I tried to tell Sehoy, and then Tahchee, but neither would listen. They insist on attributing his recovery to me." She had not noticed the children of the village slowly beginning to close in on them.

Cole pulled slightly back and favored her with a smile. Then his hand came up. "Here, you must be starving. The venison is well-cooked, the way you like it."

She had not realized how hungry she was until she began nibbling at the small pieces of venison. Afterwards, only then noticing the children, she moved toward a community well and drank from a ladle of water. When she sat on the piled rocks, the silent children gathered around. Their brightly colored tunics and turbans set off their remarkable brown faces. Everywhere she saw blue eyes, or green eyes, or pale gray eyes mixed among the dark brown ones. She laughed as the children began stroking her hair, then turned pleading eyes to Cole, hoping he would rescue her from the fond attentions of the children.

Cole clapped his hands, sending the laughing children scooting in every direction. Cole gripped Diana's shoulders and moved with her toward his horse. He assumed they would be allowed to leave now that the child was recovering. Taking the reins of his horse, Cole frowned. He and Diana would have to ride double back to their encampment, and this particular animal did not take well to two riders.

While Diana sat nearby, Cole threw the saddle and pad across the bay mare and began tightening the cinch and girth. He had just coaxed her up from the rock and positioned her in the saddle when Tahchee approached, leading the silver and white stallion.

"For Healing Woman," he said. "Son laughing. Son filling stomach. Son will live."

"We cannot take the stallion," Cole replied. "Your son would have lived regardless."

Tahchee grunted. "Son would have died!" he said on a note of finality. "Tahchee talk to father, the chief, when he return from hunting trip. White man and Healing Woman stay in Tahchee's valley.

Give land for people. You stay. Grow good corn and many good crops. Tahchee protect your people."

It was, of course, what Cole Donovan had hoped for. While the government of Virginia would have allowed him to settle the land, he had wanted the sanction of the Cherokee nation. Still, he was irate. "I do not believe we should stay in a region where a woman is kidnapped whenever you take a fancy."

"We will talk, white man, when anger is gone from your heart." Tahchee forced the lead of the stallion into Cole's hand. "You take. Insult to Tahchee to turn down gift."

It was, of course, a solution to the problem the one-rider mare had presented. "Very well. I am thankful." Putting his hands to Diana's waist, Cole easily moved her from his horse onto the new mount.

As they were riding out, the two men who had accompanied Tahchee to their encampment fell in behind them. Cole asked no questions; it was obvious they'd been sent by the chief's son to ensure that Diana returned safely to camp.

They were barraged by questions when they returned to the others an hour later. Diana, too exhausted to answer, left the chore to Cole while she sought the security of their tent. She loosened the ties of her blouse, then removed her skirt. Within moments she had pulled on a comfortable bed gown, and almost as soon as her head hit the pillow, she fell soundly asleep. She did not hear the laughter and chattering of the others gathered around the supper fire. She did not hear the sounds of the night, the rustling of the wind through the forest. She cared about nothing but the rest her body needed.

Although she paid little attention, she was aware of the diminishing voices all around her, of feet shuffling toward covered wagons and tents as people retired for the night. Soon, Cole eased into their tent, discarded his boots and shirt, and slipped beneath the blanket to hold her against his firm body. In her sleep, she turned over and her warm hands moved around to his muscular back.

Touching his lips to her forehead, Cole whispered, "Sleep, my bonny lass. You've had quite a day."

Closing his eyes, he felt the aggressive, painful stirring of his body as it adjusted to being so near to her soft, supple, inviting one.

He wished he could fall asleep as easily as she had.

But then, she had not had such a painful distraction.

Cole awoke about two in the morning, remembering that he was Jim Duncan's relief as night guard. He had only an hour left to sleep, but now found that he could not force that blissfully unconscious state upon himself, even though he tried. Diana stirred against him, her hand falling limply across his chest. Enveloping her fingers between his own, he drew them to his mouth for the gentlest of kisses. He felt her warm breath against his cheek as she snuggled against him, a tiny moan escaping her ample mouth.

"Is it time?" she asked in the tiniest voice.

Surprised, Cole asked, "Time for what, lass?"

"To milk the cow . . . Callie is cooking the breakfast."

Cole gently chuckled. "You're asleep, Diana. And so is everyone else in camp, except Jim."

Suddenly, she stirred to wakefulness. Her puzzled look brought a smile to his mouth. "You're awake, Cole?"

"Aye, lass, listening to you talk in your sleep."

"I do no such thing," she cooed, bringing her index finger up to the cleft in his chin to trace a path there. "I had such a nice sleep. I felt you against me, your arm holding me close, your breath tickling my temple. I felt so safe and secure. Don't ever leave me, Cole."

"I don't plan to, Diana. You are saddled with me for life."

"Promise?"

"Aye, lass, but 'tis a threat and not a promise."

Diana eased closer into the crook of his arm. "You have guard duty in a little while, don't you?"

"That I do. Jim will be pounding the butt of his musket on the ground in about an hour, Lass." She lifted her face, but did not verbally respond. "I was so proud of you yesterday at Tahchee's village."

"I didn't do anything," she said, shrugging, exposing her shoulder in the move. "We just happened along at the right time. The little boy would have recovered had I not been there."

"No one really knows that for sure." Again, he brought her fingers to his mouth. "Perhaps there is power in these beautiful hands. God knows, they

264

bring me to my knees in adoration of you."

Diana's gentle laugh warmed him. "I do believe you are trying to sweet-talk me, Cole Donovan!" Even as she spoke, she extracted her hands and eased them beneath the waistband of his buckskin trousers. When she had relieved him of the only garment he wore, she laughed, "That was much too easy, Cole. Where is your resistance?"

"Resistance, hell. I know of no such word." Cole hugged her to him, easing his fingers beneath the fabric of her gown to rub her shoulder. "I don't believe I am the one doing the sweet-talking, Diana Rourke."

Diana had never felt so happy. If only she could lie in Cole's arms for the rest of her life, never worrying about what had happened in Philadelphia, never thinking about life outside the one she wanted to share with Cole. She had once loathed him for his cruelty, though she now understood why he had engaged in the trickery at Rourke House. She had been furious when he'd taken her against her will and fled with her into the Alleghenies. She recalled the night she had tried to escape, how cold she had been in the snowdrifts and how Honey Boy had given away her location. Oh, how angry she had been! But of the bewildering array of emotions she had felt, there was one that could not be denied. She felt that Cole Donovan loved her as much as she loved him. She prayed she was right. After all, she carried the seed of their love within her and one day, very soon, she would have to tell him.

Cole had no inkling of the thoughts scampering about in her mind. But from the way she had relieved him of his clothing, and the way her hand lingered on his chest, the way her body pressed against his own and her slim legs entwined among his muscular ones, from the way her eyes lovingly, seductively held his, he knew she wanted the same thing he wanted.

Pulling her body across his own, his fingers eased the fabric of her loose-fitting gown down so that the mounds of soft, supple flesh could be captured, in turn, by his mouth. His body hungered for her, and as she willingly straddled the maleness of him, forgetting prelude, putting aside her need for foreplay, Cole fell into the sweet confines of her sensual prison.

Chapter 15

Cole gathered everyone together the following morning. In the predawn hours, when neither of them had been able to sleep, he and Diana had discussed many things.

Cole propped his foot on the stump of a felled tree. "We have a decision to make whether we stay or move on. Since the decision involves us all, we need to discuss it, then put it to a vote."

The outspoken Zebedee Ward was quick to point out, "You and your woman acted mighty strange when you got back here yesterday. Didn't talk about it last evenin' at supper. Mayhaps we should know what happened at that there Indian village."

Without hesitation, Cole explained everything, exactly as it had happened. In the first moment of silence, Callie Ward said, "Then are we to understand that if we stay, Diana will be viewed as their healing woman and can be taken from us at any time, regardless of whether her consent is given? If she is unable to help a sick or dying person in their village, all of our lives will be in peril."

Cole replied, "True, we got off to a rather bad start. But I believe they are friendly people, and they do have many elements of European culture among them. I do not believe we will be in mortal danger, but I do believe there will be much pressure on Diana to be, as you said, their healing woman. It would be unfair of us to accept the gift of the land for a settlement never knowing from day to day if Diana will be taken from us to perform miracles."

Jim Duncan, patting his elderly father on the shoulder, pushed himself up from his seated position. "And how do you feel about that, Mrs. Donovan?"

Diana shrugged. "I feel a little trapped," she readily admitted. "I feel that if we move on, the rest of you might blame me for relinquishing the privilege of settling here. But if we stay, you might blame me if I should, at some future time, fail Tahchee's people and they no longer view us as friends."

"I say the men vote on whether we stay or move on," Zebedee Ward proclaimed.

"I say we *all* vote on it," Cole countered, "men and women alike. After all, it is a decision that will effect all our lives."

Zebedee Ward, knowing he was in a minority of one, did not argue. There were eleven men and eight women in their group, twenty-seven in all, including the children. Cole said, "All in favor of moving on, raise your right hand." Nine hands went up, including Cole's. "All in favor of staying here and settling the land." Again nine hands moved hesitantly into the air. Cole's dark eyes moved over the group of people to settle on Diana, seated on a keg beside Callie Ward. "You have not voted, Diana," he said quietly. "The decision is now yours, whether we go or whether we stay."

Diana had seen Cole cast his vote in favor of moving on. But she knew that was not the ballot he would have cast had he not been worried about her. He was sacrificing something he very much wanted in order to protect her. Thus, she rose to her feet, her hands hanging limply at her sides. "My vote is . . ." Her words hung precariously. If a bird had chirped four miles away, she was sure she could have heard it. "We stay. My vote is that we stay."

Cole quickly closed the distance between them. "Are you sure, Diana? Is this absolutely what you want?"

"Isn't it what you want?" she replied.

"I want what is good for you, Diana. I don't feel comfortable with your decision."

"But this is where we should be," she replied, cutting a look at the other adults. "If you noticed, the women voted to move on, thinking that was what their husbands would want. But most of the men voted to stay. Now that the decision has been made, if you were to ask for another show of hands, everyone would want to stay."

Without hesitation, Cole turned to the people and asked, "Everyone who wants to stay and settle this land, raise your right hands." Just as Diana had said, every hand but one was raised, and the absent hand was Cole Donovan's. "You're right, Diana. I have been selfish." With his arm across Diana's he said, "We stay," and cheers reverberated into the early morning stillness.

In the days and weeks to follow, the men felled trees to build cabins and community houses, a trading post that Diana and Cole would operate, and, at the insistence of the women, a small chapel where they could meet and pray. Their first week in the new land, Tahchee had led a welcoming party, bringing food, tobacco, horses, and seed for planting, and pledging the backing of his braves if hostile Indians were to threaten the new settlement. Tahchee's little son had accompanied him, quickly becoming friends with the children of the settlement.

Since that pledge of friendship, Tahchee had visited regularly, summoning Diana only once to assist in the breech-birth of his sister's first child. Mother and daughter had both survived the ordeal.

Now, seven weeks later, with a warm July sun bathing their peaceful little valley, the people of Pine Creek — a name voted on by everyone, including the children — had settled into a daily regimen of friendship and mutual cooperation. There was still much work to do: building a wall to keep out predators and hostile factions, putting the finishing touches on community buildings, plotting the livery and corral down wind, of course, from the living quarters. Cole and Zebedee Ward had left three days before to file homestead documents with the proper authorities in Roanoke.

Late in the evening, the horizon turning red beneath an azure sky, Diana sat on a boulder overlooking their busy settlement, composing in her mind the announcement she would ultimately have to make to Cole. The morning of his departure he had remarked, "You're getting a bit thick in the middle, eh, Diana?" then had added humorously, "That good venison Ward brings us settles well with you, I assume." Diana had dropped her eyes from his and smiled weakly, evading his efforts to place his hand upon her slightly rounded abdomen. A suspicion had clung to his gaze but he had not questioned her, a kindness that served to make Diana's guilt insurmountable.

She wasn't sure why she was so hesitant to tell him that his child grew within her. She tried to convince herself that it was because they had just begun a new life, and because the old one still dangled precariously over their heads. He had never been anything but gentle and loving with her, yet she was fearful of his reaction to her rather untimely news.

This morning she had felt for the first time the flutters of the child within her. The wonderful, exhilarating feeling had made her smile to herself and she had been glad to be alone, to enjoy in solitude the happy emotion that had risen within her. As the day had drawn on, she made a vow that when Cole returned within the fortnight, he would be informed of the impending birth.

"Diana?"

Startled, Diana released a small cry. "Goodness, Callie, you startled me."

Callie gently laughed. "You were deep in thought. Thinking of your husband?"

Diana felt a pang of guilt. Callie still believed that Cole was her husband. What would the people of the settlement think when it came time to summon a preacher for a wedding ceremony? What would Callie think? Perhaps it was time to confide in the woman who had become her dearest friend. But even as she met Callie's friendly gaze, she knew she would continue the deception. "What has brought you out?"

"You," Callie replied, sitting on the boulder beside her younger friend. "I'm worried about you."

"Whatever for?" Diana was genuinely puzzled by Callie's statement. "I'm so happy."

"Then why don't you tell your husband about the child growing within you?"

"Because—" Diana had been about to confess her unwed state. Instantly, she caught her words. "He has so much on his mind right now," she replied evasively.

"Nonsense! I see how content he is. Make him truly happy. Tell him about the gift you will give him."

"Callie," Diana closed her eyes tightly, "Cole and I are not married." There, it was out. Let her friend think what she would, she could not take back the words now. She had told the truth, and she would not cover it up with another lie. Diana half expected Callie to turn up her nose, scoot off the rock, and put distance between them. But

272

Callie's hand fell gently to Diana's arm.

"Dearest Diana, is this why you drop your eyes when someone refers to Cole as your husband or to you as his wife? Don't you know that everyone is aware of your love for each other? If there is no bit of paper recorded in a church registry, or a county courthouse, this does not make you any less pledged to each other. Vows of love come from the heart. If you love Cole, then he is your husband. If he loves you, then you are his wife."

Silence. Diana dropped her tear-moistened eyes. Without flicking the tears away, she turned and drew Callie into her arms. "Thank you. How dear a friend you are to me. I was so frightened that my confession would lose me your friendship."

"Do you feel better now?"

"Oh, yes . . . yes. Because you know and understand, a great weight has been lifted from my shoulders."

"And you will tell Cole when he returns?"

"About the baby?"

"Yes, about the baby."

Diana drew back and took Callie's hands in her own. "He'll scarcely have dismounted his horse before I tell him. I promise."

Rising to her feet, Callie firmly gripped Diana's hand and coaxed her up. "Come, the dark is falling and you should not be outside the protection of the walls."

That evening as she slept, a quietness and inner strength filled Diana. She would count the days until Cole returned and by that time she would have composed the perfect announcement.

273

The child fluttered within her. She placed her hand lightly on her abdomen and smiled to herself. "Please, please let him be as happy as I am."

In the peace of their new settlement, Diana quickly fell asleep, her hand instinctively falling to the pillow where Cole's head should have rested beside her.

In the past six months Webster had hired more than a dozen detectives, firing them almost immediately when they failed to come up with even the smallest clue as to Diana's whereabouts. The latest gentleman, however, a short, stocky, and rather brooding Englishman named Pipps, had been much more successful in the search. Since his employment three weeks before, he had been able to trace Diana Rourke and an unknown male escort to the mountains of southwestern Virginia. Even now he awaited word concerning a rumor that a new settlement was being established in a remote region of the Appalachian Highlands. Was it mere coincidence that the Indians were referring to the small settlement as Pine Creek, the name of Rufina Chambers's trading post?

The Englishman paced back and forth in the parlor of Rourke House. It was six o'clock in the morning, and he was sure Webster Mayne would not be happy about being roused from his bed at such an hour. But Martin Pipps considered himself the best, well worth any inconvenience.

The tall, glaring Webster staggered downstairs, donning a dark blue satin robe, his feet bare and his thinning hair disheveled. He looked a bit like a wild man, and Pipps suppressed a smile. He thought Webster Mayne a pitiful excuse for a man, and worked for him only because of the good wages he paid.

"What the hell are you doing here at daybreak?" Webster bellowed, going immediately to the liquor cabinet to pour a brandy.

"Daybreak, eh, Mayne?" Pipps outstretched his wide, thickly knuckled hands. "It is an hour past daybreak."

"I wouldn't know that," Webster retorted. "I was sound asleep until two minutes ago. I will have to beat Mrs. Sanders for rousing me."

Pipps chuckled. "I scarcely believe Mrs. Sanders will stand still for a beating."

Webster threw himself heavily into the corner of the divan. "What do you want? More money?"

"The funds you have given me are sufficient for the time being. It is the truth I want, Mr. Mayne."

Webster moved faster than he had in years. Pipps had scarcely completed the short sentence before he was on his feet. "What do you mean, Pipps? Do you question my integrity? My honesty?"

"I question nothing, Mr. Mayne. I call you a liar. You have withheld valuable information."

Webster's gaunt face suffused as the blood rushed through the veins of his forehead. "You are dismissed, Pipps. I will not have you talk to me as if I were so much rubbish."

Pipps shrugged absently. "Very well, Mayne. I

will go. But without me," he waved a thick finger, "you will not find your cousin."

Webster gulped the brandy. "What makes you so sure?"

"Because I am the best at what I do. And you," Pipps took great satisfaction in announcing, "*you* are the one who killed Standish Rourke."

As quickly as Webster's face had suffused, it now drained of color. A sickly pallor clung to his sunken cheeks. "You are mad, Pipps!"

"Am I? You react like a guilty man. Have I, as you Americans say, stuck the nail on the head?"

"The saying is *struck* the nail on the head. And no, you have not done so." The man was attempting to bait him. Recovering his lost composure, Webster moved with more confidence back to the liquor cabinet to refill his glass. "How should I have reacted, Pipps? You accuse me of murdering my uncle, a man I loved very much. I *did not* murder my uncle, and such a confession would not be the truth. Now," Webster spun back, a macabre grin molding his face, "what other, ummm, 'truths' do you want?"

"It will help if I know the identity of the man who is with your niece."

Webster's eyes gleamed as he bellowed, "How should I bloody well know?"

"Ah, but you do, Mayne." Again, the thick index finger rent the air between them. "I am a good judge of character. If I am to do the job for you, I must have all the details. If I do not have all the details, I must humbly resign."

"And what have you got so far," Webster asked,

a wry smirk twisting his mouth, "that would motivate me to give you the details?"

So! He was taking the bait. John Redding had assured Pipps that he would. "I am certain that I know where Miss Rourke and the man are."

Webster leaped for him, upsetting his goblet in the move. "Where? Where are they?"

"They, Mr. Mayne? Ah, so you do know more." When Webster's enthusiasm subdued, Martin Pipps continued, "I will tell you no more, Mr. Mayne, until I know the identity of the man your cousin is with, and how they came to be together."

Silence. Webster pinched his thumb and forefinger to his closed eyes. He had to know where Diana was; he had only a few months to get his hands on her share of his dead uncle's estate. He had bought a little more time with his creditors with hastily proffered promises, but he would not be able to hold them at bay forever. Diana had to return to Philadelphia. She had to be declared mentally incompetent by the courts. That was the only way Webster's father would inherit, the only way his son could then manipulate him into bankruptcy. With that thought in mind, Webster decided he had no choice but to trust the Englishman, the only one of the men he'd hired who'd made any progress in the pursuit of his young cousin . . . if, indeed, he could believe what the man was telling him.

"Very well," Webster replied after a moment. "But what I am to tell you must go no further than this room."

No further than John Redding's ears, Pipps thought,

replying instead, "Of course, Mr. Mayne. I am a man of discretion."

Webster looked around. None of the servants was within hearing range. "I suspect the man with my cousin is Cole Donovan."

Pipps feigned surprise. "The man who is supposed to have been hanged?"

"Yes. A dying man trading his life for Donovan's and died in his stead."

"But why would a man do that?"

"I don't know!" Webster lied. "Perhaps Donovan saw to the future security of his family or something. How am I supposed to know the motives of a dying man?"

"I suspect, Mr. Mayne, because it was *you* and not Donovan who financed the trade. Am I not right?"

"Of course not! I—I . . ." Webster stammered nervously. He tried to deny the words of the Englishman, but the man was too astute for him, much too quick to detect deception. "Yes, very well, I am the one who financed the trade. My God, the man is a distant relative. I could not allow him to hang. It would have been a disgrace on the family name!"

"But he is a Donovan, not a Mayne."

"My great-grandfather was a Donovan," Webster replied wearily. "Family is family, regardless of surname."

"Perhaps you are right. But please tell me, why would your cousin flee with this—this Cole Donovan?"

"How should I know?" Exasperation quavered in

Webster's voice. He was not a morning person, and certainly was not at his best when half asleep. He had a headache, and by the laws of gravity, should be prostrate in his bed. "Perhaps the spoiled wench fell in love with him or some such silly thing."

"But how? How could that be? She was well protected in this house. How could she have formed any kind of alliance with this violent man, either in the nature of a conspiracy or of the heart?"

"The man was living here, Pipps."

"But how do you know?"

Webster frowned viciously. "Because he had my permission to live here. He was kin, for God sake!"

"Then the fitful nightmares of your cousin during her stay here? They were not mere dreams, eh? She really did see this distant relation who mirrored the looks of your great-grandfather?"

"I would assume so."

"But you declared so adamantly, Mr. Mayne, that she was insane. If you knew that she—"

"Wait!" Webster's hand flew up. "How do you know about this? Whom have you been talking to?"

Pipps was an expert at covering himself. Without hesitation he replied, "Men talk in the taverns, Mayne. I keep my mouth shut and I listen. You spread a goodly share of the tales yourself. All of Philadelphia knows that Miss Diana Rourke swore to having seen the ghost of her great-grandfather. The person she was actually seeing was

Cole Donovan, the alleged killer of your kindly uncle."

For a brief moment, Webster had thought Pipps must be acting in league with another person in order to have obtained his information. But Pipps was right on one point. Webster had spread tales, and he'd had good reasons for doing so.

"Very well, Pipps. My young cousin was seeing Cole Donovan. God only knows why he would engage in such deception against an innocent woman."

"But you knew about it."

"Of course I did! I will not deny that I need my cousin's inheritance to pay personal debts. My only crime was allowing Cole Donovan to engage in his trickery. I personally committed no crimes."

Pipps—and John Redding—would certainly refute that assertion. "Ah, but omission is as serious as commission, sir. Please, do not waste my time. I do not care what you have done. I care only that you pay me what I have earned. You put Donovan up to his masquerade in order to drive your cousin mad so that your father could inherit, not only his wife's share, but his niece's share of his brother-in-law's estate."

"That is not true."

Pipps threw up his hands in defeat. "Very well. Then we have nothing more to discuss. You have paid me sufficiently for the work I have done. We must now terminate this, umm, arrangement."

Webster's ruddy features blackened with rage. "You cannot do this! You have information for which I have paid handsomely. The least you can do is give me what I have paid for." Pipps played his cards well. His burly arms hanging limply beside his short frame, he moved confidently toward the foyer of Rourke House. Webster Mayne dogged his trail, his hand at Pipps's shoulder, attempting to halt his retreat. "You cannot do this! I have paid you well!"

Having reached the door, Pipps turned back, his hand flicking at the bony one grasping at his shoulder. "Do not whine, Mr. Mayne. I told you, I will give you the information in exchange for your truthfulness."

Webster was in a dilemma. He wanted to know where the blasted, ragamuffin wench was, and he could not allow Pipps to ride away possessing that information. His eyes narrowed venomously as he cried with vexation, "Very well, very well! I did put Donovan up to it! Everything you said is true. I did finance the switch in prison."

"And the murder! You did that too?"

Even Webster was not that desperate. His shaking hand withdrew from Pipps's broad shoulder. "No, no, of course I did not! I confess to everything . . . except that!"

Pipps smiled broadly as he pivoted on his heel and reentered the parlor with the clumsy Webster again dogging his tracks. "Very well, I will tell you what I know."

"I not only want you to tell me what you know. I want you to go to wherever she is and bring her back."

"That is not how I work, Mayne."

"You *will* do it, if you want to be paid the

balance of your fee."

What would it hurt anyway? Pipps thought. He had already relayed Diana Rourke's likely whereabouts to John Redding, who had paid him a much more handsome reward than had the wiry, bone-thin Webster.

Pipps, despite his dark visage and formidable demeanor, was well respected among the Philadelphia police. That was the primary reason John Redding had hired his services. An almost fatal bout of pneumonia had prevented John from helping Diana during the late months of winter, but he was well recovered now. He would now be able to concentrate on helping Diana Rourke and the man who was with her if, indeed, Pipps brought him the information he hoped for.

John Redding leaped from the table where he was enjoying a cup of hot coffee when the knock sounded at the door. Pipps had informed him he'd be gone no more than an hour.

Within moments, Pipps strolled into the room, rubbing his fingers over a clean jawline. The look of satisfaction in his stocky features elicited a smile from John Redding. "He confessed?"

Pipps moved into the parlor and took a chair. "He confessed to financing the switch in prison and to putting Cole Donovan up to the trickery against his cousin. He would not, however, confess to the murder of his uncle."

"But we have something to go on," John Redding said. "I pray to God your information is correct. I believe I will travel to Pine Creek myself."

"Are you up to it, Dr. Redding?"

John had tremendous admiration for the Englishman; he could well imagine the devious methods Martin had used to extract the confessions from the drunkard, Webster Mayne. Pipps was a man who prided himself on his efficiency. John was only sorry that he'd had to wait so long to help the two young people out in the Southeastern wilderness, who thought, no doubt that all the world had turned against them.

John and Pipps stared at each other with mute understanding. Then John rose, poured a cup of steaming hot coffee, and brought it to Pipps. There were many things to discuss and many plans to make.

Webster Mayne was an insufferable bastard. John's only regret was that unveiling his vicious deeds would hurt Webster's father.

John, however, would be placated with nothing less than seeing Webster behind bars for what he had done to Diana.

There was also the very remote chance Webster would slip up and reveal to the world — at least to all of Philadelphia — that he was the true killer of the gentle, likeable man who had been Diana Rourke's father.

"What are you thinking, Dr. Redding?"

Startled, John met the Englishman's dark gaze. "I'm putting our priorities in order, sir," John replied. "We must first ensure the safety of Diana Rourke and the young man who is with her. Then we must somehow extract a confession of murder out of Webster Mayne."

"And you will require my services in this endeavor?"

"I will. Are you amenable?"

The Englishman leaned forward. "When I faced Webster Mayne this morning, I was seized by a desire to throttle the man. I would like to see the man dangling from a rope. If he is as vile as my heart tells me he is, I will assist you in any way I can."

"If he is as vile . . ." John echoed grimly. "I cannot stress to you how vile the man is." With energy he said, "Drink up. There is much to be done."

"To prepare for the return of the young lady?"

"Indeed. I only hope that the scalawag, Cole Donovan, has taken good care of Miss Rourke. If not, he will wish he had been hanged that foggy January morning."

Chapter 16

Diana sat peacefully among the rhododendrons, azaleas and wild laurel. Just across the valley, the shores of a spring-fed lake teemed with life: beavers, bands of wild turkeys, foxes, squirrels, black bears, and deer. Diana sat at a vantage point overlooking the valley and the lake so that she could see everything. The forest muffled the sounds of the settlement just beyond, allowing her to fully enjoy the wildlife. Stocked with bass, chain pickerel, crappie, sunfish, and bullhead, the lake offered good fishing for the settlers and Indians, who often engaged in the sport together. Across the lake, nesting warblers and other songbirds had taken up residence in the tranquil mountains and filled the air with their gentle calls.

Diana had promised to make little Hester a cornstalk doll for her birthday, but the materials, including beeswax, rags, and a dried-apple head that Sehoy had made, sat in a small wooden box beside her. She was too excited to work on the promised doll, though she knew she would complete it by Hester's special day. Cole was expected from Roanoke, and she wanted to be the first to sight him and welcome him home.

She was wearing a new dress of pale blue cotton her friend, Callie, had sewn for her as a surprise gift. The waist was high, in the French fashion, and the skirts full, to allow for the growth of the child within her. Despite having been pulled back in combs, Diana's full, golden hair had managed to escape in the steady breeze that had blown. Occasionally, she flicked back the recalcitrant locks, only to have them return to her face with annoying persistence.

Sighing deeply, Diana drew her long legs up beneath her skirts and wrapped her bare arms around them. Taking special care not to soil her new dress, lest she be unpresentable for Cole's return, she had brought along a blanket which she attempted to straighten against the breeze.

Absently, Diana watched the eastern trail which cut through a stand of virgin hemlocks towering above expanses of ferns, mountain laurel, and honeysuckle. The deep, quiet woodland afforded her the serenity necessary for her wait. All through the morning she had been composing her announcement. "Cole, I bear your child." "Cole we are going to be parents." "Cole your seed grows within me." "Cole, there is something I must tell you. As you know, when a man and a woman are together, certain things can happen . . ." No, none would do. Callie had told her not to hem and haw. A simple, "Cole, we are going to have a baby," would, Callie thought, be quite sufficient.

But Diana felt too special for simplicity, as if she were the only woman in the world about to have a baby. This announcement was the most important aspect of her life with Cole right now. The trails of the forest before her were like labyrinthine clefts in which her thoughts were hopelessly lost. She tried thinking of other things, Aunt Rufina, the trading post, the residents of Rourke House, John Redding, the cabin where she and Cole had met the Wards . . . everything came together inside her head, then scattered to the wind just as quickly. Her gaze moved over the magestic forest and lake before her in an attempt to return peace to a befuddled mind. A rock precipice on the other side of the lake sported a relentless growth of trees, moss, and lichen. Studying its glistening loveliness, she did not see two mounted horsemen, leading five heavily-laden pack horses, exit the trail that had, moments ago, been the focal point of her intense wait.

She might have remained sitting, staring toward the precipice, if twigs had not broken beneath the hooves of one of the horses. Snapped to attention, she stared at Cole and Zebedee Ward as if she had been dreaming. Neither man had seen her sitting atop the boulder and, as her senses returned, she hopped down, moving carefully among the stones toward the trail.

Cole . . . dear Cole, she thought, darting onto the well-traveled path just a few feet in front of the lazily ambling horses.

Calming his spooked mare, Zebedee Ward huffed, "What are you trying to do, woman?"

But Diana merely whispered breathlessly, "Cole, you've returned."

Dismounting, Cole dropped the reins and the leads of two pack horses, traversed the short distance separating them, and folded Diana into his arms. "Ward, take the horses on ahead. I'll walk back with Diana."

Just at that moment, another mounted figure emerged from the woodline to the rear of them . . . a sallow, saturine man with a hawklike nose. Discomfort plagued the stranger in the dark, loose-fitting clothing. Evidently he was unused to riding, and by the time he reached them he was a whimpering wreck. "Mr. Donovan, Mr. Ward, you really must be more patient. I am doing you a service. At least give me the respect I am due."

Meeting Diana's puzzled look, Cole explained, "Our new preacher, Aldous Bernard . . . Diana Rourke."

Stunned by the introduction—and the first use of her surname in a long time—Diana whispered, "You told Zebedee I was not your wife?"

"Before Cole could answer, Zebedee Ward quipped, "Don't know what we need a Bible thumper for. Ain't good for nothin' but keepin' the women away from the kitchen."

Ignoring the older man's irreligious cynicism, Diana approached and offered her hand. "Welcome, Reverend Bernard."

Cole said, "Ride on ahead with Mr. Ward. We will be along presently."

When horses and riders had disappeared toward the settlement, Cole drew Diana into his arms, warming her mouth with a sensuous kiss. His musky, manly aroma pleasingly assaulting her senses, Diana's hands moved across his sun-warmed shoulders as she savored the gentle caress of his mouth against her own.

"Did you tell Zebedee I wasn't your wife?"

"I did," Cole replied.

Diana shrugged as if it didn't matter one way or another. "It is best. I told Callie some time ago. Oh, I did miss you so much," she admitted, her tousled head falling to his shoulder.

Cole put her slightly away from him and took her hands, to outstretch them as he lovingly appraised her appearance. "A new dress?"

Diana smiled. "Callie made it for me." Instinctively, she attempted to draw in her slightly rounded abdomen, mentally chastising herself for doing so. She had vowed to tell him her wonderful news, yet even as the promise filled her thoughts, her body sought to hide that which would soon be only too evident.

His arm across her shoulder, he slowly moved with her on the trail. "Are you sure Callie did not make this dress for me?" he questioned, humor lacing his words. "After all, I am the one enjoying it the most." Then growing serious, Cole paused and again turned her to him. "I didn't think I would last the fortnight without you, Diana."

"I imagine," Diana replied, shyly dropping her eyes, "that it was rather like a toothache. When it's gone, you miss the pain."

"I can hardly compare missing you to a toothache. Now," resting his hands across her slender shoulders, Cole continued, "tell me what is on your mind. You have taken special care to be beautiful for me, and I do not think it is just to welcome me home. Is it something you wish to tell me, lass? Something you feel you must be especially beautiful for, as if the blushing loveliness of your cheeks were not enough?"

Diana's gaze had clung to his mouth as he'd spoken, but now her eyes again dropped. All her careful compositions of the morning drifted off with the wind. Callie's instructions to be simple, her own need to beat around the bush and get to the point slowly . . . every thought, every conviction, everything was gone. Lamely, she attempted to change the subject. "Will Reverend Bernard reside at the settlement?"

Furrows of concern marred Cole's forehead. "Tell me, Diana."

Silence. Diana sighed deeply, her fingers linking against her abdomen, her tears threatening to spill. Her fingers stopped their nervous play and closed over the edges of his open shirt, tenderly, absently, only to be replaced by her crimson cheek as it came to rest against his muscular chest. "I'm going to have a baby, Cole." There, it was out. The announcement that had burdened her lay open like a knife wound. She felt his breathing suddenly cease, his arms stiffen across her shoulders.

It seemed like hours rather than the few seconds that passed before Cole's fingers moved beneath her chin. He eased her face up and did not speak until her eyes timidly met his own. "Repeat what you just said, Diana."

"Is there really a need?"

"I'm not sure. I'm afraid to trust my ears. Humor me . . . repeat what you said."

"I'm going to have a baby." Did his eyes suddenly darken as they narrowed, did perplexity crease his forehead? Did his grip on her chin tighten as his mouth pressed into a thin line?

As Diana fought the urge to turn and flee into the forest, Cole's hands at her waist immediately had her airborne. As her eyes widened in surprise, he turned in place and laughed hoarsely, "A wee bairn! What a happy homecoming! A wee bairn to bounce upon my knee." Then he flipped her over and into his strong, protective arms. The happiness conveyed in his features won the tiniest of smiles. "Tell me, lass, that you do not tease me. Tell me again . . . I want to hear your news again."

Hugging his neck tightly, Diana fought back her happy tears. "We're going to have a baby, Cole. Oh, thank you—thank you!"

Puzzled, he coaxed a bit of space between them, and his eyes met her violet gaze. "Thank you? For what, lass?"

"For not being angry. I was so afraid you would be angry."

Puzzlement creased his brow. "Why would my darling lass giving me the gift of life make me angry? I thought you knew me better than that!" Again, Diana threw her arms around his neck, eliciting a laugh from him. She was so elated that he could not sustain the moment of anger he had felt at being misunderstood. He cared only that he was home, she was in his arms . . . and they were going to have a baby. The only word that came to him in view of her silence was, "When?"

"When?" Diana drew back, taking his hands in her own. "The baby?"

"No, the parting of the Red Sea, lass. Of course, the wee bairn!" Although he had spoken sharply, his underlying affection inflected his words. He tenderly put her to her feet, then held her to him.

"I would say sometime in early October."

"My God!" Cole brought his hand to his forehead. "That's scarcely four months away!" Without hesitation, his right hand sought the roundness of her abdomen. "This isn't the good venison Ward brings down from the hills. This is a bairn. How could I have been so blind?" He might have remained there, looking at his beloved with puzzled awe, had he not heard Zebedee Ward's loud, shrill whistle, the irritating method employed at the settlement to call the settlers back from the woods. Either a meal was ready to be shared, or the community was under attack. Cole seriously doubted the latter.

Diana listened to the smooth, mellow sound of Cole's voice as they moved casually along the trail. His enthusiasm as he decided that the first item of business for their new minister would be a wedding ceremony allowed no chance for her to get a word in edgewise. Then he began posing names for both a son and a daughter, voicing immense pleasure at the possibility of one of each. Diana's heart was gladdened by his delight. How could she have so foolishly feared a negative reaction? Cole Donovan spoke as if he were the only man on the face of the earth about to become a parent. She smiled; just a few minutes ago she had felt similarly unique.

A long, weary ride north through the mountains had reduced the normally exuberant John Redding to sheer exhaustion. He carefully nursed the cup of coffee Callie Ward had put between his palms, then instructed his English-speaking Cherokee guide to see to their horses. He looked around at the well-planned settlement now known throughout the region as Pine Creek. The pleasant young Callie Ward had been quick to tell him how their original twenty-seven settlers had swelled to more than fifty in the first few weeks, and John could certainly understand why. The ground was rich, black, and fertile, and the mountains surrounded them like a protective fortress. John fancied that the courageous group had picked the most beautiful spot on the face of the earth for their settlement.

Almost before he could take a second sip from the cup, the tall form of a woman approached through the heavy gates. How lovely she looked, her hair catching the midday gleam of the sun, her pale blue gown rustling in the slight breeze moving down from the mountains. Although John had never met the man walking at her side, he was well aware of his identity. It was Cole

Donovan.

Diana had been moving absently beneath the protective wing of Cole's arms, gazing at the ground. But when she heard a familiar, "Diana Rourke!" her head shot up.

Could it be? Was the sun playing tricks on her? "Dr. Redding?" She spoke his name timorously, sure that she was dreaming. But she wasn't. Freeing herself from Cole's arm, caring not that confusion marred his sun-bronzed features, she rushed toward John Redding and hugged him warmly. "What are you doing here?" she whispered. "How did you get here? My Goodness! How did you ever talk your wife into allowing this trip?"

"By ship, then overland from Portsmouth. And . . . my wife was glad to get me out of her hair for a few weeks. Now, the question is, what are *you* doing here?"

Turning, Diana outstretched her hand to the very silent Cole. After hesitating, he began to move toward them. "John, this is Cole Donovan. He is the reason I am here."

John Redding frowned as his gaze met Cole's. He had wanted to conduct himself as a gentleman, even to be cordial until he learned the facts. But as he stared into the face of the taller man, his resolve flew to the wind. He saw before him the man who had jeopardized the life of an innocent young woman, and could not forbear accusation. "So! You are the man who kidnapped this young woman from Philadelphia!"

"N—no. John, you have—no!" Diana stammered nervously, dropping the wooden box which held

294

the half-assembled doll. "Perhaps that is the way it began, but—"

"But what!" John snapped uncharacteristically. "He had put your life in danger. And for what reason?"

"John," Diana squeezed the older man's hand, then moved beneath Cole's arm. "You have it all wrong. Cole and I are very much in love."

When heated words had suddenly sprang up, Callie, calling her daughter to her, had discreetly entered the cabin to put her family's meal on the table. Zebedee Ward's questioning look elicited Cole's assurance, "It's all right. The man has just cause," before Zebedee, too, entered his family's cabin.

Diana was plagued with apprehension. The two men looked angry enough to spring and kill without a second thought. That would never do. John was usually so mild, even in anger. But now he stood his ground like an angry bull, almost as though he hoped Cole would invite a round of fisticuffs.

Cole, however, masked his anger behind a half-cocked smile and hesitantly extended his hand. "Dr. Redding, I've heard a lot about you from my Diana."

John Redding could not be openly rude. With the same hesitation, he extended his hand, but withdrew it with haste. "This is hardly an occasion for social amenities, Mr. Donovan. I believe we have things to discuss."

Cole and Diana were both thankful that most of the settlers had gone indoors for the noonday meal. Only John's Indian guide, and one playing child, moved among the buildings. Taking the coffee cup from the firm grip of John's left hand, Diana set it upon the rail of Callie's front porch. "Please, let us go to our cabin—"

"*Our* cabin?" John echoed, with stunned severity.

"Yes, John. Our cabin." She could not prevent her exasperation. "Cole and I share our quarters. Since we are to be married, I see no harm in our living together."

John was not sure where his anger came from. With the assistance of the very efficient Mr. Pipps, he had learned enough about the genteel Scotsman to conclude that he was innocent of the crime for which he had been condemned to die. But from the first time he had seen the tall, slender Diana Rourke, John had felt an overwhelming need to protect her from all harm. Call it a paternal need; whatever it was, it could not be denied.

Giving Cole a venomous look, he conceded, "Very well. Which of these attractive dwellings belongs to you?"

Diana pointed to the north, toward a small L-shaped cabin nestled in a stand of dogwood.

Cole had stiffened defensively against the Philadelphian's hostile glare. He stood his ground when Diana began to move, followed closely by John Redding. When she turned and asked, "Cole, are you coming?" he pivoted smartly on his heel and caught up to them. The silence was unnerving.

Since Diana had sat atop the boulder all morning awaiting Cole's return, she did not have lunch prepared. She simply sliced the rest of the morning's bread, took a jar of honey from the cupboard Cole's hands had lovingly built, and placed basket and jar on the table between the two seated — and still glaring — men. "What are you trying to do? Outstare each other?" Diana's voice was crisp and remonstrative, though she might as well have spoken to a split log for all the response she got. In an attempt to take the edge off the tension, she dropped into a chair between the two, crossed her arms, and said in her sweetest voice, "Is it possible to discuss this with some degree of civility, gentlemen?" When both pursed their lips rather childishly and did not answer, Diana said firmly, "Well, gentlemen?"

"I imagine it would be sensible to relate to you what has happened in the past six months," John Redding eventually responded.

"That's a start. Please, we are both listening."

"Where shall I begin?"

"At the beginning."

"Very well. I will be brief. I am aware that Hogan Linford went to the gallows instead of," he did not meet Cole's narrowed stare, "you, Mr. Donovan. I am aware that Webster Mayne paid to have you switched in the jail and that he thereafter blackmailed you into participating in a conspiracy against Miss Rourke. When is the baby due?"

He asked the unrelated question without hesitation. Startled, Diana clambered to her feet. "Wh — what do you mean?"

John, too, arose. "I am a doctor. There is a

certain bloom in a woman when she carries a child. Call it precognition. Call it what you will. Just do not deny your delicate condition. To do so would be an affront to my profession."

While Cole pressed his thumb and forefinger to his eyes, the ashen-faced Diana responded quietly, "In about four months."

John gave Cole another of those lethal looks. "And will this man do the honorable thing, Diana, and take you as his wife?"

"We have already discussed it and it will be done."

Cole had taken just about as much of this insult to his character as he could. He stood, knocking over his chair as he did so. "Listen, Dr. John Redding," he assaulted, pointing a threatening finger. "I don't give a damn what you think of me. But I love Diana, and I will make her my wife. If you came here to make accusations and cast your black insults, then you can bloody well turn on your heels and leave!"

Considering himself properly reprimanded, John Redding pressed his mouth into a thin line. Words were temporarily lost, though a retort began to form in his mind. The silence was unbearable. Even Diana, the mediator between two hostile forces, seemed at a loss for words. Thus, it was up to John to amend the situation. "Accept my humblest apologies, Mr. Donovan. I am concerned about Miss Rourke's welfare. I do not wish to see any harm come to her."

"She cannot come to harm as long as she is with me."

"She must return to Philadelphia."

"Never." Cole seemed adamant.

"It is the only way to put Webster Mayne where he belongs."

Diana's hand rose to the slim column of her neck. "My God, John. Did he confess to my father's killing?"

"He has confessed to everything but that. I have a plan, though it may be untimely now—"

"Why?" Diana would do anything to bring Webster to justice.

"Because of your delicate condition. And the fact, Miss Rourke, that Webster might view the birth as placing his mother farther down the line to inherit."

"That is not possible. The birth of my child will in no way affect Jocelyn's inheritance."

"Webster is not a rational man, as you know. I cannot jeopardize the life of your child."

"Then what do you suggest, John?"

John outstretched his hand, favoring Diana, then Cole, with a timid smile. "Let us put our personal differences behind us, Mr. Donovan, and discuss what can be done after Diana has given birth to the child."

Cole hesitated. John Redding had been unnecessarily haughty since his arrival. Could he be trusted, Cole wondered? "The authorities still believe I murdered Standish Rourke, do they not?"

John replied to Cole's question, "They know nothing yet to the contrary. I cannot place an innocent man in mortal danger—if, indeed, you are innocent—without having proof of Webster's

299

guilt. Therefore, no one knows of your circumstances except Webster, my investigator, Mr. Pipps, and I."

"And how do you plan to extract a confession?"

"First of all," John's palms struck the table, "I will take word back to Rourke House of . . . ," a knowing grin turned up the corners of his mouth. "Ah, but we will discuss my strategy after I have partaken of some of this good bread and honey."

His wry smile frightened Diana. What in the world could the kindly, genial Dr. John Redding be up to?

July 7th, 1787

For the first time in his life, Webster Mayne was bored stiff. He did not even find solace in a goblet of his favorite sherry. Restlessly, he dressed early for an appointment, made his excuses to his father, who was working on domestic ledgers, and rode to the Library Company of Philadelphia, the largest and best public library in North America.

On the second floor of Carpenters Hall, Webster idly thumbed through worthwhile books of political theory, history, law, philosophy and revolutionary polemic. He wondered which of the volumes the delegates of the Continental Congress had looked through. For posterity's sake, the library should keep a record.

Picking up a copy of John Henry Grace's *Voyage to the East Indies,* Webster sat at one of the long library tables and leaned back. But he soon tired of the volume and closed his eyes tightly, wishing his headache would stop pounding with such ferocity.

Webster was still furious that the Englishman, Pipps, had tricked vital information out of him. After spilling his guts and admitting his treachery—except for the killing of his uncle—Pipps had given him nothing to go on, saying merely that he would investigate further. His cousin might as well be on the moon. If he ever found her, and Cole Donovan, he had vowed to plunge a knife into the latter's heart. Pipps had sent a missive that he would meet him here this morning, and if he did not arrive soon, Webster was going to leave. He would not have the man wasting his time.

Since his father was getting suspicious of Pipps's frequent visits to the house, Webster had started meeting with him elsewhere.

The day was unbearably warm, and Webster loosened his tightly knotted cravat. With a clean handkerchief, he wiped away the sweat which had risen on his brow.

He started to rise when Martin Pipps emerged from the stairway, but a slight shaking of the man's head kept Webster in his chair. Pipps approached, mumbled, "Your father is downstairs and coming your way," then moved past him as if to browse through the many books on the shelves.

Webster opened Grace's volume to a page, it didn't matter which, and appeared to be reading intently when Philip Mayne emerged from the stairs just seconds behind Pipps. He approached, clearing his throat when Webster apparently failed to notice him. "Come home, Webster."

301

Feigning surprise, Webster darted to his feet. "Father . . . excuse my absent-mindedness. I did not see you approaching."

"Come home. We need to talk."

"Is anything the matter?"

"Startling revelations," the tall, brooding man replied. "There are things I want to hear you either admit or deny."

A sinking feeling threatened Webster's equilibrium. "Have you—heard from Diana?"

"We will discuss Diana—and our distant kin, Mr. Cole Donovan—at home."

So, his machinations had caught up to him. Webster quickly sat, his trembling hand easing Grace's volume beneath his armpit. "Very well. Let me return the book to its proper place."

"Damn the book! Let the librarian put it up."

Webster did as he was told. He had never before heard such firmness in his father's voice and, frankly, it annoyed him. "Just tell me, Father, who visited you this morning?"

Philip's mouth pressed into a line of bitterness and frustration. Quietly, so as not to draw any more attention from the library patrons, he responded, "Pipps."

Webster again picked up the book. "I'll be home, Father. But first I must return this book to the shelf." Ignoring the angry glare of his father's dark eyes, Webster stepped around him and discreetly approached Martin Pipps. Grace's volume was put in the wrong place as he said to his new investigator, "What the hell have you done, Pipps? If I'm not in jail on Monday morning, meet me

302

in my rented room at Moyston's City Tavern. And you had better have an explanation."

Before leaving for Pine Creek, John had directed Pipps to go to Philip Mayne. The investigator knew exactly what would soon be discussed between the two men. He silently nodded and did not watch as Webster Mayne joined his irate father.

Following the short, tense horseback ride to Rourke House, Philip had scarcely waited for them to step into the foyer before verbally attacking his son.

"Damn you, Webster! Damn you!" Philip's normally ashen face was engorged with blood, so intense was his fury. "Why would you engage in such trickery against your own young cousin?"

Rebellion filled Webster's glazed black eyes. "Why did Pipps take so long to carry tales? It's been weeks since I last saw him!"

"Because John Redding—who paid him good wages to snare you—told him to visit me some time after he had left for Virginia."

Webster remained calm, despite his feeling of betrayal. He had paid not only for Pipps' investigatory services, but for his discretion as well. "John is in Virginia? Why?"

"How the bloody hell should I know?"

Webster sauntered past him and toward the liquor cabinet in the parlor. Claudia, who had been dusting there, had discreetly slipped out when she'd heard Master Philip's angry tone. "A brandy, father?" Strangely, Webster remained undaunted. He had expected his chicanery to catch up to

303

him. When his father did not reply, but simply stood glaring at him, Webster asked, "What did Pipps tell you?"

"I know all about Donovan and what you made him do. I know all about the unfortunate, dying man who was hanged for my brother's murder. I know everything! My God, Webster, did you hate your young cousin so much? It would not pay for you to attempt to kill her—again!—so you try to drive her mad?"

So! His father was dredging up that incident when Webster had tried to drown his three-year-old cousin. And all the while Philip had let him believe he thought he had been rescuing the little girl from the creek. A wry smile twisted Webster's mouth. "Of course it would not pay, father. If Diana dies during the year, Uncle Standish's estate, including what mother would have inherited, goes to the Philadelphia municipality. With her gone, the estate is in limbo—none of us will profit. But if she is declared insane, then mother gets it all. And when she inherits," Webster turned, lifted his glass, and favored his father with a wicked smile, "we inherit."

"I should have smothered you at birth, Webster."

Webster laughed maniacally. "Perhaps you should have, father. Now, tell me, what do you plan to do with this information?"

"I should take it to the authorities."

"Will you?"

The older man pondered the short, briskly delivered question for a moment. Having a tremendous sense of justice, Philip knew Webster's crimes should be reported. He looked into the blank eyes of his son. He saw treachery . . . deceit . . . wickedness. But still, they were the eyes of his only son. "No, I will not." Surprised at the feebleness of his voice, Philip continued with more conviction, "But when Diana is returned to Rourke House — and I will make sure she is — she will be well guarded. You will not get your hands on her, and she *will* inherit half her father's estate. We will have to make do with Jocelyn's share."

"Need I remind you that someone might still find out about mother?"

"We will not think about that."

Again, Webster lifted his glass at his father's bravado. "Very well, father."

But behind his laughing eyes, more treachery was being plotted.

How ironic . . . his own father would personally deliver the victim into the hands of her lifelong nemesis.

Chapter 17

After seeing to John Redding's comfort in lodgings built by one of the settlers who had subsequently decided to move on, Diana returned to the cabin she shared with Cole. John had come up with quite a plan to extract a confession from Webster Rourke, and the details would have to be worked out before he returned to Philadelphia. The irony of his plan made her shiver, despite the heat of the July afternoon.

When she entered her cabin, she found Cole relaxing lazily upon their bed, reading from a book John had brought from Philadelphia. "Enjoying my book?" she asked, caring not whether she received an answer. She was morbidly absorbed in John's plan.

"Very much," Cole replied. "Sir William Jones's poems possess," Cole cleared his throat, "a distinctly amorous cast. I might enjoy this more than you," he smiled, immediately launching into the recital of a verse from "A Turkish Ode of Meshihi." " 'The smiling season decks each flowery glade — Be gay: too soon the flowers of spring will fade.' "

Diana eased onto the bed beside him. "And are you going to read poems to me throughout the afternoon?"

Dropping the book, Cole drew her across his body. "Actually," he grinned with dashing appeal, "I owe it to those tired beasts out there," referring to the pack horses, he continued, "to relieve them of their burdens before seeing to personal pleasures."

"And what pleasures are those?" she questioned teasingly.

Holding her gently, Cole's right palm hit the firm mattress. "This mortal man has missed a certain sweet lass." Nipping her chin, he laughed, "Ah, the sweetness of passion! But first," easing his feet to the floor, he rose with Diana still in his arms, "I will show you what I have brought from Roanoke."

"What interest have I in flour and sugar and salt?" she replied. "I am more interested in the sweetness of passion."

Grinning, Cole took her hand and coaxed her from the cabin. The pack horses grazed in a rich patch of clover as he unpacked the various items he had brought to their new home from the "civilized" world on the eastern side of the mountains: a small, elegant crystal chandelier to grace their rustic cabin, glass panes for the windows, brass andirons for the hearth, colorful dresses with matching accessories, and frilly bed gowns for his soon-to-be bride.

Holding one of the dresses to her slender frame, the very pleased Diana danced around her amused lover. He thought her a masterpiece of grace and sensual elegance, alive and flowing, imbued with passion. It was all he could do to keep from sweeping her off her feet. The pale, luminous shades of her exquisite beauty, from the soft, subtle pink of her cheeks to the brilliant gold of her hair, held him in awe. Her eyes were happy, her expression radiant.

Gently taking the dress from her, Cole picked his favorite of the bed gowns he had purchased. Placing it across her arm, he said, "I am going to see to the horses. You, pretty lass, will be wearing this when I return to the cabin," leaning ever so close, he whispered, "with nothing on beneath."

"But—" Diana laughed, "this is indecent! Flimsy enough not to be here at all!"

"That," Cole retorted with a half-cocked grin, "is precisely why I chose it." Turning her away from him, he lightly slapped her rump. "Now, go make yourself enticing for your soon-to-be husband. After all, I went through considerable embarrassment in a lady's shop to choose that for you!"

Demurely, favoring him with a sweet smile, Diana moved toward the porch of the cabin. Reaching the door she turned and said, "Don't be long, Cole."

To which he replied between clenched teeth, "No longer than necessary. By the way," Cole approached the porch and handed a leather portfolio to her, "take this inside for me." Diana took the familiar portfolio, in which Cole kept private notes and records of domestic purchases, and continued on her way into the house. When Cole's mellow voice instantly drew her attention, she turned back. "By the way, lass, I discovered in Roanoke that we are not, as we thought, in Virginia. We are just below the border of North Carolina. We were unable to file homestead papers and will have to journey to Salem in the next few weeks. And," Cole was not sure if he should divulge this information, because he was not sure how it would affect her. "Somewhere in our travels, we have left the Alleghenies."

Moving toward the steps as he continued unloading the pack horses, Diana laughed. "Of course, these are not my mountains! I thought you knew that. I have always been aware that the Cherokee live south of my mountains. But, if it's any consolation, I did not know that we were in North Carolina."

Court spoke matter-of-factly. "Shows what I know of this vast land. You knew we had chosen to settle in the Appalachian Highlands, and yet you said nothing. I thought you would protest to the high heavens."

"The other settlers never said anything?"

"Ward didn't know where we were either. And it never seemed to come up with any of the other families," Cole responded.

"I admit I feel much farther from Aunt Rufina knowing that Allegheny soil is not beneath my feet, but—"

"We will return, if you wish."

Immediately, Diana closed the distance between them. "Whether we are in the Alleghenies or the Appalachians makes no difference. What matters is that we—you and I—are together."

Dropping the harness girth he had just unfastened, Cole pulled her into his arms. "That's my lass. It pleases me to know that you love me enough to want to stay with me. But I will admit—and I don't feel that my masculinity is threatened by doing so—I would return to the Alleghenies with you, if that was what you wanted."

Touching her mouth to his in the gentlest of kisses, she whispered, "That will not be necessary, Cole. I am happy with you, wherever it may be."

Taking his hands in a moment of thoughtful silence, she favored him with a loving smile. Soon after, she had closed the door of their cabin to begin making herself beautiful for him.

Fourteen miles to the south, a band of twenty-seven renegade Indians who had ventured hundreds of miles from the Spanish territory of Florida, sat around a campfire, roasting wild turkeys and sharing the jugs of English whiskey they'd pillaged from the homestead of murdered settlers. Most were Seminole. Their leader, Oclala, regarded himself as appointed by the gods, and sat separated from his followers by several feet. His buttoned leggings and ruffled shirt further set him apart from his half-naked brethren. In addition, crescent-shaped pendants of silver hung about his neck, and ostrich plumes adorned his cloth turban. He had taken the plumes from the hat of a captured white woman they kept with their band to teach them the white man's language, and to satisfy Oclala's sexual needs.

Oclala carried an English long rifle, one of many he had captured in battle. One day he hoped to return to his tribe in Florida, and to oust his twin brother from the coveted position of chief. His brother, as first-born, had claim to this position; Oclala had objected to this claim and, in doing so, had rebelled against the authority of his dying father. When he had attempted to take the life of the chosen brother during a hunt, Oclala had been banished, the most severe form of punishment outside of death. In the two years following his banishment he had picked up twenty-six loyal followers, including a crazy Chickasaw who dressed in women's garb and a young Seminole woman captured by Catawbas, then abandoned because of a disfiguring birthmark. Moving ever northward, Oclala had murdered and pillaged in every civilized settlement, Indian and white, in his bloody path.

Their white captive, a pretty dark-haired woman named Polly, sat away from the men, her hungry gaze upon the roasting turkeys. The leather band around her neck was fastened to a thick, rawhide leash which had been tied around a sturdy young sapling to keep her from running away. She knew if she tried, she would be killed. She'd had no nourishment in two days and prayed that the men would leave a tiny portion of food for her to eat this evening. She got only what Oclala's warriors left, and often it was nothing more than the smallest morsel of meat clinging to the well-gnawed bones of their prey.

This afternoon, however, the Indian woman who fought for Oclala every bit as fiercely as his braves, broke off a leg from one of the turkeys and brought it to their white captive. Despite her immense hunger, Polly took it cautiously, fearing the offering was another cruel torment. But the manishly dressed Seminole—referred to as Black Face because of the birthmark—allowed her to take the food. The ravished woman devoured it before Black Face could change her mind.

The Seminole woman pivoted to return to the campfire when she noticed something strange about the captive white woman who had been with them for seven months. Narrowing her dark eyes, she knelt, smiling wickedly as Polly, expecting to be struck, cringed from her nearness. Black Face crudely lifted Polly's ragged skirt and thrust her hand toward her ample belly. Polly whimpered in surprise, but breathed a sigh of relief when the Indian woman's hand withdrew without leaving physical marks upon her body.

Rising to her feet, Black Face approached her leader and announced, "Oclala's seed grow in belly of white woman."

For all the response she got — not even the arching of a thick, black eyebrow — she might as well have made an observation about the weather.

While Cole took care of their supplies and horses, Diana enjoyed a cool bath and donned the transparent bed gown Cole had brought to her. She looked at herself in the small mirror and blushed with embarrassment. The gown certainly left nothing to the imagination.

An hour later Cole entered the cabin to find her lying upon their bed with the sheet covering her slim form. She feigned sleep when he approached to sit on the bed beside her.

But Cole knew better, and was amused at her embarrassment. Didn't she realize how lovely she was, how the scant gown would flatter her lithe body? "Will you not allow me to see it?"

Keeping her eyes lightly shut, she replied with an arousing pout, "In my condition I should not be wearing something like this. Besides, I feel like a French harlot."

Her wistful violet eyes opened for him. Pure instinct and the thrill he felt as her tender fingers lightly stroked his chin compelled him to hungrily claim her mouth. "Then," he teased between light nips at her soft features, "let me see . . . what a French harlot . . . looks like." It was not difficult to direct his total concentration on her sensuously molded form beneath the single sheet. Taking the edge of the offending material, he pulled it back, drawing a breath with ecstatic awe as his hands moved to her half-naked flesh.

His hot male smell aroused Diana to wickedly wonderful heights. It mattered not that it was early afternoon. It mattered not that just across the clearing, resting on a rough-hewn bed, lay a prim and proper John Redding, a man who would certainly condemn her display of love for a man who was not yet her husband. All she cared about was that she and Cole were again together, after two long weeks of separation. Her body was hot and writhing against him, wanting only to feel him begin his explorations and enslave her against his iron-hard body.

Taking the fabric of her erotic gown, held together by a single satin bow, Cole exposed the tip of her right breast to arouse it, her frenzy of passion inviting his tongue to delve into the sweet crevices of her luscious curves. He was glad he'd bathed in a clear mountain stream that morning. He would not want to detour from the treasure lying beneath his hands for something as distracting as a cold bath.

"Out of your musky garment," Diana sweetly ordered, dragging his shirt down his muscular arms. As she spoke, she nuzzled his neck, chuckling lightly when his arousal furrowed his brows into a frown. While he kicked off his boots, Diana unfastened the buttons of his trousers, then eased them down with her warm palms.

Teasingly caressing his hips and buttocks, she soon heard Cole groan his ecstasy aloud. "You little vixen," he said huskily, ridding himself of the last of his clothing. "I should punish you for being such a tease!"

"Then punish me!" she laughed in return. "For doing this . . . and this . . . and this . . ." As she spoke, her hands lightly caressed various parts of his body. "And here," she ended on a final note, her smile fading beneath passion-darkened eyes, "you cannot deny that you want me, Cole Donovan!"

Cole drew the thin garment separating their bodies over her head and discarded it to the floor. He lowered the proud evidence of his sex down to her, but did not immediately enter her. Mesmerized by the magnificence of her, he was content for one brief moment to simply look at her, at the exquisite violet eyes which beheld him with love, at the crimson cheeks, the full, sensuous mouth begging to be captured, the fine strands of hair, which had strayed to her forehead. Ah, what a jewel was his Diana, and what a treasure to be taken!

His hands tantalizingly invaded her body, his

314

mouth assailing her womanly flesh with teasing kisses. Then he felt the ever so slight mound of her stomach and his movements ceased. Gently, he rested his head upon her abdomen. "My wee bairn," he whispered. "It grows here."

"Yes, my love," she replied, fondly touching his dark hair. "And your wee bairn will not mind us being together like this. Now hush, Cole Donovan, and show me how much you love me."

Cole ran his hands down the delicate spread of her hips, feeling the warmth of her thighs against his own. His hands lowered, drawing up her knees, squeezing them against his hard body. There, in the sweet receptacle of her womanhood, she was ready. That he did not immediately fill her brought little groans of protest, and his body stiffened with ravenous greed as he held back, teasing her, wanting her so wickedly that he was sure his gaze burned her with passion's fire. Their damp bodies molded together, complimenting each other, legs entwined, hips fused in wondrous rapture. And all the while he branded her as his private territory, his hands burning rivulets across her writhing flesh.

With intoxicating skill, Cole brought her to sensual arousal. Her hips undulated against him, begging to be filled with his manhood. When, at last, their bodies blended to seek fulfillment, Diana's hands worked with feverish intensity over the hard muscles of his back and hips. All inhibitions had vanished with the wind; all that mattered was that they lay together, taut and enflamed, she moaning at each exit, and he probing her body over and over with magnificent skill.

315

When, at last, their tantalizing motions topped ecstasy's peak, blissful torment wracked their bodies as they shuddered together, sated in each other's embrace. Then Cole took one final plunge and they lay together, his rippled muscles relaxing, her hands clinging to him in the aftermath of their thrilling love.

Then, for what seemed like hours, they lay in exquisite exhaustion, the wild and wonderful memory of their love bringing silent, peaceful sleep upon them.

Cole wanted only to spend two weeks lying in Diana's arms. He could not, however, satisfy that desire when, just before dark, alarm spread throughout the settlement. As he hastily dressed, assuring Diana, who had sat up in bed, that everything would be all right, he could hear the gruff voices of the men, the fear evident in their sharp, impatient orders to women and children.

"Hurry and dress, Diana," Cole said, arising, pulling on his boots. "I'll see what the trouble is."

He almost ran into Zebedee Ward on his own front porch. "Jim Duncan just returned," Zebedee said. "There's a band of renegade Indians moving toward us, about ten miles to the south."

"A large band?"

" 'Bout thirty."

"Does anyone know what tribe?"

"Don't know how reliable Jim's information is, but he says they're Seminoles."

Having done a bit of reading on the different

316

Indian nations of the Americas when he'd first arrived in Philadelphia, Cole protested, "That's impossible! Seminoles would have had to travel a thousand miles."

"He swears they're Seminoles. They got a white woman with 'em, trailin' behind the pack like a dog on a rope."

Cole shuddered. "There's got to be a mistake. They can't be Seminoles."

John Redding approached. "What is the trouble?"

"Renegade Indians, a small band. I believe we have enough men to take care of them should they threaten us."

John hadn't prepared for trouble in the normally peaceful region. His dark eyes mirrored his worry. "Where is Diana?" Just at that moment, she exited the cabin. She looked to Cole for an explanation, but he simply replied, "Probably a lot of worry over nothing." He managed a small smile. "A band of renegade Indians that does not approach half our number. Do not worry."

But she was too smart for that; she saw the worry in Cole's face. She had lived in the mountains long enough to know that just twenty renegade Indians against fifty white men could devastate the latter. They were vicious fighters, caring more about winning than about their own lives. But she could not worry Cole by showing fright. For him, she would have to be supportive, and with that in mind, it was not difficult to put on a facade of strength. "John, some coffee? I've just put on a pot."

John moved past Zebedee Ward and the younger man. "Sounds good." As he reached the cabin door he turned and said, "If, God forbid, you need an extra man, I'm pretty good with a musket, despite my city breeding."

When Diana and John Redding had entered the cabin, Zebedee Ward said, "Didn't want to say this in front of your lady, Donovan, but word's come from the south that this band has been lootin' and killin' along their route. Kill everybody that gets in their way, women and children, too."

Again, Cole shuddered. "We'd better prepare for the worst, and hope for the best."

"We're in trouble, Donovan."

"Don't be so damned negative," Cole said, moving toward the small band of armed men approaching them.

Inside the cabin, both nursing cups of hot coffee between their palms, Diana tried engaging John in small talk. But John Redding was not receptive. His hand went out and gently squeezed hers. "You are worried, Diana, and rightly so. But it will do no good. What will happen will happen. It is as simple as that."

"It's Cole," Diana replied. "He loves me very much, John. I do not want him to jeopardize his life on my behalf."

"Listen to yourself, Diana!" John reprimanded harshly. "Cole does not join with the men against a formidable foe simply because of you! He cares about this settlement and every man, woman and child living here. Yes, he cares about you, enough, I assume, to die for you, but he also cares about keeping this settlement safe!"

She deserved the reprimand. Extracting her hand,

318

she slowly smiled. "Just this morning you spoke of him as if he were vermin. And now you are defending him?"

John's eyes dropped. "You are right, Diana. This morning I was angry with him for taking you away from Philadelphia. I have nurtured my anger toward him for months." Looking up, he confessed, "But all the while I knew he had taken you away because you were in danger at Rourke House. That he was more perceptive than I was absolutely infuriated me!"

"But," Diana's hand fell to his in a comforting gesture, "how could you have known? Cole saw Webster kill my father. You did not. You saw in my cousin only a drunken bully. Cole saw a murderer."

At that moment, the cabin door opened. Cole entered and began gathering his weapons and ammunition. "A few of us are going to ride south. It may be necessary to enlist the aid of Tahchee's men."

Alarm darkened Diana's eyes as she closed the distance between them. "But why must you go, Cole? Let the other men go."

Dropping his weapons with an alarming clang, Cole took her by the shoulders and shook her firmly. "You know better than to say that, Diana! Don't disappoint me. I am as much a part of this settlement as any other man. Why shouldn't I ride out? Don't treat me like a wee bairn. I will not permit it!"

He had never spoken to her so sharply, and his reprimand was the second she had received in the space of a few minutes. Silently, feeling his firm, painful grasp, Diana realized how selfish she was being. It was all right for the other women's husbands and sons to risk their lives, but it was not all right for her man. Dropping her eyes, she eased her arms free of his grasp. "Forgive me, Cole." Neither had noticed John Redding walk out to the porch with his mug of coffee. Caressing his strong shoulders, Diana continued, "I was being selfish. I simply don't want to lose you, Cole." Tears moistened her violet eyes. "Please, forgive my moment of weakness."

Although the men awaited him, Cole felt that he owed her a moment of his comfort. Tenderly he took her in his arms and held her to him. "Forgive my sharp words, lass. Of course you are worried. We are all worried. But protecting you, and loving you, are all I want of life. Do not deprive me of the right."

Resting her head on his shoulder for the briefest of moments, Diana said, "Take care of yourself, Cole, and come back as quickly as possible."

"The men who are staying behind are fortifying the walls and the gate. I am entrusting you with the task of keeping the other women and children calm. Gather them into the community hall. It is the safest place for you. You might also consider," he managed a slight smile, "the possibility that we are up in arms about nothing. The renegades may pass us by. We can pray to God they do."

Folding her to him, Cole moved toward the porch. He released her only when John Redding approached, dangling an empty mug from his right hand. "Shall I accompany you?" John asked.

"I'm glad you're still here. Mildred Bruce has just gone into labor with her seventh child. Her previous six have been stillborn. Perform a miracle for the poor lady, Dr. Redding, and deliver a healthy bairn into her arms."

John smiled sadly. "I'll admit that my expertise is in bringing life, rather than with taking it. If this is where my services will best be of use, then please point the way to the lady's home."

"I will take you there," Cole offered. "Diana, after you have seen to the women and children, and the older people, will you assist Dr. Redding?"

"Of course," she replied.

Without inhibition, Cole pulled her to him and kissed her warmly. "I will be back soon."

"Yes, I know you will."

Crossing her arms, Diana moved down the steps, then half-ran toward Callie Ward's cabin without looking back.

Diana had no time to worry about Cole. She and Callie had gathered everyone together in the community hall which stood in the center of the settlement. Diana now sat beside Mildred in the Bruce cabin, comforting her and doing whatever John Redding asked of her.

The labor was long and excruciating for the middle-aged woman. At times her breathing was so shallow that she and John both feared she'd died, but then the contractions came with vicious force and she would writhe in agony and pain.

"Why do you stay with me?" she gasped in exhaustion. "My body kills all my babies."

"Not this one," John assured her, himself exhausted. "Not if I can help it."

Just past midnight on that hot summer night, Mildred Bruce gave birth to a healthy baby boy. Mother and child were resting in peaceful sleep before John slumped on a small cot off in a corner. Callie chose that moment to enter the cabin.

She approached Diana. "You go on to the community hall and sleep. I'll sit with Mildred for a while. Mrs. Duncan is watching over my children." Drawing back the sheet, she admired the dark-haired baby boy. "You will know this joy in time, Diana. There is nothing like it."

"I hope it is natural, after assisting in birthings, to be a little apprehensive," Diana said.

"It is very natural," Callie whispered so as not to disturb the exhausted doctor, "to worry not only about your baby, but about yourself as well."

"Thinking of myself," Diana said, pressing her mouth into a thin line, "is something I've done quite a bit today. Every time I turn around, I'm saying something I shouldn't. I've gotten my proper share of reprimands for my selfishness."

After she had related the day's events to Callie, the older woman said, "We are human, Diana. Do not berate yourself for the small weaknesses we all have."

Diana arose from the rocking chair beside Mildred's bed and offered it to Callie. "Thank you for sitting with Millie."

"We are all family, Diana. We do things together,

and we look out for each other."

Diana looked toward the dark corner. "What should I do with John?"

The smiling Callie whispered, "He'll be all right where he is. Let him sleep."

As she reached the cabin door, Diana turned and asked, "Any word from the men?"

"None as yet," Callie replied, with a deliberate tone of indifference. "But it has only been a few hours since they left. They can take care of themselves. Now, you go and take care of yourself. And hurry, before you wake everyone."

Before she departed, Diana said, "If I'd ever had a sister, Callie, I would have wanted her to be like you."

The smiling Callie responded, "Hush and be off with you!" Just before the door closed, she whispered, "Sister," aware that Diana had heard the loving endearment.

Chapter 18

Cole and the eight men with him came upon Oclala's campsite just past ten o'clock in the evening. So many nights previous had been clear and warm; why did nature choose this night for a violent storm? The men were soaked. Dismounting and tying off their equally drenched horses, they advanced and crouched in the thick undergrowth of the forest, just a hundred yards up the hill from the encampment of drunken, boasting Seminoles. The Indians had pitched a tent and had a good fire burning beneath. As Jim Duncan had earlier reported, they did indeed have a captive—a pretty brown-haired woman whose skin had been darkened by the hot Southern sun. She sat Indian-style in the clearing, the rain beating down and plastering the scant rags of her gown to her form, emaciated but for her abdomen, swollen with child.

"Anything we can do to help her, Donovan?" Jim Duncan asked quietly. "She looks kind of sick."

"Not with just the nine of us," Cole replied.

"We need more men."

"We can't leave the women unprotected," Zebedee Ward said gruffly. "Maybe Tahchee'll give us some of his braves."

"Tahchee's village is in their direct path," Jim reminded Cole.

Cole counted the party, including the Indian woman dressed in men's attire, who looked as though she could fight as fiercely as the rest. "With less than thirty men, they would be crazy to go up against two hundred Cherokee."

"Them bastards look about that crazy," Zebedee Ward was quick to point out. "Let's take 'em now, while they're wiped out on whiskey."

Cole rested on his right knee in the rich mountain dirt, his hands wrapped lightly around the barrel of his musket. "We cannot jeopardize the life of the white woman. They would slit her throat at the first sign of trouble. No, we will have to make careful plans. Besides," Cole gritted his teeth in frustration, "this rain has probably dampened our gun powder."

"What do you suggest, Cole?" Jim Duncan asked.

Jim's brother, Parker, said, "I don't mean to boast, but I was just about the best tracker in Tennessee. An' I know how to blend into the forest like a tree sapling." Parker Duncan was almost that thin. "Why don't I keep an eye on these bastards? I'll track their movements while you men do whatever has to be done to stop 'em and free the white woman."

Lightning rent the air. "Pray they stay put for

the night," Cole said, opposed to the idea of Parker Duncan remaining alone in close proximity to the murderous bunch.

"Be crazy to move on in this storm, Donovan," Parker replied. "But in case they do decide to pick up and move, somebody's got to know where they're at."

Silence. Cole pondered the idea for a moment. "You're right, of course." He did not want to agree with Parker's suggestion, but at the moment he had no alternative. "One of you other men volunteer to remain with him. That way one of you can keep a watch on them, and the other can ride back and forth between us. The rest of us—except you, Jim—will ride to Tahchee's village." Putting his hand on the younger Duncan's shoulder, Cole said, "You return to the settlement and inform the others of the situation. And please—try not to frighten them."

In the next few moments the younger Bruce brother had volunteered to remain with Duncan. The other seven men returned to their horses, sliding treacherously in the slick mud of the trail. Leading their mounts through a narrow gulley out of hearing range of the renegades, they mounted and took the northeast trail toward Tahchee's village.

An hour later, with the storm diminishing somewhat, Cole and the men reached the village, gave the proper signal to the sentry, and soon dismounted at Tahchee's hut. Within moments, Tahchee greeted them. "It is a strange hour, Donovan, to visit."

326

"It is not a social call, Tahchee," Cole replied. "There is trouble that affects us all, Indian and white alike." Sehoy exited the hut and stood behind her husband. "We must talk to your father, the chief."

"The chief is off on summer hunt with tribal elders. What is this trouble, Donovan?" Tahchee crossed his arms. "I do not see fire upon the horizon. The blackness of the storm has ridden away with the winds."

"It is more treacherous than that," Cole replied. "The treachery is of a two-legged kind. Renegade In—" quickly, he amended his statement, "Renegades."

"Of my tribe?" The perceptive Tahchee had been very aware of what his white brother had been about to say. "Cherokee?"

"No . . . Seminole."

"The Seminole live many miles to south." Tahchee pointed in that direction. "They do not venture far from homeland."

"These are Seminole," Cole argued. "I have no idea what they are doing here, but they have killed and plundered. They have cut a bloody path, and they will add to it the blood of your people and mine if they are not stopped."

"Tahchee have many braves. How many Seminole?"

"We counted about thirty."

Tahchee laughed mightily. "Thirty! Then what is problem, Cole Donovan?"

"The problem is that they have a captive white woman with them. We would prefer to free her

327

rather than see her killed."

"One life not worth many lives. Let Seminole kill woman quick and easy, then we kill Seminole and end their bloodbath."

Sehoy had stood by, quietly listening. Only now did she speak up, despite knowing that it went against the grain of Indian custom. "No . . . Cole Donovan is right. Woman does not deserve to die."

Strangely, Tahchee did not reprimand her, though he glared when she dared to approach and take a place beside him. He did not appreciate her display of independent thinking in the presence of his white brothers. "Cole Donovan, is it so important to save white woman?" he asked, attempting to extricate himself from the humiliation his normally humble wife had caused him.

"It is," Cole replied. "After the woman is freed, the only way to deal with the murderous bunch will be execution, I'm afraid. If it is necessary for the safety of your people and mine, then so be it."

In the next few minutes, Tahchee gathered the youngest and strongest of his braves together, then scattered the others to the perimeters of the village to set up watch and defend it if necessary. Tahchee ordered Sehoy to gather together the old people, women and children of his tribe, as the white settlers had done, though he thought the safety measure a rather melodramatic request on the part of Cole Donovan. He had, after all, informed him that there were less than thirty bloodthirsty Seminole. But he would humor the white man whose wife had saved his young son from certain death. In the weeks they had been living together in harmony, they had also become close, like brothers.

Soon, a band of seventy men mounted their horses to ride to the southwest, toward the deep gulley where the Seminoles were camped. But just as they were about to leave the village, young Byron Bruce raced his nimble young mare into their midst. Clinging to the back of his saddle was a thin, ragged, sun-browned woman who looked about to collapse.

Byron dismounted just in time for the young white captive to fall almost gracefully into his arms. Cole immediately dismounted. "How did you free the woman? And where is Jim?"

Byron Bruce was breathless with exhaustion. "She . . . them bloody Seminoles . . . they was . . ."

Cole put his hand on the boy's shoulder. "Calm down. Take some deep breaths." The lad of about seventeen did as he was told.

"They was real drunk, Mr. Donovan. Parker an' me, we seen 'em fallin' one by one into dead heaps by their campfire. Then there was just this one, a really ugly woman with half her face black as pitch. Parker, he crept up on 'em, an' he believes that Indian gal seen him as he clamped his hand over this here female's mouth. He cut the rawhide tyin' her to that tree an' he carted her off. Damn, but he's sure that black face seen him sneakin' off with her."

"And she did not alarm the others?"

Sehoy had approached with a ladle of water and

offered a sip to the lad, then to the emaciated white woman, who gulped the cool liquid. One of Cole's men approached and picked her up, and Sehoy moved ahead of them toward the hut where she had gathered the people of her tribe.

In the few moments this had taken Byron Bruce had regained his strength. He came to his feet, then flicked dust off his buckskins. "She didn't say nothin', Mr. Donovan," he said, speaking of the Seminole woman. "She just glared with them mean black eyes. It was spooky. Real spooky!"

Tahchee had dismounted his pony to stand beside Cole. "Now we go, and when we finish, renegades will be dead."

Cole's hand went up. "Let's reassess the situation. The woman probably saw Parker, and yet she did not sound the alarm. Either she was jealous of the white woman or—" he almost choked on the words, "there are more of them than we saw and they are setting a trap."

Zebedee Ward dismounted his horse. "Then we gotta decide which it is, Donovan."

Cole was sharp in his reply. "I don't think it is a matter of deciding. It is a matter of finding out."

Black Face had, indeed, seen the white man sneak up to the perimeters of their camp to free the captive Polly. She had wanted to be rid of her for many months—especially now that Oclala's seed grew within her. She herself wanted to lie with Oclala as his woman. True, she was ugly, with her hideously marked face, but if she was the only woman within reach, then Oclala would come to her to satisfy his sexual needs. It did not matter to her if he chose to hide her ugliness behind an animal skin as long as the maleness of him satisfied her own desires. She had easily rebuffed the primal needs of the other Seminoles, because she wanted only Oclala, their leader, and he had wanted only the comely, blemish-free white woman.

Black Face had given Polly's rescuer scarcely more than ten minutes before rousing her Indian brothers. Oclala, on hearing the news, struck a vicious blow to Black Face's head. How dare she allow a white man to steal away his captive woman! What would he do now when his loins ached for gratification?

The enamored Black Face viewed Oclala's blow as a trophy. She touched it, relishing it, and hoped the wondrously painful wound would never go away, because his hand — Oclala's hand! — had left it there.

Oclala might have struck Black Face again if two of his men hadn't dragged a struggling staker Duncan toward him, forcing him down to his knees before their leader. "Where is white captive?" Oclala calmly asked in his broken English.

"My friend took her away . . . where you'll never find her, you stinkin' bastard!"

Oclala said nothing as he calmly removed his knife from its sheath. Grasping the dark hair of the wide-eyed and horrified young white man, Oclala opened his throat with one swift move.

Parker Duncan was dead before his body hit the ground.

With groggy indifference, the renegades gathered their few belongings and mounted their horses. Now that the white man — their enemy — knew where they were located, they would return in great numbers to vanquish them. Oclala made the decision to turn due west along the ridge of a deep gulley. From that point he could see half a mile on either side of them. If the white men appeared with their reinforcements, then Oclala and his small band would have a chance of escape.

After they had put ten miles behind them in just over two hours, the light mist covering their trail as they traveled, Oclala ordered that Black Face be tied between two sturdy saplings for a more carefully planned punishment. She held her head high as she was stripped to the waist so that Oclala's men could beat her in turn with their globe-headed clubs. Her body jerked convulsively with each blow, but Black Face did not cry out, not even when her head eventually fell to her ample chest. Her revered leader wanted her punished and it pleased her greatly that her pain entertained him. Afterwards, his body aroused by her strength, the wounds, and the firmness of her youthful, naked figure, Oclala cut the rawhide strips from her wrists and pulled her half-conscious form down to a blanket. Dragging up her loincloth to expose the receptacle of her womanhood, he forced her thighs apart and rammed himself into her. He was still groggy from whiskey as he pounded clumsily against her, harder and harder still, his left hand supporting his weight, and his right smearing her dark body with the blood oozing from her wounds.

Puzzled by her very weak smile as he took her, Oclala probed her body until his loins exploded in primal greed.

Black Face had smiled because she was happy. It mattered not that her flesh throbbed with pain. Oclala had taken her as his woman . . . and he had not even covered her marked face with an animal skin.

Just after dawn the following morning, Cole, Tahchee and their men reached the location ten miles to the north where the renegades had spent the rest of the night. They found only the remains of a campfire and half a dozen empty whiskey jugs.

Cole Donovan was a man possessed. When they'd come upon the viciously murdered Parker Duncan, he had sworn to bring to justice the bastards who'd done it. Parker's brother, Jim, had left their party to take the body back to the settlement.

Tahchee had sent several of his braves out to scout the area. One now exited a trail from the north and said, "They have turned northeast, toward the white man's settlement."

"My God," Cole mumbled, remounting his horse. "Byron, double back four miles and cut north through the woods. You must warn our people."

"What'll you do, Mr. Donovan?"

"We'll follow their trail from here, and pray to God we reach them before they reach our homesteads."

His gray-black gaze darkened with fear. Foremost in his mind was his lovely Diana . . . and their child growing within her.

Diana was exhausted. Jim had returned to Pine Creek, just after three o'clock that morning, with his murdered brother's corpse. The body had been tenderly placed upon the table in the Duncan's cabin, and since then she had been sitting with the grieving parents. With her hand resting lightly on her dead son's chest, Liddie Duncan wept quietly. Her surviving son and her one-legged husband sat off in a corner of their cabin, nursing the painful loss of son and brother with long, deep swigs of Tennesee moonshine.

Reverend Aldous Bernard had read from the Bible for almost two hours, but now slumped in exhaustion across the table. Diana wished she had John Redding for company, but she knew he deserved the much-needed sleep he was getting after delivering Mrs. Bruce's baby.

How had their peace and serenity turned so topsy-turvy? Yesterday she had been quietly sitting atop a boulder waiting for Cole to return from Roanoke. Today one of their neighbors lay dead beneath a bloodstained sheet, awaiting construction of a coffin and a decent burial; a woman had been brought to their settlement pregnant with the savage leader's child; and her beloved was off with the other men tracking down renegade Indians who had no business being this far north.

Just before seven o'clock, young Byron Bruce galloped his exhausted mount into Pine Creek. He had ridden fast and hard, covering the miles in just over an hour. Diana rushed out to the porch of the Duncan's cabin to meet him.

"Byron, where are the men?"

"Trackin' them renegades," he replied, swiping his hat off his head in respect for Donovan's woman. He very much admired the prettiest woman in the mountains, as did all the young men in Pine Creek. "They're movin' north toward us, and Mr. Donovan wants us to fortify." The men left behind began emerging from throughout the settlement. "Them Indians is a'headin' this way," Byron repeated, accompanying Diana to the door of the cabin. "We gotta fortify."

As the men, mumbling, dispersed among the cabins to make preparations, Diana took the news indoors. "They're coming this way—the renegades." She'd spoken with soft defeat.

"What'd you say, Mrs. Donovan?"

Jim put the jug down and ambled across the large, sparsely furnished room. "The renegades, they've headed north. Cole sent Byron Bruce with orders that we fortify."

"Is he safe, Byron?"

"You mean Mr. Donovan?" She nodded. "Sure, ma'am. Last I seen him 'bout an hour ago he was

335

riled up like a stuck boar!"

That may very well have been true an hour ago. Now, however, Cole was more worried than angry. Since the trail of the renegades had ended about four miles north, with the murderous bunch again turning west, Tahchee, believing they had left the region, had ordered his men back to their village. Cole still wanted the renegades punished for the murder of Parker Duncan and all the other innocent victims of their bloody spree.

There was something he had to take care of first. He gave last minute instructions to the men, then left them camped in a clearing where the trail of the renegades turned from north to west once again.

Entering Pine Creek just before noon, the delighted Diana was in his arms the minute he dismounted his horse. His face was worried and stern, and her sad smile quickly faded. "What is wrong, Cole? Where are the other men?"

"Camped several miles from here. Where is Aldous Bernard?"

"The reverend? He's slumped across the table in the Duncan cabin. If it's about the funeral—"

"No . . . though I would suggest that Parker's coffin be built with haste." When she gave him a puzzled look, he quietly explained, "The heat, Diana."

"It is already done, Cole. Mr. Bruce built it this morning. We were awaiting the return of the men before conducting services."

Failing to reply, Cole entered the Duncan cabin. He placed his hand on Liddie Duncan's shoulder in a gesture of sympathy, then approached and shook Aldous Bernard to full wakefulness. "Mr. Bernard?"

"Mmmm?" Lifting his head, the thin gentlemen stuck a monacle to his right eye and studied Cole as if he'd just seen him for the first time. But immediately, recognition lit his eyes. "Mr. Donovan . . . the trouble over?"

"Not yet." The silent and very puzzled Diana approached from behind him. "Will you perform a wedding ceremony? Now . . . without delay?"

Diana's hand instantly eased into Cole's. "Why the rush?" she asked. "Cole, what is going on?"

Turning, taking her in his arms, he drew her to him. He was so exhausted he could hardly keep his eyes open. "We're going to get them for what they did to Parker . . . for all the innocent people they have killed. But before I ride out of here, I want to leave a wife behind, and I want a wife to return to."

Diana's heart sank with dread.

Callie, who had slipped in just moments ago to offer her condolences, said quietly, "You will need witnesses. Let us go to the community hall. The people of Pine Creek will witness the exchange of your vows. Then," her sad eyes turned to Liddie Duncan, "we will give your dear boy to the Lord."

"Aye," Liddie said quietly. "If you don't mind, I'll sit here with him until then."

Diana hugged the older woman. "I will return, Liddie." To Mr. Duncan, she said, "We all loved

Parker."

Pierce Duncan managed only to clear his throat of the huge, painful lump sitting there.

The wedding happened so quickly that when it was over Diana could recall only one or two words of the hastily spoken service. As soon as Cole had touched his mouth to hers in the gentlest of kisses and signed the hastily drawn-up marriage document, he was out the door and nudging his horse into a fast canter through the forest. He did not look back; tears stung his gray-black eyes.

"What do you suppose this is all about?" Diana asked Callie.

"He is worried."

"About what?"

"He is an honorable man. In the event something should happen to him, God forbid, he wants to be sure your child has his name."

Trembling, Diana covered Callie's small hand when it fell to her arm.

Cole spent just over an hour returning to the men. There were twenty-two of them now, enough, he hoped, to cut down the savages. Rejoining the men, they began a western trek, traveling only three miles before again turning north. The renegades were moving in a zig-zag pattern, like a drunkard's stagger between tavern and home.

At mid-afternoon Cole's men came upon the murderous bunch. They were feasting greedily at

338

the carcasses of three wild turkeys, laughing and boasting, and drinking what was left of the stolen whiskey. Cole did not watch as the leader, Oclala, covered the one woman among them. But Zebedee Ward watched as he left her weak and moaning beneath his slobbering, assaulting, drunken body. No woman, not even a vicious renegade, deserved such treatment. Half-naked, her body was black, the result of a brutal beating.

The leader was easily recognized by his gaudy attire and the heavy, silver crescents which adorned his bronze neck. That was the man Cole wanted.

"Check your weapons, men," he ordered quietly. "We're going to take them down."

"The draggle-tail, too?" Ward asked.

"I don't cater to killing women," Cole said between tightly clenched teeth. "Take her alive if you can."

"Then what we goin' ta do with 'er?"

"I don't know." In the moments to follow, Cole positioned the men in a line, belly-down upon the hill overlooking the encampment. Each man, eight of whom had two loaded weapons, had been instructed which Indians to aim for. "I'm taking the leader," Cole said, "that one over there." Pointing to Oclala, he took aim. He had a real bad feeling about this . . . a feeling that had clung to him throughout the morning and afternoon. He thanked God that Diana was his wife and that their child would rightfully bear his name. "On the count of three, fire." He looked down the line of men to either side of him. *"One . . . two . . ."*

The forest suddenly became deathly quiet, and as Cole yelled *"three!"* the shots echoed with deafening assault through the mountains. The startled renegades who were not struck in the first volley did not have a chance to react. They were either killed or mortally wounded almost before they could jump to their feet, looks of horror grotesquely twisting their painted faces.

Cole and the men stared down on a grim, bloody scene. The woman had managed to crawl behind a boulder across the clearing from where the men's muskets were stacked. If she had a weapon at all, it would be a knife which could easily be taken away from her. She was certainly in no condition to fight them.

The men of Pine Creek sat atop the ridge until all movement ceased in the gulley. Cole reloaded his musket and when he was reasonably sure that every last man was dead, he cautiously rose to his feet. "Stay here, men."

"I'll go with you, Donovan."

"No, Zebedee. I don't see the sense in two of us risking our lives." Stealthily, Cole moved down the side of the hill, his weapon moving fluidly, nervously over the grisly scene. A twig snapped beneath his boot and he crouched, rising only when he realized that he himself had made the startling noise. As he moved farther down the hill, the absence of life gave him the moment to breathe a sigh of relief. He let his guard down.

Oclala knew he was mortally wounded. He had

been struck in the lower abdomen and the exit of the fifty-four caliber musket ball had taken half his back with it. But even as he lay dying, his mouth twisted with wry amusement. He had fallen on his ever-present, ever-loaded musket. Through quickly dimming eyes, he watched the approach of the white man.

Cole saw the bloody finger wrapped around the trigger of the musket and the livid eyes of the renegade leader at almost the same moment. Dropping to his knees, the aim of the musket moved swiftly to the fore.

But it was too late for Cole Donovan as Oclala fired with deadly aim. Before Cole hit the ground, eleven fresh rounds from the men on the hill twisted Oclala's body into a convulsing, unrecognizable mass of bloody flesh.

Cole lay upon his back among the dead Indians, the rich green of the forest swirling away into foggy darkness.

His last thought was of Diana and their unborn child.

Chapter 19

Philadelphia, December 7, 1787

The first snow of the season had begun to fall during the night. Webster stood at the parlor window, his fingers raking the draperies back and forth with nervous irritation. Loosening his cravat, he watched the roadway winding toward Rourke House this early Friday morning, each passing coach or carriage absorbing his total concentration until lost from sight on the slushy roads to the west.

He was not sure why Diana had waited four months to return to Philadelphia when she could have traveled with John Redding back in August. *We could have had these four long months to drive the aggravating little wood sprite out of her blasted mind and lay claim to her inheritance on behalf of his mother.* As it was, he had only until the end of December to accomplish the task. But would that really be so difficult, considering that she had lost her husband on the very day of their marriage?

As he stood at the window, his mouth twisted in wry satisfaction. He remembered the warm August afternoon when John had returned from the new settlement of Pine Creek, North Carolina, bearing the news that Cole Donovan had been killed by a renegade Indian. It pleased him immensely that the man who had betrayed him lay rotting and putrid in the ground beneath the southern sky. He had gotten what he deserved. No longer would he interfere in his plans to take Diana's inheritance from her.

Absorbed in his morbid thoughts, Webster was scarcely aware of the carriage pulling up to the front entrance of Rourke House. He heard Mrs. Sanders cross the foyer, followed closely by her simpleminded daughter, and almost immediately, kind words were being shared between the servants, his cousin, and Dr. John Redding. Diana's voice was dry and empty, free of the vibrance he remembered from the first days, almost a year ago, that she had spent at her father's house.

Webster stood in the parlor, his arms crossed, waiting for Mrs. Sanders to escort Diana and John Redding into the room where he stood. He watched Diana's silent move across the large room, her comely figure flattered still by the somber gray gown she wore. The veil across her face hid her flawless complexion and exquisite violet eyes. She approached, her head held high, and offered her hand to Webster.

"Diana, it is good to see you again."

"Thank you, Webster," she said quietly.

"Did you have a pleasant trip?"

"It was pleasant enough."

343

John Redding approached and stood beside her, his gaze lifted smugly to Webster's. He was well aware that the younger man was furious over the counter-conspiracy involving the astute Mr. Pipps. Momentarily, he and Webster shared a brief handshake and John forced himself to ask, "Have you been well, Webster?"

As if you gave a damn, Webster thought, gritting his teeth, yet still managing some semblance of a smile. "As well as this blasted weather permits," he responded.

Diana asked, "Would you gentlemen mind if I go straight away to my rooms? I am terribly tired."

Webster bowed politely. "Of course . . . Mrs. Sanders, show my cousin to her suite." Briefly, Diana took John's hand, then moved, almost mechanically, ahead of Mrs. Sanders. Webster wished he could have seen his cousin's face. The pain that surely filled her eyes would have pleased him immensely. Webster, however, had to project a facade of sympathy and understanding in the presence of John Redding. "How is she, John?"

"You know you really do not give a damn," John replied somberly. "I have her on laudanum. Since the death of her husband she has been despondent . . . and suicidal."

John Redding's words planted an idea in his head. Suicidal! Webster's eyes moistened wickedly. Only a crazy woman would commit suicide, and Webster would have to see what he could do to help her make that decision. "Poor, poor thing," he replied, clicking his tongue annoyingly. "I will do everything possible to see to her comfort, and to her speedy recovery."

I am sure that you will, John thought sarcastically, replying instead, "Yes, she will need the support of her family."

"Has she seen her Aunt Rufina?"

"She visited for a week before journeying on to Philadelphia. Her aunt has remarried."

"Remarried? Rowanna's unsightly sister?"

"She's not a comely woman, but she is kind. She has married a man the people of the region call Hambone. Quite a likeable rogue, actually."

"Why am I not surprised at a rogue husband named Hambone?"

"I wouldn't speak ill of Rufina and her husband in the presence of Diana, were I you. She is very fond of both, and would look unfavorably upon your criticism."

That was an observation Webster did not feel required an answer. He was, after all, entitled to his own opinion. Turning to the liquor cabinet, he said, "A sherry, John?"

"Too early for me."

"Mind if I do?"

Would you care if I did? "Of course not, Webster."

Webster turned back with a flashy smile. "Tell me, John, how is my young cousin taking the death of her husband, the great masquerader?"

"Masquerader?"

"Of course, you must have heard the stories of

345

what he did to my poor cousin here, in this very house, before he kidnapped her away."

"Ah, yes. But that is in the past. Diana was very much in love with Master Donovan."

Again, Webster clicked his tongue. "Such a shame that my lovely young cousin should have been spoiled by the lust and wickedness of such a man!"

John gritted his teeth to keep from replying. He wanted to pounce and kill the arrogant ass. But he had to bide his time. Patience was the key word here. "I cannot see the point in speaking ill of the dead." Lowering his angrily raised eyebrow, he asked, "Is your father home?"

"Father." Webster had a puzzled look, as if he did not know whom John was speaking of. "Father. Father, of course! No, I'm sorry, he is away in Jersey. He will not return until the first of the year."

That is what you think! John thought. "A shame. I am sure he is anxious to see Diana again."

"Yes, it is unfortunate that his business could not wait."

"I must be going. Please tell Mrs. Donovan that I will see her again on Sunday."

"On Sunday?"

"Yes, she expressed a desire to attend church with my family."

Webster's hand fell almost menacingly on John's arms. "I would prefer that she did not, John. She is in mourning, and I believe it would be appropriate for her to remain in this house, at least until the new year."

"Indeed? I see no harm in her attending church."

"While my father is away, I am master of this house. I tell you now, John, that my cousin will not leave these grounds. Please respect my wishes."

Actually, Webster had left no room for argument. His dark eyes glared threateningly. "Very well." John bowed politely. "I will respect your wishes, though I do not understand them."

Webster and John Redding had always been at odds. But John knew one thing: he *would* come on Sunday to take Diana to church with his family.

Mrs. Sanders and Claudia scooted about, unpacking Diana's bags and separating clothing that needed to be pressed from that which could be put away in the large chest of drawers. Diana sat quietly in the Queen Anne chair beside the hearth, watching the flames flicker delicately against the black hearth. She had not removed her hat with its somber veil, nor the gray traveling gloves that hid her winter-pale skin.

Soon, the unpacking completed, Claudia slipped out of the room and Mrs. Sanders approached, wringing her hands nervously. "Is there anything I can do for you, Miss Diana?"

Diana met the older woman's gaze, almost as if she had just recognized her. "I — well, it might be nice if you didn't call me 'miss' any longer. I was married to Cole Donovan."

"Shall I call you Mrs. Donovan?"

Rising, taking the kindly woman's hands, Diana

347

replied, "It would please me greatly if we could be friends, Mrs. Sanders. I don't belong here. I feel like a simple girl taken from her simple life in the mountains and thrust into the sadness of my father's house. If it is not too uncomfortable for you while I am here, I would appreciate your calling me Diana."

Mrs. Sanders bit her trembling lip. "What do you mean, while you are here? Aren't you planning to stay? To live in the house that was your father's?"

Diana smiled sadly. "We'll talk about that later. Now—will you call me Diana?"

"Very well . . . Diana. I will bring you a nice cup of tea, with sugar and cream the way you like it."

"Thank you." Mrs. Sanders withdrew her hands. "I will be in the upstairs parlor. Will you kindly ask my cousin to come there? We have things to discuss."

"Yes, of course."

When Mrs. Sanders had gently closed the door behind her, Diana removed her hat and veil and tossed them, along with her gloves, to the chair she had just vacated. Mrs. Sanders had placed her silver brush upon the dresser. Pulling out her combs, she picked up the brush to drag it through her hair with a vengeance. She pinched her cheeks to return a little of the color that usually graced them. Then, drawing in a deep, weary sigh, she moved toward the parlor.

She had just approached the window and was

looking out at the light flurries of snow when Webster rapped at the door and entered. "Cousin, you wished to see me?"

Silence. Diana stood at the window, her fingers wrapped lightly around the heavy winter draperies. Then she spun about and a grim smile momentarily overshadowed her prettiness. "Indeed, Cousin, I do wish to speak to you."

Webster was surprised by her expression. He had expected moping sadness and tearful eyes begging for sympathy. "And what is it, Cousin?"

"In three weeks I will inherit my father's property," she began quietly, approaching a chair to ease herself lightly into it.

"You and my mother," he corrected.

Diana continued as if she had not been interrupted. "I have made arrangements to sell the house to a German family in the city. You and my uncle will have to make other living arrangements. Mrs. Sanders and her family will remain here. The new owners have agreed."

Shocked by her crisply delivered statement, Webster dropped heavily into the love seat beside the cold hearth. Melodramatically he drew his trembling hand to the lapel of his coat, but a lack of strength would not allow his fingers to grasp the fine material. "You cannot make us leave! This is our home. My mother was born in this house. I was born in this house! This house will be as much my mother's as yours! You cannot sell!"

"Well, we won't have to worry about any more Rourkes, or Donovans, or Maynes being born in

349

this house, will we?"

Webster clambered to his feet, despite the weakness in his knees. "I will fight you, Diana . . . Donovan! Why, dear God, are you being so cruel? So callous?" Fury darkened his features.

Diana, too, arose, and approached Webster. Standing just outside of arm's reach, she replied between clenched teeth, "I know what you did to me! You put my late husband up to masquerading as my great-grandfather. You tried to drive me insane so that you and your father could rob me of my inheritance. Webster Mayne, I will see this house burned to the ground before you and your family inherit it!"

"My God! My mother is a very ill woman. She hasn't left her private suite in fifteen years!"

Diana crossed her arms, an almost vicious smile turning up the corners of her lovely mouth. "I do not believe your mother is in this house! Why do you think I am so confident right now, Webster? I have not seen my Aunt Jocelyn. I have not heard her. I have heard only the mention of her name. Perhaps my Aunt Jocelyn does not even exist. You could very well be Philip Mayne's bastard, spewed from the womb of a harlot!"

Webster was not sure from what source he drew the strength not to slap his beautiful young cousin. He pivoted smartly on his heel and skulked toward the door. But then he turned, his mouth dragging at the corners, and hissing cruelly, childishly, "I'm glad Cole Donovan is dead. I wish I could have seen him die myself!"

Diana was strangely unaffected by his declaration. The parlor door slammed resoundingly behind her infuriated cousin and she listened to the sharp retreat of his boots on the polished floor. Within minutes Mrs. Sanders knocked, then entered with her tray.

"What did you say to your cousin? I have never seen him so angry."

Diana cocked her head sweetly to the side. "Why, dear Mrs. Sanders, do I look capable of angering Webster? My goodness! You know how strange his moods can be."

Mrs. Sanders set the tray on a small round table. "Aye, perhaps you're right. His moods change as quickly as the weather."

Diana sat forward to study the tray. "Mrs. Sanders, you brought two cups."

"I thought the master would still be with you."

"Do not call him master any longer. I do not like it, and he does not deserve such respect." Smiling again, she continued, "Please, won't you be so gracious as to take tea with me?"

Mrs. Sanders had never imagined that the sweet young woman could have such a cold expression on her face. She was quietly mortified. Without replying, she took the matching chair on the other side of the table and slowly poured tea into the two cups.

After a long nap, Diana arose, enjoyed the steaming bath Mrs. Sanders had drawn for her, and dressed in a loose, comfortable gown suitable for her private rooms. She then sat at the French desk and began writing a letter:

"My dearest Callie,

"We have arrived safely in Philadelphia. Traveling overland to the coast, then by ship to New England shortened the journey by many weeks. I must admit that scarcely had my pony entered the forest before I missed my beloved Pine Creek. My longing is only to return to the home we have built there, and to see you, my dear friend, and my precious son. I hope my little Drew is well and that he is being a good baby. Please give him his mother's love and a tender hug to remember me by. Yes, my friend, I know he is too young to miss me, but indulge me my fantasies. God knows, I shall not have such privileges in this dark, dreary house overlooking Philadelphia.

"To my surprise and delight, my dear friend, Dr. Redding purchased a lovely family Bible for me when we arrived in Philadelphia yesterday. I was very proud to enter my beloved husband's name in it, along with my own, and the name of our son, Andrew Cynric Donovan. I shall treasure John's thoughtful gift always, as I will treasure the lovely baby clothing your gentle hands have sewn for me.

"I shall keep my letter short. I have put my

plan in action and already it is working well. Scarcely had I been in the house an hour before my cousin was furious with me. Oh, how pleased I am with my own wickedness!

Always your friend,
Diana Donovan"

Diana smiled to herself as two bold flourishes emphasized the final word of her letter. Then she folded it in thirds, melted a little wax over the fold, and pressed the Donovan seal—which she'd brought with her from Pine Creek—into the liquid wax. Tucking it into the panier of her gown, she knew it would be safe there until she could give it to John Redding for posting.

She was inordinately pleased with herself.

By mid-afternoon Webster was too intoxicated to stand without hanging on to something sturdy. He hadn't been this furious since his days at the New London Crossroads School, when his archenemy—a theology student—had shaved a wide swatch of his hair from forehead to nape of neck after he'd passed out drunk one cold winter night.

He hated his young cousin! In his inebriated state, he swore that he would gladly forfeit his uncle's estate if he could see Diana as dead as that miserable Cole Donovan. But, alas, his creditors would not be pleased with that. He had already been extended four months beyond his deadline for paying the debts he had amassed throughout New

England.

Webster dined alone that evening, since Diana had chosen to have a supper tray brought to her private suite. Throughout the evening Webster brooded at the liquor cabinet, trying to decide what to do about his cousin. So, she knew he had hired Donovan. She should be pleased. Hadn't she fallen in love with the Scottish bastard and enjoyed the lust of his loins?

Just before midnight, Webster stumbled to his bedchamber in the west wing of the house. He collapsed to his bed, too drunk to shed himself of his clothing. The darkness of large chamber enveloped him, stifling his ability to breathe. Webster fought unsuccessfully to loosen his clothing before he suffocated. But his arms were like lead weights, and he managed only to free himself of the scarf tucked into his coat.

Suddenly, the door from the corridor opened, allowing a cold blast of air to enter the room. "Tuxford? Tuxford, get over here and help me prepare for bed." Silence. Webster tried to force his eyelids open, but they were as heavy as his arms. "Damn you, Tuxford, answer me!"

"Tuxford is not here."

The softly spoken masculine reply had the effect of immediately sobering Webster Mayne. His head jerked off the pillow and his boots landed firmly on the carpet. What a blasted nightmare he was having! He could have sworn he'd just heard . . .

Drawing in a deep, ragged breath, Webster closed his eyes tightly. "Tuxford?" he called timorously.

"Tuxford is not here," the voice repeated.

Webster's head flew around so swiftly that it could easily have torn from his neck and tumbled across the room. A cry of fear was lost deep in his chest as his bloodshot eyes raised to familiar gray-black ones. The tall, slim form of a man wearing blood-stained buckskins moved hauntingly down the length of the room. "My God . . . Cole Donovan!"

But no. No! It could not be. Webster buried his face in his hands and shook it fiercely. He had to relax. He was asleep and having a horrid nightmare. He drew in short, deep breaths, stilling the pounding of his heart, trying to quiet the violent tremors of his body. When he was sure he had accomplished that, he peeled his face from his palms and looked around.

Darkness. Nothing was there but the shadows of night. Throwing back his head, Webster laughed until tears filled his eyes and his chest heaved with pain. "You've got to stop drinking so much, you bloody fool!" Then he fell to his bed and forced himself into unconsciousness.

Because she had scarcely eaten a bite of her evening meal, Diana now felt the rumblings of hunger in her stomach. She hadn't been able to eat because she was lonely for Pine Creek, her son, and all her good friends. She was especially lonely for Cole and felt the masculine essence of him nearby, warming her, bringing a smile to her

355

mouth and a glow to her cheeks. Only a few embers crackled in the hearth, and she buried herself down into the covers to warm herself. "My darling, my love," she whispered, closing her eyes, feeling, she was sure, the gentleness of his breath against her cheek. "Where are you on this cold and lonely night?"

When no answer was forthcoming—and certainly, she did not expect one—she let her mind wander back to that terrible day when the men had brought the lifeless body of Cole Donovan back to their peaceful little settlement of Pine Creek. It was a day never to be forgotten. She shuddered as she remembered her piercing scream of horror. She remembered the hatred she had felt for the Seminole woman—the only survivor of the renegade band. Diana had never thought she could hate so deeply. Two women—Black Face, strangely tamed by the loss of all her Seminole comrades, and Polly McFadden—were destined to spend the rest of their lives at Pine Creek and remind her of that tragic afternoon. The gentle English captive, Polly, was due to give birth to Oclala's son any day. The other was pregnant, also by Oclala.

Diana lay quietly in her bed, feeling guilty for the bitter feelings she harbored against Polly, who had certainly not consented to being the captive of the vicious renegades. Her husband and her little daughter had been murdered during one of Oclala's killing sprees, and she had that horrid memory to carry with her for the rest of her life. Polly was a kind woman, carried her weight in the settlement,

356

and had many times expressed her sincere gratitude to Diana for her friendship. After the birth of her child, she and Jim Duncan planned to be married. Jim loved Polly, but he was opposed to the idea of being considered the sire, by law, of Polly's Indian bastard, although he had agreed to assume paternal responsibilities for the child.

The other woman, Black Face, was another story. While she had caused no mischief in Pine Creek thus far, no one trusted her. She had been assigned one of the empty cabins and had made herself quite useful at the loom. She had, though reluctantly, traded in her men's garb for the simple cotton dresses worn by the other women of the settlement. Because of her disfiguring birthmark, Black Face had a chip the size of a mountain on her shoulder. Callie had posed the idea to the Indian woman of taking on a more flattering name, but Black Face had staunchly refused. The name was one that her revered Oclala had given her, and she would carry it with her until her death.

Two women . . . two reminders. One day perhaps, Diana would be able to put from her mind forever that horrible day when Cole had ridden out, vibrant, full of life and loving her as she was sure no other man had loved a woman, only to be brought back to Pine Creek strapped upon a travois.

Again, Diana's stomach rumbled, a painful reminder of the dinner she had not eaten. Remembering that Mrs. Sanders had not returned to take away the tray, Diana forced herself from the warmth of her bed, donned her robe, and sat in the chair beside the covered plates. Removing them, she picked at the delicious bread and the tender beef, enjoying it almost as much as she might have when it was steaming hot.

The moonlight somehow managed to penetrate the clouds and fill the room with gray shadows. Hypnotically, her eyes lifted to those of Cole Cynric Donovan, and she felt the pang of familiarity. How could two men, born so many years apart, look so alike . . . the same classic features, dark, wavy hair . . . tall, strong builds. So different, yet so alike. Lifting her water goblet to the lifesize portrait amidst the tall mirrors, Diana whispered, "To you, great-grandfather."

"And to me?"

She had taken a swallow of the cool water, but now choked on it. Tears filled her eyes as she tried to catch her breath, coming to her feet to move about in a frantic, and rather comical circle. Then, a strong hand slapped her upon her back and she was drawn into a musky, manly embrace.

"C-Cole! What are you doing here?"

"Haunting the place," he replied, humor lacing his words.

"But you weren't to arrive until tomorrow night."

"Couldn't bear being separated from you for even a day. Sorry I gave you such a fright. How do you like my garb?" Taking her hands he spread out her slim arms, then stepped back so that she could get a full view of him.

358

Seeing the ugly, dark stain upon his shirt, she said, "It's horrible. It reminds me of the day you were killed."

Laughing, drawing her into his arms, he whispered, "Aye, my death. Tragic wasn't it?"

"Well, I won't forget it, Cole Donovan! I knew that if I returned to this musky old house you would follow me! I knew that your spirit would return to me, even if your body could not!"

"And you think this is not my body?" he teased affectionately. "I beg to differ. This body can do things to you that my spirit cannot!"

"Prove it!" she teased in return. "Take me in your arms, my love, and fill me with the essence of your being."

"Essence, my bloody eye! I've got something else in mind!" Again, her spirit, her lover, laughed his teasing laugh, picked her up in his arms and moved with her toward the bed.

Thankful to be the only occupant in the east wing of the house—the elusive Jocelyn Rourke did not count—Diana enjoyed the moments of ineffective struggle against him, sharing in his laughter, and looking forward to the passion they would share beneath the covers of her bed.

Chapter 20

Webster weaved his way downstairs the following morning and entered the kitchen area at the back of the house. Mrs. Sanders nodded but said nothing and Claudia, as usual, bowed with grand flourish, a custom Webster took as deliberate mockery.

"Girl, will you stop doing that!" Webster bellowed, immediately grasping at his pounding head. "Mrs. Sanders, bring me coffee." Silently, Mrs. Sanders poured a cup and brought it to him. Webster sat at the table, nursing the steaming cup between his palms and trying to still the violent tremor deep within him. He knew the great quantities of liquor he consumed were probably eating out his insides, but he also knew he could not stop. The stinking potation was in his blood, and the only thing that kept him from going starkraving mad in a house of madness. Taking only a few sips of the coffee, he rose calmly to his feet. "Is my mother's breakfast tray ready?"

"I have just prepared it," Mrs. Sanders replied. Webster approached the sideboard, looked over it for a moment, then took the vase containing a single late-blooming rose and set it aside. "Your mother always enjoyed the roses," she boldly reminded Webster.

"Well, she is not in a mood for it this morning," Webster replied.

"Isn't she well?" Mrs. Sanders asked, genuinely concerned, yet, in a way, baiting him.

Webster smiled wryly. "Considering her state, she couldn't be better."

He had just begun to ascend to the second floor of the house when he head the approaching Diana's steps suddenly muffled by the footcloth in the turn of the stairs. He halted his movements and waited for her appearance. Although he was still very angry with her for threatening him yesterday, he managed an expression somewhat resembling a smile. "Good morning, Cousin."

Diana gave him a dubious look. Approaching, standing on the stair just above him, she replied, "And good morning to you, Cousin. Did you sleep well?"

Only then did Webster remember his horrid nightmare. She had a strangely satisfied look on her face, and his eyes narrowed with suspicion. Could she have the power to direct the course of his dreams? "I slept very well. And you?"

"Oh, I had a bit of a distraction," she chuckled lightly. "But after that, I slept like a wee babe."

"A distraction?" Webster arched a dark eyebrow. It pleased him immensely that she might, after all, be unstable enough to see ghosts without any help from him.

"Just a little one, Cousin." She was not about to divulge that she had made wild, wonderful love to the man who planned to be Webster's worst nightmare. Her hand fell to Webster's arm as she added, "But don't you fret, my dear one." Her sarcasm was thick, like mud. "I will be just fine for the next three weeks, and then you," her hand withdrew as she chuckled wickedly, "will be out in the cold."

"As I told you yesterday, dear Cousin," Webster spat out the words, "the house will belong as much to my mother as it will to you."

"And as I told *you*," Diana replied in her sweetest voice, "I'll wager that your mother fled this madhouse years ago and hasn't been seen since. I am going to expect proof that she is even up there."

"You have no legal right."

Diana's tone did not change. "Dear Cousin, do you think I do not have my wager covered? You think about it. No one has seen my father's sister in fifteen years, except you and my Uncle Philip."

"And Claudia."

"Claudia sees ghosts. We cannot rely on her. Cousin, do you really think the magistrate will not be suspicious when I remind him that my aunt has not been seen in, what is it now, fifteen years? Oh, no, dear Cousin. Either my aunt will show herself within three weeks' time, or I will have her declared legally dead. What she would have inherited will then be mine to do with as I please. And I promise that neither you nor your father will get a brass farthing!" Webster deliberately allowed the tray carrying Jocelyn Mayne's breakfast to clatter noisily to the floor. "What a shame, Webster!" Diana continued. "You have dropped dear Aunt Jocelyn's tray. Now," leaning close to her furious, crimson-faced cousin, she whispered, "what will *you* have for breakfast?"

Then she scooted past him and moved toward the kitchen, passing Claudia who was rushing toward the stairs to clean up the mess. She had scarcely seated herself at the table when Mrs. Sanders said, "I heard you baiting your cousin, missy. You have a cruel streak. You must want your father's estate very badly."

"I couldn't care less about it. I detest Webster." Diana linked her fingers and dropped her chin to them. "Besides, you think about it, Mrs. Sanders. Have you seen my aunt in the past fifteen years?"

"No. But Claudia has."

"Has she indeed?" Mrs. Sanders did not respond. "Has a doctor ever been summoned to tend an illness? Does she have a private maid to attend her needs? Are the windows of her suite ever opened to allow fresh air? Is the hearth in her chamber ever lit on a cold night? Have you ever been asked to mend or clean her clothing? Has a seamstress ever taken measurements to keep her up with the latest fashions? Has a cobbler ever been called to make new shoes or mend old ones? Have you heard her voice in the last fifteen years?"

Mrs. Sanders shrugged, choosing only to answer the final question. "She was always quiet. What do you want for breakfast, Mrs.—Diana?"

"Whatever you've cooked will do. I'm starving."

Mrs. Sanders busied herself preparing a plate, which she soon placed on the table in front of Diana. Drawing her hands to her hips, she said, "Now let me ask you something, Diana. Why are you wearing that pretty rose-colored gown when your husband died just four months ago? Where is your somber gray? Why are you in such a happy mood today when yesterday you were brooding like a heartbroken widow? Why did I see you half-dancing through the corridor just moments ago? Why are you starving this morning when you scarcely picked at your supper?"

"How do you know I picked at my supper? My tray was not collected last evening."

"Claudia collected it this morning, while you were still sleeping."

It occurred to Diana that her chamber should not be so easily accessible to the people of Rourke House. "Your point is well taken, Mrs. Sanders," Diana replied. "Since you have seen fit not to answer my questions, then I shall not answer yours. To change the subject, I would ask that you send Tuxford for a locksmith. I wish to have a new lock put on my chamber door, with only two keys for it."

"Two keys?"

Diana smiled grimly. "In case I lose one." Taking a bite of her breakfast, she said, "Good tripe, Mrs. Sanders."

"If you like tripe," she snipped. "Tastes like swill to me."

"My goodness," Diana laughed. "You did wake up in a foul mood this morning, didn't you?"

"Harumph! Is it possible to wake up in a good mood within these walls?"

"Mrs. Sanders?"

"Ummm?"

"Why do you stay on here?"

Mrs. Sanders had been stacking pots and dishes for washing. Ceasing her movements, she turned and eyed Diana critically. "I've been here for twenty-five years. My girl was born here . . . my man died here. Who do you think will offer a house position to a woman with a mean boy like my Tuxford and an addle-brained girl?"

"What is addle-brained, mum?" Neither woman had seen Claudia enter the kitchen. She now eased the tray and dishes Webster had dropped among the others being stacked for washing.

"Put the broken dishes with the trash," Mrs. Sanders ordered, hoping her daughter would quickly forget what she had overheard.

But she did not. "Mum, what is addle-brained?"

When Mrs. Sanders did not immediately reply, Diana said, "Well, Mrs. Sanders? Doesn't your daughter deserve an answer?" Diana arose, approached the stove, and took two biscuits which she broke open on a clean white napkin. Then she filled each with a little ham and scrambled eggs, wrapped them tightly and tucked them down into the panier of her gown. Mrs. Sanders, busy composing a reply to Claudia's question, had not noticed, and Claudia thought nothing of it. Stranger things had been done in Rourke House.

"Addle-brained," Mrs. Sanders began after a moment, giving Diana an almost venomous look before returning her gaze to her daughter. "Addle-brained means you can think about many different things all at the same time. Not many people can do that."

Claudia smiled broadly. "Does that make me special?"

"It makes you very special, daughter." With that, Claudia picked up her bucket, oil soaps, and wooden box of rags so that she could do her other morning chores. A very proud smile lit her face.

"Well done, Mrs. Sanders," Diana said when Claudia had disappeared into the corridor. "You really should be much more careful what you say. One day you are going to hurt that sweet girl's feelings."

"Wouldn't mean to if I did," Mrs. Sanders pouted.

Claudia, passing Webster in the corridor, said to him in a sprightly tone, "I'm addle-brained, Master Mayne."

"I'm well aware of that," Webster replied dryly. "Go about your chores." Reentering the kitchen, Webster mumbled absently, "Strange girl, that one," then gruffly ordered, "Prepare my mother another breakfast tray." He refused to meet Diana's taunting stare.

Taking the newly prepared tray, Webster again left the kitchen. Diana, pushing her plate aside, arose and started after him. But she did not make her presence known. She trailed him in secret, up the wide stairway and into the corridor, ducking into the cover of doorways when Webster occasionally paused and looked around. Within moments he entered the east corridor, removed a key from his pocket and unlocked the door. Before he entered, he checked again to assure that he had not been followed, especially by his nosy cousin, Diana.

When he had entered the door, Diana tiptoed quickly toward it. But he had locked it from the inside. Quietly bending, she peered through the keyhole, but all she saw was Webster unlocking still another door. She caught only a glimpse of feet covered by a sheet when the inner door was opened and immediately closed. She was able to hear her cousin's greeting, "Good morning, Mother. How are we this morning?" If Webster received an answer, Diana did not hear it.

Muttering an expletive, Diana crossed her arms and moved back down the corridor. She was not sure how she would spend the day. John was not due to visit until the following day, Sunday. It was too cool to enjoy the outdoors, and the snow that had fallen the previous day had turned the ground to slush.

Thus, she turned to the attic in her hope for salvaging some good from an otherwise dreary day. She would deliver the biscuits she had taken from the kitchen to a man who was probably ravished. Peering about to be sure she was alone, she moved up the narrow stairwell toward the unused third floor, then up the even narrower steps leading to the attic. Reaching the scarred, dusty attic door, she knocked cautiously—once, then twice, then once again. The prearranged signal was instantly answered.

Opening the door just enough to accommodate her body, Cole took her arm and pulled her in. Drawing her to him, he asked, "What are you doing here? Did anyone see you?"

With a musical laugh, Diana's arms eased around his strong neck. "Everyone saw me downstairs. No one saw me come up here." Taking the napkin in which the biscuits were wrapped from her panier, she held it out to him. "Breakfast. I thought you would be hungry."

Cole's eyes narrowed in gentle perplexity. "You shouldn't take chances like this, not even to see to the needs of my stomach."

"Don't scold me," she pouted. "You must eat! Besides, if you weren't here, I would never be able to go through with the insane plan John came up with. Something else is on my mind and I want to talk to you about it."

"What is it?"

Drawing away, Diana sauntered through the many years worth of collected items scattered throughout the dusty attic, then sat on the small cot where Cole had apparently just been resting. It was still warm from his body. "Before we went away in January, did you ever see my Aunt Jocelyn? I mean, before I arrived here . . . afterwards . . . ever?"

Crossing his arms, Cole stood before her. He took a moment to think about what she had asked. "Actually, no, I never did meet the lady."

"Cole," Diana arose and approached him, easing her arms around his waist. "You know this house fairly well. Do you think there might be a way into Jocelyn's suite other than the two doors that Philip and Webster keep locked?"

"Why?"

"I just don't believe she's in there." Diana shrugged her shoulders. "I asked Mrs. Sanders about her this morning and she admitted that no one has seen or heard her in fifteen years. It occurred to me that if Jocelyn had left Rourke House many years ago, certainly my father would have asked Webster and his father to leave, also."

"And do you believe your father would have allowed fifteen years to pass without seeing his only sister?"

"If he was as bullheaded as I am, it is possible. When I hold a grudge, I hold it forever."

"But you did not hold a grudge against me."

"Ouf!" Lightly Diana hit his chest, then moved back into his arms. "That is because I fell in love with you, you wicked Scottish rogue! Now—don't change the subject. I recall Uncle Philip telling me that his wife and my father had a terrible spat before she secluded herself in her private suite."

"Diana?" The question in his mellow voice drew her gaze to his own. "We have returned to Philadelphia to extract a confession from your cousin, and only for that reason. What difference does it

369

make whether Jocelyn Mayne is or is not in those secret rooms? You do not want your inheritance, and plan to provide for your Aunt Rufina and Mrs. Sanders and her children with your share. You, as I, want only to hear Webster confess to his foul crime so that I will be vindicated and we can return to Pine Creek and our son. Now, tell your husband, why this sudden curiosity?"

"I just despise Webster. If he is hiding something sinister, then I feel I have a right to expose him for what he is."

"He could hide nothing more sinister than murder. Have you considered the effect all this might have on Philip?"

"If Jocelyn left this house fifteen years ago, Philip is as devious as his son. I want to know—I *must* know if Jocelyn Mayne is in those rooms. Why not let all the skeletons out of the closet, Cole? We have the perfect opportunity."

"If that is what you want, then I will try to find a way into the suite. But if she is in there, and if she keeps a weapon beneath her bed covers—as you did once—I don't look forward to a bullet in my gut!"

Although he had spoken with complete innocence, Diana's head snapped up, startled by the cruel reminder of his almost fatal wound. In the brief moments that Cole held her to him, she relived the agony of waiting, four months ago, and the procession of hot August days when she had feared the loss of her love and the years of loneliness in their new settlement of Pine Creek . . .

The sun had just begun its descent upon the timberline, fluid crimsons mixing with the golden glow of dusk. Mr. Bruce had arrived minutes before with the news that all the renegades, save one woman, had been killed. The people of Pine Creek hugged each other happily, crying their relief, then scattered to their separate homes to prepare special feasts for the men who were on their way back. Until much later in the evening it didn't occur to Diana that Mr. Bruce had not met her look when she'd informed him his wife and new baby were doing fine. She had been much too happy about the removal of the threat to their settlement to even consider that something might be amiss.

With John Redding for company, she had just put a hearty supper on the table when she heard the rumble of many horses entering through the gates. Tossing her apron aside, smoothing back the disheveled wisps of her golden hair, she asked John, "Do I look all right?", and without awaiting his answer, rushed out to the porch to await Cole's return. They had been married that morning in a ceremony that surely must have set a world record for haste, and she wanted only to tell Cole how very happy she was.

John gave her a moment to greet her husband alone. But when he heard Diana's frightened voice ask, "Where is Cole? Zebedee, where is Cole?" he moved quickly out to the porch where the horses had stirred up a fog of dust. Simultaneously, Diana

371

and John Redding saw the empty saddle of Cole's horse, then the travois bearing the deathly form of the man who had just that morning become her husband.

Diana froze in horror as John rushed past her and knelt beside Cole Donovan. Tearing back the thick, bloodied material of his shirt, he exposed a smooth, round hole in his right lower chest. "My God, this man is dead."

Zebedee Ward responded with husky annoyance, "He ain't dead, Mr. Medicine Man. He ain't dead."

Without even thinking about poor Diana, John shot back with equal annoyance, "Well, he might as well be!"

Her love for Cole gave Diana the strength to move her feet, though they felt like dead weights. She knelt beside John and her trembling hand moved to Cole's forehead, then traveled an affectionate path down his hairline and to his neck. "He will live," she said quietly.

Rising, John Redding took her firmly by her upper arms, pulled her to her feet, and shook her gently. "Don't fool yourself, Diana! He will not live! You might as well get that through your head right now! He *will not* live!"

Blankly, her gaze met his own. "He's going to live," she said again.

In a mixture of frustration and rage, John released her. Snapping his fingers, he ordered two men to take Cole inside. All the while he cursed the barbarity of this new region and wished he was

372

back in Philadelphia.

For two days Cole lingered between life and death. His few lucid moments were brief, long enough only for them to force a sip of water down his parched throat. If he said anything at all, it was Diana's name, and she was always beside him, holding his hand, cooling his fevered brow, dropping her head in exhaustion to the pillow beside him to snatch a few moments of rest.

Zebedee Ward had dug a grave the same day they'd brought him home. Young Byron Bruce had constructed a fine cedar coffin, ornamenting it with brass upholstery tacks removed from discarded furniture; Cole Donovan, he felt, deserved to go out in splendor. Reverend Bernard spent two days preparing the finest funeral service ever to be spoken over mortal man. Outside the perimeters of Pine Creek, Tahchee and his bravest men sat astride their horses in silent vigil.

Diana spent the early morning hours of each day making a thick meat and vegetable soup because she knew Cole would be hungry when he awakened. Indeed, when much to the surprise of everyone throughout the region he opened his eyes three days after the skirmish, he said, "Damn, lass, I'm hungry." Without betraying any signs of surprise, Diana prepared a bowl of her soup, then sat on the bed and hand-fed him.

"That was quite a nap you had," she said quietly, smiling.

Cole, extremely weak from loss of blood, had merely given her a puzzled look. "Blast, I've got a

373

headache and," Cole touched the bandages tightly restricting his chest, "this hurts. How long has it been?"

"Three days. Here," with steady fingers she brought a spoonful of the broth to his mouth, "eat this and cease your chattering, husband."

"Weren't you worried about me?"

At just that moment, John Redding, stirred from his cot by the young Bruce boy who'd been watching at the window, burst into the cabin. "Do be quiet, John," Diana said. "Cole has a headache."

John approached as if sure he was hallucinating. But Cole greeted him with a warm, if somewhat weak, smile. "I gather you have assisted my sweet lass in taking care of me?"

"That I have," John replied. "But we did not expect you to live."

Turning his head from the soup spoon, Cole took Diana's hand and held it to him. "With Healing Woman here," since arriving in the region, John had heard the legend involving Diana, "I don't think the great spirits had a chance of taking me away."

"What are you thinking, Diana?"

Rudely jarred back to the present, Diana met Cole's gray-black gaze. "You don't want to know what I was thinking."

"As long as you weren't fretting about that trivial wound I received—"

Smiling, moving into his loving embrace, Diana

replied, "Of course not! That's in the past. You are here, alive and well. You are my husband and that is all that matters." Looking around at Cole's dusty and thankfully temporary lodgings, she shuddered. "I don't like you having to stay up here. Eat your biscuits before they get cold."

"I'll eat them a little later. As for my being here, we don't want Webster discovering me in Rourke House, do we, lass? This is the safest hiding place in the house. He is too familiar with the cellar where I stayed before. By the way, did he say anything about seeing me last evening?"

"He had a rather strange look on his face when I asked him how he slept, but that was all. The oaf! He's terribly happy that you're dead."

Cole feigned shock. "I don't believe it! As close as we were, he and I?" Laughing, he added, "And I thought the man really liked me!"

"He likes you better dead," Diana laughed in return. "Now, about Jocelyn—"

Touching his mouth to Diana's warm forehead, Cole responded huskily. "To the devil with Jocelyn! I want you to stay and keep me company. Let us sit together and speak fondly of Pine Creek and our son."

"That is all fine and well, Cole Donovan!" Drawing back with a note of humor in her voice, Diana managed to give him a reproving look. "We have capers to plan! Confessions to extract!"

"I prefer confessions of love. Stay with me in this drafty old attic and I promise you will not be bored!" He grinned boyishly.

It was certainly an offer difficult to refuse. After the harsh words she had exchanged with Webster this morning, and having faced Mrs. Sanders's outspoken scorn, she was certainly receptive to a few tender moments spent with the man who was her life and love. But suppose the household should become suspicious of her sudden disappearance and conduct a search for her about the premises? Would they think to look in the attic? It was a chance she could not take.

Withdrawing from him, Diana said, "I must tell Mrs. Sanders that I have a slight headache and will rest for a little while."

"A headache! Don't pull that one on me, lass!"

Diana laughed. "You do not want them to come in search of me, do you? Cole Donovan, I don't know what I am going to do with you!"

"Promise you'll return and I won't make a scene."

The manly scent of him wafted toward her. Easing against him, she slipped her arms around his waist and held him close. "I promise I'll return as soon as possible." Offering her mouth to his searching one, she found it very difficult to leave, even for a little while.

Webster sat on the bed beside his mother and put the silver tray containing her breakfast on the large, wooden bed tray. Uncovering each plate, he sniffed the delicate aromas. "Smell that good food, Mother. That must certainly stir your appetite." Jocelyn Mayne did not respond. "Here, Mother, taste the eggs, beaten well with milk the way you like them. Not hungry?" Webster gave his mother a reproving look. "Very well, I'll try them first. There—see, I am still alive. No poison, nothing. Just eggs the way you like them. Still not hungry? I do declare, mother. Sometimes I don't know what I'm going to do with you." With a macabre grin, Webster took the lap tray and placed it on the chair. "All right, mother. I'll eat your breakfast so Mrs. Sanders will not fuss. But this really must stop. You're being terribly childish. You wouldn't want Father to be upset, would you?"

Half an hour later Webster relocked the doors and returned the tray of empty dishes to the kitchen to be washed.

Chapter 21

Diana's stealthy movement down the stairs from the attic to the third floor, then from the third floor to the second, did not go undetected by Webster Mayne, who had been searching the house for her. She had just entered the corridor floor when he suddenly loomed before her, his tall, unprepossessing appearance extracting a startled gasp from her.

"Webster, what are you trying to do? Frighten me to death?"

Webster, who had just consumed a full bottle of brandy in his mother's chamber, wryly watched his cousin draw her hand to the slim column of her neck, then tug at the high, tight ruffles of her gown. "What were you doing up there?"

"I was . . ." Diana thought quickly, lest her hesitation draw his suspicion. "This house will probably be my sole property just after the new year, and I wanted to see what was on the third floor."

"And did you see what was up there?"

"Actually, no, the chamber doors were locked." She felt comfortable with her lie, because she couldn't imagine Webster traveling any farther up than the second floor. After all, climbing the narrow stairs would take exertion and many times she'd seen Webster unable even to move from the parlor divan. But she had underestimated Webster's familiarity with the house that had been his home since birth.

"Nonsense!" Taking her in a grip strong enough to cut off the blood supply to her arm, Webster forced her back up the stairs.

"Stop it, Webster! Stop it right now!" He was hurting her, forcing her upwards so quickly that she stumbled over the dusty stairs. She tried to grab a guardrail to halt their progress, but managed only to fill the palm of her right hand with painful splinters.

In the wide, dark corridor of the third floor, Webster dragged her along, paying no heed to her angry protests. He threw open door after door, exposing bedchambers and private suites that had not been used in more than fifty years. Bedclothes and draperies hung in dry-rotted strips, and rats the size of half-grown cats scurried about the ancient carpets. Reaching the end of the corridor, Webster threw open the last of the doors, then dragged Diana into it. Pinning her against a wall, he assailed her with breath stinking of liquor, rubbing the male part of him against her slim hips. She was too shocked to scream her indignation and fear.

"You have teased and taunted me, you vicious little wood sprite," he hissed. "Cousin or not, I am going to teach you a lesson you will never forget!"

"W—Webster, let me go." Diana's voice strained, the tight restriction of her chest making it difficult to breathe. "I will say nothing about this if you will let me go now."

"Let you go?" he sneered, his right hand taking her wrists to pin them above her head, his other raking clumsily over her breasts. "No, my dear cousin! You will know what it is like to be with a real man! Not some damned Scot with a pretty face! Tell me, did you enjoy being with him? Did you whimper and moan like a lusting little harlot beneath his body?"

Diana attempted to raise her knee to the most vulnerable part of him, but he was much too close for such a movement. His reeking breath nauseated her and she tried sliding down the wall to escape him, but he would not allow it. Clumsily, he continued to molest her, trying to capture her darting mouth with his thick, slobbering lips.

Neither had heard approaching footsteps . . . Diana, because panic had deafened her . . . Webster, because lust had gripped him. Diana suddenly felt the weight of her cousin ripped from her and in the same moment she half-slid down the wall, landing heavily on her knees.

Webster caught only a glimpse of Diana's rescuer before a powerful left fist caught him full upon the jawline. He staggered backwards, tripped over a corner of the rotting carpet, and struck his head on the edge of a heavy bureau.

Diana rushed into Cole's strong arms. "H-how did you know?" she gasped.

"How did I know you were in danger?" She nodded against him, her trembling hands seeking the warmth of his jacket. "I felt it. A powerful force pulled me from the attic. I sensed your danger, Diana, as if someone—something—was whispering the warning in my ear. Did he hurt you, lass?"

"N-not really," she whispered, showing her palm. "Except for the splinters. He—Webster was going to—"

"I know, Diana. Come." Taking her in his arms, he moved with her from the room and into the dimly lit corridor. "I will take you to your chamber and we'll get those blasted bits of wood out of your hand."

"We cannot risk it. Someone might see you."

"I will be careful," he promised.

"But Webster—"

"Webster will be out for a while. He reeked of drink, and," only now could Cole manage a smile, "he's probably got a sizeable lump on his damned head."

Diana enjoyed the protection his arms afforded her. He carried her, as if she were weightless, down the narrow stairs, pausing just long enough to ensure that the servants were not about, then eased into the recess of her doorway and pushed the door open with his foot. He gently put her upon her pillows, then knelt beside her.

"Let me see your hand." Diana showed him the injured hand. Cole wet his finger to wipe away the tiny droplets of blood, then tenderly extracted the larger of the splinters from her palm. When she cringed, he asked, "Did I hurt you?"

"I'm just a big baby," she replied, pointing to one of the small, swollen areas near her thumb. "This one looks deep. Shall I fetch a needle?"

"Show me where to look and I shall fetch it."

"The blue basket, over there by the chair." Cole

had just reached the basket when a knock sounded at the door. Alarm marked Diana's face, but Cole very calmly moved through the glass doors into the sitting room and hid himself at the side of an armoire. "Who is there?" Diana asked.

"Diana, the locksmith is here," Mrs. Sanders called through the door.

"Already?" Hopping from her bed, Diana tucked her injured hand into the pocket of her gown. She approached the door, then opened it to Mrs. Sanders and a small, thin man carrying a wooden tray.

"Show him what you want," Mrs. Sanders said. "I will be down in the kitchen tending to my chores." She turned to walk away, but instantly turned back. "Have you seen Master Mayne?"

Diana felt her cheeks suffuse with color. "No, I haven't," she lied. "Perhaps he went for a ride."

"Tuxford would have known," she said. "He's the one who saddles the horses. Never mind. I'll send Claudia to look for him."

The locksmith made a quick examination of the door, then said to Diana, "Do you want to keep others out of here while you're away, or do you simply want to lock yourself in?"

"I just want to lock myself in," she replied.

"Good! Then one of these will do." Taking two brass locks from his wood tray, he showed them to her. "Which would you prefer?"

"The pretty one," she said, pointing to the one on the right. "Will it take very long to install it?"

"Just a few minutes, madam."

"I'll wait in the alcove until you're finished. Oh,"

turning back, she added, "I want the only two keys to this lock."

"As you wish," he replied absently, taking out a carpenter's measure.

Diana entered the sitting room and closed the glass doors. "Where are you, Cole?"

"Here," he whispered huskily, stepping from the cover of the armoire and standing at a point where Diana could see him, but the locksmith could not. "I don't like hiding like a blasted rat." Though he had just rescued her from a fate worse than death, his words struck a discordant note. They were doing what had to be done, and Diana was not happy that he had complained. After all, his life was as much at stake as hers. He was the one who could still go to the gallows for a murder he had not committed.

Cole must have read her thoughts. Without speaking a word, the softening of his eyes drew her to him. Caressing her arms tenderly, he said, "Forgive me, lass. This is much harder than I thought it would be."

"I know," she whispered, her anger mellowing against the warmth of him. Her face was like a book; Cole could see that something else was bothering her.

"What is the problem?" he asked.

"Webster."

"What about him?" When his voice grew louder, Diana's finger touched his mouth, her eyes darting to the door where the locksmith worked. "What about Webster?" Cole asked again, though more quietly.

"We didn't check him. Suppose he's—dead?"

"Webster dead? No such luck. His skull is probably as hard as his heart."

"Still, when the locksmith finishes, perhaps you should go check on him."

"If you wish." Pulling her body firmly against his own, Cole murmured, "But right now, I am hopelessly stuck here in your sitting alcove, beside your bedchamber, away from the secret doorway among the mirrors. How can I possibly escape?"

"Escape? Cole Donovan, one would think you don't enjoy my company," she teased.

"I don't enjoy it. I lust for it, Diana Donovan."

"Madam!" With a small cry, Diana pried herself loose from Cole's arms. "Madam, the lock is installed. Do you wish to inspect it?" As a highly irritated Cole Donovan crept back into the shadows of the armoire, Diana closed the glass doors and approached the locksmith. "Will it do, Madam?"

Diana made a show of inspecting the lock, pretending she knew what she was doing. As far as locks went, it looked fine. "May I have the keys?"

"Then it meets with your approval?"

"It is fine. The keys?" When he dropped two brass keys into her hand, she asked, "And these are the only ones that fit this lock?"

"They are."

"You're sure?"

Disapproval stained the little man's thin face. "Madam, I have no reason to lie. These *are* the only keys."

"Very well. See Mr. Sanders downstairs for your fee."

384

"I, madam, have other chores about the house. Good morning."

As soon as his clipped footsteps began to descend the steps, Diana closed the door and tried one of the new keys in it. Only when she tried unsuccessfully to open the door did Cole approach from the sitting room.

"There is something you did not think about, Diana," he said.

She turned, smiling her warmest smile. "I have thought of everything!"

"The doorway behind the mirror."

Laughing, she replied, "That one is necessary for you to come and go at will."

"Did it occur to you that Webster is also familiar with that entry into this room?" It hadn't, and Cole could see that the oversight embarrassed her. "We'll think about that later. First, I had better see if your cousin is still among the living. I'll go out through the mirrors."

Quickly closing the distance between them, Diana moved into his arms. "Will you return?"

"To what, Diana? A woman stalked by her cousin? A woman who has to install locks because she is so frightened. A woman . . .," he deliberately paused over the words, "so obsessed with striking out at her only living family that she has left her son a thousand miles away?"

His words stung, because he knew how much she loved their son, the expression of their mutual love. Diana felt her eyes moisten, her mouth tremble. Yes, she was obsessed. Her only cousin had killed her father, then had allowed an innocent man — who

385

was now her husband—to be blamed. She was obsessed with seeing justice properly served. Cole was angry. Didn't he remember that he had much more—his life—to lose? But she could not allow herself to be moved by his need to strike out. Lifting her chin, she took Cole's hand. "You asked what I want you to return to, husband. I want you to return to this." Lifting his hand to her mouth, she kissed each finger in turn, then took both his hands and lowered them to her breasts. "And these. Return to me and to the love I have for you. I will not dwell on your cruel words. Think what you will. Return to me, Cole, because no woman can love you as I do."

With tears moistening his own gray-black eyes, Cole drew her to him. "Forgive me, lass. I simply do not want to be in this house."

"I know, love. I know."

Reaching out his right hand, Cole flipped the latch on the mirrored door. "I'll check on that blasted cousin."

"Try not to hurt him."

"I'd like to kill him."

"I'd rather the hangman did that."

Kissing her briefly, Cole disappeared through the door into the darkness of the interior stairwell. Diana then turned toward the corridor, unlocked the door, and moved swiftly toward the kitchens in search of the locksmith. She could use that second lock after all.

Webster began to stir. He sat up and clutched his

aching head, trying to remember what had happened. He had gone down to the kitchen to fetch his mother's breakfast tray. He remembered sitting on the edge of her bed and her stubborn refusal to eat. What had happened then?

He sat against the bureau and tried to focus his gaze in the unfamiliar semi-dark chamber. Was he still at Rourke House? He felt strangely sober and couldn't remember the last time he'd felt like that. It wasn't his preferred state, and he resolved to guard against its happening again.

Webster might have continued sitting on the floor all morning if a huge rat hadn't scampered across his boot. He didn't favor being devoured by the vicious beast and any little friends it might summon. As he reached the door and turned around for one last look at the chamber, his memories of the morning came flooding back. He smiled wickedly, imagining that Diana had already taken news of his aggression to the others of the household, possibly even to John Redding. Well, he would have to deal with that later. For now, he had unfinished business with his dear cousin.

But the confidence with which he descended the stairs to the second floor quickly waned. How had Diana extracted herself from his clutches when he had wanted only to reduce her to a whimpering, pleading shell of a woman?

Damn! That man again! That blasted nightmare that refused to relinquish its hold on his very soul! Cole Donovan! Tightly clenching his teeth, Webster was determined that he would not allow himself to be persecuted by a dead man! Pain wracked his jaw.

Rubbing the wound, he wondered where it had come from. Certainly it could not have been inflicted by his weak young cousin. He must have hit himself when Diana had escaped from him.

Moments later he charged into her bedchamber. "Diana, you—" But she was not there. He backed out somewhat humbly, showing more life as he moved swiftly down the stairs than he'd shown in months. Mrs. Sanders was in the kitchen making preparations for the noonday meal and did not look up when he entered. "Where is my cousin?"

"In the house somewhere," she replied noncommittally. "You'd best be letting her alone."

"Why? What did she say to you?"

Mrs. Sanders only now looked up from the iron stove. "Is there something she should have said to me?"

"N-no, of course not. Where in the house is she?"

"The locksmith is here and about. She is in search of him." Webster pivoted straight into the path of the agile Claudia, catching himself before colliding with her.

"Blasted girl!" he mumbled, darting past her.

He searched the house and the grounds for half an hour and did not find Diana. Finally, faced with the temporary delay in his plans, he had Tuxford saddle his gelding. Perhaps a jaunt to his favorite inn would lighten his black mood. He had not gotten what he wanted from his beautiful, if somewhat vixenish, cousin. Perhaps one of the comely tavern girls would be more receptive to his attentions.

* * *

Diana had narrowly missed her cousin at every turn. She had been all over the grounds, eventually locating the locksmith at the smokehouse. She thought it rather strange that the cumbersome lock was being installed there, until Tuxford, sneaking up on her from behind, informed her in his gravelly voice, "Urchins been sneakin' up here and stealin' the meat."

"I see," she replied. "Did anyone think about giving the poor things something to eat?"

"Do that, Miss—Mrs. Donovan, and they'll be linin' the road expectin' handouts. Best to let 'em starve."

"If you were one of them," she quipped tartly, "you wouldn't feel that way." The big, burly man laughed as he turned and reentered the stable where a carriage horse patiently waited to be shod.

"You want something, madam?" the locksmith asked, scarcely looking up from his work.

"I have another lock to be installed upstairs. Will you return there when you've finished here?"

"I will," he replied.

"Soon?"

The gentleman gave her a haughty look. "As soon as I am finished here!"

Feeling herself properly reprimanded for her impatience, Diana returned to the house, then entered the library and chose a book from the many shelves. She waited half an hour until she heard the locksmith's voice. Arising, moving toward the back of the house, she soon escorted him up the stairs to her private chamber. He stood at the door when she entered and gave her a puzzled look.

389

"Sir, are you going to enter?"

"There is only one door, madam, and I have installed a new lock."

Diana drew her hands to her slim hips. "Sir, do you think I am going to seduce you?"

"Madam!"

Diana's fine eyebrows arched upward as she fought a grin. Keeping her voice as serious as the situation warranted, she explained, "You are exasperating me, sir. Forgive my boldness. But if you will but enter my chamber, I will show you where I need the lock." Oh, if only she could be so cruel as to make him face the mirror. She would show him that he had had absolutely nothing to worry about.

Cautiously, the locksmith stepped inside the doorway. Diana crossed the room, then easily swung the secret door open. "This is where I want the second lock installed, sir. I do not fancy the idea that some nefarious intruder," she did not, of course, refer to her husband, "might use this dark, dreary stairwell to enter my bedchamber. You, as a gentleman, must certainly understand my concern."

"Madam," the little man crossed the room and dropped his wooden tray of tools and locks with a dull thud. "Man does not question the motives of women. Men like to be rewarded with answers. Therefore—"

"You are not daring to generalize about women, are you?"

"Madam," he explained with exasperation, "I would not be so bold. Now," flicking his wrist in quite an outrageous manner, he said, "go on about your business, while I do mine."

Diana was more than relieved when the aggravating gentleman finished his work, gave her the keys, and departed from Rourke House.

Scarcely had she tried her keys in the lock than Cole's tall, dark form appeared from the cellar stairwell. "Locking me out?" he asked, arching a dark eyebrow. Cole had a strange look on his face such as she had never seen before, almost a look of fear.

"Hardly," she laughed, hoping to erase that strange look. Taking his arm, she invited him through the doorway. "I'm locking Webster out so that you and I can be alone." Without really meaning to, Cole had evaded her effort to establish intimacy. His head was a maze of thought; his eyes narrowed, their gray-black softness suddenly becoming a deep, impenetrable black. "What is the matter, Cole? Are you still angry with me?"

"No." Shrugging off her inquiry, Cole took her arm and coaxed her to a small divan. "I've gone all through the passages inside the walls. I don't know why I didn't remember it, but every room in this house is accessible through those passages . . . except one. Jocelyn's suite has been bricked up at the top of the stairwell."

"Recently?"

"No, the mortar is old, cracking in places. I would say the job was done about the same time Jocelyn isolated herself in her suite."

"Could you hear anything through the wall?"

"I thought—" Cole visibly shuddered. "I thought I heard humming, but it was strange, haunting. A chill crept over me like I have never felt before. God help me, I was afraid, Diana . . . afraid of the atrocity behind that wall. I took off from there like a startled pigeon."

"Do you think my Aunt Jocelyn is mad?"

"I don't feel it in my heart. It is more than that."

Diana, too, shuddered. "Cole, you are frightening me."

"I don't mean to, lass." Taking her in his arms, Cole gently massaged her back. Feeling the gentle trembling of her body against his own, he was truly sorry he'd frightened her. He wanted desperately to be vindicated in the death of Diana's father, but at the moment he wanted only to return to Pine Creek with Diana and rejoin their little son.

He had thought John Redding's idea, posed to him last July, a rather macabre one, and if he'd had any sense about him, he and Diana would have remained in Pine Creek where they were safe. John had admitted that no one except he and a man named Pipps, whom he trusted beyond a shadow of a doubt, knew Hogan Linford had gone to the gallows in Cole's place. Cole should have been happy with that.

But could he truly be happy in life knowing that all of Pennsylvania believed him to have murdered the gentle Standish Rourke? Could Cole be happy at Pine Creek knowing that Webster Mayne would live in luxury made possible by the wealth of his uncle, the man he had killed?

No! Justice had to be served. Cole knew he would give his life for vindication. He did not, however, feel comfortable with the precarious position Diana had put herself in. That she was in mortal danger filled him with shame and guilt. If he had not intervened that morning when Webster—

Again, Cole shuddered and his grip became almost vise-like around Diana's slender frame.

"What are you thinking, husband?"

"I am thinking that I will be glad when all this is over."

"Do you miss Drew?"

"Indeed, I do. He is part of us, born of our love, Diana. But I understand that we have ends to tie up here. Webster cannot get away with murder." Enjoying the warmth of his embrace, Diana hesitated to bring up the matter of Jocelyn Mayne. But she and Cole had become kindred spirits; he could almost read her mind. "And I have not forgotten about your aunt. One thing at a time, lass."

Just at that moment a knock came to the door. With a startled cry, Diana hopped to her feet. Then, remembering her interior lock—and the two keys in the pocket of her gown—she breathed a sigh of relief.

"Yes, who is it?"

"Mrs. Sanders. You did not have lunch, so I brought you up a tray."

"Bless her heart," Cole whispered. "I am starving."

Bringing up one of her keys, Diana approached and unlocked the door, then opened it just enough to take the tray from Mrs. Sanders. "Thank you for your kindness."

Diana started to push the door shut, but Mrs. Sanders put her hand up. "Everything all right, Diana?"

"Everything is fine. Is there anything else, Mrs. Sanders?"

"Just want to apologize for being tart this morning."

"Don't apologize, Mrs. Sanders. I wasn't very nice myself."

The older lady smiled. "You'll be down for dinner this evening?"

"Yes, I'll be down."

Because Mrs. Sanders was peering around the door, Diana again attempted to close it. "Are you sure everything is all right, Diana?"

"It couldn't be better. Webster has left the house, hasn't he?"

Her smile was warm and friendly, rather than cold and obligatory as usual. "Indeed. The house will be peaceful for a while."

Only when she again began her retreat did a thought come to Diana. "Mrs. Sanders?" She turned back. "When both Webster and his father are away, who tends to Aunt Jocelyn's meals?"

"Claudia does. She's the only one the Maynes will allow in with Jocelyn. They say she prefers it that way."

"Oh, I see."

"Any more questions, Diana?"

"No . . . thank you again for the tray."

Nodding, Mrs. Sanders moved quickly down the corridor, lest Diana's curiosity delay her once again.

Chapter 22

Diana and Cole shared the ample meal Mrs. Sanders had brought to her bedchamber. As they feasted, they also shared happy reminiscences of Pine Creek and speculated on the time that would be required to trap Webster in his own devious game.

The new locks gave Diana a sense of security. She knew she would be unable to bear the gloominess of Rourke House if Cole could not come to her private chamber at will. His presence made her feel less alone, and less in danger at the hands of her murderous cousin. She felt secure in the knowledge that, wherever she was, Cole would be watching her and protecting her from all evil, as he had this morning on the third floor of Rourke House.

Collapsing onto the bed and clasping her stomach melodramatically, Diana moaned, "Oh, I did eat too much! Imagine Mrs. Sanders bringing all that food for me to eat alone!"

"Thank God she did," Cole chuckled quietly, easing himself atop her, "or I would have had to gobble you up, lass. That is how hungry I was."

Smiling mischievously, Diana replied, "I am still willing to be dessert."

Wrapping his finger through her loose, golden hair, he gently nipped at her chin. "Are you indeed? Well, I don't see how I can pass up an offer like that. Where should I start? Here?" Teasingly, he nipped at her right ear, "Here? Or here?" Imprisoning her willing mouth against his own, Cole tasted the wine-sweetened nectar of her lips, lingering, touching, teasing her soft skin with playful nips. He moved across her chin, down the smooth column of her neck, until his tongue plunged into the cleavage created by the tightness of her gown. Using his teeth to unfasten the tiny bow holding the garment together, his hands cupped the smooth, roundness of her breasts, massaging them almost roughly between his palms. "I think I have found my dessert," he continued huskily, his mouth trailing kisses downward, his hands easing the fabric of her gown down her arms until she was bare and lovely beneath him, and vulnerable to his masterful explorations.

"Would you rather I relieved myself of my garments?" Diana offered with a taunting smile. "Or shall I cover myself and bask in the safety of my blankets?"

"Try it," he threatened without malice, "and I shall rip your blankets asunder. These blasted garments clinging to my desert are about to meet just such a fate." Without prelude, and almost with urgency, Cole's hands eased beneath her garments and traveled a path across the flat plane of her stomach. Her hips rose, making it easier for him to remove her skirts. Cole studied her full, sensual form as if he were seeing her for the first time . . . flawless ivory skin, a tiny waist blossoming into womanly hips, smooth, long legs that did not hesitate to draw up against his maleness.

"Now that I am free of my garments, shall I free you of yours?"

Without hesitation, Cole jumped to his feet, outstretching his hands. "I am at your disposal, lass. But," taking a step back, he almost laughed the words, "you must come to me this time!"

Diana sat forward, watching him with feigned horror as she held a blanket to her nakedness. "Cole Donovan! You come here this instant and please me!"

"Come to me, lass." He smiled wickedly. When she arose, still clutching the blanket, he whispered, "Without that damned thing. I want to see you full in the moonlight . . . all of you . . . all the treasures that are mine."

Coyly, Diana stood there for a moment, trying to see how securely she could wrap herself in the blanket. But, enough of teasing him when all she wanted was to be with him! She casually let her covering fall to the floor and stood before him, uninhibited, secure in his attraction to her, even now. Her body certainly did not betray that she'd given birth to a child two months ago. His look pleased her and oh, so slowly, she moved toward him.

Deftly, her fingers rose and loosened the tie of his shirt. She enjoyed the tightly controlled pleasure in his features as she removed the garment, then caressed his strong chest, trailing her fingers over his taut nipples, lower, the index finger of each hand meeting and trailing a path together downward to the waistband of his breeches. She never let her cool gaze wander from his amused one.

How amazed Cole was as in the next few moments her wild, wicked passions and bold caresses reduced him, almost, to a whimpering thing scarcely resembling a man. His wonderful, painful arousal threatened to unfoot him. "God!" he whispered huskily. "Where did you learn to please a man so?" Taking her arms, he roughly pulled her up from her knees and against his heavily breathing chest.

"From you . . . only from you. Besides, it is not just any man I please," she whispered, breathless with desire and anticipation.

Picking her up as easily as he might a child's doll, Cole moved with her toward the bed. "How do you make me feel like this, Diana?"

"Like what?" she asked, tracing her fingernails around his waist and to his firm buttocks. "My darling, I don't know what you are talking about. I am an innocent, and you—poof!—you are a seducer of my innocence."

Cole's gray-black eyes ran over her face, her sweetly pouting mouth coyly turning upwards into a smile, the slim column of her neck and the gentle pulse there, the pale rosebuds of her breasts that were just enough to fill his seeking hands. The maleness of him pounded with exultation, wanting her so deeply that he could not bear further prelude. With a husky groan, he lifted her knees and

398

positioned himself between her warm, soft thighs. Need raked his firm body as he impaled himself upon her, immediately capturing the tiny moan that escaped her mouth, feeling the gentle arch of her hips as she sought desperately to fill herself with him.

Almost as though the world were contemplating coming to a halt, Cole's mouth moved in slow motion between her mouth and her breasts, to capture each in turn, all the while his hips moved gently against her, filling her with his manhood. A groan came from deep within his throat. As his movements intensified and she easily matched his rhythm and pace, his caress of her mouth became frantic.

Diana did not feel the coolness of the winter night; she felt only the warmth emitting from their wondrously entwined bodies and enveloping the entire room in their passion for each other. She did not hear the distant sounds of the city; she heard only the sweet murmured endearments Cole whispered against her ear. She saw not the shadows dancing about the large chamber; she saw only the light dancing in Cole's magnificent eyes—the light of the love he felt for her.

A hot flush engulfed her as the spasms created by his wickedly wonderful movements elicited a tiny moan from deep within her. He delved into every secret crevice, causing her to lose all concept of time. Where was she? Back in Pine Creek, the happiest place on earth? Who was she? Diana Rourke Donovan, the luckiest woman who had ever been born?

She saw, heard, felt only the good in her life. Nothing could harm her as long as she lay with Cole, their legs entwined, their hips undulating, expressions of ecstasy straining to escape in one long, shared breath as she welcomed the thrust of his tongue. Their breathing became hot and quick as their passions reached the pinnacle and the blissful torment reached a fevered intensity. Their bodies exploded together in equal, potent release.

Afterwards, their bodies clung together in sweet, unforgettable exhaustion. Diana smoothed back the damp strands of his hair clinging to his forehead. "I adore you," he rasped hoarsely.

"And I adore you, my love," she whispered.

"May I sleep with you tonight?"

"I see no reason why not. That is what the locks are for."

"To keep me prisoner?" he chuckled, his hands gently enfolding her sweet, cherubic face between them.

"I could do that without locks," she boasted teasingly. "The locks are to keep out foes, not to imprison my obsession . . . you, my love. Now—sleep beside me all through the night. We shall dream together of Pine Creek and our darling son."

That was certainly an invitation he could not pass up. Cole's eyes closed against her softness, his hands searching across the flat plane of her body toward her hip to pull her to him. Diana nuzzled his neck, comforting herself in the arms of her husband through the long night.

They were not, however, prepared for the godawful scene that later erupted from the stairs. Webster stumbled over each step, cursing, slamming his fists against walls with such jarring force that several portraits fell noisily and clattered their way to the footcloth.

A curse escaping his own lips, Cole swung his feet to the floor and hastily began dressing. Diana scooted from the bed and across dark, cold chamber to fumble in the armoire for a bed gown and robe.

Cole had just pulled on his boots, shirt in hand, when Webster beat upon the door. "Damn you, Cousin! Why have you locked me out?"

"You must go out through the mirrors," Diana whispered in dire haste. "He cannot catch you here."

"I do not want you confronting him. He is, undoubtedly, drunk."

Even as they spoke, Mrs. Sanders was trying to reason with him in the corridor. But her effort merely met with brutality. She cried out as Webster's palm struck her face, sending her staggering to the floor. Instantly, the sound of her retreating footsteps reverberated through the second floor.

"I will not stand for this!" Diana hissed. "Please, let me take care of him, Cole." Approaching the bureau, she removed a small caliber pistol. "If he threatens me, I will kill him!"

Cole's strong hands gripped her arms. "I will not stand here and argue with you. Webster himself has created a perfect opportunity."

"What do you mean?"

"Get in your bed and snuggle down in the blankets. I'll greet Webster at the door."

"But Mrs. Sanders—"

"I heard her retreating footsteps. If I hurry, I can get to Webster before she brings Tuxford up here to control the bastard."

"But—"

Cole's eyes flashed angrily. "Do as I say, please!"

Diana shrugged. "Very well. But . . ." She simply had to get a final word in. "I don't like it!"

The heavy, bolted door reverberated beneath Webster's striking fists. He continued to scream, "Open this door, Cousin! Damn you, open this door!"

Diana positioned her trembling body beneath the covers as Cole had ordered. It was really rather ridiculous to feign sleep considering all the noise Webster was making, but she did her best. Only when she became still did Cole use the key Diana had given him earlier to unlock the door.

He stood aside as a surprised Webster found the door giving way. His cousin's covered form, illuminated by the dim moonlight, drew him toward the high tester bed. Just as Webster moved out of the path of the door, it gently closed.

Cole had stepped back into the shadows. Webster turned, his bleary eyes seeing nothing but a foggy blur of a human form. Whether it was a man or woman, only God would know. "So, little cousin, you would attempt to trick me, eh? What do you have there?" sauntering with the cocky assurance his drunken state should scarcely have allowed, he sat upon the bed. "Pillows piled end-on-end beneath your covers?" His eyes never left that vague, shadowy form.

402

Diana drew in a deep breath and held it as Webster's hand closed over her waist. Feeling her body beneath the covers, Webster quickly rose, his widened eyes darting between the shadows of the room and the covers. Diana sat up. "Webster, what are you doing in my room? How did you get in here?" The cocky sureness waned. Webster found that any words he might have spoken would not form on his tongue. As Diana sat forward and rubbed her eyes, easing her hand beneath the covers to be sure she still had her weapon, Webster tried to focus on that shadowy illusion in the corner of the room. When she was sure her pistol was still at hand, Diana reached over and turned up the lantern. "If you somehow managed to get a key to my lock, Webster, give it to me!" she demanded. "And I warn you, I have a pistol."

Her words might have been whispered to the wind. Webster's full concentration was on the man suddenly illuminated by the lantern. Shaking his head, then rubbing his eyes so briskly he was sure they'd pop into his skull, he finally managed to whisper in stunned disbelief, "Cole Donovan."

Cole stepped forward. "Don't ever . . . ever threaten my wife again!" he whispered.

"You—you're supposed to be dead."

Cole smiled the most macabre smile he could manage. "I am dead!"

"Who are you talking to?" Diana demanded.

Webster spun around, almost losing his footing. "You lied to me! You lied to all of us. John said that—" He spun back, but the corner was empty. Sucking in a ragged breath, his beady eyes darted around the room, but he saw no sign of Cole Donovan.

Fear caused Diana's eyes to moisten with tears, even though she'd watched Cole move discreetly among the furnishings by the wall of mirrors and knew he would not be far away. She'd seen his hand come up to unlock the door so that he could step behind it. With smooth sureness, Diana brought the weapon up from the covers of her bed and balanced it on her drawn-up knees. "I don't know what you are trying to pull, Webster Mayne. But I suggest you remove yourself from my bed-chamber. And never mention my dead husband's name again!"

Ignoring her threat, Webster dashed across the room and started to open the secret door. But although Cole had unlocked it to make his escape, the door jammed. No force on earth could have forced it open, and Diana took advantage of the stroke of luck. "I had a lock installed there, too, Webster. You cannot get into my chamber. Now," she held out her left hand. "Give me the key you just used on my chamber door."

"I—I have no key. The lock can only be opened from the inside. Your husband opened it—"

Suddenly, Tuxford appeared in the doorway. "Mrs. Donovan, I will take him to his chamber."

"No!" Webster screamed. "Her husband is some-where in the house. I demand that you find him!"

"Cole Donovan is dead," Tuxford reminded him. When Webster balked, Tuxford used force to re-move him from the chamber, but not before Web-ster got in a final threat.

"I swear I'll find him, Cousin! Do you think I do not know what you're doing?"

As the big, surly servant forced Webster from her bedchamber, Mrs. Sanders entered. "Are you all right, Diana?"

Putting down her pistol, Diana hopped from her bed. "Don't worry about me. Are you all right? I heard Webster hit you."

Mrs. Sanders attempted to hide her bruised cheek. "It isn't the first time."

"But it will be the last," Diana promised. "Shall I prepare a cup of tea for you?"

"I had just brought a cup up to my room," she said. "I am sure it is still hot." The older woman's hand fell to Diana's arm. "Thank you for your concern."

Diana stood and watched her disappear down the stairs, then quickly closed and locked her door. Had she been a convincing enough actress? Had she shown proper despair so that Webster would believe he really had seen the illusion of the man he hated? But something else came to mind. Cole had unlocked the secret door to step behind it. Why hadn't Webster been able to open it? Approaching the door, Diana's hand went out, but before she could touch the latch that would pop it open, Cole emerged from the darkness of the stairwell on the other side. She gave a small cry of alarm.

"How did you manage to relock the door so quickly?" Cole asked.

"I didn't. It must have jammed."

"There's no way it could jam, Diana."

405

A chill crept across Diana's shoulders. "Perhaps," she hesitated, immediately releasing a small laugh. "No, of course not."

"I know you, Diana, and I know what you are thinking," Cole replied, frowning. "Credit whomever you will. Just thank God the door jammed when it did."

"Cole?"

"What is it, lass?"

She moved into the warmth of his arms. "I want this to be over."

"So do I, my love. I do miss our wee bairn."

"Soon," she whispered. "Soon it will be over and we can go on with our lives."

Webster resisted Tuxford every step of the way toward his bedchamber. But the big man proved too strong for him, and Webster could not break the stranglehold Tuxford had on his neck. He was out of breath by the time Tuxford slung him toward his bed.

"How dare you treat me like this!" Webster hissed.

"You're drunk, Master Mayne," Tuxford responded. "A swill deserves no better treatment."

"I'll discharge you!"

Tuxford laughed hoarsely. "After twenty years of doing your bidding? I hardly think so. Tomorrow you won't even remember what happened tonight."

Webster struggled to his feet and his shaking fingers closed around the lapels of Tuxford's wool jacket. "I will, Tuxford." But his anger with Tuxford diminished as he thought of other more important things. "I saw him, Tuxford. I saw Cole Donovan in my cousin's chamber. I demand that you find him! Find him and bring him to me!"

Tuxford peeled the bony fingers away from his coat. "Master Donovan is dead. I've never known John Redding to lie."

"Except this once!" Webster argued, his eyes wide and blood-red, like a madman's. "He must have lied. Cole Donovan is in this house. He is trying to drive me mad!"

"You are already mad, Master Mayne. The swill is making mush of your brains."

"You are discharged, Tuxford!"

Again, the burly servant laughed. "Sure, Master Webster. And tomorrow you'll have me doing your bidding as usual." Shoving Webster back into his chamber, Tuxford turned to leave, then asked across his thick shoulder. "Do you need assistance preparing for bed?"

"You can bloody well go straight to hell, Tuxford!"

Tuxford scratched his head thoughtfully. "Can't very well do that now, can I? Who would saddle your horse when the taverns call your name?"

"You are insolent, Tuxford."

"I am your protector, Master Webster. I am the one who knows what you did, and what you are hiding."

The calmly delivered words managed to halfway sober Webster. "What do you mean?"

"See how short your memory is? Did you not have me guarding Cole Donovan while he engaged in deception against your young cousin? Do I not know the secret of your mother's private suite?"

"Wh—what do you mean?" he stammered again.

"Claudia is not nearly as daft as you think she is. Aye, she sees ghosts, to be sure, but sometimes her words can not be discounted. She has talked to me about things she sees and things she hears, and I am able to distinguish between truth and the ravings of a simpleminded girl. I think you're going to need me, Mayne."

Never before had Tuxford called him simply by his name. But at the moment that was the least of Webster's worries. "You will help me, won't you, Tuxford?" Desperation clung to his words.

Tuxford grinned maliciously. "For a price, Master. Aye, for a price."

John Redding had never for a minute doubted that he could trust Philip Mayne. He was well aware that there was something strange going on in the house that Philip was hiding, but he believed in his innocence insofar as his brother-in-law's death was concerned. Therefore, he had not hesitated to send word to Jersey when he'd learned that Diana would be returning to Rourke House. He prayed that Philip had received his message and was on his way back to Philadelphia.

The following morning he took the short walk to the livery and had his carriage readied for the journey to Rourke House. He had promised Diana on Friday that he would take her to church on Sunday, and to hell with what Webster Mayne had said. He hoped to arrive early enough to enjoy one of Mrs. Sanders's delicious breakfasts, and he certainly would not let any confrontations with Webster deprive him of that prospect. Claudia answered his knock at the front door, then led him to the parlor. But John Redding was not one to be bashful.

"I hope your mother has a good meal prepared, Claudia. I am famished."

"She has prepared your favorite, Dr. John," Claudia replied gaily. "Shall I seat you in the dining room?"

"While you are informing Mrs. Donovan that I am here, I shall see my way back to the kitchen."

"As you will, Dr. John," Claudia acknowledged, bowing perfunctorily.

John moved toward the kitchen and soon greeted Mrs. Sanders. Strangely, she did not face him, though she did smile warmly. "Have a chair at the table, Dr. John. I'll prepare a plate for you."

"Mrs. Sanders?" Still, she did not face him. John Redding left his chair and approached her, only to have her turn her face from him. Taking her chin, he forced the older woman to meet his gaze. Studying the ugly black welt on her cheek, John frowned. "Did Webster do this to you?"

"He did," Delicately, she removed her chin from his fingers. "But he was drunk as usual."

"Don't make excuses for him. I'll send over a salve this afternoon. Blast the man!"

"It's not the first time this has happened," she reminded him.

"It'll be the last time, Mrs. Sanders."

Mrs. Sanders met John's angry gaze. "That is just what Diana said." Her face pinched in a moment of thoughtful silence. "What are the two of you cooking up, Dr. John?"

"Peace in this house, hopefully. You needn't worry about it."

Just at that moment, Diana entered the kitchen, wearing a light gray wool dress with black trim, a hat, and gloves to match. She had pulled her hair up, with tight ringlets on the side, and her cheeks were flushed. John Redding thought her extremely pretty this morning.

"Have you eaten, John?" she asked.

"Not yet. Join me?"

"Mrs. Redding did not accompany you?"

"She has gone on to church with her mother and the children. Now—about breakfast."

"Of course." Gracefully, Diana removed her gloves, then sat at the table. "Do you mind, Mrs. Sanders, if we don't sit in the dining room? It is so much cozier in here with you . . . and much warmer."

"It pleases me that you are more comfortable here," she replied, bringing plates to both of them.

"How is your wound this morning?" Diana asked.

"A little sore. But Dr. John is going to send over a salve."

When Mrs. Sanders went about chores in other parts of the house, John said to Diana, "If Webster arises before we leave, he'll be in a fit."

"Why is that?"

"When I brought you here Friday he said you

410

were not to venture from the house even to attend church with my family."

"He has no right to control my life. I come and go as I please."

John smiled broadly. "That, my dear, is exactly why I did not listen to him."

In Mrs. Sanders's absence, Diana told John Redding what had happened the night before. He listened while he ate his breakfast. "Webster is getting extremely bold, Diana. We may have to bring our plan to a speedy conclusion."

"But is everything ready?"

"I pray Philip is on his way back from Jersey. I am awaiting his return."

"But suppose he protects Webster at any cost? After all, he is his only son."

"Philip would not condone murder, Diana."

Diana's mouth tightened. She placed her fork on the edge of her plate and turned her questioning eyes to John Redding. "John, have you seen my Aunt Jocelyn since she isolated herself in her chamber?"

"No, I haven't. She was always a healthy woman."

"Don't you think it is strange that she would confine herself for fifteen years and that no one, save Webster, Philip, and poor Claudia, has seen or heard her in all these years?"

John, too, set his fork aside. "I said Jocelyn was a healthy woman. She was a physically healthy woman, but her mental state left a lot to be desired. I have seen this before, Diana, especially in women. Jocelyn, unable to face life in an outside world, has created her own little world between the walls of her private suite. She has lived there, and she will probably die there."

"If she isn't already dead."

John choked on a morsel of food. "What do you mean, Diana?"

Diana shrugged her delicate shoulders. "After we have extracted a confession from Webster, I plan to demand a court order for the appearance of my aunt before her inheritance is cleared. I do not believe she is in this house."

John argued, "But Claudia mentions her moods at times. She is quiet, she is grouchy, she is feeling down."

"And Claudia sees ghosts," Diana reminded him, rising. "Come, let us depart for church before Webster comes down and makes a scene."

John, too, arose. "We have things to discuss." So that only Diana would hear, he asked, "How is Cole?"

"Homesick for Pine Creek. He is as anxious as I am to return to our son."

"Hopefully," John took her arm and guided her toward the foyer and the front drive where his carriage awaited, "that will be soon."

Laughing, Diana asked, "Anxious to be rid of us, John?"

"Heavens no! I am merely looking forward to the many summer jaunts to Pine Creek I will enjoy!"

The air was cool. Diana pulled her gloves back on, then took John's hand as he assisted her into the carriage. The bells of the Lutheran Church began to peal across the quiet horizon as the carriage wound over the winter-rutted road toward Philadelphia.

Diana looked up, catching a glimpse of Cole at the attic window.

Chapter 23

They'd been in Rourke House for two days and
this was the first time—even though she was with
another man—Cole had felt that Diana was truly
safe. He was further relieved when, not ten minutes later, Webster Mayne rode away from Rourke
House in the direction opposite that which led to
town. The stables were abustle this morning; Tuxford readied a smaller carriage and drove his
mother to her own church.

That left only Claudia in the house, which created the perfect opportunity for Cole to search for
some other way into Jocelyn's suite. And, Cole
frowned, this would keep his mind off his wife's
being with another man, even if it was something
as innocuous as attending church with a hundred
other people.

Cole left the attic and moved down the narrow
stairwell. He'd pulled on the tailored boots he'd
purchased in Philadelphia last year, rather than his
soft-soled buckskin boots, and his heels slipped methodically over the bare wood floors of the third
floor. When he reached the stairs and began his
descent, he heard Claudia's voice. "Who is up
there? Master Donovan?"

Cole had no doubt that she was referring to Diana's great-grandfather who had died many years ago. The young servant girl who talked to the ghosts of the house had been the subject of many conversations. "Aye, it is," Cole replied. Even though he did not hear Claudia's retreating footsteps, he continued his descent of the stairs.

When he moved from the shadows of the stairwell and into her path, she smiled, undaunted by his appearance. "Oh, it is you, Master Donovan! I didn't think it would be long after the mistress's arrival that you would show up. And a good thing you did! Master Mayne has been a bit of a rogue lately, terrorizing the mistress."

"Aye, so I've heard, Claudia." He eyed the tray she carried. "Where are you going with that?"

"To Mistress Jocelyn. She gets rather snippity if I'm late with her breakfast."

"May I accompany you?"

Claudia's eyes widened in surprise. "No, indeed! Master Mayne would have my hide."

"Webster is thoroughly reprehensible."

Claudia cocked her head to the side, a puzzled look marking her youthful face. "If that means he's not nice, I certainly agree, sir."

Cole turned on the charm. "You will let me accompany you to Jocelyn's chamber, won't you, Claudia?"

"Certainly not. Besides," she chuckled good-naturedly, "You don't need permission, or doors. You can come and go as you please. That must be the only advantage of being dead."

Stifling a chuckle of his own, Cole waved his

finger. "But I am not that kind of ghost. I *must* use doors, or I would have a bloody nose."

"Don't tease me so, Master Donovan! I have known your kind for much too long."

"And suppose, Claudia, that I said I would haunt you if I did not get my own way."

Despite the burden of the breakfast in her arms, Claudia managed a hearty laugh, caring not that the delicate chinaware clattered on the silver tray. "Master Donovan, I enjoy the ghosts of this house. I am special. Ghosts do not appear to everyone, you know. Mum says I'm special in many ways. Why," seriousness marked her brow, "I am even addle-brained. Mum says so herself! Go on about your business, sir, and might I say, you are one of the most pleasant ghosts of this house."

Thank God the girl was like a whimsical child. Cole did not take to the idea of her feelings being hurt as, indeed, they would be if she knew what the innocently delivered description of herself truly meant. But Cole merely smiled and nodded his appreciation at her kind words. Then he watched her move lightly down the corridor. He had no intention of allowing her to enter Jocelyn's suite by herself. When the key turned in the lock, he would be right behind her.

When Claudia rounded the corner toward the east wing and Cole heard the key turn in the first lock, he moved slowly along the wall. Standing at the corner, he watched her look over one shoulder, and then the other, before entering the antechamber of Jocelyn's suite. He had just moved toward the corridor door when the key to the second door

416

turned, but when he started to step into the chamber he heard the foyer door open on the floor below.

"Mrs. Sanders . . . Claudia?" Cole instantly recognized the voice of Philip Mayne. "Is anyone about?"

Gritting his teeth, cursing Philip's untimely return home, Cole crept back along the second floor corridor and up the stairwell to the third floor. Within moments he had locked himself in the attic, yet he could hear Philip's slow footsteps on the stairs.

Claudia, having set the tray down, met him in the corridor. "Welcome home, Master Mayne. I was just taking breakfast in to the mistress."

"My niece," he queried. "Is my niece here?"

"No, Master Mayne. She has accompanied Dr. Redding to church. She left only a few minutes ago. Would you care to take the mistress's breakfast tray in to her?"

Philip did not like this ugly game. Weary from his long ride, he managed to reply, "No, Claudia, you take the tray in to her."

"Shall I tell her you'll be in to see her shortly?"

Philip smiled weakly. "Yes, of course, you do that, girl." He turned to descend the stairs. Since Tuxford had not met him at the stables, he felt it was his duty to unsaddle and feed the reliable mare that had brought him home. First, he turned back. "Is my son here?"

"He rode out a little while ago," Claudia replied. "He didn't say where he was going." Claudia turned to complete the routine morning chore that had

417

long been assigned to her. Pivoting back, she said, "Master Donovan is in the house, sir. I saw him a few minutes ago."

Philip halted, gripping the stair rail. Sometimes the whimsies of the servant girl annoyed him. "Yes, I know you see your ghosts, Claudia. It does no harm."

"He wants to protect his wife."

Philip's gaze shot up, connecting with the innocent eyes of the serving girl. "What do you mean? His wife?"

"Mistress Diana's husband. He is here in the house."

"Indeed." Philip managed a small smile. Of course, Claudia would want to add the latest of the Donovan dead to her list of unseen residents. "Give him my best when again you see him."

"Yes, I will, Master Mayne. After I see to the mistress, I will prepare breakfast for you."

"I am not hungry."

"As you please." Claudia disappeared around the corner to Jocelyn's suite.

When Tuxford had brought him the short message that morning, Webster had immediately arisen from his bed, despite the pounding in his head. He should have liked to berate Tuxford for the events of the previous evening, but the message was urgent. Webster could not imagine what Martin Pipps had to see him about. After all, his "excellent leads" of the past few months had resulted in futility, not to mention the fact that the investigator had conspired with John Redding. Diana had returned to Rourke House without the assistance of Mr. Pipps, who would have all of Philadelphia—indeed, all of New England—believe that no man could match his skills in the investigative field. Though he claimed to have found Diana, he had not produced one shred of evidence that he had accomplished that task.

Webster dismounted at the Coleman Tavern, a distance of seven miles west of Rourke House. Being that it was Sunday, no liquor was being sold, but the tavern matron was offering breakfast to her visitors. Feeling his way through the smoke-filled tavern, Webster joined Pipps at a corner table and took a chair across from him. He declined the glass of milk offered him.

"For what reason have you summoned me, Pipps? Need more tales to carry to John Redding?"

"You owe me a considerable amount, Mr. Mayne. I have trapped your quarry."

"What do you mean?" Webster frowned devilishly.

"Your cousin. I know where she is. Our agreement was that when I had this information, you would pay the other half of my fee."

"I thought we had covered all this before." Webster's right foot came up to rest on his left knee. His arms crossed. He resisted the snarling smile resting just behind the sarcastic facade of his gaunt face. "And where, may I ask, is my young cousin?"

"You will pay the rest of my fee?"

"If you give me the right answer," Webster replied, baiting the investigator.

"I have located your cousin in a new settlement

just across the border from Virginia. The land registrar's office informed me that two men named Zebedee Ward and Cole Donovan filed homestead claims on behalf of nearly a dozen families. Your cousin—" Pipps' grin was filled with professional pride, "is living at this settlement. She had married the Donovan fellow, but he was killed. It is called Pine Creek and is almost due west of Roanoke, Virginia in the colony of North Carolina."

Webster linked his fingers and brought them to the back of his head. Pressing his mouth into a thin line, his eyes raked over the short, stocky gentleman's ruddy features. "So, this is the information that has taken you these many months to compile? You say my cousin is living at this settlement in North Carolina? And now . . . I am to pay you the other half of a promised fee?"

"Of course. I have worked a long time on this. I have put my other cases on hold and have given you my undivided attention."

Webster had leaned back in the straight, ladderback chair, but now the legs hit the wood floor with an alarming thud. Other men looked up from breakfast plates to eye them chastisingly. "You'll not get a blasted penny from me, Pipps! My cousin is not at Pine Creek, North Carolina, as you probably bloody well know from talking to John Redding! The only thing I have to thank you for is confirming that Cole Donovan is dead!" Why had Webster said that? The dreams, the blasted dreams he'd been having. Perhaps he would be able to deal with them knowing they were just that . . . horrid, disturbing nightmares. Hastily, he continued, "My

420

cousin—" His voice had grown alarmingly loud, drawing the attention of the tavern matron, who now tapped her foot disapprovingly. Webster quieted his voice. "My poor, widowed cousin returned to Rourke House on Friday. You have probably not even traveled further than John Redding's house!"

Pipps had to rely on his acting abilities now. He jumped to his feet, his hands balled into fists to relay an appropriate indignation. "How dare you question my integrity, sir! I was told in this settlement of Pine Creek that Diana was living there! I was told this by many people, including a Zebedee Ward and a young man named Byron Bruce. What reason would they have to lie to me, I ask you?"

"If you thought she was there, why did you not wait around to see her, to convince her to return to Philadelphia?"

"That is not what you asked me to do!"

"That is exactly what I asked you to do."

"You asked me to locate her for you, saying that you would take care of getting her back to the city!"

"That is a damn lie! Besides, man, what use is this conversation? My cousin is back at Rourke House where I want her."

The portly matron approached, rubbing her hands on a filthy apron. "You gentlemen don't hush your argument and I'll have to ask you to leave."

"I am leaving," Webster quipped rudely. "This place stinks like a pigsty!"

Pipps and Webster took the argument outside.

Although the investigator had, indeed, never been to the community of Pine Creek, he knew enough about it from John Redding that he felt he knew the place inside-out. "I will be paid, Webster Mayne," he said on a note of finality. "Or," Pipps was rather enjoying the dramatics, "I will be forced to divulge a confidence."

Webster drew in a deep breath. "I have confided nothing in you that the whole of Pennsylvania does not know."

"I know that you killed Standish Rourke."

"That is not true! You are bluffing."

"I have a witness who saw you! Now . . . will I be paid for my services?"

"No, you will not!"

"Very well." Pipps untied the reins of his horse. "The authorities will be interested to know who that person is. I will give you time to think about it, and I would suggest that you give serious consideration to the balance of my fee. Not only will I divulge the name of the witness, but I will inform the authorities that the body in the grave of Standish Rourke's murderer is not that of Cole Donovan. Don't you think, Mr. Mayne, that the prison guard will spill his guts when confronted by the proper authorities?"

Webster's gaunt features paled. "I don't know what you are talking about."

"But you do, sir. Why do you deny it now when you admitted it to me before? You are the one who arranged the exchange at the Walnut City Jail. Wouldn't it be a shame if it came out now, when your mother is about to inherit half of her brother's fortune? Tell me, Mayne, how many creditors are waiting for payment?"

Webster had no doubts that Pipps knew what he was talking about. He had been backed into a corner and now would have to take drastic measures to extricate himself from the mess he had created. Pipps was threatening to divulge information that could jeopardize Webster's financial future . . . indeed, his very life.

"I must know who else knows about this, Pipps."

"Only one other person."

"John Redding," Webster mumbled. He and John had been adversaries for as long as they had known each other. He would have to deal with both men, in his own way. "Very well, Pipps. Meet me at the stables of Rourke House tonight at eleven. You will be paid then."

"Why so late?"

"Because," Webster gritted his teeth, "I do not want anyone to see us together. After this evening, I don't ever want to see you again!"

Pipps mounted his horse, then leaned toward Webster. "Don't worry, Mr. Mayne. You will never see me again."

"And you will keep your mouth shut!"

"Indeed," Pipps drew his fingers to his forehead in a mocking salute. "I will never breathe a word about this to anyone."

"Do you know for a fact that John has spoken to no one but you about this?"

Pipps grinned sarcastically. "I know that for a fact, Mayne. He has too much respect for your father."

"Then why did he tell you?"

Again, Pipps grinned. "Every man has to tell someone his secrets. John and I have known each other for many years."

As Pipps rode east toward Philadelphia, Webster stood rooted to the ground for several minutes, his knuckles drawn to his teeth. He was so deep in thought he did not realize he'd drawn blood until it trickled down his hand.

He reached the stables of Rourke House shortly before noon. "Tuxford! Tuxford!" The man emerged from the darkness of a stable he was cleaning. "I'll need you tonight."

"For what, Master Mayne?"

"To dig a grave in the darkness of the timberline where it cannot be seen."

"I told you before, I will not kill for you."

"You would have killed Donovan!"

"No," Tuxford replied. "I threatened him, but I would never have killed him."

"Damn you, man! You dig the grave and I'll do the killing!"

"You've done it before. It should be easier this time."

"You just have that grave prepared by eleven o'clock tonight."

"I'll have to go to work on it now. Your father—"

"He has returned?"

Tuxford nodded. "Your father has requested that I do work on Dr. Redding's roof this evening. Seems the rain is comin' in."

"Isn't it a tad cold to be doing roof work?"

"The weather is why he needs it done."

"You have that grave prepared before you leave. Over there," Webster pointed toward the thick underbrush by the creek. "That'll be a good place. And," Webster threatened, "you'll say nothing about it to anyone. Ever!"

"I never do," Tuxford replied. "You know that."

Diana was sitting in the parlor of John's home, sipping a cup of tea and chatting pleasantly with his wife, when Pipps knocked at the door. Diana rose and took the man's hand when John introduced them. Rosa Redding discreetly moved to the kitchen so that her husband could conduct his business.

"Did he meet with you?" John asked.

"He did. And I do believe he's planning to kill me tonight. He asked me to meet him at the Rourke stables at eleven o'clock. As you directed, I let him think that you are the only person who knows about his heinous acts. You are probably next on his list."

"After tonight, we will not have to worry about that."

"You will have the proper authorities there, John? I don't fancy having my throat slit by this greedy swill."

Diana could certainly understand the investigator's need for reassurance. Webster had proved himself to be dangerous, and Pipps had gone beyond the call of duty to ensnare the man in his own trap. But a thought came to her. "And what about Tuxford?" Diana reminded the gentlemen.

425

"He is always at the stable. If he realizes a trap is being set for Webster, he will warn him."

"I have that covered. I've spoken to Philip about having Tuxford do some work on my roof tonight. Even now he is probably informing him."

"So that's why you left church early? You were expecting my Uncle Philip?"

"Yes, I knew he would arrive back home this • morning."

"How did you know?"

"Because I sent to Jersey for him."

"Does he know what is being planned?"

Shame washed John's features. "No, I'm afraid not. Webster is Philip's only son. I could not ask a father to conspire against his son. Philip is not a strong man. I do not wish to burden him unduly."

"And where does Cole fit into this?" Diana asked, worry pinching her brows.

"He doesn't. Not this time. Mrs. Sanders informed me that Webster has purchased ammunition for his pistol. I don't want to take the chance of your husband being hurt."

"And what about me this evening?" Pipps asked with some indignation.

"You'll be safe. Mrs. Sanders is replacing the powder Webster purchased with a harmless black herb. His weapon will not fire."

"John, I don't like this," Diana said, shuddering.

John arose from his chair and approached the divan to sit beside Diana. He took her hand and held it fondly between his own. "I have worked on this plan for almost a year, Diana, since your letter was slipped under my door on a cold January

426

night. Why this sudden apprehension?"

"Perhaps because Webster is family—"

"He is a murderer!"

Shrugging, Diana consented, "I suppose it is necessary. Webster should not get away with killing my father."

"And, hopefully, he will not accomplish the task of killing me this evening," Pipps interjected. "I rather value what is left of my life."

Diana took up her handbag and arose. "John, will you drive me home now? I wish to speak to my husband."

John, too, arose. "Very well. If everything goes smoothly this evening, Webster will be locked up tomorrow and Cole will be exonerated."

"Then there will be only one problem left to solve," Diana said quietly.

"And what problem is that?"

"My Aunt Jocelyn."

Diana had expected Cole to be a little angry at the change in plans. But he did not like the game he was playing and was noticeably relieved. It was stupid and senseless and only a fool—such as Webster Mayne—would fall for ghosts. The whole purpose of his charade was to extract a confession from Webster. If the fellow Pipps, John Redding, and the Philadelphia police authority could accomplish that this evening, then more the power to them. Cole just wanted the ordeal to end so he and Diana could leave Philadelphia.

Unfortunately, Webster had been suspicious of

Diana's frequent visits to the attic of Rourke House. Shortly after speaking with his father about affairs in Jersey, he had followed Diana up the stairs, watching from the shadows of doorways as she constantly looked over her shoulder. When he heard the attic door close, and then her voice commingled with the very familiar one of Cole Donovan, he knew instantly what they had been up to. He had listened while Cole and Diana had discussed the plan devised by John Redding and Mr. Pipps to trap him into confessing to the murder of his uncle. He heard everything.

Plans had to be changed; schedules reworked. Webster knew it was simply a matter of time before he was taken into custody for the murder of Standish Rourke. That Sunday, just two days after Diana's return to Rourke House—and the secretive return of her "dead" husband—he felt the burden of defeat. The Rourke fortune was lost to him; he would be foolish to believe otherwise.

But was it lost? He could turn this nasty affair to his own advantage. He had only to think clearly and act rationally. If he limited his intake of liquor, he felt that he was capable of both.

Strangely, Webster was unusually cheerful at the evening meal. He chatted pleasantly and did not scowl at the servants. Afterwards, Diana retired to the parlor to ply her needlework with Mrs. Sanders, and they chatted until well past ten o'clock. Then Webster appeared at the parlor door and asked Diana, "Join me in a sherry?"

"No, I . . ." What was he up to? she wondered. He did not usually speak so cordially to her. Per-

428

haps she should reconsider. "Very well. Just don't try my patience," she said. She had changed into her funereal black, suitable, she felt, for what would happen that evening. "But if you touch me in any way . . ." She left the threat hanging.

Webster laughed. "You really must forgive me, Diana. When I am drinking I do things that a prudent man would not do."

"You do things when you aren't drinking. And you are *not* a prudent man."

Undaunted by her rebuttal, Webster poured two sherries and offered one to his young cousin. "How could I possibly do things when I am not drinking? Thank God, I am seldom in the boring state of sobriety."

"That may very well be true. Tell me, Cousin, is there something you wish to discuss with me?"

Sipping his sherry, Webster replied, "Cousin, I merely wished to apologize for the harsh words that have been exchanged between us, for my drunken attack of you last evening which, thank God, you did not report, and to offer my deepest condolences for the death of your husband."

She did not understand the wry smile he attempted to hide behind his hand. "And I wish to thank you, Webster."

"Whatever for?"

"If it hadn't been for your treacherous nature, I might never have met Cole Donovan and we might never have had our few short months together."

"Then treachery is good for something, is it not?"

Diana took a little sip of her sherry. She studied

it carefully to be sure there was no suspicious white residue in the bottom of the goblet. "I wouldn't want to go that far." Setting down her goblet, Diana managed a small smile. "I must retire, Webster. I rose rather early this morning."

"Good night, Cousin."

As Diana moved up the stairs toward her bedchamber, worry creased her brow. Webster's actions were terribly suspicious. She wasn't sure what to think. She wanted to go straight to Cole, but she did not want to take the chance of having Webster follow her there.

She did not dress in her nightclothes. For the next few minutes she stood at the window facing the stables—thank God, Webster's chamber did not—and watched the shadows of half a dozen men taking positions in and around the stable. She had snuffed the light in her lamp so that the men would not witness her silent vigil at the window. She was afraid, more afraid than she had ever been.

She knew how desperately Cole wanted to join the men. But until Webster confessed to the murder of Standish Rourke, Cole's guilt was still presumed. Without Webster's confession, not only would Cole be held accountable for the murder of her father, but also that of Hogan Linford, who had gone to the gallows in his place. This was a very important night in their lives.

Diana still could not understand why John was so confident that Webster would confess tonight. Mr. Pipps had set himself up to be killed by a man who wanted desperately to keep his past

430

crimes a secret. To gamble that Webster would take pleasure in confessing to her father's crime, just before killing Mr. Pipps, was a terrible chance to take. She had seen fear in the face of the investigator that morning at John's home in Philadelphia. Why did any of them think that Webster could be prevented from killing Pipps, regardless of how many men lurked in the shadows?

Not only was Diana fearful for the life of Mr. Pipps, but she felt a little sad, also. Webster would be caught in his murder and treachery, and his father and mother would lose their only son. She would be glad when the night was over.

A rap sounded at the secret door . . . one . . . two . . . then one again. Taking the key from the vase where she had hidden it, she unlocked the door. Cole stepped into the room. His face was dark and brooding. "What is the matter, Cole?"

"Webster is leaving the house."

"The men are prepared?"

"They are."

Diana moved into his arms and held him tightly. "It'll soon be over, Cole. Webster will, at Pipps's prompting, admit that he killed my father. Why shouldn't he? He is intending to kill Mr. Pipps anyway." Oh, she did want to believe he would confess; however, that tiny spark of insight she'd always felt she possessed warned her that things might not go according to plan.

"We hope it goes that way," Cole replied to her question. "With Webster, one can never know what he will do."

Diana enjoyed the strength of Cole's hands going

around her, holding her gently, yet commandingly, his breath sweet against her forehead, his body firm, yet trembling against her own. Somewhere in the house a door opened, then closed almost too quietly to be heard. Boots clicked on the corridor floor, then began their descent of the stairs, across the foyer. The front door opened. Diana could almost feel the cold air rushing into the house, yet it was impossible to feel any breeze from the foyer at this great distance. Perhaps it was the chill that had crept over her.

"Soon," Cole soothed her against him. "Soon it will be over."

Chapter 24

Due to the heavy darkness of the December
night, Webster moved cautiously into the stable.
Tuxford usually kept a lantern burning and Webster did not like his absences, infrequent as they
were. He expected Pipps to be along any moment
and stood in the darkness, watching the hazy, overcast night block the moonlight. His eyes had
scarcely focused in the darkness before footsteps
sounded behind him. He pivoted smartly on his
heel.

"Mayne, do you have my money?"

Webster drew in a deep breath, aggravated by
the man's persistence. "Blast it, man, you startled
me! Do not worry about your money."

Pipps couldn't help but notice Webster did not
have a weapon with him. His eyes narrowed in the
darkness. Did he, perhaps, have a knife concealed,
or worse yet, a poker to bash his head in with? He
stood a good ten paces from Webster. "I asked you
if you had the balance of my fee."

"And I said, do not worry about it. There are
more pressing things to concern us now."

"And what is that?"

Webster's hands went out, putting Pipps even

more on guard than he already was. But he merely gestured as he stuttered dramatically, "It's Donovan . . . Cole Donovan . . . he's in Rourke House. I heard him speaking to my cousin! You must go for the police. The man is dangerous!"

"Cole Donovan is dead," Pipps replied quietly. "Now, where is my money?"

"You are not placing your priorities sensibly, Pipps! If you will not go for the police, then I will!"

Pipps berated himself. How could he and John Redding have been so wrong about Webster Mayne? They had expected attempted murder; they had expected a confession. And here the man stood, demanding that the police be fetched because Cole Donovan—the man they were trying to exonerate—was in Rourke House. "Mayne, are you drunk again?"

"Damn!" Stumbling in the darkness, Webster moved toward the tack room. "If you will not ride into Philadelphia, then I will!"

"No!" Webster could not possibly have seen the disappointment in the investigator's face. "I will go. You return to the house and I will be back as soon as possible."

"Good! I thought you would see reason." Webster moved briskly toward Rourke House, very aware that half a dozen men had positioned themselves in and around the stables. When he disappeared into the house, John Redding and the police constable moved from the shadows of an empty stable.

"You told me I would hear a confession of murder," the police constable, Mr. Douglas, said.

"And I thought you would!" John Redding shot back. "I do not know what Webster Mayne is doing, but I assure you he is the man who killed Standish Rourke."

"Well, I have no proof of that. As I reminded you earlier, a man was hanged for Mr. Rourke's murder. The same man, I vaguely recollect, Mr. Mayne said was now in that house."

John Redding was not about to confirm that information. He had to buy some time. "I've made a mistake, Mr. Douglas. Please return to town, and forgive me for taking you and your men away from their families on this cold, dreary night."

"Perhaps I should check the house, just to be sure—"

"No!" John had not meant to speak so sharply and immediately softened his voice. "As you are aware, Mr. Mayne is a notorious swill. I wouldn't put much stock in what he says."

"I will check the house," Douglas reiterated, the finality in his voice leaving little room for further argument. John's heart sank. How had such a perfect plan gone so awry? And how could he beat the persistent Mr. Douglas to the house so that he could warn Diana and Cole? Before he could find an answer, Douglas ordered his men, "Advance toward the house, cover the entrances. You, Jennings, accompany me indoors to conduct the search."

Within moments the men had converged on Rourke House. Horrified, Diana had watched their approach and rushed up the attic stairs to warn Cole. When the door came open, she was in Cole's arms almost before he could rise from his cot. "Something's gone wrong, Cole. The men are approaching the house. Webster returned first, and I believe I saw John and Mr. Pipps speaking. And now the constable and his men are coming to the house."

Panic tightened in Cole's chest. He gripped Diana's arms firmly. "Return to your chamber. If it is me they are looking for, I believe I can evade them. Please, return to your chamber and act as though nothing is wrong. Can you do that?"

Tears moistened her eyes; her body trembled violently. "I—I believe I can, Cole."

"Then go, lass. I'd better hurry to the third floor where I can get through to the interior walls." Shaking her gently, he continued, "You must act as though you are still the grieving widow. Damn, I knew something like this would happen! We should never have left Pine Creek."

Cole's harshly spoken words shamed her. Besides clearing Cole's name, she had also been concerned about inheriting the Rourke fortune so that her Aunt Rufina would not have to work so hard. "Perhaps we should have stayed in Pine Creek, always wondering when someone would come for you," she said quietly, her feelings hurt. "Could we have lived like that, Cole?"

"No, no, of course we couldn't have, lass. Come—I need to get within the walls before the men reach the house."

Leaving the attic, Cole and Diana moved swiftly down the narrow stairwell. Diana stood guard at the top of the stairs and watched as Cole disappeared into one of the rooms down the corridor. Then she crept downstairs and soon entered her own bedchamber. John would have expected her to remain dressed so she did not feel required to don her nightclothes. When she heard men's voices downstairs, commingled with that of Mrs. Sanders, she moved to the first floor and joined the group. She managed to look perplexed.

"What has happened, John?"

"Did Webster return?"

"I have not seen him since he left the house," she said, looking across John's shoulder toward the much taller Mr. Douglas. "What is the matter?"

"I am here, John." Webster emerged from the darkened parlor, his right hand clutching the delicate stem of a goblet containing brandy. "My friend, Mr. Pipps, rides quickly. How is it that he had the time to bring you and the authorities in answer to my summons within the matter of a few minutes?"

"We are here. That is all that matters. Please," a note of urgency hastened John's words, "tell Mr. Douglas that Mr. Donovan cannot possibly be in this house."

Crossing his arms, Webster smirked ruefully. "He *is* in this house, John. I would first check the attic. You will find evidence that he has been residing there."

Without warning, Diana charged toward him to beat on his fragile chest with her balled hands. "How can you be so cruel, Webster? My husband is dead—" Diana caught her words, but it was too late. Mr. Douglas frowned dismally. Cole was supposed to have been imprisoned even before Diana had arrived in Philadelphia a year ago; she could not even have known the man. And now she was claiming him as a husband? Her theatrics, her innocent need to protect him, would mean her love's undoing. She could tell, looking into the bland eyes of the police constable, that she had made a fatal mistake. "I mean—I don't mean that he is my—what I meant to say . . ." Oh, did it do any good to stammer denials? Those bland eyes warned her that her words were wasted.

"Where is he?" Constable Douglas asked.

"I don't know what you mean? I am under a great deal of stress."

"The lady *is* under stress," John interceded. "She did not know what she was saying."

"She is not under stress," Webster argued. "She is a liar. Cole Donovan is in this house. The treacherous man somehow managed to get an innocent man—a dying man—to go to the gallows for him, and he took my poor cousin against her will. He forced her to—" pressing his mouth into a thin line, he continued with haste, "he compromised my poor cousin's virtue. Now he has returned to this house to reclaim her. I heard his voice today, in the attic of this very house. And I want him caught! Don't you, Cousin?" Though he did not smile, Webster enjoyed those final words as he shared a look with Diana, then met the inspector's gaze. "The man is in this house. Find him. Take him away before I must deal with the fellow myself."

"I shall ask the lady to come to headquarters so

that we can discuss Mr. Donovan," Douglas said dryly.

"But there is nothing to discuss," John argued, taking Diana to his arm to hold her comfortingly.

"I insist," Douglas continued.

"There is no need."

Diana turned so quickly she felt dizzy from the move. Her mouth parted in horror. "Cole . . . Cole, you must flee." Rushing to him, she attempted to pull at his arm. "Please, you must flee!"

But Constable Douglas had already raised a loaded weapon at the young man who had so casually entered the foyer. "Are you, indeed, Cole Donovan, the man tried for the murder of Standish Rourke?"

"I am, sir. Take me into custody and you will be told the whole story. But I beg you, take my wife into protective custody. She is not safe here."

"I have seen no evidence of that."

John stepped forward. "Diana, pack a few things. You will lodge at my home for a few days."

Mr. Douglas called his man, Jennings, forward. The man carried manacles that had originally been intended for Webster Mayne. "Shackle him."

"There is no need," John argued.

"I said, shackle him."

Frantic, tears spilling down her cheeks, Diana rushed into Cole's arms. "No! No, you have no right. He has done nothing. Webster killed my father. Not Cole!"

Cole drew her to him, caring not that now half a dozen men had responded to the loud voices in the foyer. "It'll be all right, lass. Mrs. Sanders?"

The older woman came forward, sniffing back tears. "Pack a bag for my wife so that she may move to safety. John?" Cole's dark gaze moved across Diana's trembling shoulder. "Take good care of her."

In the next few minutes, Cole was shackled and led away. Webster stood to the side, gloating in his own wickedness, and a fragile and weeping Diana sat on the divan with John Redding, waiting for Mrs. Sanders to pack some clothing and necessities for her stay in town.

"How has this happened, John?"

"I don't know. Could Webster have overheard you speaking with Cole?" It did not matter that Webster stood at the liquor cabinet, pouring goblet after goblet of raw whiskey down his throat and listening to every word they spoke.

He felt extremely cocky now that the police had departed with a most unexpected quarry in tow. "Of course I overheard, John. I heard my cousin telling good old Cole Donovan everything about your plans today. And now," raising his glass in mock toast, he boasted ruthlessly, "I will look forward to seeing your husband, dear Cousin, go to the gallows . . . again!"

As Diana slumped in quiet defeat against his shoulder, John hissed, "You're a bastard, Webster Mayne!"

"That I am, Dr. Redding. That I am."

"Where is your father? I wish to speak to him."

"Father?" Again, Webster favored them with one of those wry smiles. "Father dipped a little too heavily into the laudanum. He probably will not awake for a day or so."

"You drugged him?"

Throwing back his head, Webster laughed. "Why, John Redding, would I do such a thing to my own father?"

"Yes," he answered shortly.

"How astute you are! Now, please excuse me. I have an errand to run."

Mr. Douglas had been questioning Cole for hours. He was within stone walls at the Walnut Street City Jail, with several doors between him and freedom, and yet Douglas kept him shackled. His wrists ached, his back ached, his eyes were so heavy with exhaustion that he could scarcely think straight. And yet Douglas kept asking the same questions over and over until Cole thought he would go mad.

"I told you, Douglas, I did not kill Standish Rourke. He was a good man and a friend. I saw Webster kill him. And it was Webster who bribed a guard right here at this jail to substitute a dying man—a Mr. Hogan Linford—for my life."

"And why would he do this?"

Striking his fists on the small wooden table in frustration, Cole yelled hoarsely, "I told you! So that I could assume the role of Diana's great-grandfather and try to frighten her. To be declared insane and institutionalized is the only way she could lose her inheritance!"

"And what was the guard's name?"

Drawing his trembling hands to his forehead,

Cole replied, "I don't know. How many times do I have to tell you? I don't know his name."

"You were in jail a few weeks. Surely you must remember the guard. If a man had assisted in saving my life, I would have the common courtesy to remember his name."

Cole clutched madly at his temples. He must try to remember so that the interrogation would end. He felt desperate. The guard . . . damn! Why couldn't he remember the guard's name? He closed his eyes tightly, feeling the manacles drag across the bridge of his nose. The guard—something clicked inside him. The big, burly man came to mind so clearly he might have been standing in front of him. The man's wife . . . he remembered once the plump woman had come to the prison with a special meal, because it was their twelfth wedding anniversary. Vaguely, he could remember her requesting permission to enter. She had named her husband—

"Brogan." Clenching his fists, Cole brought his wrists down. "His name was Brogan."

Douglas frowned severely. He personally did not know the man. But the man, Jennings, arose from a small desk where he had been writing down their conversation and bent to whisper into his immediate supervisor's ear. "Brogan, eh?" Douglas said after a moment. "Strange you should name the only Walnut Street City guard who has died within the past year. Murdered, it seems, by persons unknown."

Cole gritted his teeth to keep from saying, "Webster Mayne." As he felt the grating of iron against

442

his wrists, he thought of Pine Creek and all their friends, especially Callie Ward, who had been entrusted with the safety of his and Diana's son. He felt in his heart that he would never again see the peaceful settlement in the Appalachian Highlands where he had known his happiest days.

Mrs. Sanders wept gently as she selected a few of Diana's winter dresses and gathered the bare necessities she would need while in Philadelphia. She was still shocked at seeing Diana's husband, alive and well, standing there among the group of men having his gentle hands shackled in irons. What would become of him? And Diana? What would become of them all? She spent an hour packing the things because she did not want Diana to leave.

She did not hear the approach of a man's footsteps, perhaps because Webster crept into the room like the rat he was. Standing close enough to touch the woman, Webster dramatically cleared his throat. Mrs. Sanders spun, reeling to the bed where Diana's clothes were laid. In his right hand, Webster Mayne held a pistol—it was not the one she had filled with herbs—and in the left, a vial of amber liquid.

Fear filled her eyes. "M-Master Mayne, what do you want?"

Smirking devilishly, Webster held the gun to her heart and offered the vial to her. "Drink this, Mrs. Sanders." It was not a request, but an order.

"Wh-what is it?"

"Don't worry . . . it will not kill you. But it will immediately make you sick enough that Diana will have to stay here to take care of you."

"If she stays, Dr. John will stay, also."

"I've taken care of that, dear Mrs. Sanders." Just at that moment, a commotion erupted downstairs. Mrs. Sanders recognized the voice of her son. "Yes, Mrs. Sanders, that is Tuxford. It is amazing how quickly a man such as I can get to Philadelphia and back in the matter of a few minutes. Tuxford is even now telling John that his livery is afire. Now—drink this, or you will have a bullet through your heart."

"Dear Lord, my own son conspired to harm me?"

Webster chuckled, his eyes blackening maniacally. "Of course not, Mrs. Sanders. He knows nothing of this. Now, drink it!"

Mrs. Sanders did not want to die. She had Claudia—dear, dear Claudia—to think about. She could not leave that poor girl defenseless against such a maniac. In the moment that it took her to take the vial and drink it down, she knew she had to make a choice between Diana and her own daughter. Immediately, cramps seized her in her stomach and she crumpled in agony to the carpet of Diana's bedchamber.

Tossing his pistol aside, Webster rushed from the room and down the stairs. "Dr. Redding! Mrs. Sanders has fainted. She is so upset about Diana—"

"My God!" John Redding's eyes grew noticeably annoyed. "My livery burns. And Mrs. Sanders chooses this moment to faint?" He moved first to

444

the stairs, then toward the foyer where Tuxford still stood, awaiting his attention. "Diana—"

"Go to your livery, John," she ordered, taking his arm to give it a gentle squeeze. "I will see to Mrs. Sanders. Tuxford, will you remain here to drive me to Philadelphia after I see to your mother?"

"Of course," he replied, eyeing Webster Mayne critically across the young mistress's shoulder. "Shall I help you with her?"

"No, I am sure she will be all right. Just await me."

As she rushed up the stairs toward her bed-chamber, John moved quickly toward the stable and his waiting horse.

Diana found Mrs. Sanders slumped across the bed, clutching at her stomach. "Mrs. Sanders, what is the matter?"

"Master Mayne—" Her voice was weak. "He made me drink something . . . so that . . . you would have to stay in the house. Dr. John's . . . livery is not . . . afire."

Her body grew rigid with fear. Her eyes flew swiftly to the door to find Webster leaning arrogantly against the facing. "Webster, why have you done this?"

"Don't worry, *Cousin!* The old bag will not die. Come, dear." The sarcasm in his voice caused her heart to flutter wildly. She wanted to flee from the madman standing before her. "It is time that you met my mother, your dear Aunt Jocelyn." When she hesitated, Webster calmly picked up the pistol from the bureau where he had placed it. "You will come with me, Diana."

"Don't . . . go with him," Mrs. Sanders wept, the agony of the drug seizing her midriff. "Please, mistress . . ."

Diana had no alternatives. Her protector—her dear husband—had been taken away by the authorities. John had been lured away with lies, and Mrs. Sanders lay in distress. Even Philip, Webster's own father, lay unconscious in his bedchamber, overdosed on laudanum. Claudia would be about as much help as bed sheets right now, and Tuxford was loyal to Webster. Thus, Diana drew the covers over Mrs. Sanders, gently touched her lips to her cheek in a gentle kiss, and turned to accompany her pistol-wielding cousin to the chamber of a woman who had not been seen in fifteen years.

Although his grip was brutal, Diana did not feel the pain. She felt only defeat, mixed with a bit of curiosity so small that it scarcely existed at all. Webster would drag her to the empty chamber where he and Philip claimed Jocelyn Mayne had lived for fifteen years. She felt that tonight would be the last night of her life. But it didn't matter. Cole was back in jail and they would kill him. Callie would take care of their son, so it really didn't matter any longer. Without Cole she could not go on.

Webster dragged her along, eventually halting at the outer door of Jocelyn's suite. He maintained his brutal grip as he unlocked the door and dragged his young cousin into the unfamiliar sitting room. Her body slumped in defeat. Behind her, muffled through the thick walls of Rourke House, she heard the gentle moan of the housekeeper. But even that could not penetrate the veil of horror shutting out reality. She should fight, but she had lost the will.

Clink! They key turned in the lock. Slowly, the door opened and Diana was instantly aware of the damp muskiness of the large suite. "Come, meet Mother, dear Cousin. She was been so wanting you to visit. Haven't you, Mother?"

Diana had willed herself into another world . . . a world of detachment, a world where fear did not exist. No physical feelings affected her, not the painful grip of Webster's fingers, the pistol pressed to her ribs, the key clinking against coins in Webster's coat pocket. She knew only that her world had crumbled; it did not matter what tomorrow brought. It did not matter, because Webster would see that tomorrow did not exist for her.

If awareness claimed her, it did not reflect in her face. Her eyes were blank and empty, the pride with which she normally carried herself nonexistent. She slumped like a rag doll against the rigid body of her maniacal cousin. But when he forcefully turned her to face the woman who lay upon the satin sheets of the oversized walnut bed, a scream ripped from her throat and filled the house . . . over and over and over again, until she was lost in the foggy, dark, haunting vortex of unconsciousness.

The last thing she remembered was the pistol hitting the floor with a dull thud as Webster picked her up in his arms.

Two things had made John Redding suspicious. First, Tuxford had declined to return to the city with him, and second, he had seen no flames licking at the horizon in the direction of his livery. Still, the secondary enterprise provided a large enough portion of his yearly income to merit his concern. When he rode up to the livery and found it quiet, not so much as a lantern burning near its entrance, he turned and nudged his horse into a fast canter toward the Walnut City Jail.

The guard permitted him entrance to the chamber where Cole Donovan was being interrogated. "Mr. Douglas, you must accompany me to Rourke House."

Cole jumped to his feet, concern marking his brow. "Where is my wife?"

"He tricked me. Webster Mayne and his man Tuxford tricked me."

"Where is my wife?" Cole repeated more harshly.

"She is still at the house."

"Damn you, John!" He would have throttled the older man if Jennings had not pulled his weapon to aim it threateningly at him.

"You must gather your men and accompany me there. Make haste, for God's sake!" John said.

"And what makes you think Mrs. Donovan is in trouble?"

Quickly, John related the story, eliciting an urgent request from Cole Donovan. "You must allow me to accompany you! She is my wife!"

Mr. Douglas smirked. "Jennings, keep the man

here. If he moves so much as a muscle, shoot him."

Cole dropped into the chair.

Douglas gathered his men from a room where they were engaged in a game of cards. John rode on ahead, aware that Douglas and his seven men were only a half mile behind.

Chapter 25

The coldness of the December wind rushed upon Diana's skin, bringing her to partial consciousness. Still, her arms would not move and she felt lifeless in Webster's arms. Darkness surrounded them; she was not sure where they were. Above them, a gray, overcast sky hid the midnight moon from view. Below them, shells were crushed by steadily pacing footsteps. Before them, a creek babbled over smooth white rocks. The tall, stately house that was her worst nightmare slowly faded from view.

Webster reached a certain point in their journey and paused, dropping Diana roughly to her feet. His bony hands gripped her upper arms and when her face sank, he shook her violently. "Don't you want to know everything, Cousin?" he smirked.

Diana managed to meet his gaze. There was no fear in her eyes, only the strange emptiness that came with mental and physical defeat. She could no longer fight him. "Not really," she replied, trancelike.

"I will tell you anyway, dear Diana, since I am about to finish a task I started many years ago . . . when you were only three years old. I would have drowned you then if your damned mother hadn't stopped me. Don't you remember the swirling darkness of the creek enveloping you? Surely, you remember!"

"No . . . no . . ." Diana felt as if she had been drugged.

"I've lost everything because of you, Cousin . . . and because of my mother! Damn her untimely death!" he snarled. "Damn her! She was all that kept us—father and me—in this house." Smirking, he continued, "Didn't mother look pretty lying upon her bed, all aglow in death, her skin like shrunken leather across her delicate bones? Didn't you think she was pretty?" Diana swayed. She might have fallen if Webster, his teeth bared like a madman's, hadn't continued to grasp her, holding her up. "Because of you—and her—I will never see my rightful share of your father's estate. Yes, I killed him . . . and I would kill him a thousand times over if necessary. I hated him for being strong while my father was weak. I hated him for loving you, when my father couldn't have given a damn about me. I hated him for being my—our grandfather's favorite son and inheriting everything. I hated him and I hated you, you disgusting little wood brat! By God, before I lose everything, I will see you lose everything! Your husband will wrongfully die for the murder of your father, and you will die, Mrs. Cole Donovan, at the hands of the man who deserves the privilege of snuffing out your wretched life!"

"Put down your weapon!" Webster spun so quickly toward the voice in the darkness that Diana

451

was thrown off balance and stumbled toward the cold, swirling creek. John Redding's extended arm was steady, his finger firmly wrapped around the trigger of the cocked weapon. He did not move, not even when he heard Diana's body hit the water, though he panicked inside. He prayed to God the coldness would bring her out of her trancelike state. "Put down your weapon, Webster!" he repeated more harshly. "You are surrounded!" John prayed Webster would not be able to detect his bluff. He had ridden ahead of Douglas and his men.

Webster was even more panic-stricken. He spun from one direction to the other, trying to decide what to do. Trembling, he turned and fired his weapon where he'd heard Diana fall. In the same moment, John Redding's pistol fired, striking Webster in the left shoulder. He cried out, throwing his weapon with a mighty force. Somehow he managed to find the footpath back to Rourke House.

As John dove into the icy creek and pulled Diana from it, Douglas and his men rode up. "Webster Mayne!" John yelled. "I was here when he confessed to the murder of Standish Rourke. I heard him myself! His mother is dead also, and he just tried to kill Mrs. Donovan."

Douglas and his men unholstered their weapons and spread out across the grounds of Rourke House.

Webster held his arm close to his body, trying to stop the flow of blood from the shoulder wound.

He stumbled, he fell, he hit the walls as he moved in a zigzag pattern toward the second floor and his mother's chamber. He heard Mrs. Sanders moaning but he had only one thing in mind.

Entering his mother's suite, he locked the first door, then the second. Taking the lamp he had carried there hardly ten minutes before, he threw it with a mighty crash against the wall. The flames leaped at the rotting wallpaper and made a mighty inferno of the room. He stood gazing at the mummified remains of his once beautiful mother as the flames caught at the threads of hair that had once been lovely auburn tresses.

He heard the cries of alarm from the grounds . . . "Fire! Fire!" But it did not matter. He stood there, rooted to the floor, and watched the flames leap around him.

Douglas rushed back to where John Redding was tending Diana. She sputtered, drawing in quick breaths, feeling the water become ice upon her skin. "The house is afire!" Douglas screamed.

"For God's sake!" John replied. "Get everyone out! Philip Mayne, Mrs. Sanders on the second floor, Claudia in the servant's quarters near the kitchen. Send one of your men for the fire brigade!"

"No." Life returned to Diana's voice as she clutched at John's coat sleeves. "Get everyone out, John, but . . . let it burn. Let the house burn."

Douglas called to his men. "Get the people out of there! And do it quickly."

When he looked back toward John Redding, the doctor said, "You heard her. Let the house burn. I would suggest that you send a man into the city with instructions that Cole Donovan be released."

Mr. Douglas nodded his assent. "I will have to get an order from the magistrate."

"You have my testimony as to the confession of Webster Mayne! You take that to the magistrate!"

"It is done, John."

Moments later, Mrs. Sanders was being carried to the hospital on a stretcher, while Claudia and Philip Mayne were treated for smoke inhalation. Diana watched the east wing of Rourke House illuminate the gray skies with the brilliant orange flames of destruction. She did not know that a fire wall had been built between each wing of the house from foundation to roof, and was disappointed when the fire eventually died down in the predawn hours, leaving all but the east wing untouched.

In the arms of her beloved husband, Diana watched the men move back and forth among the smoldering ruins of the east wing. News was brought to them that the charred remains of one complete body had been found . . . the skeleton of a petite, middle-aged woman who could only have been Jocelyn Mayne. Also discovered was the grisly, dismembered left hand of a man, still adorned with the large emerald ring Webster Mayne had worn constantly.

What demonic power had guided Webster from the treacherous flames of a locked room and to safety? Even as a dozen men spread out over the grounds of Rourke House in search of him, Diana knew he had disappeared into the cold December night.

So many things happened that morning. Cole was officially exonerated in the death of Standish Rourke, and a warrant was issued for the arrest of the missing Webster Mayne. Tuxford was taken into custody as an accessory to various crimes, and Philip Mayne, damaged both by the news that his only son was a killer and by the police's discovery that his wife had been dead for fifteen years, was ordered confined to an asylum in southern Pennsylvania for an undisclosed length of time. No sane man would allow a dead wife to lie in her private suite and mummify for fifteen years. As for Claudia, the authorities took into consideration that she was more than a tad on the simple side.

In just a few short hours, the world had turned topsy-turvy and yet, all the questions and loose ends had been either answered or tied together. Diana could think of nothing but their future at Pine Creek. Thus, she was a little surprised that Cole's thoughts, at that precise moment, could run in so different a direction.

"What are you going to do about the burned wing of the house?" he asked.

They had been outdoors for so many hours that Diana no longer felt the cold. "I shall leave it as a reminder of greed and corruption. As a reminder that the only true happiness is a simple life, built together as man and woman build together. When we leave here after the new year, with all the debts and affairs of my late father taken care of, I don't ever want to see this house again." Turning into his arms, favoring him with a smile that was both warm and tired, Diana held him with all the strength she could muster. "Mrs. Sanders will make an efficient conservator of the house and when Uncle Philip is better, he will need her to care for him. Claudia will be happy here with all her ghosts. I don't even mind if Tuxford returns to the house when he has served his sentence. I believe he will have learned a lesson."

"And what of you, Diana? What lesson have you learned?"

Diana took her husband's hands and held them gently against her chest. "I am afraid I have learned only one lesson, Cole. I have learned that nothing is more valuable than love."

"My love, I hope, lass?"

"Aye, love." The tiny hint of her feigned Scottish brogue elicited a smile from the man who was her husband. "It will always be you, forever and always."

Holding her close, Cole whispered, "Do you realize lass, that we have never spoken of my family?"

"I assumed you had no family, or you would have told me about them."

Chuckling, Cole replied, "I have seven brothers, three sisters, a mother and father, two uncles, one aunt, three great-aunts, a dozen or so cousins, and thirty-nine nieces and nephews. One day, when Drew is a little older, we will have a grand reunion in Edinburgh. I will be proud to show off my little wood sprite."

"And all I have to offer you in the way of family

is a poor, pitiful uncle, a dear, wonderful, but somewhat crotchety aunt, and a murderous felon of a cousin."

"Don't forget Hambone. And Honey Boy. A little wood sprite should not have ordinary family."

Diana laughed. "I suppose you could call them family."

"Indeed, lass. Indeed."

That afternoon Cole and Diana tried to relax, to carry on as if nothing had happened. But the unpleasant smell of the burned east wing wafted through the part of the house untouched by the fire. It was difficult to ignore, even with all the windows open and a cold wind filling the many rooms of the house. They had Diana's ancestral home to themselves for the day, since Claudia was at hospital with her quickly recovering mother. Diana had prepared a small meal of boiled beef and potatoes, but neither had eaten much.

Cole kept a loaded pistol beside him at all times. He was not sure where Webster had fled, and if, God forbid, he was still on the premises, he wanted to be prepared for him. Douglas had left one man outside, but the devious Webster had already shown his agility by getting out of a burning room and evading a dozen men. One would be foolish to think he could not find his way back into the house, with only two men and a woman on the premises. Cole did not have the pistol beside him for mere protection; he kept it intending to kill.

After their unsuccessful effort to eat their first

meal of the day, Cole and Diana rested together in her bedchamber. A gloomy aura veiled the house. When Diana shivered despite the fire burning in the hearth, Cole asked, "Are you cold?"

"Not really," she replied. "I never realized how strange this house is. I doubt that I could have lasted a year, even to have claimed my inheritance."

"Are you saying that you are happy I kidnapped you?"

Diana managed her first true smile of the day. "You rescued me, Cole, though this foolish lass did not realize it at the time. It is hard to believe that just a year ago I was scrambling barefoot over the rocks beside Wills Creek, listening to the cries of the forest, dreading the call of my Aunt Rufina, listening to the low growl of Honey Boy at my feet, wanting adventures in my dull, boring life. Now I am a wife and a mother . . . and I am so happy that I want to pinch myself to make sure I am not dreaming."

"You are also Healing Woman," Cole chuckled.

Diana playfully hit his chest, then nestled her head against the muscle she had assaulted. "That was by God and by chance," she replied. "I simply came along at just the right moment. Little Tah-he-no would have recovered without my intervention."

"But God and chance gave us many new friends, eh, lass?"

Thinking of the somber Tahchee, the gentle Sehoy, and the many people of their village, Diana's mood lifted with the sweet memories of them. "Yes, indeed, my love, many new friends. But

Cole?"

"Aye, lass?"

"Do you believe Uncle Philip was being truthful when he said Aunt Jocelyn died in her sleep?"

"Why do you spoil the mood we were creating by bringing up these unpleasantries?"

"It is hard to concentrate. I keep thinking about that poor woman."

"I believe she died a natural death."

"But everyone said she was so healthy."

"It is something that happens, lass. I had a cousin once, a dear girl named Eileen, only twenty years old, full of vibrancy and life. We had gathered together at our estate—all the family from throughout Scotland—and we had an almost immoral feast laid out on banquet tables on a lovely August day. A group of the cousins were sitting together and Eileen said—God, I remember it so well—'I feel like fingers are crawling from the base of my neck over my scalp.' Just at that moment, her head dropped, and Eileen was dead before her lovely golden hair touched the table where we were sitting."

"My God . . . what had killed her?"

"A vein at the base of her neck had burst and the prickly feeling she had related to us was the blood enveloping her brain. So you see, lass, even the healthiest of us can die without warning."

Diana shuddered. "Tomorrow we shall summon the Lutheran minister and have a funeral for Jocelyn."

"Better late than never. A shame we're not having one for Webster."

459

"Do you think it is possible he didn't make it out of the fire?"

"There is a lot of debris and bricks that crumbled in piles. It is always possible."

"But what do you really think, Cole?"

"That the devil takes care of his own, lass."

"Then you think he is still alive?"

"Aye, that I do." Turning to his side and propping his head on his palm, Cole's gray-black gaze met her violet one. "Shall we get away from gloomy subjects? I would rather rest and enjoy being with you."

"Are you sleepy?"

Cole frowned severely. "Do I look sleepy?"

"No, lad, you don't," she replied humorously, "you have *that* look in your eyes."

"And what look is that?" When she did not reply, Cole eased his fingers through her golden tresses, coaxing her mouth to his own to be touched in the gentlest of caresses. "You mean, *this* look? A man's look of lust and need?"

"A man's look of sweet desire," she argued, smiling timidly, like a blushing bride on her wedding night. "How happy I am that you want me, Cole, and no other woman."

Brushing his ample mouth across each violet eyelid, Cole replied with husky need, "There are no other women, Diana." A grin raking his handsome face, he touched the bodice of her blouse. "I like this garment." The single tie holding the gathering top together suddenly sprang loose. "It is easy to get off of you." Cupping one of her breasts, Cole drew a circle around its tip with his tongue.

Stifling a groan of desire, Diana teased, "And suppose I am not in a mood?"

"Nonsense . . ." He held her gaze, his hand kneading the soft, supple breast he had exposed. When her face did not soften, her lips part to invite his kiss, his movements immediately ceased. "You mean, lass, you are not in a mood?"

"Would it matter?" she continued, replacing her teasing lilt with a monotone.

Withdrawing his hand from the softly sculpted and inviting flesh, he again rested his head against his palm. "Of course it matters. A man does not lie with a woman if she is not in a mood!"

"Oh? I thought it was the wife's duty—"

"Blast!" he interrupted her. "Making love is the pleasure of man and woman together, not just man." Cole was dismayed by the idea that his Diana, whose passion and womanly gentleness he had enjoyed so many times, might have lain with him simply out of duty. "Lass, we have never had this discussion before. Be honest. Have you ever been with me when you did not wish to?"

Drawing her finger to her chin to methodically tap it, Diana replied, "Let me think now. Let's see . . . there was the time that I—no, not that time. but there was another time . . . No, I don't believe that time either. Or perhaps it—"

The sweetness of his breath suddenly assailed her delicate cheek. "You are teasing me, lass! Why didn't I see it?"

"Because you are too busy worrying that I do not want you, husband. How," taking his hand, she rested it upon her heart, "could I resist the attentions of so gentle a man? To answer your question, there has never been a moment that I have lain with you against my will. It is not my duty, Cole, it is my wish and my enjoyment. If you were to rise this minute and leave me, I would explode with want of you."

"I don't think that will be my first choice, wife." Touching his fingers to her forehead, he whispered, "You feel a little feverish."

"It is the heat of the fire and of my heart." Drawing her slim, white hands to the back of his neck, she drew his mouth to her own. "Tell me that you love me, Cole," she whispered. "Not with words, but with your body. Oh, what a wicked, lusting woman I am, to want you so badly that I ache with joy."

Her tenderly spoken words evoked such a wondrously painful arousal throughout his body that Cole stiffened against her long, lithe body covered, for the moment, by the loose blouse and skirt she wore. Working his hand beneath the band of her skirt, he felt the delicate spread of her hips, warm and inviting against his caress. The crumpled sheet caught on his stockinged foot and he kicked it off, caring not where it fell. Pushing himself up from the bed, he freed himself of his clothing, his clean white shirt and black breches . . . those god-awful stockings he hated. Standing naked and aroused before her, his hands went out, inviting her up from the bed. The warmth of the hearth behind him, the heat of her body before him, he quickly, masterfully drew the offending garments from her pale, slim body, then eased her upon the bed. He held her hands at her sides as his mouth, his tongue teased the perfect rosebuds of her breasts to painfully aroused peaks. The thick, golden masses of her hair spread out like rays from a morning sun, glimmering against the fire of the hearth and blinding him with its exquisite beauty.

As Diana panted in short, ragged breaths, Cole traced a path down the shallow valley of her torso with his tongue. He continued down her delicately heaving abdomen, his hands lowering to caress her silken thighs. The muscles of his body jerked with excitement and want, and he could tell, as her thighs parted to allow for him, that she was as impatient for their joining as was he.

Without further prelude, Cole's hands moved beneath her body and shifted her toward the mass of soft pillows. As their gazes locked, he made that exciting connection, easing into the warm receptacle of her body with the skill and expertise they had long shared together.

Their minds fogged with mutual desire, nothing mattered but the sating of their bodies, one with the other. Her hardened breasts pressed wantonly to his powerful chest, their legs entwined, their hips connected, undulating, imprisoning, captivating. While he nipped at her mouth in teasing kisses, the fevered intensity of Cole's body pressed upon her, again and again, taking the pleasures she offered without inhibition.

In her wildly traveling mind, Diana remembered a warm valley deep in the Alleghenies. A creek babbled, a humid wind blew, rustling her hair, and longing reached into her heart, flooding her pure, young body with a grasping, grabbing, alluring desire that frightened her, and yet pleasured her so intensely she'd felt wondrously dizzy. That was how Cole made her feel now . . . as though she were again in that valley, her body longing for something that could only be shared between man and woman.

Diana wanted their lovemaking to go on and on, until dawn of the next day speckled the windowsill of their chamber of love. It did not matter if dawn brought snow flurries or sunshine to break the veil of gray across the morning horizon, as long as she could find herself in Cole's arms, loving, and being loved by, him. Her husband had proved to be a man of immense contradiction . . . commanding, yet vulnerable . . . strong, yet gentle . . . firm and masculine, yet sensitive and so sweetly romantic that a simple smile melted her heart. It pleased her to think that she did this to him, that she created so many emotions that living with him was like living with an enigma, a puzzle with so many delightful pieces to bring together.

Brought back to the present by the intensity of Cole's movements, Diana's hips matched his cadence, his rapturous possession plunging deeper and deeper still until she was filled with the joy of him. A tiny moan escaped her mouth, but he breathed it in with a husky groan of his own, his ample mouth nipping at her winter-pale flesh, capturing each violet eyelid, taking her mouth again and again until the erotic sensations within her became beautifully painful and insurmountable. Then the shudder of exquisite joy she had experienced with him so many times shook her deep within, simultaneous to his final, agonizing plunge.

They lay clinging together, unable to withdraw from each other, wanting that netherworld of passion to keep them prisoners forever. Breathing in unison, Cole's finely chiseled face against her pale, soft cheek, Diana held him oh, so gently, her hand flowing smoothly over the damp, sinewy muscles of his back.

Cole's fingers tunneled through her thick, rich hair. Their eyes met, mirrors of their souls and of their passion. Their sated bodies were surely made for one another.

"I adore you," Cole whispered huskily.

"More than your favorite dog back in Scotland?" she teased.

His eyes smiled in gentle harmony as they connected to her own. "Aye, lass, even more."

With a long, low groan, he withdrew from her and rolled to his side, taking the weight of her with him. His gaze now met the high, shadowed ceiling as his fingers absently disengaged the tangles their passionate lovemaking had weaved through her waist-length tresses. Arranging them upon his chest like a blanket of warmth, Cole then drew her fingers to his mouth for a final kiss before blissful, long overdue sleep overcame them both.

Their worst nightmares were over. They were free to love, to go on with their lives, to return to Pine Creek and their tiny son.

Their thoughts entertwined, paralleled, joined like fingers braided together. Their hearts beat one against the other, separated only by the flesh of their bodies pressed gently together.

Their hopes had been renewed.

Their future was ensured.

Their love was destined to go on forever.

Nothing, save God and chance, would ever again threaten the inexhaustible beauty of their love and their family.

Diana lay gently in Cole's arms, the sheet drawn up over their bodies. Soon she felt his gentle breathing against her cheek, and the rapid flutter of his eyelashes hinted at the dream world that had for the moment taken him from her.

What a year it had been! A year of death, of deception, of love — a year in which she had become a wife and a mother. She was so happy she could not sleep, and was content to feel Cole's arm gently wrapped around her.

Later, a sound broke the stillness of the large chamber swirling in its midnight shadows. A light with no visible source touched her great-grandfather's exquisite gray-black eyes and moved slowly toward the foot of her bed. The illusion of fog and depth and crisp satin suddenly swirled before her. Strangely, she was not afraid.

He stood there, just as he might have almost a century ago. Gently, he smiled and as quickly as he had appeared, he was gone into the netherworld that he had evaded for seventy years.

"Good night, great-grandfather," she whispered. "You are at peace now."

"Ummm?" Cole mumbled against her.

"Go back to sleep," Diana whispered, tears of

happiness filling her violet eyes. "Everything is all right. Everyone is happy now."

"I'm happy," he mumbled, drawing her closer to him.

"And so am I."

Epilogue

May, 1791

Diana stood at the entrance to the path which spiraled through a narrow dale. The aroma of wild flowers flourishing there, carpeting the hillsides with lilac-blue blossoms and honeysuckle, wafted through the cool morning air. It was a place she loved, where white-tailed deer and wild turkeys lived, and cardinals, wrens, and mourning doves filled the woods with their unrestrained melodies.

Suddenly, a child's high-pitched laughter erupted behind her, followed by the running footsteps of a man in pursuit of a scampering three-year-old boy, who zigzagged toward his mother with a picnic basket in town almost as large as he was.

"Drew, slow down," Diana ordered, laughing as the picnic basket and child suddenly impacted with her massive skirts. Cole had slowed down his pace and, reaching her, put his hand dramatically over his heart.

"This little scamp is trying to wear me down!" he chuckled, tousling his son's coal black hair. "I am too old for this."

"Nonsense! Come along, my merry lads," Diana said, "We have a long walk to the pond where the snow goose lives. You do want to see it, don't you, Drew?"

Drew was the image of his father, dark haired, his gray-black eyes every bit as loving as the man who now held Diana's gaze, transfixed for a moment that seemed like an eternity.

"Wait for Honey Boy, Mama," Drew said in his brisk little voice. "He's a comin', too."

"He'll come," Diana laughed, only now averting her eyes from Cole's. "But only because he thinks he'll eat all our food."

Diana was sure the big cat had learned to recognize the word "food." He came scrambling out of the timberline and pawed playfully at the basket Sehoy had woven for Diana just before her trip to her childhood Allegheny home. She, Cole, and Drew had so enjoyed the visit with Aunt Rufina and Hambone that Diana wished she could delay, for just a few weeks, their return to Pine Creek. But Cole was anxious to return to the thriving trading post in which he and Zebedee Ward were partners.

Entering the trail, they walked slowly, watching Drew dart among the rhododendrons and mountain laurel, picking bouquets which he lovingly brought to his mother, scampering after every frog and lizard he saw, paying little heed to the warnings of his protective parents. Soon, they moved onto the short footpath bordered by wild phlox, toward the pond where the elusive snow goose had been seen.

Within half an hour of leaving the trading post, Diana spread her blanket on the delicate, fresh green foliage at the shore of the pond where venerable bald cypress trees grew. The still, clear waters reflected the sky like a vast mirror, occasionally rippled by a large trout leaping gracefully, uninhibited by the presence of man.

During their morning excursion, Cole took Drew out on the pond in the boat Hambone had built. Afterwards, Drew continued to gather wild flowers: pink azaleas, crested iris, dandelions and laurel, all of which would surely wilt by the time they were carted back to his great-Aunt Rufina. Just as they were packing to leave, the snow goose landed on the pond. But in his enthusiasm, Drew immediately startled it into flight with a high-pitched squeal.

"Don't worry, son," Cole soothed him. "Perhaps tomorrow we will see it again. And you must be very, very quiet."

"Snow goose pretty as Mama, isn't it, Papa?"

"Not quite," Cole replied, taking his little son up in his arms for the long, pleasant walk back to the trading post.

Hambone had just finished restocking the stockroom and was moving toward the living quarters to rest when Drew came bouncing into the trading post just ahead of his parents, their hands joined and swinging, their laughter filling the warm May afternoon.

"Grampa," Drew leaped into the burly mountain man's waiting arms, dropping his bundle of wilted wildflowers. Having never met his Scottish grandparents, and Diana's parents being dead, he had

470

taken to calling Hambone and Rufina Grampa and Gramma. "We saw the snow goose."

"Did you, indeed, little lad?" Hambone juggled him on his strong arm. "Gramma has baked blueberry tarts—your favorite!"

Wriggling free of Hambone's arms, Drew immediately rushed through the curtains and toward the pantry where the tarts were arranged neatly in a row.

Rufina, rubbing her hands on a large white apron, emerged from the living area. "He'll be busy with those tarts for a few minutes."

"He'll get another belly-ache," Diana laughed. "You know how he loves your baking."

"Won't give him that much time," Rufina said gruffly, taking Diana's hand to give it a brief but gentle squeeze. "Sit. There is something I wish to discuss with the two of you."

"Is something wrong, Aunt Rufina?"

Sitting in her favorite rocker, Hambone on one side and Diana on the other, Cole sitting across from her on the spacious deacon's bench, Rufina smiled warmly at her loved ones. "Nothing is wrong, girl. You and your husband and your boy are all me and this old man," affectionately, she patted Hambone's knee, "have in the world. We plan to live long enough to be a problem, I guarantee you, but while we're alive we have this trading post that's been making a good living for us. You young people permitting, this old man and me would like to have formal-like papers drawn up so that when we pass on in a hundred years or so, that little lad back there will have this trading post to run or sell or do with as he pleases. When he's a full-grown man, you will still be young and you'll be running your trading post at Pine Creek. The boy will be wanting to spread his wings and by that time, this'll be a thriving business, catering to people moving in to the interior. We want him to have it."

Diana felt a lump form in her throat. Her three-and-a-half year old son would have his choice of valuable properties: the estate in Philadelphia, Rufina's trading post, and their own land at Pine Creek. It was only fair that he should be given a choice and the same opportunities that Cole and Diana had had, though Diana did not take well to the idea of so much distance separating her from her son. Closing her hand warmly over her aunt's, Diana looked first to Cole, who quietly nodded his assent, then to Rufina. "It is a kind and generous thing you do, both of you. You have many, many years together, and if this lovely land is what our son wants when he is a man, then it will make us happy, too."

Withdrawing her hand, Rufina slapped her knees through her voluminous skirts. "That is settled then! And there'll be no more discussion about it!" Diana saw through the rough exterior and smiled warmly at her aunt. "While you were off in the woods, this arrived by post." Rufina took a letter from her apron pocket and pressed it into Diana's hand.

"It's from John," Diana said delighted, glancing toward Cole. Breaking the seal, she unfolded the single sheet of paper and glanced quickly over the

472

words. A mixture of emotions crossed her brow as she began to read:

"Dearest Diana, Cole, and Little Drew,

"How happy I am that you are again in Pennsylvania. I will arrive by coach on the 18th . . ."

Diana smiled; that was only two days away.

". . . and will spend several days visiting with you. Please tell dear Rufina that I shall bring bolts of oriental silk, purchased at a good price from the docks, and several boxes of English buttons.

"There still has been no reliable word about Webster Mayne. Many rumors are circulating throughout New England, one that he has fled to England, an ugly, disfigured man, another that he was aboard the *Horatio* which sank in a mighty gale at sea last year, and even another that he is living in luxury and decadence in the Spanish colony of New Orleans.

"Philip has returned to Rourke House, a broken shell of a man, and is being cared for by Mrs. Sanders. Claudia is married and will give birth next month. We shall speak in more detail about family and friends when we see each other on the 18th.

"Enough, my good friends. And my love, until again we meet.

Affectionately,
John Redding"

Cole said dryly, "I guess that settles it, wife. We will have to stay another week, at least."

"Or two," she replied, smiling.

Drew came charging into the trading area, his face scarcely recognizable through the stain of blueberries covering his chin and cheeks. He carried one tart on a linen napkin and, scooting past the adults, bent beside the bobcat lying in his favorite corner. "This one for you, big kitty," he said, offering the tart to the cat, who really didn't show much interest. Honey Boy licked at the sugar topping and just as Drew started to take a big bite himself, his laughing mother scooped up the linen napkin, tart and all.

"I think a certain little lad has had enough of the blueberry tarts," she chuckled, taking the protesting Drew up in her arms. "It is time to wash this messy face." While Cole, Hambone and Rufina chatted pleasantly over cool lemonade, Diana tended the needs of her son, then returned with a much cleaner Drew in tow. "How does this look?" she asked, presenting him to the adoring adults.

"Much better," Cole replied, opening his arms, into which Drew rushed in order to charm his father out of a few sips of lemonade. Then his eyelids grew heavy and tired from the day's activities and he soon relaxed into the crook of his father's arm.

When they thought he was asleep, Diana, who had been dwelling on John's letter, asked, "What do you think became of Webster?"

Cole replied, "I think he's dead."

474

Hambone said, "The lucky wretch is wallowing in his own misery somewhere."

Rufina agreed with Cole. "Lost off the coast . . . fish food, for sure."

But Drew instantly surged out of what the adults had thought was a deep sleep and gestured dramatically with his little arms, jabbing and poking at the air. "When I get big like you, Papa, I shoot him with my gun and cut him with my knife and chop his head off with a big axe."

"Hush, Drew." Diana clicked her tongue, admonishing Cole, "We shouldn't speak of Webster so much in front of our son."

"And he shouldn't spend so much time with the sons of Polly Duncan and Black Face," he admonished in return. "They play those vicious war games, and I don't like it."

"They are just little boys playing little boy games," Diana explained for the hundredth time.

Hambone asked, "Are you talking about the Seminole sons of Oclala?"

"Yes." Diana shrugged. "I assure you the boys show no signs of their father's savagery."

"Not yet," Hambone responded gruffly.

Diana arose, a little agitated. "I'll put Drew to bed."

When she moved from the trading area, Cole said, "She's very sensitive about the two boys. One of them, the son of Black Face, is being tutored by his mother in the art of hostility. Polly has managed to raise a gentle boy, but he is bullied by the other. Only time will tell what becomes of them. I have a feeling that one will turn out bad, and the other good."

"And their influence on Drew?" Rufina asked.

"Only time will tell that, also."

"Time will tell what?" Diana asked, converging once again upon the group.

Cole did not want to upset her further. "Time will tell, little wife," Cole lied easily, "what will become of us all."

Diana was fairly sure they'd been discussing subjects much more specific than the general ravages of time.

Nestled within the extensive Allegheny mountains lay a heavily forested dale that reflected a day long past, its aura so primitive that time could be forgotten. It lay within easy walking distance of the trading post and it was there, after darkness fell and Drew was safely tucked in bed, that Diana and Cole walked along a trail winding through an original stand of hemlock, beech, and black cherry trees. The trail plunged deep into the forest, bringing them to a solitude that shut out all traces of the world beyond the forest. A timeless waterfall splashed into a crystal clear pond. That was where Diana chose to take Cole that evening, to her special place where the birds sojourned in joyful, and yet haunting, song.

Evening had cast a stained-glass skylight across the horizon. Deep terra cotta, golds, blues, and brilliant pinks joined together in picturesque elegance.

Cole dropped to a grassy knoll and invited Diana into the comfort of his arms. He held her, touched her, felt her cool skin respond to the very nearness of him. Her vibrance chased away exhaustion, her beauty was the bounty of life lived to fulfillment.

Her dreamy gaze across the timberline was followed closely by a long, lingering sigh. "What are you thinking, lass?"

Nestling her head against his strong shoulder, Diana moved to touch her temple to his own. The sweetness of his breath whispered upon her cheek. "I was thinking how happy I am. Are you happy, too, Cole?"

"No . . . I am beyond that . . . I am delirious."

"I hope that is good."

"It is wonderful."

They sat together for a long, long time, far past the hour of midnight. Then, with a happy laugh, Diana hopped to her feet and quickly shed herself of her loose-fitting cotton dress, the only garment she wore. Her nakedness glimmered in the moonlight as she turned and rushed playfully toward the pond. "Where are you going, Diana?" Cole asked, his body responding to the provocative loveliness of her nudity.

"Beneath the waterfall. Come, join me."

Grinning rakishly, Cole shed himself of his clothing. His slim, firmly built body soon joined hers beneath the gentle waters of an Allegheny fall.

He held her ivory body against his bronze one. Their mouths met in the sweetest of kisses and all about them the forest lulled them with its midnight song, inviting, caressing their entwined bodies with

477

the haunting loveliness of the breeze that wafted all about them.

Making sweet, wicked love beneath the fall was a new and exciting experience for both. Moments later, they dropped into a thick, lush patch of spring-green clover, content to lie together in the aftermath of their love. Very few words were spoken; they were too happy just enjoying each other.

Diana sighed deeply. Beyond all the tomorrows, there were still questions needing answers. What did the future hold for the child born of their love? How would the sons of the Seminole renegade, Oclala, affect Drew's life? Would Webster's fate ever be learned?

Perhaps one day the questions would be answered.

Perhaps in Drew's time.

Contemporary Fiction From Robin St. Thomas

Fortune's Sisters (2616, $3.95)

It was Pia's destiny to be a Hollywood star. She had complete self-confidence, breathtaking beauty, and the help of her domineering mother. But her younger sister Jeanne began to steal the spotlight meant for Pia, diverting attention away from the ruthlessly ambitious star. When her mother Mathilde started to return the advances of dashing director Wes Guest, Pia's jealousy surfaced. Her passion for Guest and desire to be the brightest star in Hollywood pitted Pia against her own family—sister against sister, mother against daughter. Pia was determined to be the only survivor in the arenas of love and fame. But neither Mathilde nor Jeanne would surrender without a fight. . . .

Lover's Masquerade (2886, $4.50)

New Orleans. A city of secrets, shrouded in mystery and magic. A city where dreams become obsessions and memories once again become reality. A city where even one trip, like a stop on Claudia Gage's book promotion tour, can lead to a perilous fall. For New Orleans is also the home of Armand Dantine, who knows the secrets that Claudia would conceal and the past she cannot remember. And he will stop at nothing to make her love him, and will not let her go again . . .